DAYLIGHT

A MERRYMOUNT SERIES

ILA SIKORSKI

Daylight

Copyright © 2025 by Ila Sikorski

Published by Ila Sikorski

All rights reserved.

No part of this book may be reproduced in any form or by any electronic or mechanical means, including information storage and retrieval systems, without written permission from the author, except for the use of brief quotations in a book review.

The story, all names, characters, and incidents portrayed in this production are fictitious. Any resemblance to actual events or locales or persons, living or dead, is entirely coincidental.

Editing by Kayla Morton with K. Morton Editing

Proofreading by Kimberly Swiszcz

Book Cover and Art by Marissa Lussier

a merrymount series
Daylight
ila sikorski

Too loud. Too quiet.
Too small. Too big.
Too smart. Too dumb.
Too broken. Too much.
This one's for you.
You're everything.

CONTENTS

The Playlist   ix
Content Note   xi
Recap O'Clock   xiii

Prologue: Red   1
Chapter 1: Red - Rock bottom, but lower   9
Chapter 2: Miller - This is me trying (a lot)   17
Chapter 3: Red - Just some pals hanging out   24
Chapter 4: Miller - Dear Old Dad   32
Chapter 5: Red - The Prophecy (Red's Version)   40
Chapter 6: Miller - Utterly, Totally, and Completely
Fucked   47
Chapter 7: Red - Ain't no thang but a chicken wang   57
Chapter 8: Miller - Baggage with a side of pasta   68
Chapter 9: Red - crushcrushcrush   82
Chapter 10: Miller - We're late for school. Again.   90
Chapter 11: Gwen - Do your worst, Gwendolyn   100
Chapter 12: Gwen - Howdy, Neighbor   109
Chapter 13: Miller - Shacking up and living in sin   122
Chapter 14: Gwen - Happy Birthday, Miller
Caswell   129
Chapter 15: Miller - What's My Age Again?   140
Chapter 16: Gwen - The friendzone is the endzone   149
Chapter 17: Gwen - Is this an ambush?   160
Chapter 18: Miller - Family Pizza Night   172
Chapter 19: Gwen - I want to fuck your brother   183
Chapter 20: Miller - Should I be scared?   190
Chapter 21: Gwen - Thanksgiving Eve   201
Chapter 22: Miller + Gwen   213
Chapter 23: Miller - Yes, ma'am   223
Chapter 24: Gwen - Can't be hateful, gotta be
grateful   233
Chapter 25: Miller - Put a ring on it   242
Chapter 26: Gwen - Pspspspsps   250

Chapter 27: Miller - Cat Daddy   260

Chapter 28: Gwen - Oh, so this is what it's supposed to feel like   268

Chapter 29: Miller - Mr. and Mrs. Claus   274

Chapter 30: Gwen - The House Meets the Mouse (Part 1)   282

Chapter 31: Miller - The House Meets the Mouse (Part 2)   288

Chapter 32: Gwen - Meet the Parents   296

Chapter 33: Gwen - Playing house   303

Chapter 34: Miller - The Book of Advice by Melanie LeClair   309

Chapter 35: Gwen - It's grand gesture time, people   317

Chapter 36: Gwen - Karma is a cat   322

Chapter 37: Miller - The Blueberry Festival   328

Epilogue: Penelope   335

Stay tuned...   339

Acknowledgments   343

The Spice Guide   345

Also by Ila Sikorski   347

About the Author   348

THE PLAYLIST

Daylight - Taylor Swift

right where you left me - Taylor Swift

Break Up In A Small Town - Sam Hunt

The Prophecy - Taylor Swift

crushcrushcrush - Paramore

What's My Age Again? - blink-182

Close To You - Gracie Abrams

Whatcha Say - Jason Derulo

Labyrinth - Taylor Swift

Married Life - Michael Giacchino

There She Goes - The La's

My Kink Is Karma - Chappell Roan

Her - JVKE

lowercase letters - Noah Richardson

CONTENT NOTE

Daylight is an adult romance novel containing:

Infidelity and emotional abuse in a past relationship, childhood trauma, anxiety, depression, open door intimacy, drinking/alcohol, pregnancy, and explicit language.

Readers who may be sensitive to these subjects, please take note.

A *Spice Guide* has been included in the back matter of the book outlining the chapters that contain explicit sexual content for readers who wish to find or avoid.

RECAP O'CLOCK

To catch you up to speed...

Margot moved to Merrymount, found out her neighbor was her failed date, got a job in the town's coffee shop, and became BFFs with the owner, Red. Failed date neighbor, Sawyer, decided he wasn't letting Margot get away this time so eventually they fell in love.

Along the way, Margot discovered she had a long lost half brother who was the product of an affair her dad had before he skipped town. Half brother, Miller, has a daughter named Penelope, and both of them eventually move into the apartment above Red's Place as their apartment was flooded.

Oh, and Sawyer's ex-girlfriend, Katie, whipped into town hella pregnant claiming the baby was Saywer's. Turns out it's not! The baby is a product of *another* affair with Katie and Red's ex-husband, Dean.

So now Red is sad and Miller is crushing from afar.

Aaaaaaaand that's what you missed in Merrymount.

PROLOGUE: RED

"*A*re you a mom?"

The question shoots through me like an arrow. My back stiffens like the sharp tip was just lodged into it, and my throat starts to feel dry. She's five years old, just a kid. She has no idea being a mom is the only thing in life I've ever dreamed about and wanted and hoped for.

The one thing in life I'll probably never be.

I muster up a smile so Penelope doesn't think she said anything wrong. Because she didn't. "No, baby girl. It's just me."

Penelope takes another bite of the peanut butter and jelly sandwich I made for her and tilts her head to the side in thought as she chews. She swallows before throwing another question out of left field. "Do you want to be a mom?"

Is it warm in here? Maybe I need to adjust the thermostat.

"I did, once upon a time."

"But not anymore?" she asks.

"Well, no." I pause. How the hell do I explain the complexities of a failed marriage and a steaming pile of self esteem mixed with abandonment issues to this child? "I mean—Yeah. *Yes.* I would love to be a mom. But it's not always so easy."

"Yeah…" She sighs, a heavy sigh making her sound well beyond her five years of life. "Daddy says the same thing."

"What do you mean?" I'm genuinely curious. Miller, Penelope's dad, has been a mystery around here for a while now, a very cute mystery. But he likes to keep to himself. I only ever see him out and about with his daughter who's now sitting in front of me with absolutely zero filter. Call me an opportunist, but I'm not passing this up.

"I don't have one, a mom," she clarifies. "Daddy says it's *complica-cated.* He says she'd *loooove* to be a mom, but *it's not always so easy.* Just like you said." The way she gestures with her hands and imitates his voice is the most adorable thing I've ever seen.

"He's not wrong. But that doesn't mean it doesn't suck. Shit. I mean—Crap. Sorry." I sheepishly turn to her, and that sad look on her face melts away just as quickly as it showed up.

"I'm allowed to say shit, but only at home. That's the rule." Penelope looks both ways making sure the coast is clear. "So, don't tell Daddy, okay?"

I hold out my pinky, and she links hers with mine. We shake once. "My lips are sealed, tiny human."

She giggles at the nickname. "It's funny when you call me that. Does everyone call you Red because of your hair?"

Instinctively, I tuck the front of my hair behind my ear. "Yes, ma'am."

"What's your real name?"

"Gwen. Or Gwendolyn. But no one really has ever called me those. It's always been just Red."

"Gwendolyn sounds like a princess name!" she exclaims.

"Funny, I think the same thing about Penelope!" I poke the tip of her nose, and she laughs.

Moving over to the butcher's block counter we have here in the back of the coffee shop, I start aimlessly rearranging trays of biscuits and scones. Penelope finishes up her sandwich, humming along to the music playing on the surround sound.

I look up at the ceiling, pointlessly trying to will my ears to pick up any bits of the conversation happening in the upstairs apartment between Miller, Margot (my employee turned best friend), and Margot's mom, Melanie.

Whatever's going down, it's no place for an innocent kid. So, I'm down here babysitting while trying to make sure everything is good and ready to go for the Blueberry Festival tomorrow. I'm distracting myself once again.

God damn it. You know, I don't even really give a shit about the festival. My parents made it this huge deal my whole life, and the second they deemed it safe to hightail it out of town, they did and never looked back.

I'm happy for them. I really am. They did everything right. They raised me in a small, safe town. They built a solid business from the ground up to hand over to me when I was ready. They supported me with tight lipped smiles when I told them I was marrying my high school boyfriend and held me when I eventually got the sense to leave him. On paper, it's all dandy and perfect.

But now they're gone, retired and living full time on a cruise ship that sails around the Bahamas. And I'm here alone, not even sure if I really care about all of this. This being my whole life and how it's played out.

I thought I'd be happy by now. I thought I'd be married with two or three kids running around a fenced in yard. Maybe we'd have a dog or a cat. I'd greet my husband at the door when he got home from work. We'd get to whisper and giggle together while decorating and wrapping gifts for holidays and birthdays after the kids went to bed.

I wanted a simple, happy life.

And I guess it is simple. It's just not so happy.

I look down, and Penelope is standing beside me. Damn,

those tiny human feet and their cat-like quietness. "*Shit.* You scared the hell out of me."

"You were staring at the wall for a while."

"I was?"

"I called your name three times."

I shake my head. "Ugh, sorry kid. Today's been kind of weird."

"No. The *grown ups* are acting weird."

"You know, you got a point, P. Come on, let's go find us something to do out front."

I let her walk ahead of me, my hand on her back guiding her out onto the coffee shop's floor. I'm guessing it's one of her friends or classmates sitting over at the kid's table, because she darts over to greet him. He's just as excited to see her, both of them jumping up and down, talking over each other. It's adorable as hell.

It's so much easier to make friends and do life when you're five. I sigh to no one but myself and find George manning the counter.

"Hey G, you're good to go. Thanks for the help." I pat him on the back and take the towel he was using to clean the counter from his hands.

George hesitates and looks around like he's about to ask if there's anything else he can do to help. He's fishing for a story, and I don't have time for it today. I stop him before the words leave his mouth. "There's nothing to stick around for. I'm not letting anyone get a show today."

I won't even pretend to know what kind of drama is unfolding upstairs, but I'll make damn sure it's not a spectacle for everyone in town to gawk over. Margot deserves better than that.

George throws his hands up in surrender. "You didn't even hear what I was gonna say."

"Didn't need to, it was written on your face. I mean it. I appreciate the help but get out."

His shoulders fall, and he claps one of my hands with his before making his way to the front. "Will you text me later?"

"I'll think about it."

I make myself busy with customers and organizing while keeping one eye on Penelope at all times. Margot comes down after about an hour, her face white, stricken with shock. I don't ask questions. I just hug her as tight as I can and tell her I'll see her in the morning. She's with Sawyer, I know she's in good hands with him.

I watch another hour pass by on the clock, wondering when it's appropriate to head upstairs and check on Miller and Melanie. After the last few stragglers of customers have left, I flip the open sign to closed.

Just as I'm about to give in to the little voice in my head telling me to meddle, I hear footsteps making their way downstairs. I keep running my hand down Penelope's hair as she lays across me in a booth. She dozed off a little bit ago, and it's been really nice to just sit here with her.

Miller and Melanie make their way over to the booth, faces mirroring Margot's from earlier, and I offer them a soft smile. "Hey," I say quietly to not wake Penelope.

"She fell asleep?" Miller slides into the booth across from us, Melanie scooching in next to him.

"Only about a half an hour ago," I tell him.

"Thanks for all of this, Red. Seriously. I'm sorry I caused so many issues today."

Melanie chimes in before I can. "I told you, no more apologizing. None of this is your fault."

"She's right. Besides, I got the good end of the deal. Hanging with this one is a breeze." I motion to Penelope. "She's a great kid."

Miller looks to his daughter with so much pure, unconditional love in his eyes that I feel like the wind just got knocked out of me. "She's my whole world." He shifts his focus to me. "Thank you," he whispers.

I nod my head silently, unsure of what else to do.

Melanie is the first to fill the awkward silence. "Well, tomorrow should be fun."

I can't help it, I bark out a laugh, causing Penelope to stir. I keep my hand running through her hair and shush her so she doesn't fully wake.

"So, do either of you care to fill me in?"

They both open their mouths and try to talk over each other, then stop. They start up again at the same time, and I hold a hand up. "Miller, spill now."

It all comes out like word vomit. "Margot and I share a dad. He told Melanie when he left them. I found out a couple years ago. Margot found out today."

My mouth hangs open. I'm pretty sure my jaw is dislocated from my skull. What the *actual* fuck is going on?

"Woah," I manage to say.

"Everyone is just trying their best. We're going to be just fine. More than fine, actually," Melanie says. She puts her arm around Miller's shoulder and squeezes once. "I'm gonna head to the back to check my phone."

Once she's out of sight, the awkward silence returns.

Holy shit. This feels like the plot of a *CW* show from when I was in high school. I can't even imagine how Margot feels right now. Or Miller. Or Melanie. Shit.

"She'll fall asleep anywhere." Miller's looking down at Penelope, watching her back rise and fall with each breath in a perfect rhythm.

The arrow I felt earlier finds its mark again. I hate that I'm immediately jealous instead of just blindly happy for them. I hate that I feel like I'll be stuck watching people live out their lives, dreams that I thought would come true for me, from the sidelines forever.

I try to gently readjust and move so I can attempt to pass Penelope off to Miller without waking her, but those pretty, green eyes flutter open and look up at me. She smiles, and when she turns her head slightly to see her dad across the booth, those eyes widen as she says sleepily, "Daddy!"

He scoots out of the booth and opens his arms for her to jump into them. She cozies up with her arms wrapped around his neck, tucking her head into the crook of it, behind the curtain of his long curls that fall just above his shoulder. Their hair has the exact same color and wave, so much so that you're unable to tell where Miller's ends and Penelope's begins.

The world feels like it stops when I see the two of them together.

Suddenly Penelope's head pops up, tiredness from just a few seconds ago vanishing. She twists her neck so she's facing me, a smile beaming on her face like a lightbulb just went off above her head. "Red…"

"Miss Red," Miller corrects.

Penelope rolls her eyes, the epitome of five year old sass. "*Miss* Red. I know you said it's not always so easy. About being a mom. But I think you'd be a good one."

I freeze. I feel my cheeks flame. All of the air just got sucked out of me. And I watch Miller's face go from confusion, to shock, to mortification in under two seconds when he sees how much one little comment affects me.

Penelope does *not* see the two adults in front of her floundering for something to say to get themselves out of this uncomfortable shit-show and continues, "I'd be the happiest ever if you were my mom! Daddy says you're really pretty so he must like you too even though he never says much when we're here! He's just shy!"

And with this, Miller throws his hand over Penelope's mouth. I shimmy out of the booth and stand, prepared to make a beeline for the back, the only safe space in this entire Godforsaken coffee shop, apparently.

Miller finds his voice again. "Penelope, you can't just say that kind of stuff to people we don't know. We've talked about this. Boundaries, babe."

She's not having it. "We *do* know Red. She hung out with me all afternoon!"

"Yes. And I appreciate that but—" He shakes his head and tucks her head back into his neck with his hand. He takes a deep breath. "We'll talk about it more when we get home, okay? Can you please say goodnight to Miss Red?"

She lifts her head again and a frustrated sigh leaves her mouth. "Goodnight, Miss Red," she grumbles and tucks her head back into him.

Miller mouths, "God, I'm so sorry."

I shake my head at him, he has enough on his plate to deal with. Before I can change my mind, I place my hand on Penelope's back and rub two small circles. "See ya later, tiny human. I had a blast hanging out with you today."

We both say our quick goodbyes, and I walk them to the front door, locking it behind them, and watch as they walk to their car.

I'm too broken, too damaged, *too much* to let myself get lost in some fantasy with the two of them. They deserve easy. They deserve more than some messed up, mouthy, truckload of baggage redhead taking up space in their lives. I need to distance myself hard from any feeling of hope or want involving Miller and Penelope Caswell.

CHAPTER 1: RED - ROCK BOTTOM, BUT LOWER

I can't fucking breathe.

I mean, I'm sure my lungs are doing their best, but their best is simply not fucking good enough right now as I try to inhale every bit of oxygen I can.

The air is thick with humidity and doing absolutely nothing to help me work through these shallow breaths. I try to focus on anything to ground myself.

I hear tires on the pavement, car doors opening and shutting, and the beeping noise of an ambulance reversing. I try to keep focusing on every sound and smell happening around me, rather than the darkness that feels like it's consuming me from the inside.

Keeping my eyes squeezed shut, I keel over one of the bushes that line the outside of the hospital I just burst out of like someone on the run.

You will not puke, Red. You will pull yourself the fuck together and not give that asshole another piece of you.

I repeat these words over and over in my head, sprinkling in some other random affirmations about being strong and smart for good measure.

It helps until it doesn't. I feel the bile rise in my throat again when another intrusive thought comes crashing through the positive mantra wall I was building in my head.

She's having his baby.

I waited for what felt like my whole life to have a baby. His baby. *Dean's baby.* And poof, here I am. Bent over outside of a hospital an hour away from home, swallowing down my own vomit, while that same Dean, my ex-husband—*Dean*—is inside with the mother of his child. Who is not me.

Now, am I possibly jumping to conclusions and Dean Fitzgerald just so happens to be visiting a random hospital the very same day Sawyer Hale's ex-girlfriend is giving birth to her mystery baby? Perhaps.

A hunch tells me I'm not, though.

The same hunch had me driving to a slum-city, cockroach infested motel at 2:00 a.m. on a random Thursday to find Dean fucking two women in said motel's equally disgusting ass bed with the wedding ring that I put on his finger the day we got married sitting on the busted nightstand.

I had the majority of his shit on the front lawn and John coming down to change the locks on the doors by the end of the day. That was a little over two years ago.

I'm fine now. I'm healed.

Okay, I'm healing. Ish.

I spent the better part of the last two years avoiding a single meaningful conversation or connection and throwing myself into my coffee shop that I maybe, sort of, have started to resent now. But yeah, I'm good. I'm so good.

"Oh, honey…" A familiar, strong, feminine voice breaks through my inner monologue, and I feel a soft hand on my back.

"I'm okay!" I shoot up, swiping under my eyes to brush any loose tears and mascara away. I twist around to face one of my favorite people on the planet, Beth Rivers, Sawyer's grandmother.

"You're not, and no one's asking you to be." She pulls me into a tight hug.

"Do you think…" I start, but I can't bring myself to finish the question.

Either that baby is her grandson's, and he didn't find out until maybe a week ago, and he'll be spending the rest of his life co-parenting with his toxic ex, or the baby is Dean's. There's no winning here.

Beth sucks in a sharp breath before releasing me to pull apart and holds me at arm's length. She waits until my eyes meet hers, and I can see tears forming on her lash line that I'm sure match my own. A sad, knowing look crosses her face when she says, "I'm gonna tell you the same thing I told Sawyer. We're gonna figure this out. All of us."

I nod my head and start to feel my breathing level out. I needed someone here to pull me back out of the dark. It's okay to still need a hand sometimes. At least, that's what my therapist keeps telling me every week during our sessions.

"Thanks, Beth, but you didn't have to come after me. You should probably head back in."

"Nah." She lets go of my arms and waves her hand at me. "Crowded as hell in there. Red, be honest with me, you feeling okay to drive?"

I give myself a once over. I'm not teetering on the edge of a breakdown as much as I was a few minutes ago. I might need to give myself a couple extra seconds to cool down in the car...But—"Yeah, I think I can manage."

"Good girl. Let's get the hell out of here then. Hop in your car. I'm following you home." She pulls the sunglasses that were perched on the top of her head down and turns to start walking away before I can object. It's a smart move on her part and a sign of the fact that no matter how old she gets, Beth Rivers knows all of her Merrymount kids well, blood related or not.

I find my keys in my purse as I get to my driver's door. I click the unlock button and hurl myself into the seat, landing with a thud. Everything feels so fucking heavy. After taking those extra seconds I thought I maybe needed that I definitely did need, I reverse out of my spot, and see Beth stopped in her old truck in the middle of the aisle in the parking lot. There isn't a drop of impatience on her face.

I spend the drive back to Merrymount skipping every single love song that comes on and looking in my rearview mirror to see Beth behind me the entire way. She follows me until I park in my driveway, and she pulls to the side of the street in front of my house.

Beth rolls down her window when I step out of my car. "Red!" she calls.

"You didn't have to follow me the *whole* way home." I shake my head smiling, walking down the driveway towards her.

"Sure I did. My job is to look after all of you. But before I take off, I wanted to say something, and I don't want you to take it the wrong way."

"Okay..." Beth Rivers is known to say the most out of pocket things, but they're all always out of love. Doesn't mean I'm not nervous for whatever wisdom she's about to bestow on me.

"You were and always will be too good for Dean Fitzgerald. If that baby is his, and God help him if it is, I'm glad you're not the one in that hospital bed."

Her words hit me hard, and I bark out an ugly laugh. I cover my mouth before I do something even worse, like snort. "Yikes, Beth."

"The harsh truth. I needed to get it out. I don't need to give you the whole speech, but I'm up the road if you need me, and if I don't hear from you, I *will* be checking in tomorrow."

She rolls up her window and gives me a look before driving away, a look that reminds me while I might feel alone sometimes, I'm never truly alone in a town like this.

It's another subtle reminder I need before heading into the

empty house I live in, the house I thought would have one day been filled with loud, loving tiny voices to greet me. The house that now only greets me with a deafening silence I can never seem to fully drown out.

* * *

I LAST until the sun sets. I pace and putter and clean every nook and cranny before I feel like I'm going out of my mind. I have to get out of that painfully empty house.

After checking the clock on the dash of my Mini Cooper for the ninetieth time and realizing all I did was waste a lot of gas driving around for two hours, I find myself at the back of the coffee shop, unlocking the door after shimmying the finicky lock a few times to let myself inside in the dead of the night in search of *anything* to do with my hands.

There's always something to clean or organize or plan. I can occupy my time until the sun comes up and maybe then my body will finally find sleep.

Trying to be mindful that it's almost 3:00 a.m. and there are sleeping people occupying the apartment above the shop, I quietly flick on a few lights and make my way through the back room. I step past stacks of to-go cups, hot sleeves, and covers I know for a fact can be sorted through to be put away. Sounds like a good starting place to me.

Once I make it to the counter, I gently toss my phone and keys onto it, opting to sit in the silence rather than attempt to play any sort of music, regardless of the volume.

The last thing I need is to wake either of the humans upstairs, because then I'd make a fumbling idiot of myself in front of Miller Caswell in the early hours of the morning after arguably one of the worst days of my life. That's something I'm trying to avoid for the rest of fucking forever.

I'd also like to avoid Miller entirely for the rest of forever, but that's not really working out for me, seeing as how his half sister is the closest friend I have slash best employee, and he's now living in the apartment I own above the coffee shop with his five year old daughter...because I offered it to them when their place fell apart from water damage.

It's not his fault I'm acting like this. He hasn't done anything wrong. I don't think he's programmed to do anything wrong actually, and that's what's so Goddamn infuriating. He's *nice*. Like, to the bone kind, and gentle, and caring.

I stumble over every other word and look like a crazed animal whenever he's around. I'll always catch him staring at me with this dumb, puppy dog look on his face. And fucking hell, it's a cute face. But just when I'm about to scream and ask *"What?!"* his even more adorable, cute puppy looking daughter will whip her head around, and I have to clap my yap shut.

Before Margot came to town, it wasn't like this. Miller was a regular ole customer that would come in and order a regular ole thing off the menu. I could think about how lickable his jawline was without guilt, because he was just some guy. He'd sit in a booth and do whatever it is he does on his laptop. I still haven't figured out what that is exactly, but that's beside the point.

We were content in our respectable strangership. Two ships passing silently in the night, or whatever. Now I'm hyper-aware of his every move, and I don't know what to do about it.

I spend the next few hours organizing and reorganizing the stacks of paper products I passed earlier in the small stock room we have in the back. I plan the baked goods orders from our supplier for the next four months, getting us through the New Year, which feels excessive, but it's fine. I type out my weekly email to my parents, filled with white lies of my happiness post-divorce and questions about their tropical travels that I'll skim the answers to whenever they grace me with a response.

I jump from task to task until I crash into a booth. I'll rest my eyes here for a couple minutes and then lock up to go home and finally sleep like the dead in my bed, hopefully. The clock on the wall says it's about fifteen minutes until 6:00 a.m. We're not open today, and I'll be out of here before Miller or Penelope wake up.

* * *

I TRY to turn over in my bed, but my face feels stuck, and I have to pry it free from the plastic covering. I jump up, bashing my knee on the table, and kick the blanket that was covering me aside to take in my surroundings.

I'm not in my bed. I'm still at the cafe because I fucking fell asleep. Based on the sun shining right through the floor to ceiling windows in the front, it's well past the fifteen minute time limit I gave myself to *rest my eyes*. God, I'm such an idiot.

There's a big circle of dried drool on the seat I'm going to have to make disappear before I sneak out of here undetected by Miller and Penelope. I pick up the crocheted blanket that got tossed on the floor in my freshly awakened panic and fold it to put back in the closet upstairs.

How, why, and when the fuck did a blanket from the closet in the upstairs apartment get down here?

Abandoning my plan to clean the booth, I rush to the back door to see Miller's car, that was parked right next to mine when I showed up earlier, is gone. I let my forehead hit the cool glass window on the door, close my eyes, and sigh to myself.

When I pry my eyes open, I catch a spot of color above the lock on the door. It's a pink sticky note with some scribblings of probably the worst handwriting I've ever seen in black ink and a small P, written with what looks like purple crayon.

Happy Sunday, Red. Penelope said to tell you that you look like Sleeping Beauty. I agree. -Miller & P

After quickly and pointlessly looking around to make sure no one is watching me, I find my phone and fold up the sticky note to tuck it into the back of my phone case. I tell myself there's no particular reason why I'm not just throwing it away. It's just there for safekeeping for the time being.

CHAPTER 2: MILLER - THIS IS ME TRYING (A LOT)

"It's only gonna be another two weeks max. I promise."

"You said the same thing two weeks ago, Ernie," I say through gritted teeth into the phone.

"I know, but these things happen with repairs and renovations. I want it to be good as new for you and that little girl of yours. Just give me some time. Red's okay with you staying at her place still, right?"

I stifle the urge to scream because Penelope is watching a movie only a few feet away in the living room of the apartment Red is letting us stay in above the cafe. "That's not the point, Ernie. Red's place is supposed to be temporary. I need to have Penelope back at home. She needs routine. She needs stability."

I've said all of this multiple times to him over the course of the last however many weeks, and I don't even know why I bother. It changes nothing. I hear my landlord, who really is trying his best, sigh on the other end of the call.

"I hear you, Miller. You're a good dad trying to do right by your daughter, I respect the hell out of it. But it's out of my hands. I wish I had better news."

"Yeah, me, too." I match Ernie's sigh. "Well, keep me posted."

He reassures me he'll follow up as soon as he can, we say our goodbyes, and I pocket my phone, rather than chuck it across the room to smash it to pieces like I would prefer.

I keep my shit together. That's what I've done since the day Penelope was born almost six years ago. That's what I'll continue to do to give my girl the very best life possible, every good opportunity I never got. I'm breaking generational curses and tossing out single teen dad stigmas.

It's exhausting and hard and heavy until I look up and see her. The dark curls and bright eyes, identical to my own. The smile that's missing a couple front teeth now. The thick, long eyelashes. She knows if she bats them at me, I'll cave on every silly request she throws my way. When I hear her giggle, it sounds like a chorus of the happiest harmonies.

"Daddy, do you think we could go there someday?" Penelope asks, noticing I'm off the phone.

I don't have to look at the TV screen to know *where* she's asking me to take her. I can hear the familiar love song playing and immediately know the exact scene she's referring to. It's not the first time she's asked and it won't be the last. Kid is obsessed with a good *happily ever after.*

I make my way over to sit next to her on the small velvet couch. She's perched on the edge, hands cradling her face in awe as the animated canoe carries the lost princess and the charming thief through the water to watch the lanterns float up to the sky.

I don't feed into the misogynistic bullshit that these movies are only for girls. I'm man enough to appreciate the magic in it all. So I wrap my arms around my princess and pull her onto my lap to say, "Not today—"

"But someday," she finishes for me.

"You know it." I kiss the top of her head. "But hey, it looks like we're gonna be staying here a little bit longer. I'm sorry."

She pops off my lap and turns to face me. "We get to keep staying at Red's?!"

If Red Bozelli had a fan club, Penelope Caswell would be the founder and president. Where I find this situation to be unbearably uncomfortable, my girl thinks this is one giant party.

"Miss Red," I remind her. "Just a little bit longer. I thought we'd be home before school started tomorrow but…"

"Who cares?!" Penelope jumps on the couch and starts bouncing around. "I can't wait to tell her!"

"How about we politely *ask* on our way out? We need to finish up that school supply list." I grab the remote off the coffee table and hit the power button to shut the TV off.

Penelope jumps off the couch and sprints over to the door that opens to the staircase that leads to the cafe below us. We almost never use the door to the right, which leads right out to the back lot where our car is parked. We can't miss an opportunity to see Miss Red, now can we?

She quickly shoves her little feet into her favorite jelly shoes and turns to me with an impatient look on her face. "Well? Are you ready?" she asks.

I shake my head and laugh as I get up from the couch and find my own pair of shoes next to the door. "Yeah, Miss Impatient, I am."

That's all the permission Penelope needs to practically dive down the stairs. She no longer feels the need to wait until I get to the bottom landing to throw the door open and make a beeline for Red behind the counter.

"Red, Red, Red! Daddy needs to talk to you!"

I'm shutting the door that leads upstairs behind me when I see Red look up from her phone. Penelope immediately has her full attention. She crouches down into a squat to get eye level with her.

"Eh, Daddy can wait. I'd rather talk to *you*." Red grabs Penelope and squishes her into a hug. Penelope's laughter trills through the shop, one of my favorite sounds in the world.

I feel a shiver go down my entire spine. I can't have this woman continuing to call me *daddy*.

"Good morning," I greet Red, pretending she has no effect on me, like I always do.

Without letting Penelope go, her eyes meet mine. The dark smudges under them haven't left or lightened in over a week. "Hi."

What would I give to get more than one or two word responses out of Red? Just about anything.

But she's going through a lot right now, and I can't help but recognize my daughter and me squatting in her apartment might be adding to that already extremely full plate of hers.

"You got a minute?" I ask.

"Sure." She releases Penelope and pats her lightly on the back. "I set aside a french toast bagel for you, if you're hungry." Red gestures to the kids table over in the corner that has basically become Penelope's second home this summer.

"Heck yeah!" Penelope high fives Red and dashes over.

"I have some bad news," I start.

Red faces me with a look of concern. "What's wrong?"

"I just got off the phone with my landlord. He's saying it'll be another two weeks, at least. I'm sorry, we should have been out of your hair sooner. I understand if we need to—"

"That's it?" she interrupts.

I lean against the counter. "I can't guarantee it'll only be the two weeks so it's no problem, I'll get us packed up and out—"

"No," she places her hand on my bicep. "I meant...that's all that's wrong? You need to stay longer?"

I try to not jump at the physical contact. Normally Red is trying to put an ocean's worth of distance between us. I switched my deodorant *and* cologne thinking she thought I smelled bad. Then when I realized that wasn't it, I stayed firmly away. She has boundaries, and I don't want to cross them. She deals with her piece of shit ex-husband plowing through every single one of them enough.

I sigh. "Yeah. And again, I'm really sorry. Say the word, and we're out."

"It's not a problem, Miller. I've told you that a bunch of times. Stay as long as you need. Hell, just stay, period. I really don't mind."

Her eyes go wide as if she realized what kind of statement just came out of her mouth. I'm sure mine do the same.

A strand of hair falls in front of her face. It takes every ounce of self control in my body to not reach out and tuck it behind her ear. Her hand leaves my arm, and she swipes the hair away before I can change my mind.

Boundaries, Miller.

"No, no. Absolutely not. I promise as soon as Ernie gives me the go ahead, your apartment will be wholly yours again."

I don't miss the quick drop of her mask. I haven't figured out all of the triggers, and I don't think she knows that I know, but the sadness is there. It's a familiar loneliness I clocked early on because it matches my own. The world only gets glimpses into Red's real emotions.

"My offer stands, okay?"

"Noted and appreciated." I wink at her, and she offers me a small smile, a fucking gold medal in my world.

"So, what do you two cool kids have going on today? Is she excited for the big day tomorrow?"

I'm caught off guard by Red trying to continue the conversation longer than it needs to go. Normally, she's cutting me off and bolting, and I'm stuck trying to chase her down. Sometimes figuratively, sometimes literally.

But then I remember she's probably trying to do everything in her power to keep her mind distracted while waiting for the news of Katie St. James's baby's paternity results. It's been a couple of days since we all found out Katie gave birth and allegedly doesn't have a clue who the father is between my sister's boyfriend, Sawyer, and Red's douchebag ex, Dean.

Sawyer was Katie's ex-boyfriend who she was cheating on with Dean. Apparently for years. I don't know, it's fucking messy. Small towns are weird.

"She's pumped. I wish I loved school as much as she does. We have a couple more things to grab from the supply list. I don't remember first grade needing so much shit."

Then again, it's not like I have the best idea of what you might need for the first grade. And even if I did, my parents never contributed. My dad straight up refused and my mom…she didn't have the energy.

"Do you need help with any of it? Margot should be here any minute, and I'm always down for a good Target trip."

I again practice the art of pretending to not be shocked by her new found comfortability around me. "Help? Shopping? With Penelope? And me? You know I'd be there, right?"

Red rolls her eyes. "Yes, I assumed you'd be there. Come on, you're acting like I avoid you like the plague or something."

"You do." Margot's voice causes both of us to turn, and I see my sister walk through the doorway from the back.

Well, at least Margot said it and not me.

"I do not," Red quips. Margot and I both level her with a look that tells her she's full of shit.

"You two aren't allowed to gang up on me. It's not fair. You're like the fucking twins from *The Shining*. Anyway, Margot, nice of you to join us."

"I'm not even late," my sister counters.

"That's beside the point."

"It's quite literally *not*…"

I stop whatever ridiculous back and forth is about to go down between these two. Red, because she knows she's being weird. And Margot, because she never wants to be wrong. Ever.

"Alright, Red, let's go." I reach out and grab Red's hand, lacing my fingers through hers, and fight through the electric shock that jolts up my arm and through my entire fucking body.

I try to convince myself it's completely one-sided when I watch Red's lips part slightly. I try to suppress every hopeful thought in my head when she doesn't immediately let go. Her hand is so soft, and I have to forget how it feels when she tightens her grip. I completely ignore Margot's jaw unhinging from the rest of her head as I guide Red and me around the counter to scoop Penelope on our way out.

The only thing I don't let myself skip over is how Red drops my hand as soon as Penelope sees us walking over. I'm not hurt by it. I appreciate her recognizing a line that needs to be drawn. I remind myself that while I might have once naively dreamed of a life with an actual partner, someone to share it all with, that's not how my cards played out.

CHAPTER 3: RED - JUST SOME PALS HANGING OUT

Shopping isn't so bad. I'm rather fond of it. I do it *all* the time. I love perusing and buying all kinds of things. One might even call shopping a hobby of mine. A pastime if you will. Some possibly would tell you I'm highly skilled in the art of shopping.

So there's absolutely no reason for me to be on the verge of physically combusting while sitting in the passenger seat of Miller Caswell's extremely practical, safe, and reliable Toyota Camry as he drives us to the closest Target.

I feel bad for setting my expectations so low, but it's like, really freaking clean in here.

Sure, you can tell a tiny human occupies the backseat based on the stickers scattered across the rear passenger door, some peeling on the corners from age, plopped on there with no rhyme or reason. But it's otherwise practically spotless.

I turn around to see said tiny human, Penelope, snug as a bug in the five-point harness car seat behind me. She dons head-phones with cat ears on the top over her perfect brown curls. I'm jealous of those curls. I'd have to sit in front of a mirror with a 1.5" wand for at least an hour to even hold a candle to them.

She shoots me one of those mega-watt smiles that takes my breath away with how unfiltered and carefree it is as she bops her head along to the music she has playing. I spent all of my summer vacations in middle and high school—and an occasional as-needed night here or there still to this day—babysitting Merrymount kiddos. So I've spent plenty of time with children of all ages. I have to tell you, Penelope Caswell is a special fucking kid.

But as I move to face the front again, I remember I'm supposed to be attempting some semblance of normalcy with the man to my left. The man whose very large hands with veins that just kind of *do something for me* are wrapped around the steering wheel. I keep staring at the thin gold pinky ring with a *P* engraved in the center sitting on his finger, and I don't know why I'm so irrationally nervous.

Being in Miller's vicinity makes me jumpy. The tips of my ears get warm, and my heart does this weird pitter patter thing that has me considering making a cardiologist appointment as soon as possible. The way he makes sure my eyes are meeting his when he talks to me sends tiny shivers to my toes, and I don't know where they came from. That terrifies me.

I'm not the brightest bulb in the tanning bed. I didn't pay much attention in school. I've always known I would only need to know enough to take the cafe over when my parents deemed me fit. I'm okay with it, and I get by just fine. But damn, I've never felt dumber than when I have to attempt a full conversation with Miller because there are cartoon bluebirds twittering in my brain when he looks at me.

He doesn't make me feel less than because of it either, and that scares me, too.

I watch Miller glance up at the rearview mirror. His eyes must find the same scene I did because he smiles before focusing back on the road. He's so pretty it hurts.

And I don't mean that in a bad way. Quite the opposite, actually. I think I rather like how entirely different he is from every other guy in this Godforsaken town. Miller is a little above eye level with me when we're standing next to each other. So, if I had to guess, he's about 6′. He keeps his hair long, and the brown waves stop just before his shoulders.

He has a young face. Like, I'm sure Miller will be carded and look twenty-two for the next twenty years. But, God. It's a good face. The green gene is for sure strong with this family because his eyes match Margot's and Penelope's perfectly, but his are framed by the darkest, jet black eyelashes that I would pay a shit ton of money for. I can't see them underneath his sunglasses, but I have them memorized by now.

Not that I was paying attention or anything.

"You're telling me all I had to do to get you to look at me was chauffeur you around?"

I jump in my seat at his voice when I realize I was just caught straight up ogling Miller Caswell.

"What? No. You uh, you have something…there." I wave my hand at absolutely nothing and look out the window.

He doesn't take the bait. He doesn't even loosen his grip on the wheel to pretend to brush off the nonexistent *thing*. It's annoying. It's hot. *No—It's infuriating.*

"Do you need anything in particular here?" Miller asks. He flips the blinker on to turn right into the plaza's parking lot once the light turns green.

"Not really," I answer honestly, appreciating the hell out of the subject change. "Maybe some candles? A book if I see one? Target will tell *me* what I need."

Miller laughs as he puts the car in park. "Fair enough. You want to meet at the check out in say…" He looks down at the old watch on his wrist. "Half an hour?"

"I'm good to tag along with you guys if that's alright."

Penelope answers before Miller has a chance. "Duh!" I turn to see her fling her headphones on the seat next to her and unclick her carseat. "You can help me pick out my first day outfit! Daddy's not very much help."

Ouch. I see Miller's cheeks go red. While he always dresses nice, in my opinion, I don't remember thinking my dad was the expert at clothing options when I was a kid either. So, I get what she means.

I don't know where Penelope's mom is…but I know it's definitely not Merrymount, and I know she's not making any effort to fill in the gaps Miller might miss along the way. I know I don't *know* her, but unless there's a damn good reason she's absent from their lives, I hate her. I'd say I'm sorry, but I'm not.

"Well, that settles it then, P. Let's find you the best outfit any first grader has ever seen."

* * *

THERE ARE ABOUT three or four extra bags of shit we absolutely did not need in the trunk of Miller's car, and Penelope is currently playing tag with a couple of kids from her class in the baseball field next to the park she convinced us to stop at on the way back to the cafe.

I called Margot when we first got here and successfully managed to get her to ramble for ten minutes until she finally caught on that I was partially using her as a buffer between me and Miller. She hung up without saying goodbye.

So now Miller and I are sitting on a bench, a solid foot of space between us, in silence. It's not comfortable. I'm sitting with my back ramrod straight, the pinnacle of perfect posture. Miller has moved his resting arm off the back of the bench more times than I can count in a very short amount of time. I try to inconspicuously peer at him and see him smirking.

"Is something funny?" I ask him.

"Tell me something."

"What do you mean?" I finally turn to face him and he runs

his hand through his hair. He tugs on the ends before releasing his fingers. He does it a lot, and I track the milliseconds of that move every damn time.

"I want you to tell me something, Red. Anything."

"Why?" I realize I'm answering every question with a question, but I can't seem to stop.

"Because one minute you're trying your hardest to pretend I don't exist, but then you do things like place a recurring order of my kid's favorite bagel for the cafe without asking. I'm not good at reading into things. I want to know that we can be friends, and to do that, we should know each other. At least a little bit."

Friends.

I don't think I've ever hated an f-word more. It's irrational to have such a negative reaction to friendship with Miller. He's a good guy and related to my best friend. I *am* letting him and that kid of his live in the apartment I own. In fact, I would love it if they stayed. It's nice seeing that place have life in it again. But I've told myself repeatedly that anything more than this is impossible. It's not in the cards for me.

So why does it suck to hear he just wants to be friends? I'll dissect this during another late-night swan dive into overthinking. I box up the feelings I'm so desperately trying to keep locked and mentally watch myself chuck said box into a dark, empty corner of my brain.

"What do you want to know?"

Miller pauses, pretending to be lost in thought. I watch him run two fingers down the sharp lines of his jaw. "Where'd the nickname Red come from?"

I laugh because it's the most ridiculous thing he could have come up with. I guess I should appreciate the softball question. But then I see he's not laughing with me, and his head has tilted slightly.

I release my hair from the claw clip that was holding it up, letting the heavy bulk of it cascade down my back as I shake my head and ruffle the layers out with my hands. Miller's pupils dilate to the point where they almost completely swallow the green surrounding them.

"My parents say the doctors handed me to them swaddled in a stark white blanket, and the only pop of color was the full head of fiery hair on the top of my head. They were so shocked by it, the only thing they managed to say was *Red*. It stuck—for obvious reasons—after that."

I clock the half second of confusion on Miller's face and then it disappears. I could have imagined it.

"Hmm, that makes sense." He doesn't sound like it makes sense to him at all, actually. "So…What is your legal name?"

"Gwen. Gwendolyn, actually." I tuck a piece of hair that falls in my face behind my ear.

"Gwendolyn," Miller repeats like he's testing it out and committing it to memory. It sounds nice.

"My mom read somewhere that it could bring good luck or something."

"But *she* doesn't call you Gwen or Gwendolyn?"

"No," I laugh. "Really, no one does. I don't think people even remember my real name most of the time."

"Do you not like it?" he asks.

"My real name or my nickname?"

"Both."

I take a moment to look over at Penelope. I watch her laughing and running with her friends, all so young with so much ahead of them. There's no pressure to be better or live up to anything yet. They get to just exist. I remember being her age, thinking everyone was going to know Gwendolyn Grace Bozelli's name some day. Jokes on me with that one.

"I can't blame people for not remembering my name when I forget it most of the time. I used to correct people when I was younger, you know? But everyone saw and heard what they wanted to see and hear. Merrymount is a very stuck in our ways kind of town. And there's nothing inherently bad about being Red. It's fine. But…" I trail off.

"But?" he coaxes me to continue.

Am I really about to drop some deeply suppressed, hidden secret to Miller Caswell simply because he asked?

"But sometimes when I'm alone, I admit only to myself that Red and Gwen feel like two different people. And sometimes, I don't feel like either of them."

Well, good thing that sounded absolutely batshit crazy.

And on another non-sarcastic note, it's a good thing Penelope is bolting over here, waving like a maniac, to change the subject.

"Daddy! Miss Red! You gotta see this!" she yells.

Miller jumps up from the bench, scanning the area for any signs of something amiss. I bounce up with him, remembering two sets of eyes are better than one when it comes to kids.

Over protective dad Miller is doing something to me.

I'm not admitting what that something is.

"What's wrong, baby girl?" Miller asks, voice slightly raised with concern. As Penelope reaches us, huffing and puffing, Miller's hands land on her shoulders, and he does a full assessment of her.

Penelope rolls her eyes so far back I have to stifle a laugh and hope they don't get stuck in the back of her head. "Daddy, nothing is *wrong*. Look!" She opens her mouth into a wide smile and pinches her top front tooth with her little fingers, wiggling the tooth back and forth.

The stress melts off Miller, and I'm finally able to get a lung full of air knowing Penelope's okay. She's just a tad excited about a new loose tooth.

"Another one?!" Miller exclaims, a smile taking over his face as he bends over to examine it.

"Imgonnaberich!" Penelope garbles while continuing to try to wiggle the tooth free.

"Jeez, kid. You've been keeping the Tooth Fairy in business." Miller twists his head to me. "Third one this year, crazy, right?"

I nod my head, smiling at both of them. "Cutest jack-o-lantern I've ever seen."

"I'm hungry. Is it okay if we go home now?" Penelope asks.

Miller lifts Penelope up onto his shoulders, making it look like the easiest thing in the world. Her giggles, that can be heard probably everywhere, make the perfect last day of summer vacation soundtrack.

"Me too, kid. Let's go. Gwendolyn." Miller looks to me, and I do a full halt, eyes probably bugging out of my head. "Pizza sound good to you?"

"I…uh, umm. Sure?"

It's the only half sentence I can muster up. It does the trick though because Miller and Penelope both smile at me before they start their trot back to the car, Penelope bouncing up in the air.

Cheers to pizza with my friends, Miller and Penelope, I guess.

CHAPTER 4: MILLER - DEAR OLD DAD

"Okay, now do a twirl for me!"

I watch my sister, Margot, happily direct my daughter, her niece, with a big ole camera strapped around her neck. Penelope shimmies and twirls for every picture Margot snaps. They've been at it for about an hour now. I'm not sure how long photoshoots like this normally last, but I'm not gonna be the guy to interrupt them or try to end it early.

When Margot asked me to borrow Penelope to practice portrait style shoots, I barely let her finish the sentence before I was telling her yes.

Penelope and I aren't broke. She never has to need for anything, and she only *wants* occasionally. I've worked my ass off for the past seven years to give us every chance at comfort and stability.

But professional pictures weren't ever in the budget, and I have beat myself up about it. Our apartment has a bunch of 4x6 images I printed at the drugstore and put in random frames, all pictures I took on my cell phone. So Margot offering me the chance to let my girl feel special and get big moments of her life like this captured? Sold. Done. Best fucking sister and aunt award, and she's only been at it for a couple months.

I never let myself visualize this as a possible reality before now. Family beyond the two of us wasn't anything I gave myself time to want. I thought finding a long lost half sister from a shared piece of shit father was something people only ever read about.

But that's Merrymount for ya.

I think Margot needed the distraction of this photoshoot, too. It feels like the entire town is waiting on the paternity results of Katie St. James's baby–if Sawyer is the father and what this means for Margot and Sawyer together. Plus, she's processing mine and my kid's entire existence. On top of probably reopening some fatherly wounds.

I stopped by Margot's cottage the other day and found her at the edge of the river, staring out at the water. I noticed Sawyer's Jeep wasn't in their shared driveway. I walked up next to her, we looked at each other, and neither of us said anything.

After about five or so minutes of quiet, Margot screamed. It made the hair on my neck stand straight at the pent up frustration and hurt I could hear. The geese that were silently wading in the water only a second before went flying into the sky. It felt like it was years in the making and these last few hits just came at her hard.

She told me she can only focus on one big thing at a time, and I get it, so we haven't approached the subject of dear old dad. I get her need to take a break from the heavy.

For as fucking shitty as this all is, I'm glad Penelope and I land in the good distraction category of it all.

Penelope is, to no one's surprise, a natural in front of the camera. If I wasn't so protective of her, I'd have tried to get her into some sort of modeling a while ago. Of course I'm biased, but she really has always been the cutest fucking kid. I got stopped no less than four or five times every time we left the apartment when she was a baby. It was cool, but it freaked me out.

I don't leave much room for the unknown when it comes to Penelope. Keeping her safe, healthy, and happy are my top priorities. They're my driving force to keep going.

"I think that about covers it, lil P," Margot calls as she looks down at the small screen on her camera, flicking through the last round of pictures she snapped.

Penelope dashes over to me, crashing into my chest as she wraps her arms around my neck. Doesn't matter if we've been apart an hour or an entire day, there's no better feeling in the world than her being back in my arms.

"Daddy, did you *see* all of the pictures Auntie M took?! I'm like a movie star!"

"Sure did, kid. You looked beautiful," I tell her for the nine millionth time in her life.

I panic-bought this book right before Penelope was born about raising daughters, and it talked a lot about this whole words of affirmation thing. I grew up with my dad calling me a fucking dumbass for every single thing I did or said, so I needed all the help I could get. My list of good role models was nonexistent.

Penelope was only hours old when I first started telling her,
You are kind.
You are smart.
You are brave.
You are strong.
You are beautiful.

I wanted her to be the most confident, sure of herself, and supported girl this world has ever seen. Almost six years later, I still want that. I'll want and work for that forever.

"Miller, do you realize you have a mini model on your hands?" Margot states as she meets us at the bench I'm sitting on.

"I've known that since the day she was born. You're the only photographer I'll trust with her though."

Margot rolls her eyes. "I'm not a real photographer. But, I appreciate it. I'll be needing her in the future, and you, too. Family session! I can already picture it."

"Maybe Miss Red will want to do it too!" Penelope exclaims.

Margot recovers faster than I can, swallowing a laugh. "I bet she'd *love* that. Hey, lil P, how about you go practice on the monkey bars for a little? You said earlier you wanted to."

Penelope's eyes light up and she turns to the playground. "We have time?" The question is directed at me.

"Go, have fun. Auntie M and I will be here when you're ready to go."

Before bolting off, Penelope runs up and gives me another quick hug. She does the same to Margot, and then she's off.

The two of us watch her sprint to the jungle gym, immediately jumping into conversation with the few other kids who were already playing. I don't know where she gets her extrovertism because it sure as shit isn't from me.

"She's pretty attached to Red, huh?" Margot asks.

"She's obsessed. I'm just thankful she can't reach the deadbolt on the door, or she'd bust out of the apartment in the mornings to see her before I'm ready to head out."

"I mean, can you blame her?"

"Not at all." It's out of my mouth before I can think better of it, and I watch Margot's eyebrows start to wiggle.

"So, what's the deal with you two?"

Let the meddling begin.

"Aside from her letting us stay at her place while we're homeless? Nothing." If I say it enough times outloud, I'll believe it.

"C'mon, I see the way you two act around each other. There haven't been any new developments?"

"Gwen has more important stuff going on."

"Gwen, is it?" I don't miss the prodding tone in Margot's voice.

"Red. You know what I meant. Besides, that important stuff involves you, so maybe we should redirect this conversation. How are you holding up?"

Margot slumps against the back of the bench. She's so short that her feet don't even reach the ground with the angle she's chosen to sit at. She blows the hair that fell in front of her face up and away. "I'm fine."

"Fine?" It's my turn to probe.

"I can't hope for either outcome because they both fucking suck. On one hand, I'm about to be, like, a step mom-*ish*. Which like—absolutely no offense to step moms—I don't want to do with Katie. And on the other hand, Red's about to watch the worst non girls' girl I've ever fucking met get the life she wanted with the guy she thought she was going to spend her life with. So, yeah, it's just…fine. I guess."

It's the farthest thing from fine, but I get where she's coming from. We're all thinking that exact same thing. Who knew two people could cause so much damage in such a small amount of time?

"How's Sawyer taking things?" I ask.

"Better than before, and honestly, that's all I can ask for. He doesn't deserve this."

"Being a surprise dad isn't the worst thing in the world."

"Miller, shit." Margot sits up and grabs my arm, worry written all over her face. "Of course it's not. You're the best dad. Penelope's amazing."

"Woah, hey. I didn't take it personally. I just—I know he doesn't know me that well, but if he needs…If he needs anyone with some experience, I'm here. I know it's not the same—"

Margot squeezes my arm before releasing it and leans back again. "Thank you. Really, thank you. I'll let him know. Speaking of dads…Do you mind if I ask you a question?"

"Shoot." I think I have a feeling that I know where this is going.

"What was he like? I mean, how did you know how to do all of the right things?" She looks towards Penelope, watching her cheer on a boy her age as he swings from bar to bar.

"By being the exact opposite of everything he is. He's not a good person, Margot. You didn't miss out."

She nods her head, and I take that as an invitation to continue, "He was…mean. To the bone, nasty. I don't remember a single *I love you* or *Way to go, kid* or any sort of positivity from him. And he beat my mom down every chance he got to the point where she just never said *anything.* Our house was silent, unless he was angry. It was walking on eggshells every second of the day until I heard his snores from the recliner in the living room.

"You know he refused to plan my mom a funeral when she died? He had her cremated and threw the urn in a closet."

"Miller, oh my God. I'm so sorry," Margot whispers.

"I used to obsessively write my eighteenth birthday down over and over again in the margins of notebooks in school, counting down the days until I could get out. A little bit after I turned sixteen, I found out my girlfriend was pregnant. I spent every minute that I wasn't working on my school issued laptop figuring out how to get emancipated because I knew I wasn't bringing any baby of mine home to him."

"Did he know?" she asks.

"No. He knew I had a job at the bank. I got a part time teller position, and he would do drive-bys to make sure I wasn't lying about where I was. My manager knew the gist of things and let me do my research and homework in one of the empty offices."

"But he had to have found out eventually?"

"The courts sent him summons paperwork for the hearing. I knew it was coming and saved every dime I made to get a small studio apartment, to prove my ability to be self-sufficient to the judge and to get away from him. The landlord took my pay stubs, sheer determination, and the application for emancipation as an act of faith. I'll be thankful until I'm dead for that kindness."

I'll never forget that court hearing. I prepared for the worst. I wore the best suit I could find at the thrift store to appear responsible and ready. I triple checked with the cashier that it looked good enough.

I thought my dad would come into that room swinging, fighting tooth and nail to keep me under him. But he didn't. It was the opposite. He was three sheets to the wind and asked the judge where he had to sign to get rid of me. I was handed the declaration of emancipation only ten minutes later and left the courthouse feeling freer than ever before.

I went back to that small, studio apartment I had just signed the lease on a week before, grabbed the envelope of cash I had hidden under my mattress, and finally went to the closest Walmart to stock up on every baby-related thing I read about needing.

That day felt like a reset on my life. I knew shit was about to get a hell of a lot harder, but I didn't care. The struggles from then on would have meaning and purpose. Everything would be on my terms and it wouldn't be weighed down by anyone.

"Jesus, Miller. And you did all of this…alone?"

I know where Margot's headed with this.

I'm not ready to talk about it though.

"Nah." I bump into her with my shoulder. "I haven't been alone since the day I found out about Penelope Grace."

We both face the playground to see my girl recreating the shimmy and twirl poses from earlier for her friends, laughing with a grin that reaches so far it's basically touching her ears.

Margot does this little shake thing—the tell she's about to cry but trying not to—and turns to me with her head tilted. "Her middle name is Grace?"

"Mhm." I wave to Penelope when she spots us.

My saving grace.

It's what I told the nurse who handed me the birth certificate paperwork. As I was filling it out, her first name was easy. I saw her, and I just knew. But I was stuck on the middle name.

I thought, *Grace, Grace...Penelope Grace Caswell. That's a good name.*

"Interesting," Margot says slyly.

"Why?"

"That's Red's middle name, too."

And for the rest of the afternoon, there was only one question on repeat in my mind.

Are you allowed two saving graces in your life?

CHAPTER 5: RED - THE PROPHECY
(RED'S VERSION)

I haven't left my bed in days.

That's not true. I emerge from the cave of comforters I've created to pee occasionally. Sometimes I even take a swig of water when I find a half empty plastic bottle on my bedroom floor.

I have nothing left in me.

I'll never admit this out loud, and I'm going to hell for it, but I clutched onto the tiniest bit of hope that Dean wasn't the father of that baby. I thought maybe, just maybe, I wouldn't have to watch my dream unfold into a nightmare.

But when Margot showed up at my front door two days ago, wanting to gently break the news to me in person like the good friend she is, I watched that hope disappear. And like the shitty friend I am, I crumbled.

Thankfully, I managed to keep it together until Margot left. I put on my bravest mask, assuring her I was going to be okay. I played off taking the next couple of days to clear my head. Do I think she believed me? Not entirely. But it was enough to ensure no one would attempt to break down my door while I wallowed.

I've spent the past forty-eight or so hours watching every

scrap of what I had meticulously thought out and planned as my future melt away into nothing. I've re-lived all of the fights with Dean about children and the infidelity and the divorce and the attempts to rebuild after the fact, just to fall apart all over again.

Years. I wasted years of my life with nothing to show for it.

You know when mentally you feel done with the tears, but your body tells you it's not finished yet? My face feels permanently puffy from crying, and I'm at the point where I'm over it.

Dean hasn't called, not that I thought or hoped he would. But the silence scares me all the same. I have to keep wondering if he's going to show up, God forbid with Katie. I've practiced a lot of grace and patience in my life, but that's all gone out the window when it relates to those two pieces of shit.

I don't want to hate Katie. I never wanted to hate her. I, along with everyone else in this town, gave liking her my best shot. When she wanted to get into it, I walked away, every damn time. I'm not so sure I could do that now. Don't think I'd want to either.

I think about how easy it was for Miller to clock Dean's behavior at the bar this past summer, and how he put an end to it with his fist, right then and there, no questions asked. It wasn't to be the bigger man or to showboat his masculinity. It wasn't about anything aside from standing up for his people.

"Fuck!" I scream to no one but myself. I throw the comforter off the bed and sit up, squinting at the sliver of bright sunlight streaming in from the window next to my bed.

I'm so sick of running in circles in my brain. I'm so sick of *all of it.*

Flopping off the bed, I move to stand, but I haven't been upright in a while so everything feels a little wobbly and dizzying. I'm most definitely dehydrated, and I couldn't tell you the last time I ate something. My appetite has been nonexistent.

I fumble my way to the bathroom connected to my bedroom, kicking the piles of clothes that are scattered on the floor out of the way. I purposely avoid the mirror, just like I have every other time I've walked by one the past couple days, and grab my toothbrush out of its holder on the counter.

Standing upright for the next two minutes feels impossible so once I have the toothpaste applied, I sit my ass on the covered toilet. The fact that I'm making an effort with my dental hygiene is good enough for me.

I attempt to run my free hand through my hair, and my fingers immediately get tangled in the rat's nest I've let form on my head.

"Okay, *that's* fucking disgusting," I mumble to myself over the electric toothbrush buzzing in my mouth.

I spit and rinse with mouthwash and finally face the depressed bitch in the mirror.

It's me. I'm the depressed bitch in the mirror.

The bags under my eyes look like I applied multiple layers of purple eyeshadow. The blotches of red all over my face may very well be permanent now. My hair looks greasy, dull, and like it'll take an entire bottle of detangler after multiple rounds of shampoo and conditioner to come close to correcting.

I'm self aware enough to recognize this is a new level of embarrassingly down bad.

I strip out of the old crew neck I've been living in and turn the shower nozzle to the hottest setting possible. The bathroom fills up with steam, and the mirror shows me mercy by fogging quickly, letting me temporarily forget the creature I've turned into staring back at me.

Stepping out of the shower thirty minutes later feels like a rebirth.

I spend the next thirty brushing my hair.

I do my skincare routine.

I find a baby blue matching lounge set to change into.

I mentally check off each small accomplishment and internally high five myself with every win.

The soft knock on my front door startles me. I haven't checked my phone in a while, but it's not like I've been expecting anyone. My texts to Margot and Daisy in our group chat have placated them enough so they give me space. I wouldn't be surprised if Beth showed up unannounced but—and I know it sounds weird—that knock wasn't a Beth Rivers knock.

Dashing to the windows, I gently peek around the curtain.

There's no one on my porch.

I swear to fucking Christ if I was just dingdong ditched I'm about to commit a crime.

For some reason, this is the thing that sets me off. I sprint down the stairs and swing open my front door with all the strength I can muster, letting it slam into the wall and rock the picture frames hanging there.

My eyes search my driveway and then down the street to see if I can catch a glimpse of the culprit. I step onto the porch to keep looking for any sign of *something* and almost trip on whatever is at my feet.

I look down to see a paper bag with a pink sticky note and familiar chicken scratch handwriting attached to the top. I snatch it up and run back into the house, again slamming the door, this time closed.

I run into the kitchen and plop the bag onto the island, avoiding the note. I'm not ready to read it yet. I have to process all of this bit by bit.

Carefully unraveling the bag, I see there are two clear topped plastic containers, and I pull them out to inspect their contents. One has a salad with a small cup of dressing sitting on the top. The other is about to burst open, filled with penne and red sauce. It's still warm.

Suddenly, I'm ravenous. I pop the top off the Tupperware and pick up a noodle with my fingers, plopping it into my mouth, forgoing the need for a fork. I can't explain it, but the simplicity of pasta right now is so goddamn comforting. I don't even know how he knew this is exactly what I needed.

I almost miss whatever is square shaped and wrapped in tinfoil in the bag. I grab it and peel a piece of the tinfoil away to find a vanilla cream frosted brownie with pink sprinkles on top. It's clearly homemade, and I feel my heart crack.

I've missed the cafe. I've missed seeing my regulars and putting smiles on peoples' faces.

But I haven't let myself admit that I've missed the normalcy of seeing Miller and Penelope the most, until now.

I pull the sticky note from the bag as I keep eating the pasta, finally grabbing a fork to finish it like a civilized person.

It's going to get better, Gwen. But until then, pasta. Penelope asked to make brownies today. See you soon.

-Miller & P.

I fold up the small piece of paper to tuck into the back of my phone case later. I watch a tear fall onto the granite, narrowly missing the note. I wipe my eyes to avoid any others spilling out and ruining something so precious.

He…thought of me. He's also still exclusively calling me Gwen and has been since our afternoon in the park, which is still fucking weird, but that's beside the point right now.

Miller thought of me enough to package up leftovers and drive them over here, on top of working his regular job (honestly, I still don't know what that is), helping out at the cafe,—Margot has texted me updates—and raising his daughter all on his own. While I've shut out the entire world to throw myself a pity party.

I don't know how to process all of this rationally. I mean, he's just an inherently good person despite all of the bullshit he's been handed throughout his life, and this probably is just a product of that. So there's nothing to read into.

I remind myself of that every time I pick up and unfold that tiny, pink piece of paper over the next several hours to reread the words he wrote. Later, I finally shimmy it into my phone case, right on top of the first one he left at the cafe.

I spend the rest of the evening on the couch, rather than in my bed. I commit to going to the cafe tomorrow. I plug my phone in to charge overnight. When it comes to life after being dead all day, it lights up with missed texts. I consider ignoring them all and letting them be a tomorrow problem, but I realize I probably won't sleep well if I don't at least *check* to see who's been reaching out.

> MARGOT
>
> Miss you. Book club got rowdy today. I think they need you to keep them in check.
>
> MARGOT
>
> Miller asked about you today. Again.
>
> MARGOT
>
> Can I give him your number?
>
> MARGOT
>
> If you don't answer in the next 5 minutes, I'm doing it.
>
> BETH RIVERS
>
> Margot tells me you haven't been out of the house in days. You're worrying me, kid.
>
> UNKNOWN NUMBER
>
> Hey, Gwen. It's me. I hope the porch drop off wasn't an overstep.
>
> UNKNOWN NUMBER
>
> Miller. This is Miller Caswell. I should have clarified that.

A laugh escapes me for the first time in days. It sounds unnatural and choppy, but God, does it feel good. I'm not ready to respond to anyone yet, but today was a good first step towards whatever comes next.

Maybe Miller's right. Maybe it will get better.

CHAPTER 6: MILLER - UTTERLY, TOTALLY, AND COMPLETELY FUCKED

It's been well over a week since I've heard from our landlord, Ernie. It's two weeks past the date he told us the apartment would be ready. I'd like to say I've remained calm about the whole thing, but the slew of less than pleasant voice-mails I've left him today would tell a different story.

Something's up, and I'm pretty sure I know I'm not gonna like whatever the outcome is.

I tried my hardest to think positively, to will things into working out. I put my all into making sure Penelope is set and settled in school. I emailed her teacher last week to check in, she assured me P is one of the politest, happiest, smartest kids in the class. I'm not surprised but I love hearing it.

We've fallen into a new normal, and the days have been fine. They're filled with work and pitching in at the cafe. The after-noons and evenings are booked and busy with homework and dinner that we've porch dropped at Gwen's before we start P's bedtime routine.

We haven't talked about it besides Gwen thanking Penelope every single day with a hug that always feels like it lasts just a bit longer each time. I took a picture yesterday. I've been meaning to send it to Gwen, but every time I pull up our text thread, I can't bring myself to do it. We haven't texted since the first night Penelope and I brought her dinner. Her response to my fucking moronic message is the last thing there.

GWENDOLYN

hi miller caswell. it's me, red or gwen or
gwendolyn or whatever lol. i hope you're right.
about it getting better. thank you.

She doesn't mention the notes. I haven't brought them up either, but I continue to leave one with every delivery. I mean, she probably just tosses them. It's dumb.

Nights are tough when Penelope's asleep and I have nothing to distract me from the fact that I just fucking wish I had someone to unwind and talk out the day with. I have to over-think living in this apartment, and if we've overstayed our welcome, and what our next move is going to be.

Gus Burton stops by to hang sometimes, which is something I'm getting used to but appreciating a shit ton. He's Sawyer's best friend and from what Margot tells me, basically his brother.

I don't know what was going through my head when I invited him over the first time. I splurged on the new *PS5* a while back and…a friend sounded nice. I keep in touch online with some of the guys I went to school with, but my life has always been so significantly different from theirs in all aspects that getting together hasn't been a thing.

Jesus, that's lame as hell.

Gus is quiet as fuck. Not much to say except game talk when we're playing, but I like him. He's a good guy. I've thought about asking Sawyer if he wants to join sometime, and I probably will, but he and Margot are enjoying their time together right now with the weight lifted off their shoulders knowing Sawyer *isn't* the new dad in town.

So, things have been fine, I guess. But my luck is about to run out. I feel my phone vibrate in my back pocket and pull it out to see Ernie's name come across the screen with an incoming call.

"Nice of you to fucking call me back, Ernie," I answer. My patience for this guy ran out a week ago.

"Miller, kid. I'm sorry to leave you hanging. Please. Understand I've had a lot going on." I can hear his heavy ass breathing into the phone and look up in fucking prayer that I can keep it together.

"Yeah, and me and Penelope haven't, not knowing what was going on with our *home*," I snap.

"I know, I know. Listen—I get it. Miller, come on. I gotta have a chat with you."

I inhale and run through the worst case scenario. No end date on the repairs, or something went wrong and our stuff got damaged. I don't remember what my renters insurance covers. Fuck.

I exhale, and he takes that as his cue to proceed. "I sold the building."

Oh. Nope. That's definitely the worst case scenario.

"You're joking." He's joking.

"The repairs felt like they were adding up to be more than the place was worth to me. This whole thing has been such a headache, it's hard on an old man."

"You're barely fucking forty, Ernie."

"You'll know what I mean when you're my age. I'm sorry, I didn't wanna have to do this to you. I'm gonna go ahead and give you back your last month's rent and deposit in full, of course. The buyers are talking about wanting to demo but…" He trails off, clearly not knowing what to say. "I don't know the logistics. But maybe you could ask Red about renting from her officially?"

I'm so fucked.

"Yeah. Yeah, I get it. Thanks, about the rent. I, um—" I clear my throat and try to process the next steps. I give myself a second to breathe so I don't threaten to knock this guy out.

"Thank you. For the call, Ernie. I'll…We'll be in touch or whatever, okay?" I need to get off the phone.

Ernie's taken aback by my abruptness. "Oh, of course. Yes, Miller. Again, I'm sor—"

"Yeah, you're sorry. Thank you." I end the call and throw my phone down the couch. It bounces on the cushion and falls to the hardwood floor, facing screen down.

With my luck, it's shattered and I'm going to either have to deal with shards of glass in my thumb or fork up cash we definitely need to be saving now that our living situation is fucked.

Realistically, I'm more than sure Gwen would let us stay long term. But what I'm not so sure on is if I'm comfortable with that.

I don't like owing people things; I don't do favors or handouts. Everything I have, besides this short stay I begrudgingly agreed to for the sake of my daughter's living situation, is because I've worked my ass off for it.

Checking the time on my watch, I see my lunch break is up, and I have about two hours until I need to get P from school to figure my shit out. I blew Ernie off so fast I didn't even get the chance to ask how long we had to clear our stuff out or anything.

Shutting down conversations like that is a deadbeat dad trait that I picked up on that's hard to break. I'm dealing with it.

I grab my cell off the floor and inspect it to confirm I didn't just screw myself even more with a broken phone before heading back down to the cafe.

Gwen jumps up from where she's leaning against the counter when she hears me shut the door.

"Sorry!" I try to get out as fast as possible. She's always been kind of jumpy, but since the news spread about Dean and the baby, she's been even more on edge, and I feel real shitty contributing to that in any way.

She looks up and those eyes—*fuck*—filled with so much hurt and pain that she won't let out, look up to meet mine. I forget every hard thing I'm about to have to deal with. I'd do anything to take away a fraction of what she's feeling, she's the least deserving of this kind of heartbreak over and over again.

I felt bad the night at The Bar when I punched Dean. Yeah, I knew him from around town as the asshole cop who thought his shit didn't stink, but he didn't do anything to *me* personally. And while I still stood by my decision because he *was* mouthing off to Margot, a part of me felt gross about it.

But at least three years of cheating and lying that resulted in a baby with another woman? When you had someone like Gwendolyn Bozelli?

I wish I hit him twice.

"Oh! Miller, hey. No, not your fault. Don't apologize." She shakes her head, and I watch her hair practically dance around her face. She takes one step forward. "Wait, what's wrong?"

How does somebody who goes out of their way to avoid me ninety-nine percent of the time recognize right off the bat when something isn't right? I feel like I put so much energy into trying to catch everything, and Gwen just does it effortlessly.

"Nothing's wrong," I half mumble as I walk to my regular booth in the corner. My work laptop is there, right where I left it before my lunch break.

Gwen follows me and sits down on the other side of the table. "You're a bad liar, Miller."

"Sorry," I repeat, opening my laptop to see three new password reset requests, a chat asking for help with some document attachments, and an email from my manager, all waiting for my attention. All of the tasks are marked urgent when each sender and I all know they're not.

"Stop saying sorry and tell me what's going on, and I'll forgive you." There's a lightness to her voice I haven't heard in a while, and it makes me pause enough to glance up at her to see she's smiling. It's one of those big ones that makes me think I forget how to breathe.

I smirk back at her, appreciating the distraction from my

downward spiral she doesn't even know she's offering me by just giving me this lick of attention.

"Let me clean up my inbox, and I'm all yours." *Why did I just say that?*

Her cheeks darken, and I feel my own heat up. Embarrassing as fuck.

"What do you do for work anyway?" she asks.

I'm happy to pivot this conversation more than she knows. "I'm the IT guy for Coastal Savings."

"You work at the bank?!" She's making it sound like I save kittens from trees or routinely perform open heart surgery.

I get started on the password reset requests first while I think of how to respond to her without launching into a long ass story she doesn't actually care to hear. "Yeah, I got a part-time job as a teller when I was sixteen. My manager, Steph, saw what I was juggling…trying to finish school, learning how to adjust to life with a newborn. She took a chance on me, and I'll never forget it. I've always been good with computers and shit so when an IT position opened, she got me in the door."

Steph was one of the first adults who took me seriously and saw my potential aside from the judge who granted my emancipation. She was able to look past the outside layer of a teen dad who grew up in a shitty environment. She didn't judge me for it. Instead, she encouraged me to keep up with my trainings and helped me make sure I was up to date on different opportunities.

"I get to work from home now, or wherever." I motion to her cafe we're sitting in. "Ninety percent of the time. The other ten percent, I'm only there for big meetings or hands on stuff, it's not often. It lessens the burden of finding childcare for sick days and vacations, and I don't mind the job."

"That's so cool."

"I'm a glorified nerd. Not sure many people would consider that cool."

"Good thing I'm not many people then," she retorts.

My fingers pause on my keyboard. Is Gwen…flirting with me? I look to see her fingers lightly tapping on the table in some sort of pattern, those pretty lips tipped up. She has her other elbow on the table, hand propping her head up at a tilt. The dark smudges under her eyes are still there, but there's also joy, no matter how small it is.

"That you are not," I finally respond as I hit send on my last email.

"Did you always know this is what you wanted to do?"

"I didn't have time to think about it. I had a small window to figure out what I was good at and how to make a stable career out of it. This was the easy thing that stuck."

Gwen sits with that for a minute while I pull up the rental website to get started on my search for mine and Penelope's new form of stable.

"You do everything for her, huh?"

"Yeah, she's not exactly super independent yet. We're working on turning six over here."

Gwen laughs. "No, I mean you do everything for *her*. Every move you make is for her best interest. It's really admirable, Miller."

"Oh. Well, yeah. She's my world. I'm what they call a *helicopter dad* according to Google. Which is where I get most of my parenting info, just so you know. But I don't mind the title. I'm proud as fuck about it, if I'm being honest."

She nods her head in understanding. "I'd be proud too. Now, can you tell me what had you coming down the stairs looking like the world just came crashing down?"

"It basically did," I answer truthfully, focusing on the screen as I aimlessly scroll through what looks to be a very dismal results page with a whole lot of nothing.

I don't want to burden her with this. Today is the first time I'm seeing a glimpse of the real Gwen again and fucking it up by making her feel like she needs to help us feels counterproductive.

Maybe knowing—or hoping—we're close to the end of this arrangement is helping her feel more comfortable around me. I don't want to go back on that progress.

She pulls the laptop away from me and glances at the screen. "Wait. Why are you looking at apartments?" She fully takes the laptop into her hands to get a better look. "And *why* is the search radius outside of Merrymount? Miller, what the hell is going on?"

"It's fine, Gwen. I promise." I try to take my laptop back but she's refusing to let go, holding it hostage until I give her the real response she's looking for.

"Are you…Are you moving? Did I do something? What about your old apartment?"

I sigh. Okay, we're doing this. "Ernie—"

"Your landlord?" she interrupts.

"Yeah, he called a little bit ago. He sold the building."

Gwen's hands finally release my computer and fly to cover her mouth. "Oh my God."

"It's not great," I say in defeat.

"But…" I'm watching her process this in real time, seeing the gears turning in her head, piecing together how she can single-handedly fix this. Because that's what Gwen does.

"I don't get it," she continues. "Why are you looking at apartments? Especially ones out of Merrymount? You can't be serious."

"If that's all that's available, I don't really have a choice."

"What the fuck does that mean? Is upstairs too small? We could switch. You two can have my house or…I don't know. Come on, this is stupid. You're not moving."

I shake my head. This is the complete opposite of what I wanted to do. I don't want to stress her out.

"No, we just don't need to be taking up your space anymore. We overstayed our welcome as it is. Gwen, you have no idea how much you've helped out. But I have to give Penelope a home."

She winces, and I'm afraid I said the wrong thing. I do that a lot.

"Merrymount is your home," she mumbles and looks down.

"Gwen…"

"No. This is fucking ridiculous, okay? I have a place. Here. In town. This is me officially advertising it for rent." She puts her hands to her face to make a megaphone. "You heard it here first, two bedroom apartment for rent above Red's Place!"

Chris, Merrymount's favorite goofy part-time cashier and bartender, looks up from his spot on a barstool at the counter. "Really? I've been looking to move out of my grandma's with no luck."

Gwen scoffs. "Not you, Chris."

His shoulders slump and he goes back to do whatever it was he was doing on his phone.

Gwen's eyes meet mine again. "Say yes."

"You don't understand—"

"Yes, I do. More than you know. You think you'd be asking for too much. You're so engrained to handle it all on your own that you don't see those around you *want* to help. Let me. From someone who gets it."

I run my hand through my hair, pulling at the ends. I put my head to the table.

Gwen waits. She doesn't add anything else to sway me in either direction. She gives me the time I need to process all of it, and I could kiss her for seeing so much of me without knowing it.

Fucking Christ, do I want to kiss her.

I don't let myself dwell on that often, but that thought is so Goddamn loud in my head right now, the only thing that pulls me back is hearing her do that little finger tap pattern on the table top again.

"Rent," I demand.

Gwen smiles because she knows she's got me. "That pasta you make, every Thursday night."

"You do realize it's just store bought sauce and pasta?"

"Don't care." She holds out her right hand, silently asking me to shake on this insanely imbalanced deal she's offering me.

"No way. The scales are way off."

"Fine. Can you keep helping with the dishes when you're not busy? It's like, my least favorite part of this place, and Margot's slow."

"You want me to bring you mediocre pasta on Thursday nights—something I've been doing anyway—and dishes...and that's going to be the rent I pay to live in your apartment?"

"Yes." There's no room for an alternative in her voice, and her hand is still outstretched.

"I have one amendment."

"I'm listening," she coaxes.

"The Thursday dinner is no longer a drop off. The three of us will eat together, okay?"

I watch Gwen swallow and mull over how she's going to respond. It takes her a couple seconds to internally argue with herself, but I don't care. If we're going to do this, I need to know she's going to be comfortable having me around.

"Deal." She nods her head once in confirmation.

"This is insane." I grab her hand and fight through the charged current racing through my arm to shake on it and add, "Thank you."

Her grip tightens around mine as she smiles in triumph from winning this battle. "You're welcome."

On top of unexpectedly packing up our entire apartment, I now have to somehow come up with a plan to tell Penelope the news of our new home without her physically combusting. The effort I'm about to put into that is pointless, I'm sure.

CHAPTER 7: RED - AIN'T NO THANG
BUT A CHICKEN WANG

My bare feet hit the hardwood floor of my bedroom, and I take in one of my most favorite smells in the world wafting in from the window I have cracked next to my bed.

It's the smell of leaves beginning to change and cool air that makes you grab your oldest, comfiest hoodie. I breathe in the scent of football games, apple picking, pumpkin carving, and bonfires that last all night.

It's the end of September. The start of my most favorite time of the year.

Fall.

You're assigned a season at birth. Don't ask questions, it's just one of the rules. My season is fall. I love everything about it and trying to put that feeling into words wouldn't do it justice, so it's a *if you know, you know* type of thing. Capeesh?

I've been feeling the temperature drop and the days shorten for a couple weeks now, waiting for the switch to flip between seasons. I slowly and quietly said goodbye to summer while trying to settle into life post breakdown.

I start my morning routine: wash my face, brush my teeth,

and tame my out of control hair. I change into a clean pair of cheeky underwear, a new pair of long cable-knit socks, and throw on my old Merrymount High Varsity Cheer hoodie, tucking my thumbs into the holes of the sleeves I've created from wear and tear over the years. This sweatshirt has been through it all with me and it falls about halfway down my thighs, so it's perfect for a no pants day.

I pad my way into the kitchen, grabbing the s'mores iced coffee in a mason jar I brewed last night from the fridge. I'm throwing this flavor on the menu next week, and I want to make sure it's just right before I release it to the masses of Merrymount.

The first sip after a drop of creamer tells me I have nothing to worry about when it comes to pleasing my customers at Red's. This shit is good.

I crack open the window above my sink to let that crisp, fresh air in, and I find my laptop on my kitchen table, where I left it last night before I went to bed. I sit down, facing the French doors that lead to my backyard. I watch my laptop come to life as I open it up and inhale another glorious sip of caffeine.

All around, I'm feeling better. There's a list of people to thank for that, and at the top of that list is my therapist, Lisa, whose picture just popped up in the corner of my computer screen. I tap accept on the notification to start our meeting for this week's session.

"Good Morning, Red," Lisa greets me with a bright smile, one I've come to lean on and love over the last couple years.

"Anotha glorious morning! Makes me sick!" I say over my cup in my best Winnie Sanderson impersonation.

"Ah, so you feel it in the air today as well, huh?" Lisa was assigned fall as her season at birth, too. I'm convinced it's one of the reasons I've stuck with her through this process for so long. She gets me.

"It's starting, Lisa. I can practically feel the leaves crunching already."

"How are you feeling today, honey?"

The main reason I clicked with Lisa almost instantly, is she's perfectly informal. The slew of consultation appointments I had with other therapists immediately following my separation from Dean taught me I could never reach my full potential of clear mind and mental stability if I constantly felt like I was having to put on an act for the person who was supposed to be helping me.

I met with a few professionals in their stuffy offices with stale hard candy sitting in a bowl next to the leather chair they directed me to sit in, and I wanted to crawl out of my skin right then and there. One male therapist's first question like, right out the gate, was "Do you think there's anything *you* might have contributed to your marriage ending?"

It was the last time I set up an appointment with a male therapist.

Some weren't so bad. Most weren't awful. But none of them felt like they could work with me to tackle untangling everything going on in my head. Until Lisa.

She calls me honey and listens to my rambles, following up on every point, whether there are five or fifteen. And she calls me out on my bullshit, something I do appreciate from time to time.

I finally settle on a generic answer, although an honest one. "I'm feeling good."

"Good?" Lisa adjusts her thick, tortoiseshell framed glasses that always find themselves teetering on the edge of her nose. "Good is good, Red. What has this week looked like?"

"The usual. Nothing crazy has happened at the cafe. I stayed late yesterday to have dinner with Miller and Penelope."

Lisa looks into her laptop's camera. "You had dinner with them last night?"

"Uh, yeah."

"And how was that?"

"Miller made salmon, and I thought there was no way Penelope would touch it. But she did! She ate her whole plate and asked for seconds. I don't blame her, it was wicked good. Can you believe neither of them has ever tried sushi? Insane. I told them we'd have to order take out sometime. I was ready to head home but Penelope asked if I wanted to watch the rest of the movie she had on earlier, and I had nothing to do. So, like, why not? But to no one's surprise, she passed out well before the end. But then Miller put on *The Bachelorette*, and I obviously had to see who was being sent home…so, yeah."

"So, you'd say you had a good time?"

I'm not sure where she's going with this. "Yes." I've learned it's easier to answer her questions before demanding explanations.

"And this was a spur of the moment decision, not connected to the informal, verbal contract you have with Miller about his and his daughter's living arrangement?"

I now see where she's going with this. "Yes," I admit.

I watch Lisa lean back into her chair and interlace her fingers together on her lap. Her notebook and pen are perched on the chair's armrest. Her tight, jet black curls are gathered in a loose ponytail on the top of her head. She pretends to ponder for a minute.

"Interesting."

I huff a sigh. "Out with it, Lisa. What's so *interesting*?" I throw up air quotes for extra emphasis so she gets that I'm onto her shenanigans.

"You have barely strayed from this rigid routine of yours for… almost two years now? Maybe more?" Lisa waits for me to nod my head.

She continues, "Except with Margot. And now the Caswells."

"Yeah, Lis. I found friends. Who knew?"

"You've had friends all along. You've been the one guarding your castle."

Okay, Lisa's metaphors are kind of annoying sometimes.

"Do you see some of your walls starting to come down?" she asks me.

I don't fucking know is how I want to respond. But, of course, I do not. I take my time mulling it over in my head. I think about how I don't jump at the sight of Miller coming down the stairs anymore and rather, greet him with a smile like a normal human being.

I don't hesitate to join Penelope in whatever activity she wants me to participate in, whether it's a random dance party or donut eating contest. (Miller squashed that one pretty quick. He said it was a choking hazard. He was right, but I pouted alongside P in solidarity.)

Margot has been opening the cafe, and I've been heading in a little later. We work with each other on scheduling, and Miller fills in when needed. I've even thought about officially hiring someone else part time. You know, besides tapping George in from the pizza shop when I'm in a bind. It's not all on me now, I feel lighter.

The only thing that I've actually planned is Thursday night pasta, and it doesn't feel like a chore at all. I look forward to it.

Now that I really sit here with it all, I realize life has shifted, and I didn't even notice it happening.

"Woah," I say.

"Woah is right, Red. I'm really proud of you. Nothing that has been thrown at you has been easy. Showing up for yourself every day is no small task. But granting yourself grace and freedom, something you have struggled with for some time, is so beautiful and rewarding. It doesn't have to be big and heavy. These baby steps you're making are laying an incredibly strong foundation."

We dive into the rest of this week's session without any other major breakthroughs. I beat around the bush when Lisa brings up my lack of communication with my parents, and thankfully, she doesn't push me on it. I think I've made enough progress this week in her eyes that she's willing to look past it.

Once I sign off with Lisa, I get started on housework I've neglected lately, beginning with my very sad monstera plants that have seen better days. I hope some water and sunlight can bring them back to life. Poor little droopy babies.

I flop onto my couch after attending to my greenery, dishes, and laundry. Satisfied with the work I put in, I grab the remote to throw on one of my comfort shows as a break. The sounds of Gavin DeGraw float through my living room, and I let my eyes flutter closed, not needing to see to know what's going on in this episode because I've seen it so many times. A nap doesn't sound so bad right now.

* * *

I LOOK between the extra butter popcorn in my left hand and the movie theater popcorn in my right. I repeat this several times, unable to make a decision.

"They're not expired. I checked this morning when I got in." Chris's voice snaps me out of my pattern, and I face the teenage pain in my ass cashier at the front of Merrymount's little market, The Store. It's been staple in my life, since I grew up two doors down at the cafe.

Chris is also somewhat of a staple around town. He's young— I think he just recently turned eighteen. He's not really a pain in my ass. Well, not all of the time. His grandma paid me a lot of money over the years to keep him entertained while babysitting. He's weird as fuck, but like, everyone is. He just hasn't quite figured out his place yet, and I think that's perfectly fine.

I let my arms drop, still holding onto each package. "Ugh."

"I promise! I take the quality control of this place very seriously!"

"Chris, shut up." I lift the two boxes of popcorn. "I don't know which one to pick."

"Seriously?" He tilts his head and adjusts his giant, black

framed glasses that make his eyes bug out a little. "The obvious answer is movie theater."

Good enough for me. I place the extra butter back on the shelf and walk to the register. "Sold."

I don't know why I'm overthinking this. It's microwavable popcorn.

Am I making a pit stop at The Store for this one specific thing to subtly hint at and hopefully score an invite to a movie night with Miller and Penelope for the second night in a row?

Who's to say?

But aside from the butter trip-up, I'm feeling on fucking fire today.

Taking a day to rest and reset isn't something I've allowed myself in a very long time, and I know I have a long way to go, but past me is really fucking proud of current me for putting in the work to find pockets of slow joy.

After my very satisfying couch nap, I took my time getting ready before my weekly—but is sort of becoming way more than once a week—dinner with Miller and Penelope. It was nice to sit in front of my vanity and play with my makeup again. I finally felt like I could put mascara on without fear of it streaking down my face from tears. I even curled my hair—just for the hell of it. Okay, not for the hell of it. I might have sort of noticed Miller staring at my hair when it's like this one or twice and thought maybe I should try it out again. For like, science.

Chris lets out a low whistle when I reach his register. It's harmless because, well, it's Chris. I changed his diapers as a baby and consoled him when he cried after he lost his first tooth.

"Red, might I just say—"

But boy, does he try. "Chris, if you're about to hit on me, you may not."

He immediately looks down to scan the box of popcorn. "Yes, ma'am."

As much as I do not need Chris Roberts painfully trying to

make a move, the attempt tells me that I must have done something right. It's the confidence boost I needed before heading over to the cafe.

"So, what's shakin'?" I ask Chris as he takes his sweet time bagging the one item I'm buying.

"Nothing. Grandma is trying to get me to enroll at the community college. I'm not sure I want to."

I check the time on my phone. "I have a few minutes, want to talk it out?"

"I don't need to burden you with my woes."

"God, you're so fucking dramatic. C'mon, Chris. Give me the pros and cons."

He sighs, and it takes everything in me to not flick him in annoyance. I don't even know why he's putting on this act. It's not like he's ever had a problem asking me for help in literally every aspect of his life. Despite how many times I've told him I do *not* ever need the dirty details.

"I really don't want to bother you, Red."

"You're not bothering me. I'm offering!" I throw my hands up, about ready to tell him nevermind and dash the hell out of here.

"Well, since you asked…"

Fucking finally.

"If you didn't have Red's, where would you be?"

"Honestly? I've never thought about it. The place literally has my name on the door and has since I learned how to walk. But, I'm pretty sure it's normal to not have your entire life planned out at eighteen."

"It feels like everyone in this town does, though. Everyone except me."

"That's simply not true," I retort.

Chris shrugs his shoulders. Seeing him dejected like this isn't something I enjoy. I'd rather him try to hit on me again.

"Chris." I gently shove his arm. "What's holding you back from at least trying?"

"Failing," he answers immediately.

"Now *that* is something I know a thing or two about. I've failed with a lot of stuff, and I turned out fine! Failed tests, failed gym, hell—I even failed my marriage!" I will use self deprecating humor to get him out of this funk. I don't care.

The door jingles the same bell trill I have at Red's, and I turn my head to see Daisy Stiles walk in as Chris says, "Red, I think everyone would agree leaving Dean Fitzgerald is the best thing that could have ever happened to you."

"A-fucking-men to that, my dude," Daisy says.

"Alright, we're not dogpiling on me. Not today."

Daisy leans her head into my shoulder. I feel the long, black curls of her hair tickle my arm, her signature daisy crocheted bandana sitting perfectly in place on the top of her head. She knows it's very much so on the nose, just like being named after a flower by her two florist parents. She's never cared what anyone thought about her though, and it's something I admire a lot.

"We're not dogpiling, we're just still celebrating your freedom," she says.

"Yeah, yeah, yeah. Feels the same," I respond.

Chris finally hands me the plastic bag with my single box of popcorn, and I tap my card on the reader to pay.

"It's not," Daisy replies. "Anyway, any plans tonight? I was gonna text Margot, but it's Thursday so Sawyer's probably fucking her against a washing machine."

We both turn our heads to Chris when we hear him choke on air. He shakes his head to let us know he's good as he takes a sip of water. We all know his unrequited infatuation with Sawyer Hale and pay no mind to it. Margot blew into town and now gets to live out his dream. He's still trying to swallow it. Literally.

Daisy continues, "And I was going to see what Beth was up to. I have some ad ideas to run by her. But when I pulled up to the riverside, I saw Gus was still there and decided my day didn't need ruining by that oaf."

Their hatred for each other truly knows no bounds, and as much as I would fucking love to meddle, I don't have the time or energy to unpack a decade's worth of rivalry over seemingly nothing. It works just fine this way.

"Sorry, Daze. I have dinner with Miller and Penelope. I don't have anything going on this weekend though, we could plan something with Margot?"

She tries to hide her disappointment, but I don't miss the way her face falls. I know she hates being home, but I also know if I tried to invite her right now, she'd decline, thinking she's a burden or something.

"No worries! Of course we can do something, text the group chat when you're free."

"I get off in an hour. I don't have plans…" Chris throws out.

Daisy smirks. "Good to know, Christopher. The twins have a new Lego set they probably wouldn't mind some help with. Pop over next door to be a doll and help them out?" She tilts her head slightly and lets those big, brown eyes widen. I count to three in my head while I watch Chris fall into a trance. Daisy pulls her bottom lip in with her teeth for good measure.

I know this act well. Daze and I have never had a problem tag teaming and leveling up our flirt game to get what we want in certain situations. Pawning off Chris to keep her eleven-year-old twin brothers occupied? An easy move. A smart one.

He nods. "Sure, sure. Sounds fun, yeah. Of course, Daisy."

Daisy leans over the counter, smacking a kiss on his cheek. "Ugh, you're the best. They're gonna love that." She straightens back up and stands on her toes to quickly pop a kiss on my cheek before she leaves. "Text me when you're home after dinner, 'kay?"

"Yes, captain," I answer.

Once the door shuts, and both Chris and I watch Daisy saunter back over to The Fuzzy Leaf, her family's flower shop, I hear Chris let out a frustrated sigh. "I fell for it again, didn't I?"

I clap a hand on his shoulder before I make my way out.

"Yeah, my dude, you did. Don't let it get you down though. And hey, about school?" He perks up, and I wish I had some more solid advice for him than I do, but I give it my best shot. "Carpenter Valley Community lets you try out classes for two weeks before having to commit. So, no money lost if you hate it and bail. Tell Judy you're gonna give it a shot."

Chances are, his grandmother just wants to see him doing *something*. Like I said, he's a good kid. Just needs a solid kick in the ass sometimes.

The relief on his face when he hears a solution that requires almost no commitment is laughable. "Thanks, Red. I don't know how you do it, knowing everything about everyone. You're the best."

"It ain't no thang but a chicken wang, Chris."

I leave The Store feeling positive. I walk down the little alley between the Main Street buildings to reach the back, humming one of my favorite songs and swinging my plastic bag like an idiot. I reach the only unlabeled door. It leads directly into the apartment above the cafe where I know I'm about to have dinner with two people who have quickly become fixtures in my life.

I ignore the pang of worry I feel when I think about how I'm probably more attached to them than I'm letting on. Miller and Penelope are my tenants, my best friend's family, my...friends. None of this is a big deal.

God fucking damn it, I sound like Margot.

CHAPTER 8: MILLER - BAGGAGE WITH A SIDE OF PASTA

I turn the burner off on the stove when I hear a knock on the door. It's faint enough that Penelope didn't hear it from her bedroom so I'm able to make my way over without having to fight my almost six year old to open it.

And thank fucking God for that, because when I open the door I'm faced with perfection and the real life version of most of my daydreams lately.

Gwendolyn Bozelli is leaning against the doorway. Her beautiful fucking face, with a closed lip smile that I pretend is reserved just for me, is surrounded by her thick hair that she clearly took her time curling before coming over here. The waves fall around her cheeks, over her shoulders, and stop right where my eyes find her—for lack of a better term while my brain is short circuiting—perfect fucking rack.

I swear I'm a respectable, stand up guy. Everyone's body is beautiful. I put in the work to make sure objectifying women is something I never partake in. But Gwen has this tank top thing that's basically painted on her, and where fabric normally covers, it's a V, and the bottom point of that V is low. There isn't a spot of skin on her chest that isn't covered by cute little freckles.

I'm pretending I don't notice the tiny balls poking from behind her shirt. I'm choosing to actively not think about Gwen with pierced nipples. That's not something that's my business. I fill my head with visuals of anything else to distract myself.

The jeans she has on are also tight as fuck and I know that when she blows past me, I need my vision to avert to anywhere that's not the ass that I know is being hugged by the denim.

"Hi," she greets me. I blink to bring myself back to reality. She doesn't move. Normally, she'd just walk right in. I mean, this is technically her place.

"H-hi." I just fumbled a one fucking word greeting.

Gwen's smile opens and it reaches so far, the corners of her eyes crinkle, and it takes everything in me to not crash my mouth into hers. I don't know what the fuck is happening to me.

This is when I realize she knows. She can fully see I'm completely struck by her standing in the doorway, and she loves it. She's shining so bright from my attention, and I've barely even gotten the chance to drown her in it.

"You look beautiful, Gwen. You always look beautiful. You're stunning." Okay, that was a lot.

I see the skin under the freckles on her face darken as she says, "Thank you." She moves her hand to tuck her hair behind her ear but before I know what the hell I'm doing, I find my hand stopping hers to do it myself.

Gwen's just as shocked as I am when I pull my arm back. She quickly slides through the doorway, kicks off her sneakers, and walks to the kitchen island to place the plastic bag she brought with her onto it.

I'm still standing here with the door open like an idiot.

"Daddy, when is Red—" Penelope starts to ask from her room. I see her head poke out. "Red!" she screeches and sprints the few steps over to Gwen.

"Hello there, my favorite tiny human. I've been waiting to see you all day," Gwen says.

"You should've come over sooner! Daddy let me hang posters in my room. You have to see!" Penelope releases her grip around Gwen's waist, only to grab hold of the woman's hand to drag her into the newly-decorated bedroom.

"You don't need to hold me hostage, P. I'm a willing participant," Gwen says with a laugh.

I finally shut the front door and head back to the stove to finish dinner. I can hear Penelope rambling off every member of the Heeler family to Gwen as she gives her the grand tour of her room.

When I told Penelope we were staying, she immediately jumped into her strong argument about needing her room to be perfect. She was sure to quote how I had previously told her we weren't putting anything on the walls because this was supposed to just be temporary, but now it isn't.

What they don't tell you about raising a smart kid is that arguing with them is next to impossible. They always have a point and ninety percent of the time, the point is solid.

So, her new bedroom that overlooks the main street of a small town in Massachusetts is now covered in posters of a cartoon Australian cattle dog family.

Moving the rest of our stuff from our old place to here actually wasn't terrible, entirely because we actually had *help* for once. I thought about asking Sawyer but then got in my head about bothering him, so I was ready to tackle the project on my own. I hoped to get everything at least cleaned out and in boxes in the new apartment in one weekend.

My plan didn't unfold that way though, because Gus and Sawyer showed up unannounced bright and early that Saturday with Gus' truck, ready to unload and unpack.

I guess I should have read more into Margot asking for a key to the apartment at Ernie's. She told me she wanted to do laundry because the washing machine at the cottages was acting up. Turns out she picked up through the grapevine it was moving weekend for the Caswells and took it upon herself to put Gus and Sawyer to work.

Looking back, I should have seen this coming. But I can't stress enough how not used to the idea of a village I am. But when I was able to hand the keys back to Ernie by the end of just one day and had everyone over for pizza and beers, I was thankful as hell.

By the time the girls finally emerge from Penelope's bedroom, I have two bowls set with silverware in front of the two barstools at the island, and I have mine on the other side, where I'll stand. I've been trying to find a single barstool that matches these two with no luck so I'm going to end up just ordering a new set of three.

I don't mind standing, but I know from the way Gwen scrunches her face every time we all have dinner together, she feels like she's putting me out. I want her to feel comfortable here.

I finally got her to stop arguing with me about the seating arrangements when she's here. I'm cool with forking over money for another stool so we don't have to do it again.

Gwen hoists Penelope up onto her barstool before I have the chance to. She does it without a second thought, and it feels dumb for me to think of it as big of a deal as I do, but I've never had anyone else helping out like this. I don't want to get used to it, and I don't want her to think she's obligated.

"Thanks, Red," P mumbles while jamming as much pasta into her tiny mouth as she can on the first bite. The manners are there, the execution I guess needs some work.

"No choking, please," I remind her.

I wait for Gwen to take a bite. I don't want to get my hopes up, but I really do hope she notices a difference. I might have used company time today to Pinterest the fuck out of a sauce recipe, opting to skip the cheap store bought jar I usually use. I might be trying to impress her.

"Holyfuckingshit," Gwen says while covering her mouth with her hand. She swallows and adds, "Miller, what the hell?"

I fork my own bite in my mouth with a smirk and look at Gwen like I haven't the slightest clue as to what she's talking about. She scoops up another bite. Another muffled moan. Not my intended response, but I can't say I hate hearing it.

Penelope ignores both of us, eating and lightly kicking her little feet against the island.

"Why does this taste so good? I mean, thank you. I appreciate every meal you've ever made for me. But Miller, this is like, really freaking good."

"I tried a recipe I found online. Instead of the jar."

"For the record, I liked the jar sauce."

"I know." I feel my face heat up no matter how hard I fight it, and I keep my gaze down in my bowl. Maybe this was a stupid idea after all.

Gwen's hand wraps around my wrist, and I pause. God, her skin is always so soft.

"But I hate to be the bearer of bad news and tell you I love this like, twenty times more. I promise to help next time, but we can never go back to the jar."

We.

I'm not gonna dwell on how fucking sweet that sounds.

She still hasn't let go of my arm.

"You got yourself a deal, Gwendolyn."

She lets her hand rest for another moment before releasing me to continue eating.

Penelope finally voices her opinion. "I don't know what the heck you two are talking about. Tastes the same to me."

The small kitchen fills with laughter from all three of us, and it sounds just as fucking sweet as the idea of a *we* when it comes to me and Gwen.

But again, I'm not going to dwell on that.

* * *

"MOVING HER IS *NOT* AN OPTION, MILLER."

Penelope fell asleep halfway through the movie she picked for us all to watch. Movie night was non-negotiable the second she realized Gwen brought popcorn. She's snuggled up on Gwen's lap and even though the credits are now rolling for the movie we put on *after* the first, Gwen still isn't ready for me to move my daughter to bed.

"She has school in the morning," I argue, albeit lamely.

I don't want to have to move her either. Seeing the two of them like this, so natural and so normal, makes my chest tighten. I catch my left hand rubbing small circles there to loosen it. My right hand stays firmly planted on the couch because the last time Gwen adjusted herself, her thigh rested on the tips of my fingers. And yeah, there's a layer of denim between my skin and hers, but it's contact I'm not giving up right now.

Gwen looks down with my favorite soft smile at Penelope, wrapped in a big fuzzy blanket that's covered in avocados with googly eyes. She smoothes out the top of Penelope's hair and leans down to get close to her ear.

"Hey, sweet, tiny human," Gwen whispers. "Daddy's shutting the party down. We have to go brush our teeth, okay?"

Penelope's eyes flutter open, then close. She opens them again to half moons and nods her head once in a *still half asleep but will listen to anything you say* state.

This is where I'm supposed to swoop in and handle the bedtime routine because I'm her dad and that's what I do every night. But Gwen keeps Penelope cocooned in that fuzzy blanket and lifts her up, cradle style, and walks to the bathroom.

When she reaches the door, she turns back to me and mouths, "I got this, okay?"

She doesn't wait for me to respond. The next thing I know,

the back of that beautiful head of hair is swaying into the bathroom.

It's crazy to me that just a few short months ago, this entire scenario would have seemed out of the question. I can honestly say I never thought I would trust anyone else with my daughter beyond the daycare I had to go through however many interviews with to feel comfortable.

But now I can hear Gwen singing a song about shiny teeth while Penelope's electric toothbrush powers away in the bathroom as I sit on the couch. I'm seemingly tapped out of parental duties for the time being by the hilarious, loud, and drop dead gorgeous woman in the next room over.

Gwen made Penelope shoot water out of her nose earlier at dinner when she literally licked her bowl clean to demonstrate how much she loved the homemade sauce.

The laughing continued when the three of us tried to finish a single game of *Operation*. We couldn't, for the record. Gwen would make the zapping sound right before I could pull anything out of the pretend patient, causing me to jump and lose, every time.

When we all finally got settled on the couch, P and Gwen housed an entire bag of popcorn during the previews, before the movie even started. When I had the audacity to ask why we weren't skipping the previews, Gwen told me I was a funsucker trying to ruin the movie goer experience. That caused Penelope to fall off the couch, cackling.

My face hurts from smiling so much tonight. I've never seen Penelope feed off someone else's energy so easily. I feel like a broken record, but things just feel different. It's a slow change with a big impact ever since the group of people we've been surrounding ourselves with came into our lives.

After I put our drinkware in the sink to clean once Gwen leaves and trash the empty microwavable popcorn bags, I quietly walk towards Penelope's bedroom. I don't mean to eavesdrop, but it's a small space.

"Why don't we pick out your outfit for school tomorrow? Make things easier on Daddy in the morning," Gwen says.

I don't hear Penelope respond, but she must give the go ahead because I hear the opening and closing of drawers.

Gwen might not be a mom yet, but she sure has that natural motherly instinct so many people online talk about when I'm late night doom scrolling for advice. It doesn't come easy to me like it does so clearly for her. She's the one who suggested pajamas *before* we started our movie night, anticipating P falling asleep before I could think of it.

I remember the look on her face clear as day when Penelope slipped up that one time in the cafe, talking about Gwen and how she'd make a great mom. I remember how a deep sadness took over every feature and how I couldn't think of a single thing to say that would make it better. But I knew I wanted to.

I lean in the doorway and watch Gwen mull over options before presenting them to a very sleepy P, laying in bed with her head propped up on one arm.

"It might be chilly tomorrow. Do you know what you have for a special? It's Friday. I always had gym on Fridays. Maybe a sweater over one of these?" She holds up two T-shirts that look the same to me, but Penelope points to the one on the left.

"That's a good choice." I offer out my opinion so Gwen knows I'm there, and I'm not just standing off to the side like a deadbeat creep.

Penelope rolls her eyes, a bad habit of hers since the early age of two that I've had negative luck in breaking. "Daddy can't tell the difference."

"Most men can't, girlie. But that's okay," Gwen responds.

Gwen finds the drawer of black leggings, grabs a pair to lay out with the shirt and sweater they picked out together, and then immediately picks up one of the dozens of books we have stacked next to P's bed. She sits on the edge of the bed, and one hand reaches out to rub circles on Penelope's back, the other holding the book up to read.

Before I know what I'm doing, I'm pulling my phone out of my pocket and snapping a picture. I've done this a couple times now, catching P and Gwen doing random, little things together. I don't know what I'm saving them all for. I really need to share them with Gwen, and I will eventually, but these are the kind of moments that need to be documented.

Margot calls them quiet happys.

I flick on Penelope's ridiculous amount of nightlights while Gwen is finishing up the story. Once Gwen says *the end* and P is back to sleep, I lean over and kiss the top of my daughter's head, wishing her sweet dreams like I do every night, and gently close the door behind me as Gwen and I walk back out into the living room.

While Gwen and I have found a comfortable common ground with Penelope, we still have absolutely no clue how to act when it's just the two of us. That's more than apparent now standing here in the dim light.

"Thank you," I start.

"For what?"

"You just put my kid to bed, Gwen."

"Oh." She scrunches her nose and shakes her head. "That's like…That's not something you need to thank me for."

"I do. It's a big deal to me."

"Why?" Gwen walks to the sink, turns the faucet on, and starts doing the dishes.

Absolutely fucking not happening.

I follow her and switch the water off. "Okay, one—You're not cleaning up. We invite you over for dinner, not chores." She switches the water back on, ignoring me.

"Two—" Water off. I keep my hand on the knob to stop her from fighting me on it again and turn my head to look at her.

"You do everything for everyone. It might not be a big deal to you and honestly, it kind of pisses me off that everyone around here doesn't see an issue with that. But it's huge to me. Penelope's bedtime routine is something only I have done every single day since we came home from the hospital."

Gwen's hand covers mine. Her pinky traces the engraved *P* on my ring. I had it made for Penelope's first birthday to celebrate reaching such a big milestone, and I haven't taken it off since. I feel goosebumps break out up my arm. She doesn't look at me though, keeping her focus down.

"I know," she breathes. "But this is all I know."

It sounds more like a confession than I think she intended.

I place my other hand on top of hers. "I don't want you to think I don't appreciate—"

"I don't!" she interrupts.

"Let me finish." I raise an eyebrow at her, and she sticks out her tongue. "I appreciate everything you do. Penelope does too. But we really just like having you around, no strings attached."

Although, I really wouldn't mind being attached.

"So, I can't do the dishes?"

"How about this..." I release my hand from hers and bump her with my hip to take her place in front of the sink. "I wash, you dry."

"If I accept this deal, can I ask you something?" she asks.

I turn the water back on and soap up the sponge while answering her. "Yes."

"Where is Penelope's mom?"

Fuuuuuuuuuuuck.

I'm not oblivious to the fact that I'm a young, single dad, raising a little girl on my own, and people certainly have questions about it. I know I could tell Gwen I don't want to talk about it and she'd drop it. I'm pretty positive she wouldn't get upset and would even completely understand my need to shut this down.

I normally shut it down, every single time something like this happens. I did it with the daycare, her preschool and kindergarten teachers, and even Margot and Melanie when each of them has asked. I stand by the fact that it's absolutely nobody else's business where Penelope's biological mother is.

It's still my first instinct. But I mull over how to respond while scrubbing pasta sauce out of our bowls from earlier.

"We don't have to talk about it. I'm sorry, that was a huge fucking overstep, and it's none of my business and—"

"Penelope doesn't have a mom."

Gwen pauses. She silently takes the clean bowl from my hand to dry and waits. She lets the silence stretch until I hand her the last utensil. "Miller, I'm sorry. I was cool with dropping it, but I think you're going to have to elaborate now."

I sigh. "Yeah, I kind of walked myself into that one."

She puts the hand towel down and walks around the island to sit in one of the barstools. Her barstool. She props her head up with her hands, her elbows resting on the butcher block. Those big eyes stare at me, and I decide right here and now that my past is Gwen's business. If I have any shot in the world of having someone like this woman in front of me on my team, I have to be willing to let her in.

I opt to stay on this side of the island. Taking a deep breath in, I prepare to shell out history I thought I would be keeping buried until Penelope was older and curious. I run both of my hands through my hair, and when I look up, I see Gwen watching my every move attentively.

"Her name is Sara. We were sixteen years old when she got pregnant, and neither of us had a home we could successfully or safely raise a baby in, so we started running through all of our options. I was agreeing with anything she wanted to do. The guilt was eating me alive that I hadn't been more careful. We didn't know what the fuck we were doing."

"I know this is kind of personal but...was abortion one of the options?"

"Yes," I say without hesitation. "We spent days on her bedroom floor looking up costs and clinics. But ultimately, Sara decided she wanted to go through with the pregnancy. It was her choice."

I've always considered myself a pretty open minded guy, but after witnessing pregnancy and childbirth and now raising a daughter of my own, I'm three hundred percent in it for a woman's right to her own Goddamn body.

Relief floods through me when I see Gwen nod her head in understanding and agreement. Not that I thought she wouldn't, it just feels nice to know she gets it.

"And adoption?" she asks.

"And that's where my choice came into play. Sara wanted to give birth, but she did not want to be a mother. She never lied about it or kept it a secret. She didn't lay it out for me like some big ultimatum either. I was signing up to raise this unborn baby on my own, or I was signing the papers alongside Sara to relinquish my rights."

"When did you decide to keep her?"

"Oh, it was never a question for me. Sure, I was scared out of my fucking mind. Yeah, I thought I was probably going to fail in almost every way possible. But I knew I loved her from the second I found out she existed. Sara and I stopped being…*involved* with each other pretty much as soon as we found out she was pregnant, but we stayed friendly. I don't say this to be a dick, but it was never going to be this big love story for us, baby or not. So it wasn't a hard transition for us. No giant break up. I went to every doctor's appointment, and she sent me videos of her bump when Penelope was kicking. I got a lot of updates from her."

"You can stop me at any time but, were you there? For the birth?"

I finally start to smile again. This is a story I'll never get sick of telling. "Yep. Best fucking day of my life. Sara was a champ.

The labor was long, and I'm pretty sure her epidural wore off by the time they had her start pushing. The TV in the room for some reason had the same movie playing on a fucking loop. But…Gwen, when I heard Penelope cry for the first time?"

I get lost in the memory for a minute, and Gwen's hand reaching for mine brings me back. There's a lot of physical affection going on lately, and I'm not used to it, but I'm not mad about it either.

"When I heard her cry," I start again. "I swear to God, for the first time in my freshly seventeen years of life, I knew it was all worth it."

Gwen starts tracing the veins on the top of my hand lightly with her finger, and I feel that touch shoot straight up my arm.

"The way you describe it…it sounds like the most beautiful thing in the world. It doesn't feel real," she says more to herself, than to me.

Her tracing stops, and she looks up at me. "How could she walk away from that?"

I thread my fingers through hers, needing to connect with her, so hopefully she feels as much as she hears me when I explain this next part.

"It wasn't her time. It might never be her time. Not everyone was born to be a mom or a dad. We see men walk away from children they father every single day with no repercussions. Some jump in and out of kids' lives at their leisure with no remorse. And society is, for the most part, fine with it. It'd be wrong to villainize a woman for the same. Sara made her choice. She was honest and upfront. I have nothing but respect for her. She gave me Penelope."

I let Gwen sit with that. She doesn't have to agree with it right away either. I get it. It took me longer than I'd like to admit to get to this headspace. I spent a lot of late nights resentful of Sara. I wanted to scream. I wanted to ask her how and why, but it wouldn't have changed her mind, and it would have done more harm than good. I regret the anger enough.

Gwen surprises me when she finally responds. "Do I think she's missing out on two of the coolest people I know? Yes. Do I understand her decision? Honestly, not entirely. Not really even a little bit. But do I respect her for the sheer strength she possesses and her ability to choose herself? Yeah. Hell yeah."

I blow out a breath. "Thank you."

"But can she…change her mind? Has she ever reached out?"

I shake my head. "No, and I don't think we'll ever hear from her. She signed off on her parental rights twenty-four hours after giving birth. Legally, it's like she never existed to Penelope, it's only my name on the birth certificate. Personally, we agreed Penelope is entitled to know who Sara is if she asks when appropriate. I have her family health history if it's ever needed. I've tried to cover all the bases to do right by both of them. It's not perfect but—"

"Miller, that's more than anyone could ever even think of, are you kidding? Especially with you being so young. You act like you're not moving mountains every day for that little girl."

"Nah." I wave her off and instantly regret letting go just to brush off one of the nicest things anyone's ever said to me like a fucking idiot. "I'm just being her dad."

She scrunches her nose, and I love watching her freckles dance across the bridge of it. She shakes her head, and I clock every wave of those pretty curls. She's cute as fuck when she's annoyed with me. "I wish you could see yourself, Miller Caswell."

She's more than cute when she uses my full name like that. I don't stand a chance keeping up with a real woman like this.

It's at this very moment I decide I'm gonna try like hell to from here on out anyway. I lean across the island, being sure to not invade her space, but shortening the gap.

"I like my view just fine over here, Gwendolyn Bozelli."

CHAPTER 9: RED - CRUSHCRUSHCRUSH

I went to bed and woke up thinking the same thing.
I like the way Miller was looking at me.

In fact, I like it a lot.

I'm not unfamiliar with people looking at me. Gawking some-times. I'm tall. I have fire engine red hair that stops traffic. Boys have never been shy around me. I'm even comfortable admitting I've used the attention as an ego boost a time or two. But at the end of the day, I always knew it was surface level, shallow, superficial.

The way Miller has been looking at me though? It has me feeling like I could jump off the deep end, and I wouldn't mind drowning.

But then I reign it the fuck back in because who am I kidding? He's way too young, and I'm not what he and P need when I'm still picking up the broken pieces of myself that fell out along the way.

It sure is fun getting to play pretend though.

I open my closet and place my newest sticky note from Miller (& P) on the back of the door, next to all of the others. Once I learned the notes weren't a one off thing, I quickly realized I wasn't going to be able to keep shoving them into the back of my phone case, and there was no part of me that even considered throwing them away.

So they go…here.

I let my finger rest on the small paper for a second, rereading the simple sentence for the twenty-fifth time since I got in my car last night to drive home after saying goodnight to Miller, and discovering he packed up the last serving of pasta and snuck the Tupperware into my bag before I left. My now favorite, signature square note with chicken scratch handwriting was stuck to the top. The color varies by the day, and last night's was purple.

Thursdays have quickly turned into the Caswells' favorite day of the week.

-Miller & P.

I smile like an idiot alone in my room, close the door, and flick off the light on my way out to head downstairs.

I grab my insulated water bottle from the fridge that I filled last night and swipe my bag from the counter. I double check I have my planner, an extra charger, and keys before locking the front door. When I reach the bottom of my bungalow's front steps, I instinctively look to the house that was formerly Mrs. Johnson's next door.

Mrs. Johnson was the sweetest next door neighbor you could ever ask for. I was ecstatic that she moved in when I was in middle school. She bought the small cape after her husband passed because she couldn't bear to stay in the house they built their life in without him.

I clung onto that story with all the hope in the world that I'd end up with a kind of love like that, not caring about the end. I'd bring Mrs. Johnson cafe pastries, and we'd share coffee over the years, me listening to her replay memories. I was devastated when she passed last year, but she was ninety-seven and lived a good life.

Her kids are grown and have their own established lives in other states, so the house has been sitting empty for a while now.

Today's different though. Today, there's a realtor banging a For Sale sign into the edge of the front yard.

I guess her kids must have decided to sell the place.

I wave to the realtor (who the Johnson children must have hired from out of town because I don't recognize her) so she doesn't have to warn potential buyers of some bitch next door.

After I back out of my driveway to head to the cafe, I think about who the buyers might end up being. Maybe an older couple looking to live in a nice, quiet town? Or a new family, just starting out, wanted a safe place to raise their babies?

I could make them a welcome to the neighborhood basket with things from the cafe and flowers from Daisy's shop. I could even see if Miller wanted to make a jar of that homemade sauce for them. I remind myself to make a note of it in my planner for when I see moving trucks hauling a new beginning in.

* * *

"Best fucking coffee I've ever had."

"Sawyer, you say that to anyone who hands you a cup," I say while chuckling.

"And it's true every time, I swear." One of my oldest friends shoots me one of those megawatt smiles that has always had every girl, and Chris, in Merrymount drooling over.

It never had that effect on me though. I've been watching Sawyer Hale behave like a grumpy idiot for far too long. We've acted like the town's honorary siblings since we were kids. Good thing too, seeing as he's stupidly in love with the pixie girl standing next to me behind the counter.

Margot barks out a laugh, and I watch her eyes glaze over in that same stupidly-in-love kind of way when that smile of Sawyer's is redirected to her. Sawyer leans over the counter, and

Margot meets him in the middle, their noses almost touching, Sawyer having to bend almost in half, Margot having to stand on her toes.

I have to look away.

I love them both, so much. I love that they are so much each other's person that it was obvious from the start. Well, to everyone except them, but they caught up.

But it still stings to see that kind of love on display. I hate myself for having to admit that.

I grab a towel to wipe down some freshly vacant tables to make myself busy and give them some privacy. Book Club should be here soon, and I can't imagine a world where Judy wouldn't throw a temper tantrum if *her* table wasn't ready for her arrival.

This is one of the things I love about Red's Place. It's the one thing in my life that doesn't come with many surprises. Aside from sometimes being the host of small town drama unfolding, the day-to-day is almost mundane. I know what to expect, right down to who's coming in on what day, and what they're going to order.

I like the simplicity of it. I like the routine. The rug doesn't feel like it's going to be pulled out from under me. I know what's coming next, and I have a back up plan for my back up plan most days.

Right on cue, Judy and her gaggle of ladies come trotting through the front door.

"Red! I could kiss you on the mouth!" Judy calls.

I hear Margot mutter, "She better get in line behind Miller then."

I whip my head to her. She blows me a kiss.

"Bitch," I mouth.

"You love me," she replies before getting started on the Book Club ladies' drinks.

It's true. I do.

"And what did I do to deserve this honor, Jude?" I ask, refer-ring to her offered kiss.

"My boy is going to college!" Judy exclaims, getting herself situated in a chair at the head of the two tables we push together for them.

Ah, yes. I forgot about my little pep talk with Chris. With how Judy's acting, I'm taking an educated guess that Chris failed to mention the two week drop period. But, whatever. I got him to the door. He can handle the rest.

"Happy to help," I say and lean over to plant a kiss on Judy's cheek.

"You always know what to say to him. I don't know how you do it. Whenever you decide to finally settle down and have a boatload of babies of your own, they're going to be so lucky."

Sucker punch.

It's always a fucking sucker punch.

Judy means well. They all do when they say shit like this. But throwing around the word *finally* like I didn't plan my entire life around becoming a mother? Like I didn't have to be the one to watch it go up in smoke and then clean up the mess afterwards? It hurts, and I'm so sick of the kind-hearted reminders.

I shake it off though. No one needs to see me meltdown over something no one else can control. I mold my face into an expression of indifference. "Yeah, yep. You bet."

Margot notices though. "Hey, I think I just heard the timer go off in the back. Did you have something going? Maybe in the dryer?"

She's offering an out I desperately need but would have never asked for.

I make a beeline for the back and crash right into a solid wall.

Nope. That's a chest. Two hands wrap around my upper arms, bracing me from falling backwards, and before I even look up, I know who I'm about to face.

"Fuck, Miller. I'm so sorry, are you okay?"

He doesn't answer me. He keeps his hands firmly grasped and guides me away from the room of people watching. So I just keep rambling. "I didn't even look where I was going. That was so stupid. Did we butt heads? No, my head feels fine. Shit, what an idiot."

Miller's hands suddenly move to my waist, and he swiftly hoists me up until my ass hits the counter. His hands release me, and I instantly miss his touch. If I wasn't so frazzled, I'd probably ask how that was so easy for him.

I'm not one of the small girls. Dean never had an issue with reminding me of that.

"Gwen," Miller starts.

I finally look up from the spot on his chest I fixated on to avoid his eye contact. Those bright, green eyes are full of such a deep concern that I immediately feel so silly stressing this guy out on the daily over *nothing*.

"What happened?" he asks quietly.

"Nothing," I quickly answer.

"This game where we go back and forth is fun, but today I'd really like it if we skip all that, and you tell me what's bothering you so bad you smacked into me going no less than lightning speed."

"Look, I'm sorry I bumped into you. The dryer has towels I need to fold, and I didn't see you there."

"You didn't see me, okay. Did you hear me?"

"Huh?" I ask.

"Did you hear me? When I called your name?"

I hesitate because no, I did not hear him. I didn't even know he was there. Clearly. And my silence is apparently all the answer he needs.

"Gwen, tell me what happened. Please."

"It's embarrassing, and I embarrass myself around you enough. No need for another play-by-play." I try to brush him off, but Miller's fucking on one today because he doesn't back down. He cages me in, his palms hit the counter on either side of me.

I should feel trapped. This should be suffocating and uncomfortable. Miller's crossing a line and getting in my space and not taking no for an answer.

I should be shoving him away and yelling at him about boundaries.

But he has a tiny birthmark on the right side of his top lip I never noticed until right now.

And the way he keeps flexing his jaw, internally working out what to say to me because I'm being a stubborn pain in the ass is making me feel squirmy.

It's not the bad kind of squirmy, either.

He blows out a breath. "I just need to know if someone hurt you."

I shake my head. "No, no. I let my own feelings get hurt."

Miller closes his eyes. I count to five before he opens them again. "For the record, I'm not buying it. But I'll drop it if you ask."

I trace the *P* on his ring. "Thank you," I whisper.

He checks the time on his watch. "What if…"

I tilt my head to the side. I don't know where he's going with this. It seems like he might not be sure either as he mulls it over in his head.

"What if I helped you fold those towels, and we take off? We can dismiss P from school a little early and get ice cream or something."

This time I don't hesitate. I nod my head once and hop off the counter. Miller backs up just enough for my feet to land right in front of him, my nipples are practically touching his T-shirt. If I got any closer, all I would have to do is tip up my chin slightly to—

Woah woah woah. Slow it down, Red.

I do what any normal person would do in a situation like this.

I put my right hand up and wait for Miller to catch on. He doesn't. So, I take matters into my own hands and grab his arm with my left hand and force a high five.

"Let's fucking go!" I exclaim.

He shakes his head laughing, letting his waves flow around him, and I realize I definitely want to keep pulling those kinds of laughs out of him.

CHAPTER 10: MILLER - WE'RE LATE FOR SCHOOL. AGAIN.

"Puuuuh-leeaaaaase," Penelope whines, enunciating each individual letter in the word. Her spoon clangs into the empty cereal bowl in front of her, and she kicks her tiny feet as they dangle from the barstool she's sitting on.

I turn my head away from the scrambled eggs I'm trying not to burn to face her, pointing the spatula at my perfect, very opinionated, extremely determined almost six-year-old.

"I don't get why I have to be Anna."

Penelope giggles and sticks that button nose I love so much up in the air. "Because I said so, and it's my birthday."

"It's my birthday too, punk," I remind her.

"Yeah, but you've had more than me. It's my turn."

She has always been this smart, and the hardest thing I've ever had to learn is how to keep up with her. I don't even know why I'm bothering to pretend to put up a fight. If the kid wants me to dress up as a Disney Princess on Halloween, our shared birthday, then so be it.

I sigh, prepared to give in to this ridiculous request in the name of fatherhood. "And you're sure you want to be Olaf."

She nods her head aggressively, sure as shit, just like she always is. "Do you think Red would want to be Elsa?"

"Uh, I don't know if she planned on going trick-or-treating."

Penelope has tried to include Gwen in every part of our lives since we moved in above the cafe. Gwen is at our place more nights for dinner than not. Penelope jumps to invite her to run errands with us or go to the park just about every other day. Mostly, she tries to weasel an ice cream trip with all three of us. It hits me in the chest every time.

I'm lacking somewhere. As much as I've tried to make up for the fact that I gave her a mother who checked out before she was even discharged from the hospital, I'm falling short. While Sara deserves her peace, it can also be true that Penelope deserves to have a mom who wants to show up for anything and everything. And the fact of the matter is, that didn't happen.

"But we could ask her! And I know she'd say yes! She loves Frozen, just like me! She told me! We watched it, remember?" It's like a lightbulb went off above her head, and now she's shouting out every thought zinging through her brain.

"Can't forget your rendition of *Let It Go*, P," I say.

"What's a rendition?" she asks.

"Like how you danced and sang it. Rendition is like…" I pause to think of how to word this in a way she'll understand and hopefully it sticks. "It's like your version of something," I answer.

Penelope thinks about that for a minute. She rests her chin on her fist to tilt her head to the side and everything. "Like Taylor's Version?"

Yeah, I should have seen that one coming. I smile at her and shake my head before turning back to the stove. "Yeah, P, like Taylor's Version."

"Cool." You can hear the satisfaction in her voice. It's adorable as hell.

Selfishly, I love how much she loves having Gwen around. The three of us have so much fun together that I'm starting to forget why I always thought we could never add someone else to our little family when someone like Gwen shows up and is present so naturally.

And the past few nights, after we put Penelope to bed—which feels domestic as fuck, by the way—Gwen's been staying just a little later each time. We've discovered we have the same bad taste in comedy movies and have committed to rewatching each other's favorites.

My goal is to pull as many laughs out of her as I can. She's so Goddamn beautiful when she smiles, but especially when she laughs.

"I guess it wouldn't hurt to ask her," I answer Penelope. "But if she says no, that's final. No trying to change her mind like you do with me."

Penelope's off the stool and barreling into me, wrapping her arms around my waist within seconds. "Thanks, Daddy." She releases me and books it into her bedroom to hopefully get dressed so we're not late for school. Again.

I hear a drawer slam shut, and I call out, "Please try to match your socks!"

"Not happening!" she yells back.

Well, I guess I'm picking my battles today, and that's not one of them. I turn the burner off and transfer my eggs to a plate that already has a bagel waiting for me so I can scarf it down before we have to head out to school.

I sit my ass in the same barstool Penelope was just occupying and take a couple minutes for myself to eat and get lost in my head. I really wouldn't mind seeing Gwen in that ice queen dress if Penelope somehow convinces her to come with us.

I say "somehow" like Gwen has said no to this kid even once. She's just as bad as I am with Penelope, and it melts my fucking heart, even when she's still keen on keeping me at arm's length.

Baby steps though.

I scarf down my breakfast and place the dishes in the sink, leaving them for an after school drop-off kind of problem.

Penelope loved the idea of the bus last year even though it felt like my worst nightmare sending her on it every day. I always gave her the option of riding in with me or letting me pick her up. But, she stuck with it all year and seemed to like it.

Until she didn't.

I noticed a change in her morning attitude early this spring. It was subtle enough where I second guessed myself about questioning it which led me to beating myself the fuck up for not addressing it sooner.

She was grumpier than usual. Didn't want to get dressed, dragged her feet through every step of our usual routine. For a little, I chalked it up to growing pains.

But Penelope was dealing with a bully on the bus and had no idea how to talk about it. One morning after another really out of character battle between us, I finally asked if something was bothering her, and it was like the floodgates opened.

This fucking little twerp of a third grader was picking on Penelope for anything and everything: the clothes she wore, her missing teeth, the way she had her hair. I guess he was relentless.

She told me a few of the other kids had started to notice and stuck up for her, but this kid never let up.

I don't give a shit if I'm not supposed to have beef with an eight-year-old. I did, and I still do.

I called the school for a meeting immediately. I talked to the bus driver and the principal. It was handled well enough where I'm sure there wouldn't have been more issues, but I don't care. Penelope finally agreed to riding with me in the mornings and afternoons, and I'm thankful for that, because she was riding with me either way.

We continued the pick-up and drop-off routine at the start of this school year with little conversation around it. It's better this way.

Well, except for the fact that the two of us can't get our shit together to leave on time some mornings.

"Penelope Grace, we need to *go!*" I yell, putting her lunch bag into her backpack and zipping it up.

"I'm coming!" she huffs while finally leaving her room.

I hold out the straps of her backpack, and she loops her arms through. We both slip our shoes on and are barreling down the stairs in record time.

Forgetting about the like, eighth tardy slip Penelope's probably going to be given, the both of us stop dead in our tracks when we reach the cafe.

Apparently Penelope and I aren't the only ones with Halloween on the brain this morning.

By the looks of the place, Gwen must have gotten here hours ago, although I didn't hear her car or any movement down here at all this morning.

There are a few of the morning regulars, quietly sipping their coffee and reading the paper or checking their phones. A few people are leaning against the counter, waiting for Margot to finish their orders. She waves to me when she has a free hand, and I wave back.

Sawyer and Gus are the loudest in here, sitting on two barstools, hanging out while Margot works, before they head off for what I assume is a day of work at the riverside.

When they see me and Penelope, they stop their conversation.

"Morning Caswells!" Sawyer calls out, holding up his mug. Gus nods once at me and shoots Penelope a peace sign. She matches his greeting back.

There's something downright hilarious about a dude as big as Gus Burton—he's got to be at least 6'5" and built like a house— throw out a peace sign to a five-year-old without a care in the world about who might judge him.

Not that anyone would openly judge him. They'd be in the ground.

"Hey!" Gwen calls from the floor. She's sitting on her knees under a pile of fake spider webs. Her head pops out, and she's fucking *beaming.*

I don't move. I don't know if I'm afraid I'm gonna spook her or what, but I know I'm sure as shit not going to be the reason the light I've been craving to pull out of her fades away when it's finally back and shining so goddamn bright.

Penelope's not as cautious as I am, never has been, probably never will be. She's never had to walk on eggshells in her own home to avoid punishment, so I understand and love her carefree spirit. It's one of the things I worked so hard to protect. Penelope books it to Gwen's side, ducking underneath the layers of white material to join her.

"Good morning, my little witch." Gwen pulls a witch's hat from the big bin of decorations that's opened on the floor and plops it onto Penelope's head.

"It looks crazy in here!" Penelope says with so much amazement in her voice. This kid fucking loves a holiday, especially one that lands on her birthday.

"A good kind of crazy?" Gwen asks, chuckling.

"Duh!" Penelope starts helping Gwen loop the spider webs through the hooks I now see she's placed around the counter.

Mrs. Harrison in the front office is definitely going to ream me out for the late morning whenever I finally get P there.

"I was hoping you'd say that. Halloween is my *favorite,*" Gwen tells her.

"Oh, is it?" I chime in.

Gwen's eyes meet mine and the rest of the day can go to shit for all I care because the smile on this beautiful woman's face is aimed at me, and she's not trying to hide it even a little bit for the first time.

"Yep!" she answers. "Always has been. Do you guys celebrate?"

"'Course we do! With cake and ice cream!" Penelope yells.

Gwen tilts her head slightly, and God, it's cute as fuck. "Well...

I was thinking more along the lines of tricks and/or treats. But cake and ice cream, that's cool, too. I can get down with that."

"Oh! We trick-or-treat, too! Do you? Because if you do…" Penelope hesitates, something she rarely does. Usually, mostly always, Penelope Caswell is one hundred percent sure of herself in everything she does. But to her, there's no one cooler than Gwen. And I can tell my girl is nervous as hell she's about to be turned down.

"If you do like to trick-or-treat, Penelope and I were wondering if you would like to join us this year," I finish for her, pushing my own nerves aside.

P lets out the biggest sigh her tiny body can hold. "Yeah. Yeah, we were wondering that."

"Are you fucking kidding?!" Gwen shrieks and jumps up.

Not the response I was expecting.

I was aiming for a forced *sure* to not disappoint Penelope, and I would have told her to not worry about it when I came back from dropping P off at school. We could have come up with a plan or something. I don't know.

But Gwen grabs Penelope up into her arms, knocking the witch's hat clear off P's head, and clutches my daughter into her chest. "Yesyesyesyes!" she chants. "Obviously yes."

I hear Sawyer laugh as he says, "You just made her year, Miller. Red is the queen of Halloween around here. All this?" Sawyer gestures around the cafe at all of the decorations. "Normally starts at the end of August, sometimes sooner. This is nothing."

"I follow Disney's decorating schedule. They're in charge," Gwen declares.

"It's true," Gus chimes in between bites of his bagel. There's another on his plate waiting for him, too. "Red hands out the good candy."

"Full size candy bars, of course," Gwen says proudly.

You can't tell me it's not some sort of fate that her favorite holiday happens to be my birthday. I mean, you could tell me that. I wouldn't believe you though.

"I'd expect nothing less from you, Gwen. So, do birthday boys and girls get extra candy on Halloween?"

There's that head tilt again, but Penelope has no issues clearing things up for her.

"Because it's our birthday!" she cheers. She flails, throwing herself back, and Gwen has to fight like hell to keep Penelope from crashing to the tiled floors.

"Wait." Gwen whips her head between me and Penelope. "What? You two have the *same* birthday?"

I nod and take the coffee Margot hands me. I take a sip of that new s'mores flavor Gwen just started serving up, burning the absolute shit out of my mouth. It's so good though. She really needs to keep this in the regular rotation. "Mhm."

"That is…"

Penelope cuts her off as Gwen places her back on her feet, "So fucking cool, right?!"

The cafe goes silent just to immediately burst into laughter. Gwen has a hand slapped over her mouth, clearly trying to stand in solidarity with me as I gape at Penelope with a face that I'm more than sure gives off the *what the fuck* message I'm trying to send to my kid.

Margot is doubled over, hiding behind the counter and swiping tears from her eyes. Sawyer is holding his stomach cracking up, while Gus hits him on the back sputtering out, "So fucking cool, lil P!"

My sailor-mouthed child turns to me. She has the right idea to at least pretend to look ashamed as she shrugs her shoulders, mouthing, "*Sorry.*"

I run both hands through my hair, pulling. I think about how if this is my biggest issue, it's smooth sailing. We've gone over the rules—we don't use curse words to insult someone and there's always a time and place. *Normally* these rules are easily abided by.

But then again, that means she's comfortable. Here. In Red's Place with these people.

I finally laugh, bringing my child that I love more than anything into me. "Dude."

"Whoops," she says, hugging me back.

Conversations resume around us. Penelope hops up on Sawyer's lap, immediately jumping into a story for him, Gus, and Margot to hear. I try another sip of my coffee and deem it safe to drink.

Gwen walks towards me and reaches over the counter to grab her phone. Her eyes widen when it lights up in her hands, and she pulls the phone closer to her face to read the screen. All of the glowing happiness that was just pouring out of her melts away instantly.

Her smile morphes into a scowl, and she starts furiously tapping the screen with her thumbs. She then smashes her right thumb on one key over and over again. I'm assuming the delete button? She swipes out of whatever she was in, hits the lock button, and tosses her phone, letting it crash into the counter along the wall.

I watch Gwen keep her head down and take a deep breath. She puts on a mask of cheer before looking up. When her eyes lock on mine, she immediately realizes I just witnessed all of that. I want so badly for this to be the time when I ask her what's going on and she finally tells me.

Finally, maybe wants to let me in. At least get a foot in the door.

But we're standing in the middle of a coffee shop. The coffee shop she owns, surrounded by retro blow molds of ghosts and pumpkins and fake cobwebs. Our friends, my sister, my daughter around us. She has to be Red right now.

And—*Shit. We are so fucking late for school.*

"Gwen?" I whisper. I'm pretty sure I'm the only one who noticed, and I don't want to draw attention when it's obvious that's the exact opposite of what she needs right now. But she also needs to know I'm here.

Gwen shakes her head. "I'm good, I'm fine."

I gently wrap my hand around her elbow. She doesn't flinch away. Instead, she leans into me, just a little bit. "You don't have to be fine all the time, you know."

Her voice doesn't reach above a whisper. "But if I say it enough times, maybe it'll be true."

The moment's over before I can respond. She shakes me off and walks back over to her box of decorations, that fake halfass smile plastered on her face.

I don't know why I'm so pissed. Maybe I do, though. Maybe I know deep down there's only one person who's going to shake Gwen up that bad when she was just riding a high.

I keep my eyes on Gwen and call out, "Penelope, we're late for school. Let's go."

Once Penelope finishes her goodbyes, and we're about to head through the back to the car, I stop in front of Gwen. She doesn't look up from a string of orange lights she's untangling, but she pauses so I know she's listening when I lean into her ear. "Meet me upstairs when I get back. Please."

I wait for her to tell me no and push me away. I wait to be crushed even though I'm expecting the blow.

She nods once and softly says, "Okay."

I'm fixing this. If it includes my fist connecting with Dean's stupid fucking face *again*, so be it.

CHAPTER 11: GWEN - DO YOUR WORST, GWENDOLYN

THE WORST MISTAKE OF MY LIFE

We need to talk, Red.

THE WORST MISTAKE OF MY LIFE

I'm trying to not make a scene at the cafe.

THE WORST MISTAKE OF MY LIFE

Ignoring me won't make this go away, Red.

ME

won't know if we don't try!

THE WORST MISTAKE OF MY LIFE

Really? That's how you finally respond?

THE WORST MISTAKE OF MY LIFE

You're being childish. It's not attractive.

I start to type out exactly how little of a fuck I give about what he finds attractive but stop before I hit send.

I'm immediately angry with myself for letting him get to me enough that I broke my silence. But God, Dean Fitzgerald is so irritatingly insufferable. I don't know how I wasted years of my life on him.

I haven't heard from him in *months.* I had finally gotten to the point where I was enjoying the silence, rather than looking over my shoulder any chance I got. It was the longest we've probably ever gone without seeing or talking to each other since elementary school. Why break the streak now? What could possibly be so important?

That's what's sending me over the edge. I think I'm at a point where I could handle seeing him in passing. If he tried to pester me at work, I'd have no problem shooing him away. Margot is dying for an excuse to rip him apart as it is.

But utter the phrase *we need to talk,* and I'm sent into a tailspin. Something's up, and I have zero desire to face what it is.

Maybe he knocked someone else up. That feels like it would be a Katie problem now, though.

Wouldn't that be rich? He spends years telling me he's not ready, years of placating me with the *let's revisit this conversation next year.* Just to run around and be the town sperm donor.

If this is about wanting the house again, he's so fucking cracked out of his mind, I'll just laugh in his face. I'll laugh and laugh till tears stream down my cheeks. And then when he finally accepts I'm too crazy to deal with that he walks away—maybe walks all the way out of Merrymount—I'll throw a Goddamn party, mark my words.

I'm still fantasizing about a Dean-free life when I hear the door that leads to the back alley unlock. I look up from my spot on the couch to see Miller walk in, and he doesn't look happy.

Now is probably not the best time to admit how hot he is when he's angry, is it?

His hair looks like it's had his hands run through it hundreds of times within the last thirty minutes since he left the cafe to bring Penelope to school. His usually soft features are sharpened by narrowed eyes and the clenching of his jaw.

"I'm pissed, but not at you, and I need you to know that," he says to break the silence.

"Okay. Me too. Wanna come have a seat and talk it out?" I pat the cushion next to me.

Miller paces the small space between the living room and the kitchen, seemingly ignoring my question. He can't be this worked up because I was upset, right? I mean, it's not even a big deal. People have shitty exes. We deal with them. I don't even *know* if there really is an issue, or if it's just Dean trying to start shit for fun.

Because he's bored.

He was always fucking *bored.*

"It was your douchebag ex that texted you, right?"

"Yeah, but—"

"What does he want?"

"I don't know, and that's what freaked me out," I answer honestly.

Miller stops and comes to sit down next to me. He keeps enough distance for zero accidental touching, and I'm pretty sure it is intentional.

"I hate that he has the power to mess you up like that."

"There's another thing we can agree on." I laugh but it falls flat.

"Have you spoken at all since...?" He leaves the question open ended.

"No. He hasn't reached out...until now. And I was content to pretend he didn't exist."

Whatever space that was between us suddenly ceases to exist because Miller leans and lays his head on my shoulder. It's so gentle. He lets out the biggest sigh, like he's been holding it in for a while. "I'm sorry," he says.

He's warm. His hair is just as soft as I thought it would be. I like this a lot.

I huff. "For what? Did you cheat on me and get the meanest

girl in town pregnant behind everyone's back? And now poke into my business for funsies? Don't bother answering. I got you. No, you didn't. Don't say sorry on someone else's behalf, especially when they wouldn't mean it if it was coming from them. Save the apology for when you actually piss me off, Miller."

It's Miller's turn to laugh, except this time I can feel his body shake, and his soft hair tickles my neck. A second later, I can't contain it, and I'm joining him in a laughing fit. We both fall back into the couch and while his head is no longer resting on my shoulder, he's still leaning against me.

I love when he laughs like this. It's with his whole self and unabashed. It makes me wish more people laughed like this. It's contagious.

Miller pulls himself together first, rubbing his hand on his chest. "I like when you're fiery like that."

"Har-har," I say in a deadpan voice. "Very funny."

"Huh?" He sits up straight.

"Fiery? A redhead joke, really?"

I look at him and see the confusion painted all over his face. Now I'm confused.

"It…wasn't a redhead joke?" I ask.

"Uh, no. I meant fiery…like, feisty. Umm, you know? Like, snappy? I'm running out of adjectives here, Gwen." There goes his hand running through his hair again. "This morning has sucked, I'm sorry. I just meant…I like when you stick up for yourself. When you say what you want. I like your confidence."

Well, I'm an asshole.

"Damn it, I'm sorry. You're not who I need to be snapping at."

Miller shrugs and that boyish smirk is back on his face. "Do your worst, Gwendolyn. It doesn't bother me."

How did I go so long without hearing my name? Why does it always sound so pretty when he says it?

Dean was my *husband* and the only time he ever didn't call me

Red was when the officiant had us say our vows. Even in his proposal it was, *"Red, wanna get married?"*

Romance was in fact—very much so—dead.

"He says we need to talk," I finally admit out loud.

"Dean?" Miller asks.

I nod.

"Do you?"

"Do what?"

"Do you need to talk to him? Is there anything you feel like you have to say?"

I sit with that for a minute. It's a good question. I mean, I haven't said *anything* to Dean. About any of it. I've successfully dodged every attempt at conversations about the marriage, the cheating, the separation that led to divorce, and then…this whole mess.

I've gotten really good at ghosting Dean. And for a while, it was because it all felt too heavy and too hard to do anything else. I was dealing with keeping myself together. But now, I just really like the freedom. Thinking about having to sit down with him and rehash whatever he deems important sounds like the biggest waste of my time.

I've been too busy filling my days with things and people, like the guy to my right for example, to consider loaning any of my time to a waste of space like *Dean.* Blech.

My eye catches the tv stand, a row of tiny Polaroid pictures framed in equally tiny frames occupy the shelf under the TV. I smile, because it's practically identical to the set up I have at my house. Tiny things in our lives always find a way of overlapping. It's a silly thing to notice but, anyway…

You can tell every single picture was taken through a child's lens of the world. Miller, caught off guard with a goofy grin, making breakfast in the kitchen to our left. Margot, a dollop of ice cream on her nose, holding a waffle cone at the farm stand. A group picture of about fifty stuffed animals, piled high on Penelope's bed.

"Frankly, no," I finally respond.

I feel Miller's shoulders start to jitter before I hear him laugh. "Atta girl. But hey, you were really shaken up. And it's not the first time I've seen it. Come on, Gwen." His shoulder nudges mine. "We're…friends. Let me in."

I could have imagined his pause before the word friends. I don't want to read into what that might mean, though. Instead, I choose to do exactly what he asked for once.

"It's just, *ugh*. Why do I let myself get like this? This is new to me, and I don't like it. I never used to freeze up or shut down. It's like the older I get, the less sure of myself I am, of *who* I am." I rest my elbows on my thighs and cradle my head in my hands. My hair falls to the sides of my face, blocking Miller from my view.

It's like my own version of a confessional, and I'm suddenly word vomiting. "Everyone is so used to being able to expect this…this cookie cutter version of me. Every single day. I'm the fun time, but I'm the reliable one. You come to me with a problem, I'm solving it and making sure you're laughing and fed before I send you on your way. You destroy every version I had of a future, but I'm still expected to answer when you call. I'm a glorified doormat, Miller, and I fucking hate it."

"Have you ever told anyone that?"

I shake my head and decide I've already committed to this honesty hour. "Why would anyone need me around if I wasn't that version of Red?"

And that's the loudest voice in the back of my head, always has been.

I keep blabbing. "The second I stop being that person to everyone, I'm faceless, nameless. I'm not talented or super smart. I'm not saving lives or breaking records or rocking worlds. For fuck's sake, I'm the walking cliché of a cheerleader who peaked in her small town high school. I have the matching divorce papers with my high school sweetheart to prove it."

Miller stares back at me and blinks. He blinks again like he can't believe what he's hearing.

"Hold that thought." Before I know what's happening, Miller is up and walking into Penelope's room.

He comes back fairly quickly with a hardcover children's book and thrusts it into my lap. "Here. We have a second copy. We actually have a third packed away somewhere, too. In case something ever happened to copies one and two. I uh…" He scratches his head, looking like he's regretting this whole thing. "I picked this book up right before Penelope was born. It could be really stupid but, read it."

I quietly flip through each page. Everyone starts with *Repeat after me...*

I am kind.

I am smart.

I am brave.

I am strong.

I am beautiful.

Miller bends into a squat in front of me when I close the book. I look up to meet his gaze because it's Miller, and I know he's waiting for me to. It hits me like a ton of bricks that over the past couple of months, through a bunch of little moments, I've gotten to know a lot of the pieces that make up Miller.

And he's gotten to know some of mine too. Not Red's. Not the doormat's.

"I'm gonna be real with you, Gwen. I don't think I can hear all of the reasons why you believe those things about yourself. I have a feeling I know who they'll lead back to and while I got away with it before, I don't know if I'd be lucky enough to walk away with a clean record if I had to deck Dean again. And just so we're clear, I *want* to deck Dean again."

"Get in line," I mutter. "You said you have another one of these?" I hold the book up.

He nods.

"Is it okay if I borrow this one?"

"It's yours."

"Oh, no. I'm going to bring it back. This is Penelope's. I'm not stealing from my girl."

Miller's cheeks go pink. I can't pretend I didn't see that.

The flirting is fun. The company is better. The friendship we've found here works. But, I'm scared to even think about rocking that by leaning into this... this...*God, am I really about to admit this?* This *crush* I have on Miller?

"I, uh. I need to get back downstairs. I'm sure you have work?"

Miller stands and nods again. I follow suit.

The next thing I know he's crushing me into a hug. My arms instinctually wrap around his waist, and I tuck my head into the crook of his neck. He always smells so fresh and clean but being so close to him like this, it's intoxicating. I try to inconspicuously breathe him in. I could live here in this safe little cocoon—

What the actual fuck is wrong with me?

I let my arms fall and stand up straight. Miller stretches his arms up until a strip of skin shows just above his belt. I avert my gaze to make sure I don't get caught openly staring.

But his eyes find mine with a knowing look that says he absolutely saw me checking out the lines that I'm sure as shit lead to a very nice V. He shows me mercy by not bringing it up though.

"Will you let me know if he starts to bother you again?"

If he asked me this a couple months ago, honestly, even a couple days ago, I would have brushed him off, letting him know I could handle it myself. I might have even lied and said yes, just to be nice and never mention it again.

But he keeps showing up, judgment free, ready to roll at any pace I need, and I think I need to start meeting him in the middle.

"I will. If you promise to not run off and get arrested pulling dumb shit in my defense. I don't want to pay your bail, and Penelope needs her dad."

I need you, too is what I want to add. But I don't.

He looks at me like he wants to say something. But he doesn't.

"But hey," I add. "Are *you* okay?"

"I'm afraid if Penelope is late for school again, the front office lady is going to file a truancy charge against me or something." Miller shudders, and it takes a lot of willpower to not full blown cackle in his face.

"Mrs. Harrison? *Please.*" I wave my hand. "She pretends to be tough as shit, but it's an act."

"She scares me, Gwen. She scares me real bad."

I assure Miller he has nothing to worry about, and he seems to at least sort of absorb what I have to say.

We say our goodbyes and Miller waits until I'm at the bottom of the stairs before closing his door.

I get back to work on finishing my *very late by my standards* spooky decorating while expertly avoiding Margot's *demanding answers* face, while I'm sure Miller is booting up his laptop for a day of…whatever an IT specialist at a bank does.

I think we're both playing it safe. I think it's better this way.

CHAPTER 12: GWEN - HOWDY, NEIGHBOR

J stare at the sold sign. It stares back at me.

For some reason, I didn't expect Mrs. Johnson's house to sell so fast. Sure, it's a nice neighborhood in a cute small town, but really, what's the demand for property in Merrymount?

It's only been on the market a couple weeks. I don't know the ins and outs of realty given the only two places I've ever lived have been here in this town and both were given to me by my parents, but this feels sudden.

I'm rooted in place in the middle of the sidewalk with my hands on my hips, heavy breathing after a crisp early evening run.

While it's what I would consider chilly, I still have to wipe the sweat from my forehead and focus on getting air in my lungs. I don't think I need to reach for the inhaler I keep in my little running pack just yet.

Don't ask why the asthmatic girl likes to run to clear her head. I just do.

I haven't heard from Dean in a few days, and it's messing with me. I thought ignoring him was in my best interest, but now I'm dealing with the unknown. And I know that he knows something like this would bother me to no end.

So, I refuse to play into his little mind games. I know his tricks. I've lived through them too many times. I can handle my overthinking on my own, like a big girl.

What I don't expect is to see Dean motherfucking Fitzgerald waltz out the front door of Mrs. Johnson's freshly sold house.

I'm so caught off guard I don't give myself a second to think before words are just falling out of my mouth. "What in the everloving hell are you doing here?"

"Howdy, neighbor." Dean holds up and jingles a set of keys. There's the most rancid, vile, putrid, mortifying, every other *disgusting ass adjective* you can think of smirk on his face.

I want to saw it off with a rusty nail file.

"Get away from Mrs. Johnson's house. You'll stink the place up. She deserves better."

"Mrs. Johnson is dead, Red. And this isn't her house anymore. It's mine." He jingles those stupid keys again, and I have half a mind to stab him with them.

What are the chances that I actually *didn't* finish my run, and I passed out somewhere along the way due to an asthma attack, and this is just some big hallucination? That's like, way more likely than what just came out of Dean's mouth…right?

"From the way you're standing there, gaping like a fish, which isn't very becoming by the way, I'm assuming you had no idea we bought the place?"

"We?"

As if on cue, Katie St. James steps through the doorway behind Dean, holding their bastard baby.

I stare at the newborn for the first time. Most newborns aren't cute (despite what most parents say. It's not a dig, they just usually look like they need some more time to cook), and unfortunately, he's not the exception. But it's shocking to see how many of his features really do mirror Dean's. The paternity test was very clearly a waste of money and resources, but hey, what do I know?

Okay, no more jabs at the child. He's a victim here, after all.

My head is definitely still spinning, and I'm really not having a good time right now, but I *am* surprised by how little I feel about…him. Dean's son. The baby. Whatever his name is.

The longing I normally feel, the ache in my heart, the desire to reach out and tickle tiny toes, all of that is nowhere to be found right now. It's kind of confusing.

"Slow to catch up, Red? Always was a struggle for you." Venom laces every word of Katie's faux singsong voice.

I pull myself together, mentally throwing every single emotion I possess into a box and chucking it into the darkest corner of my brain. I pull my shoulders back to reach my full height. The move would normally put me at eye level with Dean, —something he *hates*—but I'm still standing here on the sidewalk like an idiot, while they're at the top of Mrs. Johnson's front steps.

"No, *Kathryn.* I'm just surprised."

"You wouldn't have been surprised if you answered my texts," Dean chimes in.

"You were texting her?" I watch Katie swap the baby from one hip to the other to turn to Dean in seething anger.

I interrupt before I'm forced to be the audience to their squabble.

"I mean, I'm just surprised you two are doing this. Like, you're not even a little embarrassed?"

They both try to talk over each other, with Dean saying, "Financially, it makes sense" and Katie snapping, "We're in love."

I roll my eyes, channeling my inner Penelope. "Well, isn't that…lovely. Congrats, really. Couldn't have happened to better people. Don't be surprised if I forget to drop off a welcome basket."

Get me the hell out of here.

"Red…" Dean starts, but doesn't continue.

For a split second, his voice reminds me of who he used to be to me. What I thought our life was going to look like. It's a fleeting moment where I almost think he could be sincere.

But then I hear a baby wail and realize it's *his* baby. A product of reality that I need to keep at the forefront of my mind. Katie starts bouncing, trying to soothe her son. It's choppy and unnatural to watch, and I find myself wanting to reach out and help.

Katie lets out a frustrated sigh and tries to pass the crying baby to Dean, but he marches off the steps, walking up to the front gate of the fence.

I instinctually step back and toward the direction of my house. I don't actually think this scene could get worse, but I'm not about to wait around to find out.

"As fun as this was, I should get going," I shout over the sobs. The poor kid isn't letting up and his face is beat red at this point. This isn't my problem, I need to go. But— "For fuck's sake, Katie. He's hungry. Feed him."

Her demon eyes find mine. I definitely just poked the bear, but come on, she's standing here monitoring Dean like he needs supervision just because I'm out here. I guess that's the price you pay when you "find love" in infidelity.

"And how would *you* know that?" she snaps.

She's trying to get a rise out of me, and unfortunately for her, my compartmentalization skills are off the charts thanks to her deadbeat baby daddy, so I have nothing to offer here except unwelcomed, but clearly very much needed advice.

"His head is bobbing looking for your boob. You're breastfeeding, right? The cues are there, you need to watch for them. Google dot com, babe." And with that, I dash the short distance to my house and slam the door shut.

I peep through my blinds to see Mr. Little Baby Accident latch and immediately calm down.

I know I should have more grace and patience with a new mom. It's the hardest job in the world. It's a huge transition. It's a lot of learning. But I'm a human with big feelings, and before Katie was a mother, she was a nightmare first.

She's still a nightmare. This whole thing feels like one bad dream I'm begging to wake up from.

How could he do this to me?

Because he never actually cared, I remind myself.

Everything else wasn't enough? He had to move in *next door?*

I put my back to my front door and slide all the way down until my ass hits the floor, and I throw my head in my hands.

There are no tears coming. I don't have anything left in me. I threw my all into putting up a wall out there in front of Dean and Katie, and now that wall feels so solid, I don't know where I would begin trying to break it down.

I don't think I want to either. This emptiness feels safer. I can't hurt anymore.

At least that's what I tell myself while I sit on my entryway's floor, listening to the sounds of my new neighbors bickering and moving trucks backing up and unloading next door.

I don't know how much time passes. I don't think I care.

* * *

"Don't do this to me. Not tonight, I'm begging," I plead with the lock on the back door, uselessly shimmying the knob.

It's 1:00 a.m., and I once again find myself fleeing to the cafe in the middle of the night because I can't sleep. And you know what, maybe I'm subconsciously fleeing to someone else. But I'll use the cafe as a front. Except this time the lock that's been giving us problems on and off for months has finally decided now is the time to fully and completely shit the bed.

I've somehow gotten the key jammed so far back that I think the entire thing is going to have to get replaced. But, I hold my phone's flashlight up and try one more time to at least wiggle the key out.

With one more last ditch attempt to pull, I feel a ridge of the key dislodge and then stick again. I give one more aggressive tug, and I have to catch myself as I fly back.

Once I'm on solid feet again, I hold up the piece of metal in my hand. It's the top half of the key. The bottom part is still stuck in the lock.

Excellent.

I don't even know why I dragged my feet on getting this fixed, John's Locksmith is right down the street, and I see him or his busybody husband at least twice a day.

Lazy. Scatterbrained. Space cadet.

These are a few things Dean used to mutter to himself, but loud enough so I'd hear, whenever anything like this would happen.

It's not that I enjoy forgetting to address things. It's just that there's so much. All of the time. I'm bad at delegating and prioritizing and sticking to lists, but I *try.* I try so fucking hard.

But sometimes, like right now, the effort isn't good enough, and I land myself in a situation, and I have no choice but to agree with past Dean.

I am a lazy, scatterbrained space cadet who has left myself with no other option except to get back in my car and drive my ass home. I'll have to deal with the lock later this morning, when it's socially acceptable, and I'm not at risk of disturbing the normal residents of Merrymount who are probably peacefully sleeping.

I let out a deep sigh and blindly chuck the remaining bit of the broken key and it noisily clangs off the dumpster. *Whoops.*

A light flicking on above the door that leads up to the apartment catches my attention, and I calculate that I have about four seconds to hightail it to my car and peel out of here before Miller catches me.

I spend those four seconds thinking about how much I don't want to do that.

The door with the lock that isn't broken opens and I see his hair first. It's exceptionally messy. Bedhead looks good on him.

You know what else looks good on him? The round, black framed glasses sitting on his face that I've never seen before.

That's a new Miller fact unlocked.

I expect him to be rubbing his face or yawning, maybe dazed or confused as to what's going on around him. But his eyes are clear and concerned and directed right at me.

They're also a little bigger due to the lenses. Damn, how blind is Miller?

"Gwen?" he asks.

"Hi," I sheepishly say.

"It's 1:00 o'clock in the morning."

The words fall out of my mouth. "He bought the house next door."

Thankfully, it doesn't take Miller long to catch up. Understanding dawns on his face, and while logically the concern should melt away—because physically I'm fine—it hardens.

"That's fucking insane. You know that, right?"

I shrug my shoulders, trying to not let on how badly I needed to hear him say that. "Honestly, I kind of thought I was overreacting."

"If you told me you keyed his car and put dog shit on his front step, it still wouldn't have been an overreaction."

I shuffle my feet and hoist my bag up on my shoulder while giggling. "Don't go giving me any ideas."

"I'll call Margot over here right now to watch P so I can join you."

For some reason, I don't think he's joking. I attempt to wave him off and take one small step back.

"Come upstairs." Not a question.

"I…I was about to head home." I lamely loll my head in the general direction of my car.

"And now you're coming upstairs." There's really no room for argument in his voice, and I have to say, authoritative Miller is working for me.

It's working so well I walk right through the doorway, under Miller's arm he's had braced on the frame, and march my sorry ass up the stairs.

I kick my shoes off and line them up next to Penelope's favorite jellies and hang my bag on the coat rack before falling face first into the couch. For someone who was pretending to be adamant about leaving, I'm having no issue making myself at home.

"Are you hungry?" Miller asks while locking the door.

Lifting my head off the couch cushion, I keep my voice low to not wake Penelope in her room. "You don't have to cook for me."

"Who said anything about cooking?" Miller opens one of the cabinets and pulls out a box of Cinnamon Toast Crunch. He grabs two bowls from the drying rack and two spoons from the drawer. He places one set in my designated seat at the island and keeps his set on the other side.

I hear the dry cereal being poured into one of the ceramic bowls, and I will my body to get up. I snatch the milk from the fridge, trying to help at least a little. I get situated on my barstool and watch Miller pour the perfect amount of milk over both of our mounds of sugary goodness.

He leans against the island and scoops a spoonful up into his mouth. The only sound is him chewing, and I'm the idiot sitting here mesmerized over a guy munching on children's cereal in the middle of the night.

He swallows, and I watch his adam's apple bob. The only light is coming from the light over the stove, and a small lamp in the living room so everything feels soft and quiet.

"Gwen?"

I snap out of my daze and the spoon I didn't realize I was gripping crashes into the bowl. It sounds so much louder than it probably is, and I'm nervous I just woke Penelope up.

"Sorry!" I whisper-shout.

"Don't be sorry. Eat your cereal before it gets soggy." He points at me with his spoon and a classic Miller smirk on his face.

"Aye, aye." I mock salute with my spoon before finally diving in.

We eat in comfortable silence, and it feels so much like a regular night that a deep pang rattles through me when I remember the reason why I'm sitting here in this kitchen right now.

"He bought the fucking house next to me," I finally say again after a loud exhale. "I'm going to have to...*see* him. He just couldn't let it go, huh? He had to blow everything up and then stick around to...I don't even know what exactly he's sticking around for."

I don't know if I'm rambling to Miller or myself, but I can't stop now. "Like, why bother? That's what's killing me. It's been how long now? I'm not going back. I was *never* going back. There's no love there. We literally have nothing between us. I've been racking my brain all night trying to figure it out, and I just can't."

"Do you want my opinion?" Miller asks as he clears our dishes, placing them in the sink.

I nod once. It's a small thing, but I appreciate how he approaches boundaries.

"It's a power thing. Guys like that...they don't care if you're done with them, or if you've walked away and said no. I don't know if Margot's mentioned our dad, or even how much she remembers from her own experience with him, but he's that kind of guy. They're miserable to their core and take it out on everyone around them."

"But you're not like that," I counter.

"I could have been. I don't know the kind of person I would have been if Penelope didn't come along. Hell, I still could turn into that."

"I don't believe that for a second. You're good, Miller. You're one of the good ones."

He gives me a soft smile, and I get the pleasure of watching his cheeks turn pink. "I try, harder than I want to let on. But, forget about me. Did you have to see him today?"

"Oh, not just him. The whole happy family. It felt like a bad movie. And he was jingling the keys, taunting me. I can still hear them ringing in my damn ears." I try to stifle the rogue yawn that hits me with no success.

Miller's face twists up in disgust before my yawn triggers his own. "I'm sorry for waking you up," I add.

"You didn't. I hadn't gone to bed yet," he answers as he runs his right hand through his hair. His left hand is still planted on the island in front of me. His pinky ring glinting slightly in the dim light.

"Partying hard? Or was something keeping you up?" I can't solve my problems, but maybe I can help with his.

"Nights are tough for me," he says after a beat.

"Has it always been like that?" I readjust myself on the stool, resting my head on my arm and tucking one of my legs under my butt to get comfy.

"Yeah, but I'm used to it. I've been running off a few hours of sleep a night for as long as I can remember. It helped the first year of Penelope's life, I'll tell ya that." He laughs.

"Oh, was she a tough sleeper as a baby?" If she was, you'd have no idea now. That kid can pass out anywhere.

"It wasn't her fault. Her little belly couldn't handle a lot of the formulas. It took us a while to get it right and until we did, she was up every few hours. It sucked being so helpless. I remember rocking her, bartering with any being up in the sky who'd give her a break."

"Is she lactose intolerant?" I'm sure Penelope is in fact, *not* lactose intolerant. But I'd rather learn more about her and her dad than rehash the bullshit going on back on my street.

"Thankfully, no. You've seen her throw back pints of ice cream. She was just sensitive for a bit. But hey, I know you're trying to change the subject. This whole thing is fucked up. They can't make you uncomfortable in your own house."

Well, so much for that plan…

"I know, I know," I huff. "I just—I don't know. My skin was crawling knowing they were right there. But, it's ridiculous. I'll get over it. I'm gonna head back." Another yawn escapes me, and I shimmy off the barstool.

Next thing I know, Miller is on my side of the island, and his hand is gripping my wrist. His fingers wrap around me so delicately that it tickles. His chest presses into my arm. The shadows and the quiet are making this a lot more intimate than I think he intended, and I find myself stuck in place, holding my breath.

His voice doesn't go above a whisper as he leans into my ear. I feel goosebumps rise all over. "Why do you always run away from me, Gwen?"

Because you and your daughter deserve better. Because it's easier to leave, rather than be left. Because I'm so fucking scared to let myself believe that someone will find a home in me, just to be another temporary resting place or helping hand.

I admit to none of those truths though. I take the cowardly route and pull from Miller's hand, losing the comforting feeling of his thumb gently rubbing circles on the inside of my wrist. I wrap my arms around his neck and give a quick squeeze, breathing in the fresh smell of his shampoo.

"I'm not running. I'm just…I'm tired. We should both get some sleep."

Miller looks like he's about to object. Maybe if I was a different version of myself, I'd let him.

But I don't leave room for the *what could be's*. I say nothing when I get to the door and slip my shoes on. Miller silently follows me, picking my bag up off the hook and holding it out for me. His facial expression tells me everything he's not saying. He's sorry, and he wishes I'd stay.

I don't tell him I'm sorry too, but I am. And I don't tell him I wish I was staying, but I do.

I don't think I could handle a friendship with Miller Caswell that included sleepovers, where I get to wake up in the morning to him and Penelope. I fear I wouldn't recover when the game of playing pretend ended.

Miller unlocks the door and walks me down the stairs. He opens my car door for me and tells me to let him know when I get home. I thank him for everything and assure him I'll be okay.

It feels forced and dull, and I hate it. But I have to stick to these stupid, self-imposed boundaries I created. If I tell myself it's safer and better this way enough times, maybe I'll finally start to believe it.

When I pull into my driveway ten minutes later, I see there's still a light on upstairs at ~~Mrs. Johnson's~~ Dean's house. The window is cracked, and I hear the crying before I'm even fully out of my car.

The arguing between the two bozos who are in charge of taking care of that crying baby is somehow louder, though.

"It's your turn to feed him, Dean! I can't do this every night!"

"Sorry I don't have milk tits!"

Laughing to myself, I make my way inside. I'm not the one having the worst night, and I'm taking that small win. Forgoing turning on any lights, I blindly climb the stairs to crash into my bed.

Before letting my eyes close, I make sure to send off a text to Miller to confirm I made it home safely. I'm assuming he's fast asleep by now, but I see my phone light up before I can even set it down on my nightstand.

MILLER

Get some rest. Bowl of cereal with your name on it here whenever you need it. Always.

CHAPTER 13: MILLER - SHACKING UP AND LIVING IN SIN

"What about those fancy cookies with the designs on them?" Gus suggests. He's sitting in a chair next to me in the Rivers main building. The chair is entirely too small for him to actually sit in, so he's straddling the back.

"I feel like those taste like cardboard sometimes, though," Margot chimes in from her chair behind the desk Sawyer set up for her.

"Normally, we just do a small ice cream cake..."

Penelope and I stopped at Rivers River on the way home from the grocery store this afternoon when we saw Margot's car parked out front. I thought it'd be nice to say hi before the busyness of the weekend started. Gus and Sawyer were just finishing up their day, and Margot was helping Beth with paperwork in the office.

Sawyer offered to teach Penelope to fish a little while ago, and he decided today should be the day to make good on that promise when he saw us walking up. He's fully leaned into the whole uncle thing and honestly, it's really fucking awesome.

It's cool to see how easily everyone fits in here. Only a few months ago, Margot and I barely existed to each other and these

"

people, and now we feel like one giant family. It's like it was always supposed to be this way. Penelope and I are able to walk into a place and not have only each other to cling to. We're welcomed with open arms.

Except I'm still not completely used to the idea of switching up our little traditions, and although it might be an oversight on my part, I'm kind of caught off guard by how easily everyone just shows up. But I love that Penelope is about to have a crowd of people celebrating her birthday. She deserves it all.

Margot puts down the pen she was using to jot down notes on the back of an old receipt. She's not in the least bit organized, but her heart is there. Her eyes soften with a knowing look. She looks just like her mom when she does it.

"We can make an ice cream cake work. But the small size isn't gonna cut it this year. Let us be a part of the day, Miller. For both of you."

"Don't think I don't want you there," I start.

"I don't. But I know it's hard. I'm still learning too." Margot looks out the window, and I follow her line of sight to see Sawyer guiding Penelope to toss the fishing line.

She gets it. Margot spent her whole life thinking it would always just be her and Melanie, and then somehow she ended up here in Merrymount surrounded by people who only want to love her. She's leaning into it though, and I love to see how comfortable she's made herself here.

"My vote is still sugar cookies," Gus says.

"Noted, my dude," Margot assures him. "But it's Miller's and Penelope's birthday so we're giving them the final decision."

Gus leans over, tilting the chair with him. "Red loves sugar cookies."

"Cookies it is, then," I decide with absolutely no further thought. He could just be saying that so I'd vote in his favor, but I'm not taking the chance.

Margot rolls her eyes but circles the word *cookies* on her list. "Speaking of Red…"

"You make moves on that yet?" Gus asks.

"Gus, you can't just fucking ask like that," Margot scoffs.

"Why not? We're all wondering the same thing!"

"I'm trying," I admit.

Both of their heads whip to me. These people see me and Gwen interact at the cafe. Everyone is aware that I have a giant crush on her, and that I'm willing to follow her around like a lost puppy if needed. They know Gwen sometimes comes over for dinners, and that she loves hanging out with P, but all of the other stuff…the late nights and the notes, those are ours.

So they really don't have a clue that I've been chipping away at Gwen Bozelli's extremely solid walls for weeks now. I'm not sure if I'm getting any closer, but I'll try until she tells me to stop.

"Do you want to walk us through your version of trying?" Margot asks.

"Nope." I lean back in my chair and put my hands behind my head, relaxed and ready for the verbal beatdown Margot is about to deliver. Everybody around here is always in everyone's business, and it works some, but I'm keeping Gwen and me private.

"But we can help! I know Red. Gus knows Red." Margot points to herself and Gus, respectively, when Beth strides through the door with Daisy in tow. "And Beth and Daisy know Red!"

"Oh, are we conspiring for another love match?" Beth rubs her hands together as she walks over to her desk next to Margot's like she has some diabolical plan. She pats Gus's head and kisses the top of Margot's on the way by.

"What do you mean, another?" Margot asks and I hear Daisy giggle.

"You thought my boy wooed you all on his own?" Beth's question is lightheartedly directed at Margot who immediately flusters.

"Well—No, but I—You know what? Nevermind. It's better to be on this side of of any planning. Yes, Beth. We are officially conspiring."

Daisy makes a disgusted noise, waving her hand in front of her nose. "If only it didn't smell like wet dog in here."

"Careful, Daze. Don't go acting like you'd lift a manicured finger for anyone. It'd give Miller here the wrong impression."

"Excuse me?" Daisy snaps.

Gus's voice reaches about five octaves higher than usual, in a mocking tone. "Oh, you're excused, Daisy darling."

"Real fucking mature of y—"

"You wanna talk about maturity?"

Before their back-and-forth turns into an all out brawl, Beth interrupts without looking up from her desk. "Will you two ever make it five whole minutes without the drama? You know what? Not today. Gus, go home. Daisy, get out."

Margot and I look at each other, eyes wide, waiting to see what happens next.

Gus nods once, standing to his full height, and towering over every single one of us. He places the chair back in its place in front of Beth's desk.

"Sorry, Beth," he mumbles before silently waving goodbye.

If looks could kill, the glare Daisy shoots at Gus when they reach the door at the same time would have wiped him off the planet.

"I'm sorry, Beth," she says. "I'll see you Monday."

Gus matches Daisy's pointed look while begrudgingly pushing the door open for her. Daisy doesn't even have to duck to walk under his arm and through the door.

"Christ, they're exhausting." Beth exhales once we hear each of their footsteps fade across the gravel parking lot.

"There has to be *something* that'll crack this rivalry," Margot offers. You can see the gears turning in her brain.

"I'm not in the business of meddling with those two anymore. I pass the torch to you. Now, more important matters. Miller?"

"Me?" Shit.

"Yes, you. I love Red like a daughter. She's special and good. You see all of this, correct?"

"Of course," I answer.

"Fabulous." Beth smacks her hands together. "Let's not beat around the bush. Red deserves to be loved, wholly and completely. It doesn't need to be grand or loud, just to the bone honest. She needs someone who can show up."

"I can do that." I feel like I'm at a job interview for a position that I don't remember applying to.

"Knew you could, kid. Good enough for me." Beth winks.

"So, Miller…speaking of showing up," Margot starts.

"Yeah?"

"Any chance you'd consider maybe thinking about letting me and Sawyer take P for the night one of these weekends? It'd give you some alone time with Red. We have everything you could need for the perfect sleepover at the cottage! I have all of the emergency numbers saved just in case. I was even CPR certified!"

"Marge, I trust you with my daughter."

"But this is a big deal and I know—"

"I'm serious, Margot. Yes. Please. I think Penelope would love that."

She's not wrong, it is a big deal. But I've been thinking about this for a while now. I've been letting Margot and Sawyer take Penelope out for months, and after how much P loved her night with Beth and Melanie, this is the easiest next step.

This is good for Penelope. And me, if I'm actually going to be real with myself. I don't like to admit to needing a break and taking time for myself. I love being a dad. I love being *her* dad, but I forget I'm supposed to be a guy in my twenties sometimes too.

But, wait—

"*We* have everything all set up?" I ask her. I know the answer, we all do. Margot's just too chickenshit to own up to it. Well, I'm not giving her that option anymore.

Margot nervously shoots a quick glance at Beth who appears completely unphased. "*We—*" she enunciates the word and pauses like she's testing it out. "Alright, fine. I moved into Sawyer's."

Beth looks up from the paperwork she was pretending to sort. "Can you believe she thinks we all didn't know?"

"*What?!*" Margot yells.

"I think the real question is, why do you think we'd care?" I ask.

"Because moving in with someone is a big deal, and it was really fast, and I don't know! I don't like this!"

"You don't like what, baby girl?" Beth says. "You're happy. And shacking up, living in sin! This is the fun part!"

Margot shakes her head, pretending to tune Beth out. "Don't say shacking up and living in sin ever again."

"You kids are such prudes," Beth humphs. "I'm gonna go join the fun ones outside."

"She knows not to say that in front of Penelope, right?" I ask Margot after Beth is out of earshot.

We're one week out from six years old. I'm not ready for that conversation yet. I debate heading out to monitor, but I don't want any of them to think I'm that bad of a helicopter parent. I can loosen the reins. I can be chill.

I don't need to control everything like my father.

"Eh, P will be fine," Margot tries to assure me.

"So, wow, living together? That's cool."

Margot smiles. "It is. It feels right, even if it was early. I'm just…Do you ever feel weird about being thrown into"—Margot waves her hands around—"All of this?"

"Every day, Marge. I didn't think shit like this existed, you know? Like, it was exclusively for movies and books. I thought Penelope's Disney movies were more believable."

"But it's better this way," she says.

"Oh, one hundo percent."

The only thing I'd change is my standing with the town's cafe owner, and I feel like my luck might be changing on that front soon, anyway.

Margot smiles softly. "Would you mind if I invited my mom next weekend?"

"Already did," I tell her.

"I shouldn't even be surprised."

She shouldn't. It was the first text I sent after Margot insisted on this joint birthday party after trick-or-treating.

I'm lucky enough to have found a special friendship with Melanie LeClair, and I don't take it for granted. I loved my mom. I'm sure deep down, buried underneath all of the bullshit my father pumped into her, she was a good person. She was just so lost. She didn't know how to find herself anymore.

I don't damn her or hold her choices against her. She was always doing her best in an impossible situation. She thought the only way she could escape was with how she went, and I've made peace with that.

But Melanie has unknowingly filled a good chunk of that void by welcoming me and my daughter into her orbit, and Margot graciously accepts that. It's easy to love them both.

"Do you think she'd ever move to Merrymount?" I ask.

"My mom? I mean, she loves that swim school, but...I don't know. It'd be nice, huh?"

"Yeah," I say. "The more the merrier in Merrymount."

Margot snorts. "Add that to the never say again list."

CHAPTER 14: GWEN - HAPPY BIRTHDAY, MILLER CASWELL

I've been arguing with myself—both in my head and out loud—for what feels like hours now. But when I look at the time on my phone, I see it's barely been sixty minutes. Do I continue to sit here and torture myself until I eventually find sleep or abandon ship to run to Miller?

The distance between Mrs. Johnson's house and mine used to feel a lot further than it does right now. Especially since the new assholes next door have no regard for quiet hours or peace in any capacity.

And while we're on the subject, who the hell throws a baby shower like, months after the baby is born? And on a Thursday?

Stupid as fuck parents, that's who.

I don't know if this could even constitute a baby shower. I mean, I realize that's what the dumb sign on their front lawn says, and the table piled high with pastel blue gift bags feels related, but it's well after 11:00 p.m. Music is still blaring from a speaker set up in their backyard, and party goers are still drinking heavily around a bonfire.

The last time I peeked out of my window, I could only recognize a few faces, some of Dean's douchebag buddies from the police department and both sets of new grandparents who must be in town visiting for the occasion. Other than that, it's a bunch of randos who are probably only over there for the free booze.

Good for them. Real classy.

I aggressively throw my comforter across my bed and heave myself up to pace.

I'm wasting precious time allotted for sleep and rest, listening to the idiocy out my window. I'm pissed because I've been looking forward to tomorrow for weeks, and I don't want to be spending it dodging yawns and covering bags under my eyes.

First, Miller and P invited me to crash their trick-or-treating plans. That alone feels like the highest honor. Then Margot mentioned a birthday party for the two of them. I've been in psycho planner mode ever since, one of my best sides, in my opinion.

After letting Penelope change her mind a good five or six times on costumes, we nailed a theme and decided to keep it a surprise for Miller. I had to finally give her a deadline so I could get to crafting. I got to dust off my old sewing machine that I used to alter my clothes in high school and tailor local little girls' dance costumes.

I'm not judging Miller. He's been doing his best. But this child only knows of costumes you buy at the *store*. Can you believe that? They will be homemade with love only from here on out as far as I'm concerned.

The cafe is already decorated for Halloween, so it made the most sense to plan for the birthday party to be there. Penelope has no idea, and I think she's going to lose her mind when she sees what Margot and I have conjured up with the help of our friends. The cafe has been a do not enter zone for her since Tuesday and between me, Miller, and Margot, we've successfully kept lil P in the dark, much to her dismay.

I've had to cut most of my nights with Miller and P short to prepare, and that part hasn't been fun, but I already know it's going to be so worth it to see their faces light up. Miller obviously knows we have something planned, but when Margot got the go ahead from him, we tapped him out.

After Miller found and brought me upstairs the night Dean and Katie moved in, something cracked in me, like the walls I thought I had perfected weren't so impenetrable after all.

I find myself missing the two of them when we're not together. I reach for my phone to shoot a text off to Miller when I see something that reminds me of either of them. I run to Miller when something funny happens at the cafe. I save my best treats for when Penelope dashes into the cafe after school.

The only thing I haven't come close to is a repeat of that night. I've kept myself rooted firmly on the friendship side of my feelings. The dim lighting and stillness and familiarity of that apartment felt too personal, too close to something we couldn't come back from.

The way Miller's voice sounded when he asked why I always run away…It's been replaying in my head on a loop. It was raw and sent shivers down my spine, tingling at the base. I know that if I landed myself in that type of situation again, I'd want to prove him wrong.

I liked his closeness and the way his raspy breath reached my neck. I liked how easily he saw me but respected me enough to let things be. I'm just too scared of so many things.

I don't want to be scared anymore though.

An idea pops into my head, and it's the kind where if I try to leave it be, I know I'll regret it.

I stop my pacing and sit on the edge of my bed, grabbing my phone from the nightstand and staring at it. Pulling up our text thread, I quickly type out a message. I'm half hoping Miller responds and half hoping he might actually be sleeping at a reasonable time for once.

ME

hi.

But of course he isn't asleep. His reply appears not even a minute later.

MILLER

It's awfully late, Gwendolyn.

ME

were you sleeping?

It's a dumb question, but I actually have no idea if this is going to blow up in my face, and now I'm stalling by asking a ridiculous, very obvious thing in hopes of coming up with a game plan.

MILLER

You know, I've never been booty called before.

The sound that leaves my throat is the opposite of ladylike.

ME

and the streak continues!!!

ME

care for some company though?

MILLER

Light's on for you. :)

I thumbs up his text and swipe my favorite pair of sweatpants from my drawer. They're bright red and say lifeguard across the ass. They're silly and usually reserved for my rot on the couch days, but I know Miller won't care, and they're comfy as hell.

Massachusetts probably won't see a night above sixty degrees until late May, so I grab one of my thicker hoodies from my closet, smiling like a dork at my post-it note door on the way out.

The newest addition is a doodle of three ghosts, the one in the middle being smaller. Miller's handwriting—that somehow manages to get worse?—under it reads:

Me, you, and P??? :)

He thinks I'll crack on the costume surprise. He's wrong.

I make a quick stop in the kitchen to rummage through my junk drawer, grab what I need, and shove it into my bag.

When I reach my driveway and hear the distinct voice of an extremely drunk Dean, I stop dead in my tracks. His voice is a lot louder than it should be if it's coming from *his* backyard where *he* should be.

Nope. No way. Not tonight, Satan.

I chance a look to my left and see Dean's back is to me, his hand is holding his cell to his ear, and thankfully I don't think he heard me exit my house because his slurred words don't stop.

"Baby, baby, baby…" he coos into the phone, and I will myself to not gag. "No, nothing's going on. Just some of my buddies letting off some steam on a Thursday night. Tomorrow night's a big night for us. Gotta keep the pretty little women like you safe."

Fucking. Ew. Everything coming out of his mouth makes my skin crawl. I have no desire to wait around to hear anymore of whatever the hell this is. His roster of mistresses is no longer my problem.

I very silently tip toe to my car when I see Dean round the corner of his property, moving further away from me, still blabbering away to whatever poor girl is on the receiving end of his bullshit. I start the car and leave no time for it to warm up, throwing it in reverse immediately.

My phone lights up, and I glance over at it when I get to the stop sign at the end of my street.

MILLER

Cinnamon Toast Crunch or Fruity Pebbles?

Another text comes through.

It doesn't feel like I'm running away from anything tonight. It feels like I'm on my way to exactly where I'm supposed to be, and it feels really fucking good to know that.

* * *

THE LIGHT IS INDEED on when I pull into the back of the cafe. And Miller, with unruly bedhead, bouncing his knee, is sitting on the bottom step of the staircase, waiting for me.

He jogs over when I put my car in park. I pop open my door, and Miller grabs the handle to hold it for me as I get out.

"Hey," he says with the easiest smile on his face, and I immediately know I made the right call, ditching my place of doom and gloom for this.

"Hey there." I turn around and bend over, leaning across the center console to grab my bag. When I face Miller again, I catch his head quickly snap up to meet mine and see him swallow hard.

"Miller." I raise an eyebrow, trying my hardest to hold back the giggles that are trying to escape me.

He throws both hands up in surrender. "I'm sorry! The letters! They're so big! And it's— You—" He takes a deep breath, and I can no longer hold it in and let my laugh fall out.

Miller realizes I'm not even a little bit offended he was obviously checking out my ass and laughs it off, relief painted on his face.

"You came," he finally says.

I hold up my phone. "I did ask first, right? I didn't imagine that?"

"No, you're right. You did. It's just…"

I look at my phone screen again, checking the time. I don't let him finish his thought before I grab his hand and pull him with me towards the stairs. "Let's go, we're gonna be late!"

"Late for what?" Miller's fingers intertwine with mine, and it makes my whole body feel warm in the cool air of a late October night.

"I'm not ruining the surprise with three minutes to spare, come *on!*" I lower my voice when we reach the top and step into the apartment.

I leave Miller at the door and quickly skip over to the kitchen. I keep my back to him as I assemble my surprise at the counter, reaching for the chocolate chip muffins I know are stashed in the fruit basket and plucking one out of its plastic container to place on a small plate I grab from the cabinet.

I pull the candle and lighter out of my bag, sticking the bottom of the candle into the muffin, I light it. I guard the flame with the palm of my hand as I turn and watch the clock on the stove, waiting for it to switch over to 12:00 before facing him.

"Happy Birthday, Miller Caswell."

His stare switches between me and the candle no less than four times. His eyes are wide, and his mouth is slightly ajar. He looks like a surprised puppy, and it's the cutest thing in the world.

I hold the plate up, prompting Miller to do what everyone should do on their birthday. "Go on, make a wish."

I watch his eyelids close, and he blows out the flame. When he opens his eyes, pools of bright green practically twinkle at me. That little freckle above his lip is taunting me. Miller's face is inches from mine when he gently takes the plate between us and sets it down on the island.

He doesn't make a sound, and neither do I. I'm stuck, captivated, by this ever-so-serious but secretly funny, determined and driven, soft but scrappy, incredibly smart boy in front of me.

I don't think I could look away even if I wanted to. His jaw flexes, and I watch his eyes track my movements as I pull my bottom lip in with my teeth.

The air feels charged, and while I'm sure if I was watching this from the outside, I'd be able to catch up faster, the reality is I'm not. I'm locked in place, confused and hopeful and feeling a little silly because oh my God, imagine this is entirely one sided, and I—

Miller's hands cradle my face, the warmness of them contrasting the cool metal of his ring that touches the back of my neck, and his mouth crashes into mine.

Thankfully my body moves instinctually since my mind stopped working. My hands wrap around his raised arms as he pulls me so I'm flush with his chest. I taste his toothpaste and chapstick and breathe in the scent that's so inexplicably Miller.

His fingers curl into my hair as he kisses me deeply, and a sound I've never heard a day in my life escapes from my mouth.

Miller doesn't pull away, but each kiss becomes more shallow as his smile spreads. His hands release my hair, and they start to roam. They lightly graze my neck, shoulders, and arms.

Once his fingers reach mine, they intertwine, and he squeezes once. Goosebumps appear in the wake of his touch and soon enough we're giggling into each other. It feels like here, in the dim light of this tiny apartment, is the silliest, happiest place in the world.

I want to bottle up this feeling to keep for the rest of forever.

He presses his forehead to mine, and I place my palm on his chest, watching it rise and fall through heavy lidded eyes. Each deep breath he takes has him coming down from a high that I know matches my own.

I'm trying to not let my pestering thoughts of doubt and dread sneak into this moment, but I'm downright terrified to say anything right now and break the spell.

I kept this crush on Miller suppressed for months. I told myself a million and one times that attempting to pursue anything beyond casual cordialness was reckless, a mistake waiting to happen.

Things worked. He and Penelope got to live here, safe and comfortable. We had a good thing going with this friendship, and now I'm scared we just went ahead and fucked it all up.

Because after exactly one kiss at the stroke of midnight, I realize I can never go back to how things were before. This one kiss changed the wiring in my brain that thought it knew what a kiss was supposed to feel like.

Miller's hands release mine, and when he wraps his arms around me, they find a home at the small of my back. It feels like he doesn't want to let me go, and I have zero objections.

"Can I tell you something?" he whispers. I silently nod in answer, still too scared to speak.

"That was the first time I've ever blown out a birthday candle."

"*What?*" I pull back, and I'm sure my face hides absolutely no part of how confused I am.

Miller tucks my head under his chin and shrugs. "We didn't celebrate birthdays at home. And when Penelope was born, well, my birthday became hers." There's no resentment in his voice. He'd happily give up every part of himself for her.

"But that's— Miller, it's your *birthday*," I argue.

"Listen, if I knew all I had to do was close my eyes and make a wish to end up in the position I'm currently in, I would have been lighting that shit up and huffing and puffing a long time ago." I feel his laugh vibrate against me.

"Well, good thing we got this practice out of the way then. There's another cake with your name on it for later. Penelope's too, of course. But last year was the *last time* you ever go without a birthday wish," I declare before muttering to myself, "Insanity."

I hear Miller give me a harumph. "You ride hard for your people. Gwen. I wish you'd do the same for yourself."

"That's rich coming from you."

"Eh, at least I'm self-aware."

"Hey!" We finally break apart, and I instantly miss being wrapped up in him. I'm clingy as fuck within minutes. Attractive. Cool. I have this completely under control.

"I'm kidding! Sort of." Miller picks up the muffin, pulls out the candle, and takes a bite. He breaks another piece off and pops it into my mouth.

We lean against the island, quietly sharing a midnight muffin, as if this is completely normal and a part of our day-to-day. I look around and my vision stops at Penelope's bedroom door for the first time.

There are metallic pink and purple streamers hung from the doorframe to the floor that she'll have to walk through to get out when she wakes up in the morning. There's a giant mylar balloon in the shape of a six with a half dozen Disney Princess balloons surrounding it, all floating in place thanks to the sparkly weight they're tied to on the floor.

A banner is hung on the wall that reads *"Happy Birthday, Penelope!"* in a swirly pink font.

I have no fucking idea how I missed all of this when I came in earlier.

I look at Miller, who's already watching me stand here slack jawed in amazement over the kind of dad this man is, completely on his own.

"You're the best dad," I tell him.

"She's the best kid," he answers.

My arms snake around his neck, and I lift my chin so my lips graze his, testing it out again, as if to make sure the first time wasn't a fluke. But when he meets me in the middle, I'm reminded of how easily familiar this already feels.

We don't talk about it, whatever this is, even though we probably should. Instead, Miller asks if I want to help him finish setting up the rest of the decorations he bought while watching reruns of The Office.

He signs *Daddy* on a card and silently holds the pen out to me. I pause. This feels like a big deal.

Is it a big deal? Get a grip. It's Penelope's birthday card.

Without further overthought, I sign *Gwen* (with a heart, of course) right next to his scrawl.

We build a pyramid of pink frosted sprinkled donuts on a platter, reusing the candle I brought. We stick it in the very top for Miller to light again when Penelope wakes.

I scooch closer to him on the couch when we're done setting up, gladly cuddling up under the throw blanket he holds up for me to join him in. It's just for a few minutes—then I'll go back home. He kisses the top of my head once I settle, and I think about how this is the coziest I've ever felt in my life.

We drift off to sleep, tangled together, at some point in the very early hours of the morning. In sleep, I completely forget about driving back to an empty house and every reason I had prepared as to why this might not be the best idea.

CHAPTER 15: MILLER - WHAT'S MY AGE AGAIN?

*O*ctober 31st.

On this day six years ago at 6:03 a.m., a marker was placed on the timeline of my life.

There was "before I heard my daughter's first cry" and there was "after." I was standing in the after, thinking about how the before felt like the faintest, far away place.

The world shook that day. *My* world was completely rocked to its core.

I remember the light from the sunrise was just starting to peek through the blinds in the hospital room, signaling the start of a new day and my new beginning.

I was holding these medical grade scissors with shaky hands. I was half listening to the doctors and nurses in the room coach me on how to cut this insane looking blue cord that was connected to the newborn I couldn't take my eyes off of.

So it's fitting that once again, exactly six years to the day later, a new marker is placed on the timeline of my life.

There was "before I knew what it was like to kiss Gwendolyn Bozelli," and then there was "after."

Don't ask me about the before, it doesn't exist to me now.

What *do* exist are the same rays of light I remember so vividly from the day Penelope was born just starting to dance on the hardwood floors, coming through Penelope's bedroom window that overlooks Main Street. The rising sun is sending bursts of light, much brighter than the ones from the day Penelope was born, glittering as the streamers in my daughter's doorway gently sway.

But that doesn't make sense because then that would mean it's at least 7:00 a.m., and surely Gwen and I didn't fall asleep on the couch, and there's no way—

"Daddy!" Penelope calls from her bed.

There's absolutely no way I would be that irresponsible. Except clearly, I am.

My newly six-year-old daughter comes barreling out of her room, throwing the strips of pink and purple up high, before I can fully process what's unfolding. She stops dead in her tracks when she reaches the living room. She looks to the balloons, back at the streamers and banner, and to the island with the donuts and a gift bag. When Penelope turns back to me, her Bluey nightgown is hanging off one shoulder, and she's staring at me with her head tilted.

Correction, she's not staring at me. She's now fixated on her real life idol still passed out across my chest.

"P!" My voice doesn't sound like my own. "You're awake!"

I try to jostle Gwen under the blanket, hoping to stir her awake without freaking her out. Although, I'm guessing that is going to be a wasted effort because I *know* she's going to freak out.

Fair. I'm kind of freaking out, too.

"Red?" Penelope asks.

I feel Gwen twitch. I look down to see her frozen in place, eyes wide. It feels like time stands still, giving us a few seconds to silently come up with a game plan.

Unfortunately, I've got nothing. Less than nothing. I swallow hard, silently begging for some backup here because I have no fucking idea what I'm doing.

Gwen reads my face and pulls her shit together faster than I can. She shoots up, and the blanket goes flying. She starts brushing herself off and patting her hair down.

"Well, if it isn't the *birthday girl!*" Gwen shrieks.

"Did you come over to surprise me?!" Penelope yells as she dashes over, jumping right into Gwen's arms.

"You bet I did, tiny human. Or should I say not-so-tiny human? SIX?! Six whole years old?! Happy Birthday, Penelope." Gwen spins her around, the two of them laughing.

This is what it's supposed to feel like.

I finally snap out of my stupor and lift off the couch, deciding the discarded blanket needs to be folded immediately. It'll keep my hands busy while I work through how to explain this situation to my kid.

It feels like such a sleazy dick move to have a random woman have a sleepover in our home. Penelope had to wake up to me cuddling on the couch, blindsided. I'm not supposed to be this selfish.

I can't be making decisions that affect the both of us without thinking it through more carefully than this. I need to be sure.

Then I feel guilty because Gwen isn't some random woman, not to me or Penelope. And it kind of feels like P wasn't as blindsided as I might be making her out to be. Or is that me trying to justify recklessness?

I'm twenty ~~two~~ three years old, and some days I feel like I don't know shit about shit.

Fuck. I'm twenty-three years old. I don't know how I feel about that either.

I shake my head as Gwen waltzes herself and P over to the kitchen, plopping Penelope in front of her on the island, next to the donut tower.

I follow their lead and have to abruptly stop myself from

coming up behind Gwen to wrap her in my arms with P, like this is any other morning in some alternate reality.

I stick to this reality and grab the lighter from the drawer to light the candle stuck in the top donut, respectfully *next* to Gwen. I lean over and kiss Penelope on the cheek.

"Happy Birthday, Penelope. Best—"

"Day of my life!!! Happy Birthday, Daddy!" she finishes for me in a screech and wraps her arms around my neck. She gives me a kiss on the cheek right back. I've said the same thing to her every morning on this day since she was born. She started saying it back to me on her fourth birthday, when it finally connected for her that it was my birthday too.

I love all of our traditions, big and small. They're important to me. But this one's special.

I wait until she releases me and sits back up to flick the lighter on. Gwen moves her arm in front of P as she leans toward the lit candle, an instinctual need to protect from even the smallest potential danger.

We sing happy birthday and I wonder to myself, like I do every year, what she's wishing for as she blows out the candle.

How can I be better for my little girl? Where do I come up short? Is she happy? Does she feel safe and loved? Is the gift I got her good enough because I couldn't afford a trip to Disney or tickets to a Taylor Swift concert?

Okay, that last one is specific to this year and something I just have to accept, but still. I want to get it all right.

I go to pull the candle out and divy up the donuts when Gwen's hand wraps around mine to stop me. She pushes our joined hands down and doesn't let go. Then, she reaches out her other hand and grabs the lighter from the island.

"Hold your horses there, Mr. Nobody Likes You When You're Twenty-Three." She relights the candle.

"Well, I'm certainly hoping you make me the exception to that rule," I say with a laugh, twisting my wrist to intertwine my fingers with hers. She's stunning all of the time, but she looks so pretty in the morning.

We have shit to talk through. This can't be done in a flighty way, but accidental sleepovers and mistakes be damned, I want this. I want her to want it, too.

She shakes her head at me before looking at Penelope and nodding once. They repeat the song we just sang to Penelope, and I make another wish.

Well, it's the same wish I made earlier. I thought doubling down might help make it come true.

* * *

"I'm not wearing this," I call from my room.

I stare into the mirror in horror to see myself in lime green tights and an imitation snake-skin onesie. Two giant as fuck googly eyes—I swear one of them is a lazy eye—and a floppy prop tongue are hot glued to the baseball hat sitting on my head. It matches the damn tights. The reptilian tail sewn onto a belt these two ladies actually think I'm a sucker enough to put on is still sitting on my bed.

I have to give credit when it's due though. For pulling this together in two weeks, this costume is impressive as hell. I haven't seen one thing Gwen doesn't excel at in every way. It's insane.

When I was trying to be the cool dad giving Gwen and Penelope creative freedom to come up with our costumes, I thought surely nothing could be worse than me as Princess Anna. I could rock a gender bent sister. That's fun, it's different. I was on board and was ready to reap the rewards of seeing Gwendolyn in some variation of that sparkly ice queen dress.

I'd do anything for my kid, and I've quickly learned I'd do just about anything for the woman laughing maniacally outside my door.

But the cool, sly smolder guy was *right fucking there.*

"Oh, yes you are!" Gwen yells from the other side of the door. "You promised! You signed!"

"A sticky note is not a legally binding contract, Gwendolyn!"

"You know who would disagree?"

"Uh, you?" I guess as I finally toss the hat onto the bed and ruffle my hair back out.

"Dr. Meredith Grey and Dr. Derek Shepherd. You're going to argue with two world-renowned surgeons?" I see the doorknob jiggle just a little. It's not locked. She can bust in here if she wants. But the door doesn't move.

"Fake ones? Yes." I need to peel this monstrosity of a costume off. I'm gonna do it. They're not gonna get me to cave. I'm a twenty-three-year-old man, an adult with a job and a kid—

I hear the click of the door opening first. Then Gwen's head pops in, but she looks…different?

"What happened to your hair?" I ask. I probably could have worded that better but I can't figure out what's off about it. It looks bigger, fuller I guess. But also maybe darker?

After our half-awkward morning together, Gwen only went home to quickly shower, change, and grab everything she said she would need for trick-or-treating later. When she got back to the cafe, after checking on Chris, who she finally hired as much-needed help, she whisked Penelope away to Margot and Sawyer's place to get ready. I haven't seen either of them in hours, taking some unexpected time to myself to sort my brain out.

We haven't had time to talk about anything, and neither of us knows where the other is at with things.

She enters the room, and I immediately forget what I just asked or why it even mattered. Don't care what she did differently to her hair. My brain is malfunctioning or *something* because holymotherfuckingshit.

Whatever fabric she used to pull this dress together literally molds to her skin. Every curve and dip is on full display. The sleeves go down her arms, widening on the ends. The length of it pools at the bottom, hiding her feet, but I can tell she's standing a little bit taller. There's a shiny gold chain fastened around her waist, the links of it jingling lightly.

I connect the dots and the big, frizzier curls finally make sense, although I do not remember ever getting a hard-on from the Mother Gothel in the cartoon.

And I definitely can't get one now when I'm standing here dressed as a stupid fucking lizard.

"Don't hate on the wig. It's kind of itchy, but I had to commit, okay?" Gwen places one hand on her hip, popping it out. Why did that make this whole thing like, ten times sexier?

Also, a wig makes sense now that I spend more than half a second thinking about it.

"I'm not hating on a single thing, I can promise you that." I take the opportunity to look her up and down again. This time she must see the heat in my gaze because the pout on her face suddenly lifts up, along with her arms as she twirls for me.

I miss the confidence I had last night in the dark, when I wasn't trying to shoot my shot with a knockout of a woman who's a million miles out of my league on a normal day, let alone in spandex and tights. But like I said, I'm giving it my all anyway.

"You knew what you were doing when you picked this out," is what I land on.

"Correction, I *hoped* it would be received well. Well enough to get you to agree to put that hat and tail back on to take the birthday girl for some good old fashioned tricks and treats with me." She bats her long lashes at me and clasps her hands together in front of her.

Yeah, there's no way in hell I'm saying no to that.

I begrudgingly grab the remaining costume pieces from the bed, plopping the hat back on my head and fastening the belt. Once I'm done I lift my head to look at her again.

"That's what I like to see!" she cheers while doing an excited little jump in place.

"I'm gonna get you back for this." I'm full of shit.

She holds out her hand with a devilish look in her eyes. "You pull off the perfect Pascal, and I swear I'll wear whatever you want at an occasion of your choosing."

I grab her hand and pull her towards me, I'm not met with any resistance though. Her chest hits mine. "A deal's a deal."

I want to kiss her again. I want to ruin the make-up painted so prettily on her face. I want to push her up against this door and tell her how, if I had my way, the occasion she's talking about would be an uninterrupted date in my bed, and I'd be telling her to wear absolutely nothing.

But I want to do all of this preferably while not cosplaying a sidekick. So, I settle for giving her a quick peck on the cheek. Her lips form a small O when I pull away. I'm not going to tell her the smile she then gives me is the only payment I'd ever need to agree to anything she asks.

A flash of tulle comes bursting through the doorway. "The clock says 4:58 p.m. We need to go *now!* Trick or treat starts at five! That's in two minutes, people!"

Gwen and I really need to talk about what's next. I know where I'm headed, but I need to make sure we're on the same page for Penelope. And for me, too.

Penelope's dress finally comes to a halt, and she stands before us looking a hell of a lot older than six, in my opinion. Her hair is braided and hanging off one shoulder with little flowers threaded throughout. The poofy dress is covered in ribbons and sparkles and honestly, looks way better than the ones you could ever buy in a store.

The best part is how unbelievably happy she looks, covered in glitter that I'll be finding in the crevices and corners of every-where for the rest of time. It's a small price to pay to see my girl like this.

I squat down to her level.

"Princess Rapunzel."

She nods, trying to hold in her giggles while she bops my hat. I continue, "Do you think we can put aside our differences with Mother Gothel and let her accompany us this evening?"

She looks to Gwen, who plays along, looking extremely apologetic. "Please, your highness. It would mean so much to me."

This sends Penelope over the edge, hysterically laughing until she finally gets out, "You guys are crazy."

I hoist Penelope up into my arms, carrying her out into the living room. "I'm taking that as a yes. Let's go!"

Gwen follows us out, grabbing the trick-or-treat bag and a couple bottles of water.

P and I have been under strict instructions to not enter the cafe this week, so I continue to follow the rules set by the woman currently singing "Mother Knows Best" as we walk down the staircase leading directly to the back alley.

I place Penelope back on the ground when we get outside, and the three of us walk around to the front of Main Street. P takes her candy bag from Gwen and asks if she can go meet her school friends who are huddled together in a variety of classic costumes up ahead. Before I can finish the word yes, she's off.

Gwen and I make eye contact, and I just really fucking hope she can see how big this is for us, for me. We have someone (who actually knows what they're doing) to help with hair and makeup. Someone to grab the bag on the way out when I have my hands full. Someone to watch my kid flourish with me.

I want her to see how much I want this and know that it's real.

CHAPTER 16: GWEN - THE FRIENDZONE IS THE ENDZONE

After walking Penelope through two different neighborhoods, collecting an entire pillowcase worth of candy, I get the text from Margot letting me know everything back at the cafe is ready to rock and roll for the perfect joint birthday party. After a quick pit-stop in the apartment upstairs, I walk P and Miller into a dark cafe, just for the lights to be thrown on and everyone close to us to yell *"Happy Birthday!"* in our faces.

Neither Miller or Penelope could win any performance awards. Their acting skills are shit. So I know the shock on both of their faces is genuine, and my heart swells with pride that I pulled this off.

I swear I see liquid lining Miller's eyes, the green in them popping more than usual, if possible. They're bright against the black shirt he changed into before coming here. I didn't think he would appreciate the grand entrance dressed as a chameleon so I suggested an outfit change before the "small cake I had stored in the cafe." I also desperately needed to get that wig off my head.

Miller scoops Penelope up, still in her full princess attire because while Miller was stripping costume pieces before we even got to the top of the staircase, she wouldn't entertain the thought of taking her dress off until absolutely necessary. She's shaking from excitement, and he whispers in her ear. It's their own little moment to take this in, and I get to witness it.

How lucky am I?

I don't remember the last time I felt this happy. I know this whole thing got a little complicated last night after our kiss and accidental sleepover, but that's not a today thought. Today is for loud happys, as Margot would say.

Once Miller lets Penelope down, she full blown sprints into Melanie's waiting arms. Margot, Sawyer, Gus, Beth, and Daisy all crowd around them with Gus and Daisy keeping at least two people in between them.

Miller finally, and I do mean *finally*—I've been waiting for this —looks to me.

"Gwendolyn," he breathes.

"Miller," I faux confidently address him, stepping just a little closer.

"You did this, didn't you?"

"Well, I mean, *clearly* I had help." I gesture to the room of people and party decorations in front of us.

"I've never—No one's ever—"

I stop him. "I know. And you know what I think? I think it's a fucking crime no one has ever shown up for you the way you deserve."

"This is too much."

"Frankly, if I knew what you told me last night earlier, it would have been a hell of a lot bigger of a night."

He shakes his head and puts his arm around my shoulders. His hand squeezes my bicep and I lean my head on his shoulder. "You're something else, Gwen."

"Funny, I'm pretty sure I've said the same thing about you."

Miller answers by quickly kissing the top of my head, and it warms my entire body.

I want this. I want more. But not-so-great thoughts are seeping in. The risk feels too big. I saw Miller's face this morning when he realized the position we were in. He didn't say anything, but I also feel like he didn't have to. He's scared to rock the boat, and I, unfortunately, completely understand. I wish I could be blissfully ignorant and take what I want without consequence, but that's not how things are. It's as simple as that.

Our invisible bubble of solitude in the midst of a crowded room bursts when Melanie addresses Miller, calling him over to her while Penelope rehashes our trick-or-treat adventures to Gus, who looks like he really does care about whatever story she's telling. But he's also eyeing the open bag of candy P dropped on the table so she could greet everyone with a look that tells me he might have a small ulterior motive behind his attentiveness.

Miller makes his way over to the group of people and the table they're surrounding, covered with gifts and with a cake in the middle. The way Melanie now has him in a death grip of a hug would have most bystanders believing he is her son, returning home from war after years apart.

She holds Margot and the rest of us the same way though. I think it's just how she loves.

"Mom, you're going to snap Miller's spine in half. Let him go. Jesus, woman. It's like, barely been a month since you've been in town," Margot groans.

"Watch your mouth, Margot Dorothea. Let me miss my people," Melanie says with absolutely no bite in her voice around Miller's shoulder, still not letting go.

I smile to myself. I love their relationship. I love their back-and-forth banter. I think most daughters with moms who have just never really gotten them would see it and feel the same.

Melanie grabs me next.

"There's my other girl," she says into my ear. "Beth's been keeping me in the loop, more so than my daughter who continues to tell me to mind my own business, but how have you been?"

"Good," I answer honestly. And how good does it fucking feel to know I'm telling her the truth?

"I was hoping that's what you'd say." The smirk on her face when she looks between me and Miller says everything it needs to.

I hate to be the one to disappoint her, but I should set the expectations now. "Yeah, Miller has unexpectedly turned into a really good friend." I look out of the corner of my eye to Miller a few steps away from me, and I swear I see his shoulders droop, even just slightly, while he chats with Beth.

Melanie eyes me funnily, and I try my hardest to look anywhere *but* at her, but she doesn't let that stop her from speaking her mind. "Don't do that, sweetie."

"Do what?" I can play dumb.

"Settle for less than what you want and deserve because you're scared."

"I'm not *scared*—" I try to argue. I am scared. She doesn't need to know that, though. No one does.

Melanie does this funny scrunch with her face that is so inherently Margot and rubs my arm in the most motherly way. I feel homesick for a feeling I don't remember ever experiencing, which is weird.

"Okay, okay. I won't press it, but just know, sometimes the risk really is worth the reward. Give it some thought."

I nod to assure her that I hear her loud and clear before retreating to the safety of the other side of the cafe counter to grab Penelope's gift from where I stashed it earlier.

Shopping for little girls, especially ones as cool as Penelope, is the easiest, most fun thing in the world. I had to reign myself in multiple times while going up and down aisles in stores, knowing I'd be receiving shit from Miller if I went overboard.

He'd rant about silly things like spoiling her, and it all being too much. Ridiculous. I don't have time for it.

We watch Penelope open gifts, and we all collectively sing happy birthday twice, once for Lil P and once for Miller. If you passed the cafe's front window and looked in, you'd see a picture-perfect night with a group of people, some once strangers turned friends, and now family.

Gus and Daisy manage to not rip each other to shreds. Penelope dances around all of us, laughing and singing with the new mini karaoke machine I got her. (You're welcome, Miller.)

We order Chinese take-out, and I don't remember The Little Red Dragon's crab rangoons ever tasting so good, but that just might be due to Miller saving the last one for me specifically because he remembered they're my favorite.

I send everyone home with leftovers. Margot, Sawyer, and Melanie—who's staying in Margot's cottage—stay to help clean up despite my protests. Penelope cuddles up in her favorite corner booth with the Swiftie blanket Daisy had custom made for her, and falls asleep before any of us even have a chance to wish her goodnight. Half of the flowers in her braid have fallen out but she's still covered in glitter and tulle from the dress I'm convinced we're going to have to bribe her to get off. To me, it's the sign of a perfect birthday.

My heart is full, so full that it feels heavy.

Miller locks the door behind our last guests. The clock on the wall says it's after 11:00 p.m., and the exhaustion feels like it's about to hit. I finish tying up the last trash bag to bring to the dumpster on my way out.

"Gwen, I don't have words for what you did today." His voice almost knocks me out. It's low and gravely and...strained? I turn my head to see he has a hand rubbing his chest, like there's a pain there he's trying to settle.

Melanie's words about how I have the option to not run away just because I'm scared play in my head. She's probably right, and most would agree with her. But taking that next step, actually acknowledging what is growing between Miller and me, feels so dangerous.

I've already lived through an implosion. I don't know if I'd survive another one. Adding the complexities of Penelope heightens my fears. It has nothing to do with love. I already know everything I feel for that girl is unconditional and strong. But the thought of not getting to be a fixture in her life, throwing away that stability for something that might very well be temporary…I just don't know.

I miss who I was when I was sure of myself and every decision I made. I miss the blind trust in myself, before I knew what it meant to lose it all. Like, when I was seventeen, and I thought I knew in my heart of hearts Dean Fitzgerald was the man I was going to marry.

Sometimes I wish I asked myself a few more follow up questions to that knowledge like "But is he the guy you *should* marry?" or "Will you *stay* married?"

It probably would have saved me a lot of time and helped me avoid the doubt that now clouds every thought I have now, doubt that feels like it doesn't deserve to be here, but unfortunately still is.

I didn't want to do this tonight. I wanted tonight to only be fun.

"This morning can't happen again." The words fall out of my mouth before I think better of it.

Miller nods. "I…Yeah, no, it can't. Wait, which part?" He takes a few steps closer.

"All of it." My voice doesn't sound like my own, and the hurt on Miller's face when he registers what I'm saying has me wishing I could take it all back.

But I don't. Instead, I keep digging this damn hole. "It's just, we're friends, right? Friends can kiss, but maybe it shouldn't be around Penelope because then she'd get the wrong idea. We don't want to confuse things. I mean her. I mean—" Miller just keeps fucking nodding, and I take a deep breath. "I'm almost thirty, a bitter divorcee living next door to my ex-husband. You're twenty-three with the world's most perfect daughter. It's—"

"It doesn't work. Got it." Miller's words are short and clipped, he stuffs his hands into the front pockets of his jeans. I suddenly miss the sweatpants he normally wears, the ones that he's constantly pulling up because the guy has absolutely no hips or ass.

He looks anywhere but at me.

This doesn't feel right. He's agreeing with me. On paper, he's making this a very easy break so we can continue doing what we were doing before we let fleeting feelings get in the way.

It doesn't feel simple like that though.

"But we're still friends," I say while ringing my hands together.

"You said that."

Miller stands two feet away from me in harsh, overhead lighting in the middle of the night. Our voices remain low to not wake the sleeping child still in the room with us. It's a mix of our normal with a new that just isn't sitting right with me.

I was supposed to feel better and lighter nipping this in the bud. It was supposed to be easy because what are we even talking about? It was one kiss.

"Great. Good talk. Well, the party's over so I guess—" I reach to pick the trash bag up and leave, but Miller steps towards me again and I freeze.

"Just so we're abundantly clear, you want to be friends.

Friends who sometimes kiss, just never in front of my kid." His hand reaches up to cup my neck, the same way he did last night, and I instinctively lean into his touch.

"Yes?" No. That sounds wrong. That's not even close to what I want. This isn't about what I want. It's about what's safe.

His thumb rubs the spot behind my ear. The twinkle I swore I saw in his eyes earlier is nowhere to be found, and the slight tip in his lips is the furthest thing from a real Miller Caswell smile. But still he says, "I can do that."

When he leans in, my dumbass lets my eyelids fall closed, expecting the same kind of kiss that felt like it flipped my world upside down only last night. Instead, I'm slapped in the face with the reality I created when his other hand picks up the trash bag at our feet. The rustling of the plastic causes me to open my eyes again.

"I'll carry this out for you." The hand holding me releases, leaving a cool, empty spot in its wake. Miller hoists the bag up and grabs a second one on his way out the back. I stay standing in the middle of the cafe wondering what the hell I just did.

I fucked up. That's what I did.

"Thanks," I say to no one. I make sure to give P a quick kiss on the head to say goodnight before retrieving my bag from under the counter.

Miller's walking back from the dumpster by the time I get outside. He must have grabbed my keys off the rack because my car is already running, a gesture I appreciate when the cold air nips my face.

"Thanks," I repeat when I take my clanky lanyard back.

"What are friends for?" he responds. It's sarcastic and I hate it.

"Miller..."

"Sorry. I just kind of thought...You know what? It really doesn't matter what I thought. This is cool. Thank you, and I mean that. This really was...this was really the best birthday either of us could have asked for." He holds the driver's door open for me. The last thing I want to do is get in, but I do.

"You both only deserve the best."

He smiles and shuts my door. I immediately roll down the window, delaying the inevitable goodbye. I can see him internally arguing with himself but he leans on his forearms with his head poking into the car. "I'm sorry. For shutting down like that. I'm not mad at you. Penelope and I are lucky to have you as a friend and a part of our lives. You're allowed to set boundaries. You're just…"

He doesn't finish his sentence even though I'm desperately hanging onto every word. Someone with something more than false confidence would probably let things naturally trail off here. But, unfortunately, that's not me. "I'm what, Miller?"

He stands up straight, letting his hands retreat back to the safety of his pockets, backing up a step to let me reverse out of my spot. "You're everything, Gwen. You're worth it all and then some, but I'll take whatever you give me. Text me so I know you're home safe."

Miller doesn't wait for me to answer. He turns and walks back inside. He doesn't leave the doorway though. I see the silhouette of his hair until I turn the corner at the end of the alley.

I spend the rest of my drive home in silence, aside from the sounds of the wind whipping through my window because I didn't even bother to roll it up. I bang my hand on the steering wheel, chastising myself for twisting my thoughts into words I didn't mean.

I pull into my driveway and look at my pitch black empty house. Lovely. I didn't even leave a light on for myself. I roll my window up, kill the engine, and fight against the pit in my stomach to pull out my phone to shoot a text off to Miller before trudging inside.

ME

home.

I see the dots that show he's typing as soon as my text shows as delivered.

MILLER

There's a bag of candy and a note in your purse. I put it there before you clarified things. If you could just throw that away, that'd be great. I'm sorry.

MILLER

I meant the note. Not the candy. That's yours, obviously.

MILLER

The note is yours too but I understand your position and I didn't know I would be adding to things you probably don't need right now.

The pit in my stomach now feels like it's about to swallow me whole.

I shuffle around the chaotic contents that make up the inside of my purse to find the small Ziploc bag filled with peanut butter cups and little boxes of Nerds, the perfect mix of sweet and sour, left by Miller just for me.

Tears prickle behind my eyes before I even manage to pull the sticky note off the bag. I don't deserve this one, I know I don't. But I turn it over to read anyway, because what's one more mistake to end the evening. The words are so small to all fit on the tiny square so I have to squint to decipher them.

You read about first kisses like that. You see movies every day end just the same. You sit and wonder if the real thing could ever compare.

I then notice there's another note attached to the back of this one. I pull them apart with shaky hands.

I get to now say kissing Gwendolyn Bozelli for the first time blows every single one of them out of the water. Stories could be written about how it felt.

A tear falls and lands directly in the middle of the small note. The water causes the ink to instantly smudge, and I think about how this absolutely couldn't get worse.

Until a demon spawned from hell itself in the form of my ex-husband and current neighbor taps on my window causing me to throw the notes, candy, and my purse flying.

CHAPTER 17: GWEN - IS THIS AN AMBUSH?

"What the fuck is wrong with you, Dean?" I snap as I push the door open, hoping it knocks his ass on the ground. It doesn't, and I'm disappointed when he easily takes a step back.

"Awfully late for you to just be getting home, don't you think?" He's still in uniform, but I can smell the alcohol on his breath. He must have gone out drinking after his shift. Shocker.

He looks like shit, and I mean that whole heartedly. His hair started thinning a while ago and I suggested he roll with it and keep it short. But it seems like he's decided to let the straggly pieces that are still hanging on for dear life flap away on the top. He probably tries to blame the sunken in dark circles under his eyes on the baby he fathered, but we all know it's from his drinking that borders on problematic. And his skin is so dry it could make the desert look like an oasis. I try to make sure I don't visibly wrinkle my face in disgust.

"It's none of your business where I am or when I'm there." God, I *don't* need this right now. I try to brush past him, but he steps in front of me, blocking my path to the front door of my house.

"It's always going to be my business." His words slur, and I hold back from gagging. I need to keep things in check. He's drunk, and we're alone out here in the middle of the night. I'm not scared of him anymore, but I'm also not stupid. I know when to pick and choose my battles to stay safe.

Dean has never hit me. I'm not handing out awards for it or anything. There have been a few occasions where I've thought the blow was coming, but it always stops just in time. He's always walked the line so perfectly.

But I recognize things have changed, and he might not walk the line as well anymore, so I have to be careful.

I take a deep breath and will myself into a false sense of calm until I can get myself inside. "Dean, please go home. It's only a short walk in that direction." I point towards his house, where his cruiser sits in the driveway, the driver's door is still open.

"You weren't handing out candy. You always hand out candy on the porch. You used to get mad at me when I made plans. You never came with me."

"Yeah, sorry I didn't want to go get trashed with your loser fucking friends," I say without thinking. *Okay, not in the script, Gwen. Hold it together.*

"So, where were you?"

"I'm not doing this." I don't want to aggravate him further, but I'm also not about to roll over and give him what he wants.

"You were with that punk, weren't you? The one with the kid?"

"He's not a—You know what? I hate that you think you can do this. Please leave."

"That's a yes." Dean laughs, and the hairs on my arm stand up. "Pathetic," he spits.

"Let. It. Go." I shoulder check him as hard as I can in an attempt to clear the way. I realize my mistake immediately. His hand grips around my bicep right before I'm in the clear.

I feel his hot breath on my neck, and I deserve an award for not throwing up the contents of my stomach right here on the spot. "You think that gives you the family you *begged* me for, Red? You think this fixes your sad, little heart? You're wasting your time."

His words sting, but they're not as damaging as they used to be. I scoop up that small win and hold it tight to get me through these next two minutes.

I need to placate him. I need to diffuse the situation. If I don't compartmentalize now, things could go from bad to worse and avoiding that is my goal. I need to remember the Goddamn goal. So, I don't let his words touch me. They're meaningless, just like he is. Besides, it's nothing I haven't thought of myself, as shown by my actions earlier.

"Okay, Dean. You're right. I'm just gonna head in and think about how wrong I was." I use the softest voice I can manage to make myself smaller. By some miracle, it works, and his hand releases from me just enough to let me pull away and hop and skip to my steps.

He's still standing in the same place I left him when I get my door unlocked. "I'm not going anywhere, Red. You're mine! You always fucking have been!" he calls.

I can't slam the door fast enough.

* * *

It's been two days.

Two days since I've slept. Slept at night, at least. There are usually a couple hours during the day I manage to nap on the couch after I've checked out my windows five or six times, assuring myself no one is home next door or in my driveway.

I lied when I said I wasn't scared. Sticking to the truth now, my interaction with Dean has rocked me. I don't want to close my eyes at night in fear he's out there. I made sure I was home before the sun went down the one time I did manage to leave the house since Halloween.

I feel like a prisoner in my own home, and I fucking hate it.

When I snuck out to check in on the cafe yesterday, I hoped to run into Miller, but it seems like he might be avoiding me.

Actually, he's definitely avoiding me, confirmed by the fact that I only got to see Penelope because Margot brought her down to hang with us while we de-spookified the cafe in preparation for my Winter Wonderland takeover I'm hoping to tackle in the next couple of days. I'm not slacking like I did with Halloween, no matter how I'm feeling on the inside.

Maybe the merriness will fix me.

My stomach grumbles to remind me I do still need to eat in order to survive. I could order pizza. But then I run the risk of George or John on delivery tonight, and I'm not too keen on having to explain the state of me or my house.

Where normally I would throw myself into every chore I could think of and then some to distract myself, the fact of the matter is, I'm exhausted, mentally and physically. My poor house is suffering the consequences because of it.

Everything looks and feels like it needs a deep clean. Dusting, laundry, mopping, vacuuming, organizing, the *works*. But every time I think I'm ready to dive into something, I sink further into the couch. Or my bed. Or honestly, sometimes the floor if I'm really not feeling it.

"It" being…life.

I'm tired of my life being run by Dean Fitzgerald, both directly and indirectly. I'm sick of making decisions based on things he's said or done. I'm over being this meek mouse, jumping at every little thing, especially the things that might actually be good for me. I'm cowering in my house like a little bitch, and it's gotta stop.

I shoot up from my spot on the couch with an idea and grab my phone. I dial one of the few numbers I know by heart.

The call picks up on the third ring. "George's Pizza, this is George!"

"G—it's me. Can I place a pick up order?"

"Red? You want to add something else?"

I'm…confused.

"Wait, hold on. Miller just walked in." He must pull the phone away from his face because he sounds farther away and sort of muffled, but I can still hear him. "Hey kid, I've got the three pizzas here ready to go. But Red's on the line, let me see if she needs me to add anything."

George addresses me again, "Red—"

I can hear Miller in the background and George pauses. "George, no! She doesn't know!"

The call ends without another word.

What the fuck.

I pull up my text thread with Miller. The one that's been untouched for two days. My thumbs dart across the screen, and I hit send before I can think twice about it.

ME

what the hell was that?

The dots that are normally instantaneous don't appear. Five minutes go by, then ten.

Miller doesn't respond.

I pace the length of the living room to the kitchen. I contemplate calling him but chicken out once I get his contact pulled up. I must have misheard him. The call must've dropped, and I'm a jerk for leaving George hanging like that.

Rummaging through the contents of my mostly barren cabinets, the only thing I find that could resemble a reasonable meal is a can of Spaghettios I've had sitting in here for a while. It's probably leftover from one of the times I babysat Daisy's little brothers.

I'm digging through a drawer, looking for my can opener

when I hear a car pull into my driveway, followed immediately by another one.

Abandoning the dismal plan of eating cold O's out of the can, I rush to my front window to peek behind the curtains. Miller's car is parked next to Sawyer's Jeep. Margot and Penelope are walking hand in hand up to my porch with Miller and Sawyer trailing behind. Sawyer has a case of beer in his hands from a local brewery he's obsessed with, and Miller's carrying three boxes of George's giant pizzas.

I do a quick scan of the state of my house. Post-house party trash is the vibe it's giving, and I have no time to rectify that. Thankfully, the four humans who are about to bust down my door won't judge me. I can spiral about a lot of things, but apparently not their unwavering loyalty.

Even Miller's, to whom I owe a whole conversation and apology.

"You're hermiting again, and none of us are allowing it!" Margot yells from outside.

Small fists rap against the wood. "Miss Gwen! Open up! It's chilly!"

That gets me to whip the door open. "Did you just call me Gwen?" I look down to Penelope, who still has her hand raised, ready to continue knocking. She's in her pajamas and holding her favorite stuffed cat.

"*Miss* Gwen," she corrects. "The G and the W together confused me, but Daddy helped me sound it out. You signed my card, remember?!" P then lowers her voice, "Daddy says I still have to put the miss in front of your name. He says that's what's *polite*." She holds up air quotes, and I do really think she thinks we're the only two who can hear her. God, she cracks me up.

Miller shakes his head at his daughter, and the rest of us try to not lose our shit on the spot.

"Hi," he says sheepishly.

"Hi," I answer.

"Oh for Christ's sake. Get out of the way, Caswell." Sawyer brushes past, walking straight into the kitchen. Penelope follows after him without prompting, curiously whipping her head in every direction to check out this new place.

"Sure, make yourself at home, Sawyer. No worries."

"I have for the last twenty or so years, Red," Sawyer calls without looking back.

"He's just a bit grumpy because we were…*preoccupied* when Miller called. But we're happy to be here!" Margot raises up onto her toes and kisses me on the cheek before passing through the doorway, taking the pizzas from Miller's arms with her.

Miller tries to shake the disgusted look off his face with no success. "Literally no one here needed to know that, Marge."

"That's what you get for calling me Marge, *Mills!*" Margot shouts.

"Is anyone going to tell me what's going on?" I finally ask.

The three already inside ignore me. Miller is the only one to respond. "Family pizza night. For the record, I did come up with the idea about an hour ago so nothing is set in stone. But it seems pretty solid, so we're running with it."

"And you guys couldn't have done this…at either of your places?" I think I'm missing something here.

"Well, Margot said you've sort of locked yourself away again. So, we had to bring the party to you."

"But, I'm not family."

Miller smiles like he knows something I don't, and it almost knocks me down. He is so painfully handsome, I think it's a crime that he wastes his time at the bank when he should be walking in NYFW or something. He's wearing a worn black leather jacket with a thin red stripe going down each sleeve. It's open with a plain black T-shirt underneath, one of his hundred, I'm sure. He has on the same jeans from the other night, cuffed to meet the top of his black laced-up boots. That crush I had in high school on Sodapop from *The Outsiders* is making a lot more sense right about now.

He doesn't acknowledge the fact I just dropped on him, running his hand through his dark curls. "You gonna invite me in?"

"I didn't realize you were waiting."

"I've got nothing but time when it comes to you, Gwendolyn."

I—I think there's a hidden meaning in that. The shiver that wiggles down my spine would agree. But I step aside to usher him through without questioning it.

He takes in his surroundings as he walks down the short hallway that leads into the kitchen, stopping to check out the pictures of me throughout my years of school framed on the wall.

As my parents' one and only child, the majority of photos in the house are of just me. I do realize with living here alone that does make me look completely self-centered, but the reality is I just never got around to decorating the place the way I wanted to. When Dean and I moved in, I was busy perfecting the cafe. And when he left, I just didn't care.

Miller pauses on the one picture my parents ever hung from my wedding. Which, looking back now, probably should have been a sign of how bad shit was going to go down. It's a shot that was taken from behind. It's a candid where I'm facing a full length mirror, smoothing out my dress.

Dean's mom hired the hair stylist and she opted for a tight, high bun. Not what I would have picked, but I didn't have the energy to argue. It gave me a headache an hour into the day. You can see the apprehension tattooed on my face. I told myself they were normal wedding day jitters, but I remember thinking I always expected it to feel different.

I look objectively beautiful. I'm sure that's why my parents picked this picture to showcase. But it's not me. I don't think it ever was.

"I hope you don't take this the wrong way. You're beautiful. You always are, but this isn't it."

"Isn't what?" I ask with a laugh.

"It's just not *you*, ya know?" He turns his head to me and looks at me like it's the most obvious thing in the world. "I mean, your *hair*. That's like, your identifier. You told me that once, it's been that way since you were born. It's big and beautiful and you have it slicked back and trapped away for what? You can't tell me you picked this."

I walk over to stand next to him, inspecting the photo alongside him. "I didn't, but it also didn't seem like the thing to make a fuss about. I mean, like you said, I look fine."

"You look more than fine, Gwen. But it was your wedding day. You're in the white dress and everything," Miller argues. He's very invested in this, and I'm not sure why. It was never a big deal to me. Being married and starting a family was, but the giant, frilly wedding was something I was more than okay with living without.

"Does it even matter now?" I don't ask it in a self-deprecating way. It's just truly not worth the time. As a matter of fact…

I yank the frame off the wall, open my hallway closet up, and chuck it inside. It topples down the mountain of other useless junk I've let accumulate in there and lands with a soft thud before I shut the door.

You know what? That felt damn good.

"Uh…" Miller says. I wait for him to finish his thought, but he doesn't.

I clap my hands together. "And this concludes our tour. Please make your way into the kitchen."

I hear Margot pulling plates out of cupboards, and Penelope telling Sawyer a very over-the-top story from her day at school. I still don't really know why everyone is here, but it's nice to feel like there's life and joy in this house again.

Miller doesn't move from where he's standing. "You doing okay?" he asks in a voice low enough for no one else to hear.

I quickly nod and immediately feel guilty for lying. I really haven't been okay, but Miller is the last person who should have to try to pick up my broken pieces. I pushed him away. I deserve to handle this on my own.

"You wanna try that again, Gwen?"

"Is this impromptu family pizza night secretly an ambush, *Miller?*"

"What? No. Yes. I mean—No. Sort of?" He raises his shoulders with a sheepish look. "Look, as your...friend. I wanted to check on you. Your other friends in there wanted to do the same." He tilts his head to the kitchen where absolutely no one is paying us any mind.

His hesitation on the word friend makes me want to punch myself in the face. Why am I the way that I am?

"Well, thank you. I appreciate the thought and the effort to wrangle the crew together. Besides, when I called George, it was to place an order for pick up to bring over to you so..."

"Same brain." Miller shoots me one of those smiles that light up his whole face, but then he gets serious. "But really, is this about the other night? Because I feel like shit."

"Wait, what? Why?" Yes, my current hermitting as Margot calls it is because of the other night, but it has nothing to do with Miller.

"I acted like such a dick. You're allowed to say anything you want to me, in fact I prefer it. I'm not good at communication but I won't shut down like that again. I'm really working on it. I wanted to give you some time yesterday and had planned on coming over here earlier, but the day got away from me at work, and then Penelope got home from school..."

I get distracted by the way he tugs on his hair. I think about how I wasted the opportunity to tangle my own fingers through it the other night and how I still don't know how it feels to pull it while we're… *Focus, Gwen.*

"What I'm trying to say is, I'm sorry. Please don't hide out because of me."

Okay, I need to nip this in the bud now.

"I'm not hiding out because of you. After our…*conversation* the other night, when I got home…" Oh, God. I do not want to do this. Miller has been begging for an excuse to knock Dean out, and while I have no desire to protect Dean, I'm concerned about Miller's future. He can't risk getting into trouble over me.

"What happened?"

"When I got home, Dean was here. In the driveway. He was trying to piss me off or scare me, or I don't know. I guess it worked. I fucking hate that he's right there." I look in the general direction of the house next door. Miller doesn't follow my movement. Instead his eyes stay laser focused on me.

"Did he touch you?" His voice is cold, absolutely nothing like the Miller I've gotten to know. But I'm not scared. My body recognizes I'm safe.

My hand instinctively wraps around my bicep where Dean grabbed me and I realize my mistake when Miller tracks the movement. "He was drunk."

"Did. He. Touch. You."

"I told him to leave. He wouldn't. I tried to pass him. He tried to stop me. It worked for half a second. I'm fine."

"You're fine? This piece of shit thinks you're his property, Gwen."

"Oh, I am well aware…" I mumble, remembering Dean's words about how what I do and who I see will always be his business.

"This stops now."

I don't have time to think or react before Miller is moving past me in the opposite direction of the kitchen, back out through my front door.

Shit.

CHAPTER 18: MILLER - FAMILY PIZZA NIGHT

I slam my fist into the door repeatedly, picturing doing the very same to Dean's piece of shit face. Didn't check to see if anyone was home, don't give a fuck. I'll find him if he's not here.

I hear movement behind me and whip around to defend myself, fist still raised, and immediately drop it when I see it's Sawyer.

"Sawyer, hey." I catch my breath. "I'm good here."

"You're about to land yourself a night in county jail if you don't fucking cool it. Come on, let's go back to Red's."

I don't move from my spot on the top step. "He's harassing her. I'm done sitting back and letting it happen."

"He's been harassing her and everyone else around here for years, Miller. Believe me, you're not the first person to want to knock him out. But this isn't going to fix it. It'll make things a hell of a lot worse. For you and her."

I hear what he's saying, I really do. But I've seen first hand what a man like that can do to a woman. I lost my mom because of it. I barely had a mom to begin with because of it. I care too much about Gwen to let her get caught up in all of that, no matter how she feels about me.

"Yeah, well, something has to change."

"Let's figure it out then. Come on. Come back and have some pizza." Sawyer steps up and throws an arm around my shoulders, trying to guide me away from Dean's house. I don't fight him on it. The fog of blinding anger is starting to clear, and I realize he might have a point.

"Fuck, I'm sorry." Sawyer's only a handful of years older and a couple inches taller than me, but I feel like a little kid around him.

"Don't be. You're not thinking anything I haven't, although I'm guessing from what Margot has told me, your reasoning might be a little different than mine. Which leads me to ask, how are things going with Red? It seemed like something maybe shifted the other night with you two."

"And then they shifted right back. Nothing's going on. We're friends."

"But you want more?" Instead of reentering Gwen's front door, Sawyer pivots, and I follow him along the side of the house towards the backyard.

I've never had anyone to talk shit out with like this. I don't know how much I'm supposed to say or what I'm even asking for. I don't do relationships. I stuff my hands in my front pockets and watch the leaves crunch underneath my boots.

"I'll take that as a yes…" Sawyer answers himself.

We stop at the firepit Gwen has built into her back patio. It's cute as hell out here. There are wooden chairs that lean back circled around the stone pit. String lights criss-cross over the top of the area, and tiki torches line the perimeter. A grill that looks like it's never been used a day in its life has its own little spot a safe enough distance away from the house. There are covers over a row of four bushes against the back siding, already winterized for the first frost.

I look around, taking everything in. This is a backyard you *live* in. It's so easy to picture barbecues and roasting marshmallows by the fire. There's a place to pitch a tent in this backyard and make those core memories you see families making in all of those movies. It's the white picket fence dream back here.

Gwen puts so much thought into every aspect of life and never comes up short. It fucking blows me away. Who wouldn't want more with a woman like this?

"I'd take anything she's willing to give me," I blurt out.

"Have you told her that?" Sawyer asks.

"You're asking if I told Gwen that I'm basically following her around like a pathetic dog?"

"I wouldn't say it like that...But, yeah. I guess, sort of? Look, Gus set me straight when I was lost on how to handle things with Margot. Let me try to pass along some help to you."

I shrug noncommittally when internally, I'm so Goddamn grateful someone might actually have some solid advice on what I should be doing here because I'm in way over my head.

"Red's never going to assume she's anyone's first choice. Especially you, given the fact that you have Penelope and all. She always wants to do the right thing, the *safe* thing, to make everyone around her happy. Dean did a fucking number on her, man. And—" Sawyer looks to the house, confirming the girls aren't watching or listening from the window before continuing. "She'll never admit how much her parents' leaving affected her, but it did. She goes through the worst divorce this town has seen in I don't even know how long, and they take off to sail around a loop in the Bahamas not even six months later. It was kind of fucked up."

"She never really mentions them," I say, shocked.

"I'm guessing it still hurts. Jean and Larry love Red, and they're decent people. They've done a lot for Merrymount. But in my opinion, they're not the best parents."

"I can't imagine abandoning P like that, even when she's an adult."

"I get it. I feel the same way, but it's a part of the reason why Red's pretty closed off when it comes to new relationships. You and Margot and Penelope really shook things up for a lot of us."

"So, what do I do?" I feel like an idiot.

"You keep showing up. You *tell* her this is more than some friendship of convenience. Nothing has to be rushed. You can still take things slow for Penelope's sake."

"I can do that."

"I know you can. It's why we're all here tonight. Things are going to be okay, Miller. We'll figure out what to do about Dean if it gets worse. Come on, let's head back inside before Margot houses all of the pizza, and we're left with the crust she refuses to eat." Sawyer walks up to the French doors at the back of the house, and I follow.

Before Sawyer opens the door, he turns to me again. "This stays between us, yeah?"

"Yeah, of course," I assure him. I have no desire to break Sawyer's trust. I'm beyond thankful for the insight and appreciate the fact that he was the one to talk me off the ledge before I did something really stupid.

Sawyer wasn't kidding about Margot's ability to throw back pizza. When we enter the kitchen, her plate already has the remnants of four slices and she's grabbing a fifth out of the box. Gwen's plate doesn't look much different. Penelope is still munching on her one piece of cheese pizza. She's perpetually the slowest eater on the planet.

No one mentions my disappearing act when Sawyer and I join the table. The only acknowledgement comes from Gwen in the form of her mouthing *"you good?"* She takes my quick nod as a sufficient answer.

Penelope entertains us by recapping her school day, bringing out belly laughs from the whole table when she tells us a particularly hilarious story from lunch. Between the five of us, all three boxes of pizza are demolished in no time. Margot and Sawyer stay a little bit after we clean up from eating, but say their goodbyes before Penelope...and I...are ready to leave.

When the last bits of sunlight fade away, I give Penelope the five minute warning that we need to head home because it's a school night. I don't want to leave and neither does she, but responsibilities. A big part of me wishes Gwen would just come back to the apartment with us. Selfishly, because I want more time with her, but also because I don't fucking trust Dean being that close next door to her. I should order her mace or something.

Sawyer said I need to tell her what I want. He also said I could take things slow. Those two things feel like they're on opposite ends of the world right now. I want to bring her home and have her sleep in my bed. I want to set a good example for Penelope and not jump into things with someone.

This is the whole reason I never touched the idea of dating. It felt impossible to try to figure out how to balance everything, to be someone a partner would need and still be the best dad. It was easier to just shut that part of my brain down, putting all of my focus toward Penelope. I couldn't imagine someone coming along who would have me wanting to deviate from that life.

Until Gwen.

Now I sit on Gwen's couch and battle with my brain while watching her and Penelope lay on the floor side by side, drawing mustaches on people's faces in the magazine Gwen had laying out on her coffee table. Each new one P holds up to show me gets more and more ridiculous.

My focus shifts to the TV. Gwen apparently has every streaming service known to man and threw on the Disney one when we moved from the kitchen to the living room. She also pulled out a whole bin of toys from the closet she chucked her wedding picture in earlier. She said she's kept them around for whenever she babysits kids around town. Repeating what I already know, this woman thinks of everything.

Small picture frames line the bottom shelf on her TV stand. I lean in a little and squint to see if I can make out the photos with no success. I walk over and squat down to inspect them up close.

They're vacation pictures—Gwen in every stage of her life—in Walt Disney World. Now, I've never been myself, but I've watched enough 90s sitcom specials where the cast went on vacation there, and had Penelope beg me to take her through every commercial we've ever seen of the place to recognize it right off the bat.

Gwen posing in front of the castle. Gwen smiling with different characters. Gwen eating one of those pretzels shaped like a mouse the size of her head. Her smile is infectious. It's obvious in every single picture that this is her happy place.

I wish so badly I could make that happen for Penelope. It makes me want to relook at finances and budget my way into making it happen sooner rather than later.

One of the last pictures in the row seems to be more recent, Gwen looking close to how she does now, and I pick the frame up to inspect it more closely. I recognize those lanterns…

"There's a Tangled section in Disney World?" I ask out loud. I feel like I'd remember this if I saw it before.

I hold up the frame, and turn to Gwen who looks up from the latest swirly creation she's created on the model she and Penelope have picked as their next victim. "What? Oh. Yeah! I mean, it's not anything—"

"*What?!*" Penelope screeches, and I fear I just made a grave mistake bringing this up in front of her. She jumps up from the floor and crashes into me, yanking the frame from my hand. P then notices the rest of the pictures, and she picks up each one with awe in her eyes.

"It's so magical," Penelope says with so much wonder and whimsy.

Gwen scoots over to join us. She explains where she was and when each picture was taken with extreme detail, walking Penelope through "The Most Magical Place On Earth." Penelope hangs on to every word, and before I know it, the five minutes I gave her is long since past. She's snuggled up in one of her favorite spots, Gwen's lap, watching Gwen flip through other photo albums that were stored behind the original pictures.

I think Gwen's having just as much fun as P, reliving her fondest memories.

We get to learn that Gwen's parents have some sort of time-share with Disney that allowed them to go every year. It's a grand family tradition for two people who didn't seem too keen on keeping that sort of magic alive once their daughter reached adulthood, but I guess that's not my business.

There isn't a question of Penelope's that Gwen can't answer, and soon enough, P is fighting yawns and sleepy eyes.

"Hate to be the one to break up the history lesson but..." I chime in.

"When can we go to Disney, Daddy?" Penelope asks, completely ignoring my segway into making the journey back to our apartment.

I try to stifle my sigh to no avail. I have a savings account at the bank that directly deposits a small amount of my paycheck weekly to save for this specific trip, but it never feels like enough.

"As soon as we can, baby girl. I promise. But right now, we have to get home to bed." I ruffle her head and as tired as those eyes were about five seconds ago, they still muster up the ability to send a pointed look my way.

"Just think about how special it'll be when you *do* go!" Gwen adds, clearly trying to turn this around for me. Always the fixer. "I was just a baby when I went for the first time, so all I have are these pictures. You'll have loads of pictures, but even more magical, you'll have the memories. You'll get to cherish them forever." There's a longing, faraway look on her face that hits my fucking chest.

The fairy godmother-esque speech seems to work because anything Gwen says works on Penelope, and P nods with a soft smile. "That sounds nice."

I swear I see a lightbulb go off above Gwen's head, an idea that she must be choosing to keep a secret because the *aha* face disappears before I can even tilt my head in question.

Gwen helps Penelope stand from their pretzel position on the floor, photo albums and scrapbooks scattered around them. Once I hoist Penelope up and get her situated against my side, I extend my hand for Gwen so I can pull her up.

She stands and before I think of anything to stop myself, I pull her into me—into *us*—and P's little arm snakes across Gwen's back. If I'm going to take Sawyer's advice (which I am. I'm uneducated, not dumb), I need to show Gwen we choose her. And we're gonna keep choosing her. I'm committed to the long haul of this process, but I know it'll be worth it.

I won't have her doubt like she did the other day ever again.

She's the first to break apart our embrace. "Shit! I don't have any leftovers to send you home with."

"We're going home to go to sleep. Gwen. It's all good. We demolished those pizzas," I assure her.

"I know. But you came here and this was so nice and I—I'm supposed to send you home with something!" Gwen runs to the kitchen and rummages around for probably just about anything to hand off.

I almost do it. I almost tell her she can send me home with a kiss. She set it up perfectly. But I ultimately chicken out because as much as I want to be the smooth guy, I'm a fumbling idiot.

I snatch up Penelope's stuffed cat and head to the front door to also collect P's shoes, because there's no way she's agreeing to walk to the car right now. "Gwen! Come lock this door behind us."

I'll wait on the other side until I hear it click. Hell, if I knew she'd say yes, I'd have her grab an overnight bag and sleep at the apartment. I'd take the couch, obviously, but I don't like the idea of her sleeping here alone next door to that fucking asshat.

Gwen meets us in the entryway. She's holding two clementines, a Slimjim, and a snack sized bag of pretzels. She dumps it all into one of the to-go bags she has at the cafe and holds it out for me to take, but then realizes I've run out of hands to carry anything else.

She flings open the closet and steps into slippers with cowboy hats on them. "I'll walk you out."

Penelope's asleep before I can click the last lock on her carseat, her head lolling to the side, mouth slightly ajar. Nothing motivates this kid to sleep more than the thought of me making her march up the staircase to the apartment. Now she knows she's guaranteed a free ride up in my arms.

Gwen is standing by the front of my car, fidgeting with her hands, when I close the back door. "Thanks again, for coming over tonight. I really think I needed it, but I have a hard time voicing the things I need sometimes. Which is crazy because we all know I have *no* problem voicing a lot of other things..."

She's still rambling away. Using those soft, pretty hands of her to get the words out. The only reason I'd ever consider taking things slow is passed out safely in the car behind me.

I cradle Gwen's face in my hands, just like I did the other night, and she falls silent. I hold her gaze for two seconds, just enough time for one blink, giving her this moment to object if she really wants to, to see if she really meant it when she said this couldn't happen again. But thank mother fucking God she doesn't because I capture her lips with my own, and she doesn't hesitate to meet me.

Kissing Gwen is like waking up on the first day of summer.

It's warm and inviting and feels like a new beginning. The sparks I felt from brushes of touch before can't hold a candle to the fireworks that feel like they're popping off in my head.

The outside world ceases to exist when her fingers entangle in the curls that brush the back of my neck.

I press my forehead into hers during the come down, knowing we're standing in the middle of her driveway and at some point we have to separate, as much as that's the opposite of what I want. I need to say this now before I lose the courage.

"I feel like we keep getting our wires crossed. We spend so much time together and talk about everything except the thing that might make us better because we're scared. Well, at least I know I am. I want you, Gwen. Real bad."

She shakes her head against mine, eyes still closed. "Miller," she starts.

"If you're objecting because you really think we're meant to just be friends, I'll hear you out. But if it's not that, I'm asking you to trust me."

"I trust you," she whispers. Three words that make me feel like I could fucking fly.

"Good. That's good. So, here's the plan—"

Those pretty eyes fly open. "You have a plan?"

I kiss her freckled forehead and pull away slightly. "Okay, so I don't have a *plan* plan. But, I'm gonna get this kid home to bed, and then I'm gonna call you. We still have to finish *Accepted,* so we can sync up and watch it together until you fall asleep…if you want."

Was that really stupid? Do people even do weird shit like that in real life, or am I projecting some false idea of dating from TV shows? Damn, I need more real life experience.

If I made myself a fool with that suggestion, Gwen doesn't let it show because she's beaming. She nods her head repeatedly with excitement. "I want. I mean, oh my God, I sound like a cavewoman. Yes, I want that very much."

"It's a date, Gwendolyn." I kiss her one more time, enjoying the feel of her smiling through it a whole lot.

"Drive safe!" she calls when I get into the car.

I roll the window down to respond. "Always do. Precious cargo back there." I hook my thumb to the backseat like a doofus.

I'm gonna woo the fuck out of that woman. As soon as I figure out what wooing someone actually means.

CHAPTER 19: GWEN - I WANT TO FUCK YOUR BROTHER

"**S**o, do you think I could talk to you guys about something?" I ask Margot and Daisy.

It's the question I've held off asking all night. I meant to bring it up sooner, but I keep chickening out. It's just the three of us here in the cafe after hours because Margot and Daisy graciously agreed to help me start end of year holiday prep.

I need to get menus finalized, decorations planned out, scheduling done, and every other little thing in between sorted. The Blueberry Festival committee is already about to start up again, and as much as I want to blow them off, I feel very stuck and obligated. So, I guess I need to add that to my never ending list, too.

My parents—absolute shocker to no one—have made the "extremely hard" decision to not return to Merrymount at all this year. So, I guess all of this falls on me. Which is why I'm so thankful to have Margot's and Daisy's support. I've managed to fill the night with snacks and drinks and plans to distract from the other big thing I need support on.

Daisy gives Margot a look that makes me feel wicked out of

the loop. Margot then looks at me. "Are you fucking my brother?"

The spiked hot chocolate I just took a sip of sputters out of my mouth. "No!" I exclaim.

"Damn it," Margot mutters, pulling her phone out. After a couple taps, Daisy's phone pings. I recognize that notification tone.

"Did you just send her money?!" I'm yelling.

"I was sure you were fucking. But Daze said you still look like you haven't been laid in a while. She was right." Margot slumps in her chair.

"You can't bet on my sex life!" Why am I still yelling?

"Oh my God, nevermind the bet," Daisy starts while rolling her eyes. "What's up? Is Dean bothering you again?"

"Thankfully, no." I'm glad I can answer that honestly and also really hate that it's the first thing people need to ask. I don't want to be attached to that jerk in any way, shape, or form.

"So it *is* about Miller," Margot states.

"Yes, you nosey bitch."

Margot doesn't take me calling her a bitch negatively. She just smiles smugly behind her own mug of spiked hot chocolate. This is one of the reasons why we clicked so easily when she moved to town. She gets me.

"Spill before I lose my mind," Daisy says dramatically, sipping her lemonade. My sober queen.

If Margot can be crass then so can I. "I *want* to fuck your brother."

The smile that breaks out across Margot's face is the farthest thing from what anyone would call cute. It's more like the shit-eating grin the Grinch uses when he realizes he's about to pull off the greatest heist Whoville has ever seen. I'm downright terrified.

"Well, well, well," she sings.

"Wow," Daisy says in a monotone voice. "Not a single soul in this entire town could have guessed that with the way you two move as a unit the past however many weeks."

I'm ninety percent sure I'm blushing just *thinking* about the past couple of weeks.

Miller was actually serious about watching a movie together after he got P settled in bed after the *"family pizza night"* they planned and after that, things resumed to almost complete normalcy between us.

I'm thankful for the ambush. It sparked the idea for my Christmas gift for the two of them. It's over the top, completely ridiculous, and I know I'll be talking Miller off the ledge about how insane it all is. But it's going to be so worth it. Only about a month left until I can finally clue them in.

It's been an absolute blast spending time with them again. I'm at the apartment most nights after work. I'm helping P with homework, helping Miller with dinner, and filling in the bedtime routine gaps. We've been taking Penelope to the park to get some outside play time in before it's really too cold to do so.

Miller never fails to let me know how much I'm appreciated, extra emphasis on his thankfulness for *me* and not just for what I can do. I love it.

The only thing that has slightly changed is that Miller and I get very comfy and cozy together on the couch after P goes to bed, but it doesn't go much further than that. He's so Goddamn respectful, and while I'm bursting on the inside to heat things up, I understand his need to take things slow. It's actually kind of nice to know there's a mile long list of things we get to look forward to.

Each evening, I set an alarm on my phone, too. So when we both do eventually fall asleep (because we do almost every single night), we have a backup to wake us up before Penelope notices. I think with anyone else, I would feel dirty sneaking out the door in the dark. But Miller makes me laugh, and he holds my hand all the way to my car. He stays awake on the phone with me until our teeth are brushed, and we're both in our own beds. And there's always a new sticky note in my bag for me to find and add to my collection on my closet door.

I don't think about Dean and his bullshit. In fact, I haven't seen even a shadow of him since our last encounter. It's been glorious.

But I'm starting to feel stuck. "I don't know how to do it."

"Sex?" Margot asks. I smack my hand to my face, but she continues, "I'm sure it's been a while, but I'm also sure you know what you're doing. I could give you pointers! Sometimes I do this thing to Sawyer's—"

"For fuck's sake, Margot. I know how to have sex. I don't know how to initiate the next step. Like, I don't want to make him uncomfortable, and we also have the little issue... Okay, wait. Penelope is *not* an issue, but we can't exactly make things happen, at least not the first time, with her in the room next to us, you know? I don't even know if that's where his head is at either because—"

"Oh, I'm sure we can guess where his head is at..." Daisy mumbles.

I shoot her a pointed look. "I'm serious, Daze! I don't want to mess this up."

"Are you concussed? Did you forget you're Red fucking Bozelli? The girl who has had every head turn her way when she walks into a room since the beginning of time? Men would lick the floor for you. Miller is fantastic, but he isn't safe from your spell. Get the hell up." Daisy's pep talk isn't sweet, but you can always count on her honesty, and that's what I need right now.

"She's right, babe," Margot adds. "I don't think it's possible for you to mess things up just by wanting more. He obviously wants that, too. You just need to tell him. With your big girl words. And as far as alone time goes…Uh, hello." She dramatically waves her free hand. "Auntie M here, reporting for duty and just about begging to get that wild child for a sleepover. Let me talk to Miller?"

"It just feels very all or nothing. I don't want to end up with nothing again." It's an admission I didn't plan on letting slip out.

Margot's small hand lands on my thigh. "Red…"

"No, hear me out, okay?" I shake my head to try to will the tears to stay locked in. "We're in murky water now, right? Kissing here and there. Hanging out every day. It's nice and it's fun. We take the next step, right? We date or whatever. I start sleeping here, they sleep at my place. We become this domesticated trio. Bam! We break up over…I don't even know what we break up over, but we do, okay? Then what?"

"You can't think like that, Red. Besides, I hate to break it to you, but you're already the domesticated trio you described. You're already invested. and they are, too," Daisy says.

Her truth bomb lands heavy in my gut. I have successfully and strategically kept everyone at arm's length since the downfall of my marriage, and now that I've broken my own rules, I'm so scared.

"How are you so sure about you and Sawyer?" This is where Margot will tell me she's worried every day about them breaking up. I can't be the only person who anticipates the end like this.

She shrugs her shoulders. "He's my person. There isn't a time-line that exists where we don't find each other."

Well, what the fuck.

"What the lovesick idiot over here is trying to say is, you don't know what's going to happen down the road. It doesn't mean your complete and total happiness right now isn't worth it."

The tears are impossible to stop. "Guys, come on. I needed advice, not an emotional beat down."

Both girls abandon their drinks and pull me into a group hug that probably looks ridiculous to anyone who might be passing by. "We heard you and decided you didn't know what you needed," Margot says into my sweater.

"Thank you," I say in between sniffles.

"You're so strong, Red. I've looked up to you for years. It's time you get what you've always deserved," Daisy tells me while rubbing circles on my back.

Once I pull myself the hell together and the three of us check off a couple more things on my to-do list, I look to my last bullet point. "Thanksgiving," is all I say.

Margot jumps right into things. "Mom's already in. I invited her to stay at the cottages, but she's ditching us for Beth again. Miller and Penelope are obviously coming. Gus, too." With that, Daisy pretends to gag.

"I'm out," Daisy declares, and I throw daggers at her with my eyes. "Not because of Gus!" she adds in her own defense. "My mom invited her sister, and she said we need to put on the perfect family act to impress her." She slumps in her chair.

"Mary Jane cannot control your life and deem you the built-in babysitter forever, Daze. If you don't want to spend Thanksgiving with them, you know you're more than welcome here," I remind her.

"I still live under her roof. One day I'll get out, but—Yeah. Just —one day."

I nod my head and don't push it.

I've always been close with Daisy. Her parents opened up the flower shop, The Fuzzy Leaf, right next door to Red's Place at just about the same time as my parents opened Red's. Growing up, I used to spend a lot of time at her house, until one day my mom said I couldn't go over there anymore. She never told me why, and I never asked Daisy, out of fear I'd offend her. Besides, it all worked out when I realized she could still come hang at my place.

Daisy is honest and true, but the girl has secrets. As much as I worked hard to put up walls the past few years, she's the real architect. I've had to learn to love her from afar. Which is why I never press her when she shuts down like this.

We vote for a traditional Thanksgiving meal and divvy up who's going to bring what, compiling a list to send out in a group text. I offer up the cafe to host since it's the easiest place to get everyone together comfortably. When we finally check the time, it's well past when we said we would head home.

Sawyer pulls up to the front of the cafe within fifteen minutes of Margot texting him to drive us both home since neither of us should be getting behind the wheel after drinking two bottles of Beth's spiked hot cocoa. Every year around this time, she drops old fashioned glass milk bottles of it by the back door of the cafe weekly without my asking. When I'm locking up, I'm still mulling over the advice Daze and Margot gave me.

As I get into the backseat of Sawyer's Jeep, before he pulls away, I look to the upstairs window and smile when I can see a night light emitting a purple glow throughout the room. Penelope has made the space so inexplicably hers that it makes me want to dance with freaking glee. I think about how much she's already attached herself to my heart.

I need to talk to Miller.

CHAPTER 20: MILLER - SHOULD I BE SCARED?

I feel like I've barely had the chance to talk to Gwen lately. Between the cafe and planning our big Thanksgiving, she's been running around like a chicken with its head cut off, and I've been chasing her around trying to keep up. It felt like she was ready to take the next step—whatever that means—and then plans halted. I'm trying to figure out why without assuming the worst.

The "worst" would be that she realizes I'm just some kid with half a clue compared to her before I have the chance to be the exception. She's not totally avoiding me though, so I'm taking it as a win and running with my slim chances.

Now that the holiday week is here, school is closed, and I took the week off work. We haven't had to be worrying about homework or arrival times or getting to bed at a decent hour for P. I've gotten to spend some solid time with Penelope, and I've been free to help Gwen wherever and whenever needed. I'm feeling positive as hell about it all.

As positive as I can be right now while borderline killing myself hauling canoes from the water to their winter racks with Gus and Sawyer.

Make friends, they said. It'll be fun, they said.

I mess around with computers for a living. I'm not built like these guys. This shit sucks. But I can't lie, I was kind of excited when Sawyer texted me and asked if I wanted to help. I dropped P off at Beth's this morning, where Melanie is staying for the week, so the three of them can make cookies.

Even though Beth invited me to stay, with a look that told me I might want to reconsider my plans for the day, and despite my gut telling me agreeing to help Sawyer was most likely a bad idea, I met the fucking lumberjacks over here shortly after.

I regret not joining the cookie committee.

"Let's break after this set, yeah?" Gus calls behind me. His voice doesn't sound strained at all. He's not even a little out of breath. He's single-handedly carried nine of these fucking monsters from the river, up the hill, and onto the rack without breaking a sweat in the time it's taken me to handle…three. And that's with Sawyer's help.

"Sounds good," I strain to get out while carrying the back end of the canoe Sawyer has the front of. It's cold as shit out here, to the point where I can see my breath with every huff and puff, and yet sweat is still sticking my shirt to my back.

Gus shoots ahead of us—I swear this is a game to him—and locks the canoe into place, securing it with straps. He takes the one we're holding when we reach him to repeat the process.

"You're…an animal," I say before chugging water.

"Buddy, we gotta get you out here more if you thought this was anything." Gus laughs while clapping me on the back. I struggle to not keel over.

"You're doing great, Miller," Sawyer interjects. "What August is trying to say is, we appreciate the help. Gets us out of here faster and in turn, gets us to The Bar faster for Thanksgiving Eve." The two of them high five, and I feel like I've missed something important.

"Uh, what?"

"Thanksgiving Eve," Gus states matter of factly.

"Yep. Heard that." I nod my head. "So, what? You just…go to the bar?"

Both of their jaws go slack like I just told them I've never breathed air.

"Guys, what am I missing?"

"It's Thanksgiving Eve. You grab your best friend"—Gus puts his arm around Sawyer—"And you go to the townie bar and meet up with everyone who ever went to your high school. You get drunk and shoot the shit. Then you wake up, probably hungover, and head to the high school Thanksgiving Day football game and laugh about the night before you head back for the turkey meal. It's *Thanksgiving Eve.*"

I'm not sure if I'm more surprised by the amount of words Gus just actually said, or the fact that he willingly and seemingly excitedly surrounds himself with people from high school for an entire night. I can't say I really get it, but I'm not about to voice that thought.

I barely saw the people I went to school with when I was there. I can't imagine spending a night catching up. But then again, if Gus and Sawyer are going that means others who went to school with them might, which means…

"Red lives for Thanksgiving Eve, by the way. Did we mention that?" Sawyer asks.

"Well, she did, until…" Gus adds.

"If you think we look ridiculous getting excited, just know this is Deanie's fucking superbowl. The good news is, his gang has dwindled, where ours seems to be growing just fine. So, we should be good to go without issues tonight."

"Oh, well I'm not—" I start to explain my responsibilities as a parent when Sawyer claps a hand on my shoulder.

"You're coming. Gran and Mel are watching lil P. They'll be fine, just like they are now. Margot's handling Red. We're meeting them at The Bar. Gus and Daze have even been nice enough to agree to keep their mouths to themselves, right?" Sawyer turns to Gus who shrugs his shoulders non-committedly.

"Did you guys all plan this behind my back?"

"No," Sawyer quickly says.

"We planned it behind *both* of your backs," Gus adds.

Sawyer backs up their plan. "It's time to get out of your head and do something about how you're feeling. You can't hide behind Penelope forever. That's not fair to anyone."

I lean my back against the wood building and brush my hair back to look up at the sky. They're probably right. In fact, I know they are. But it still feels weird to have people around me in my business.

I could say no. They can't actually drag me out or hold my kid hostage, but thinking about going in that direction doesn't make me feel good at all.

"You're sure Gwen's going to be there?"

Gus claps his hands together and a grin breaks out on Sawyer's face. "Sure as shit, my dude," Sawyer assures me. "There's no way Margot fails this mission. She's invested."

A night with Gwen sounds pretty fucking mint.

I let my hand slide down my face. "Fuck me, I guess I'm going to The Bar tonight."

THINGS ARE…ROWDY in the Rivers household tonight. Sawyer and Gus have been crushing beers since we secured the last canoe into place this afternoon, telling me it was cause for celebration in the highest degree. My daughter is running around with a chef's hat and one of her princess dresses on, chasing Melanie who said this was the most cardio she's done since Margot was P's age.

Beth is singing along to the country music she has blasting

through speakers while I stand here in the middle of the kitchen feeling seven different kinds of overstimulated.

I'm not used to this. I'll say it until I'm blue in the face. Growing up, my house was only loud if there was a football game on and Michael Caswell's team was losing, or my dad was screaming at me. There were never big moments of happiness and the good kind of chaos, just doom, gloom, and destruction.

When the guys and I wrapped up at the riverside, I popped over to the apartment to pack P an overnight bag. I'll also admit to checking the cafe for Gwen, but Chris told me Margot had already swept her away. He was on closing duty today, but assured me he was bartending tonight, and he'd see me there. I'm not sure if that was supposed to make me feel better? But, sure, whatever. The guy's weird.

When I got back to Beth's, I pulled Penelope outside to talk to her away from everyone. I wanted to make sure she was comfortable staying with Beth and Melanie again. This is her second sleepover ever. It's a big deal and while I'm open to change and branching out, if my girl isn't one hundred percent on board, I'm out.

But it's clear Penelope thrives in this kind of environment. I could barely finish my sentence before she was jumping into my arms, screaming into my ear about how excited she was to have a night with her two grandmas.

We're not related in the slightest, but I'm not correcting her. I know they won't either.

Penelope's squeals of delight are the one bit of normalcy I'm clinging to so I don't have to excuse myself outside. It's stupid, because if anyone else told me they needed a minute to breathe, I'd get it. I'd insist they do what they have to do. Mental health matters, yadda yadda, shit my parenting books say.

I, for some dumbass reason, feel like I have to be stronger. I've overcome worse. Some noise and chaos with well meaning people really shouldn't be a big deal. But it is, and I really wish Gwen was here.

I settle for the next best thing and pull my phone out of my pocket and sit down at Beth's kitchen table. I send off a text and wait for the three dots to appear on the screen.

ME

What are the chances I get to buy the most beautiful woman in Merrymount a drink tonight?

GWENDOLYN

no need. i drink for free tonight. ;)

ME

Is this another small town thing I don't know about? Like the entire concept of "Thanksgiving Eve" ???

GWENDOLYN

it's a silly tradition, but i benefit from it which means you'll also get to benefit from it. so no making jokes, got it?

ME

I'm scared

ME

Should I be scared?

GWENDOLYN

prom kings and queens of merrymount high get free drinks at the bar on thanksgiving eve every year. and on that note, margot said she's going to fling my phone out of the moving car later if i don't put it down right now. see you soon!

A second later a picture comes through of Gwen and Margot, cheeks pressed together, doing duck faces at the camera. Gwen's hair is pinned up in those giant ass roll things and it looks like there's a caterpillar resting on one of Margot's eyelids.

I stare at the picture probably longer than I should because I don't hear when Beth comes up behind me and leans over my shoulder to inspect my screen. I startle when she says, "Two gorgeous girls."

I fumble my phone until it lands on the table. "Holy shit!"

Beth walks over to the speaker still blaring music to turn it down. "Sorry! Didn't mean to scare you. You were just lost in your head there for a minute. Not surprised though when she's on your mind."

"She's not…I wasn't…Okay, yeah. You got me," I admit.

"Want some sage advice from an old bat?"

I give my best harumph. "Beth, you're not old."

"Says the spry twenty-something-year-old." She points her ladle at me. "Anyway, I love Red like one of my own. Rock her world, kid." Beth winks and turns back to the pot of soup she's tending to.

"Uh…" The chair scrapes against the hardwoods when I spring to get up. "Yeah, cool. Umm you have my number and stuff. Please—" I bump into the hutch as I walk backwards toward the front door. I can't get the fuck out of here fast enough. "Call me. If Penelope needs anything or—"

Beth doesn't even look up from the stove top, but I can hear the smile in her voice. "Goodbye, Miller, my boy. Your girl is safe here with us. Go have fun now."

"Goodnight, Penelope Grace! I love you!" I call up the stairs.

I wait only until I hear her echoey reply, "Love you, Daddy!" and I throw myself out the door to suck in a giant gulp of fresh air.

Did Beth Rivers just tell me to rock Gwen's world?

I walk down the top two steps of the porch and halt. Wait. Penelope is sleeping here. At Beth's. I'm sleeping…not here. Nope. I most definitely am not sleeping at Beth Rivers' house.

And Gwen is…I mean, I guess I can't totally speak for her, but I'm pretty sure is also *not* sleeping here.

Are we about to spend the night together? Like, me and her

not accidentally falling asleep half sitting up on the couch, jolting awake to an alarm at 1:00 a.m. to sneak her out the back door like teenagers?

Hoooooolyshit.

I snatch my new Rivers' River baseball hat off my head to tug at my hair. Continuing down the steps, I pace the front yard while I wait for Sawyer and Gus to appear from wherever they ran off to. I didn't join their pregame, so I offered to drive us to the bar. Daisy has offered to be DD if I decide to drink.

And maybe I will have a couple, since my date's apparently local royalty with the bar tab hook up, and I have reliable childcare. And they're a ten minute drive from any place I'd end up tonight, because I'm still a dad first.

Alright, let's run through this. Gwen and I, we're…friendsish. Friendish? Not a word. Whatever.

We're doing everything a couple does, hell, what most families do most days of the week. She cuddles up to me on the couch, and we hold hands. There's kissing and touching and it's kind of insane how good all of it feels. How good *she* feels with me. But we don't talk about it. It really feels like the time to talk about it.

But we're gonna have some fun first.

I hear the guys before I see them half running, half tumbling down the hill from Gus' cabin that sits back a little on Beth's lot. They're definitely both already a little drunk.

"Miller! Miller Caswell! You ready to fucking paaaaaaarty?!" Sawyer yells, even though he's less than ten feet in front of me.

I laugh through my nerves. "I don't think I have much of a choice."

"Now you're getting it!" Gus says as he pulls two cans of beer from his back pockets. How do they even…? Before I can finish the question, I watch the two of them cheers and puncture their cans with pocket knives before shotgunning them back.

"I know that's right!" Gus takes both empty and crushed cans to toss in the trash next to Beth's house before hopping in the passenger seat of his truck.

I hold up my keys. "Guys, we're taking my car. Let's go."

They both fumble to fight for the front seat with Sawyer ultimately accepting defeat to sprawl out in the backseat. I let Gus handle the music while Sawyer starts a speech that leads me to believe he might be more intoxicated than I thought.

He leans over the center console, sticking his head in between Gus and me up front. "I can't wait to see Margot. I miss her. It's so weird to miss someone so much that you see everyday, you know? But God, she's just so pretty, ya know? And she has these freckles that look like little stars. And—"

"Hale, we know what your girlfriend looks like. We know you're obsessed with her. Shut the fuck up." Gus palms Sawyer's face, pushing him back. "Sorry," Gus directs at me. "The guy has two drunk nights in him a year. And as"—He looks back to see Sawyer rolling the window down to poke his head out— "Annoying as this might seem, it's better than when he's moping about his parents. So, I let him have this one."

I nod in understanding, keeping focused on the dark road ahead of us as I drive along the winding back road that leads us to Main Street. The rest of the quick drive includes Sawyer trying to sing along to songs he definitely doesn't know the words to sober, let alone drunk, and Gus trying to catch me up to speed on the who's who of the night.

I don't remember a single name he gives me, nor do I think it'll matter when we get to the bar. I'm coming out for Gwen and Gwen alone.

I'm glad they forced this. I would have never shown up here on my own, and as outside of my comfort zone this is, I have a good feeling about tonight. As long as Dean doesn't make an appearance that kills the mood.

I pull around to the back of the buildings to park in my normal spot behind the cafe because every spot in the front is taken, it's car after car all the way down the street. Some cars are definitely not in legal spots, but I don't think anyone in town cares tonight.

Margot's car is parked in Gwen's spot, but it's empty so I'm guessing they already made their way inside. There's a line formed outside the bar and it looks like there's a security guard at the door? In Merrymount? Seriously? At least it's not Dean.

"What's up with the detail?" I ask Gus as we find our place in the back of the line.

"Rodney, he owns The Bar, hires security every year to make sure they don't go over capacity. It's a fire code thing, and it only ever becomes a problem on this night. And sometimes guys get too outta control and need to be thrown out. It happens." He shrugs.

A few people ahead of us turn around to say hi when they recognize Gus and Sawyer. Sawyer proudly introduces me as his brother-in-law with hard claps on the back every time. Some-where along the hellos, we're pushed to the front of the line where the giant dude in all black steps aside to let us in after checking only my I.D. We all get stamped on the tops of our right hands, and I look down to see a blue inked blueberry.

Quintessential Merrymount.

We walk inside, and I stop dead in my fucking tracks when I see her.

How could you not see her? Gwendolyn Bozelli isn't just the center of this small town bar, she's the center of the whole Goddamn universe as far as I'm concerned.

Either my mind is playing tricks on me, or there is literally a spotlight shining on her as she stands to the side of the bar, smiling and chatting away with Margot and Daisy. She has that full head of hair down in big curls that fall down her back, stop-ping right above her ass. I clock the outfit choice almost immedi-ately. It's the same one that made part of my brain stop working when she showed up at the apartment in it. That black tank that sticks to her body like second skin, and jeans that hug every perfect fucking curve.

It's definitely too cold for that tank top but you won't catch me complaining.

Gwen has a drink in hand, and she's toying with the straw as she listens to Margot say something that causes her to tip her head back in laughter. Sawyer barrels past me when he finally spots Margot up ahead. The three girls turn their heads in our direction when they hear him over the music and chatter of everyone else in this overpacked bar.

"Pixie girl!" Sawyer yells as he picks Margot up and spins her around, not a care in the world about anyone or anything else.

I watch Gwen smile and snatch Margot's drink before it goes flying. She places it safely on the bar, and I follow her eyes as they start darting every which way around the crowded room.

I look around to see if I can spot what she's looking for until my eyes find hers again and they're laser focused on me. Her lips perk up in a smirk as she drags the small straw across her bottom lip. I think I'm jealous of a straw.

Me. She was looking for me.

Any doubt that I'm right leaves my mind when she points a single finger at me and pulls it into herself, invisibly dragging me to her.

Oh, I'm fucked.

CHAPTER 21: GWEN - THANKSGIVING EVE

I'm gonna have fun with this boy tonight.

Miller looks so unbelievably out of his element, lost in a crowd of people he doesn't know. But he found *me*. I have no plans of letting him out of my sight for a minute.

He has his dark wash jeans cuffed over the tops of his boots again, and he's wearing a dark green sweatshirt with the hood resting over a baseball cap. He has his hands tucked into his front pockets, the lanyard that holds his keys and every keychain Penelope picks out for him sticking out of the left one, too.

His curls are peeking out from under the hat, and for once I'm glad they're tucked away. Those are my curls to tangle my fingers in. My curls to admire.

I have no fucking clue where this possessiveness is coming from, but when I notice a few of the girls who graduated after me follow my line of sight to Miller, I decide I need to lean into it before someone else thinks they're leaving here with him tonight.

Anyone else. They can have literally any other guy in this bar. But not Miller. Because without even a word exchanged between us, I know with the way he winks at me before crossing the floor that he's coming home with me.

And I'm downright fucking giddy over it.

I've been giddy all day, actually. Margot intercepted me at the cafe this morning, thinking she was calling all the shots on how this day was going to go, and I let her think that. I let her whisk me back to my house, and we got to spend the day together with Daisy watching trashy TV, raiding my pantry for snacks, and getting each other ready for the night.

Thanksgiving Eve is the definition of peaked in high school behavior, and I don't give a shit. It's stupid and small town, but it's *fun.* No one cares who was popular or the smartest. We all grew up in Merrymount, and there's one night a year where we celebrate that with drinks and dancing and honestly, there's a lot of hooking up.

Triple knock before you enter any bathroom or closet in The Bar on a night like this.

Miller finally invades my space, grabbing the vodka cran I've been sipping on waiting for his arrival, and haphazardly places it on the bartop. I don't have time to get a breath in before he's kissing me in the middle of this crowded room as if we're the only two people to have ever existed.

He tastes like the mango chapstick he's always misplacing and the gingerbread coffee I haven't put on the menu at the cafe yet.

I can faintly hear hoots and hollers over the music, but that can't be for us. I do not care if it is.

His hands wrap around my waist and dip into my back pockets to pull me closer. Miller palms my ass through the denim. I follow his lead—as if I had a choice in the matter.

His tongue grazes my bottom lip, the same way I was just toying with my straw, and I feel heat pool in my belly. This is a version of Miller I've never seen before, and I'm a woman obsessed.

There was a time in my life where I used to make grocery lists during stuff like this. I wanted so badly to feel *anything* even close to passion and heat and desire. Now I'm holding back from moaning into Miller's mouth, from begging him to get us the hell out of here.

Before I make a fool of myself in front of an entire town that has watched me grow up, Miller pulls back slightly, just enough for me to be able to look him in the eyes.

"I have to tell you something," he breathes into me.

I let the tiniest bit of panic and doubt creep in for half a second. I think about who I am, who he is, and where we are. I remember that the world works against me, and I'm not destined for happy or easy, especially with someone like Miller.

But then Miller's eyes widen, and he shakes his head so fast I'm worried he'll give himself whiplash. "No, no, no. Wait, that was such a shitty way to word that. Hold on—"

I don't get to hear what he meant to say. I don't know what the something is that he has to tell me because suddenly an arm loops around my waist from behind where Miller's hands just were and pulls me back. I hear Margot laughing in my ear, and *Christ* do I love this girl but right now, I'm ready to throw hands to get back to her brother.

A very drunk Sawyer clasps his hand on Miller's shoulder, holding him in place by the bar with the guys, while I'm whisked to the makeshift dance floor in the middle of the room.

"Margot, I was kind of in the middle of something," I half shout.

"Oh, I'm aware. We're all aware. You weren't exactly being inconspicuous. He can wait. I know you're going home with him." Margot finally stops and turns to me. "And I *don't* need the details. Actually, heavy emphasis on not *wanting* to know the details. I'm so happy for you and love this so, so much. But right now, we dance."

The floor in here is perpetually sticky. You have to basically flash the DJ they hire for tonight for him to play a song you request. There's a good chance a drink or two will splash on you throughout the night. But when I hear the opening chords of

Gracie Abrams' *Close To You*, I'm reminded there's absolutely nowhere else in the world I'd rather be.

I decide to lean into the comfortability of this night with these people. And right at this very moment, there's nothing else I'd rather do than shake my ass in a smokey, dark, crowded room with my girls.

Daisy meets us in the crowd, and our hands fly up right before the first chorus hits. I let the beat take me away.

I've never been a dancer, per se, but I've loved losing myself in music for as long as I can remember. I feel my hair bouncing around my face, and I sing along to every word. Margot and Daisy scream sing right back in my face as we laugh and make sure Merrymount feels like downtown Miami during Spring Break.

We don't stop after the first song ends, jumping immediately into the next and bumping into a few of the girls I used to cheer with. I can already feel sweat on my neck, but I don't care.

The last person I want to be thinking about tonight pops up in the corner of my eye as I twirl around Margot. I had a feeling it would be too good to expect he wouldn't show up. I ignore him, choosing to blow a kiss to one of my old classmates who happens to pass by. When I twirl back, he's gone.

Good. Let's keep it that way.

Unfortunately, Thanksgiving Eve is one of the few things Dean and I agreed on. Well, that's not even the whole truth. We both love this night, and that's about where it ends. I'm here for fun and catching up. I love getting to see and hear about how people are thriving year after year. He's here to relive the glory days and try to one up everyone with his mock success. Before our marriage imploded, the glory days included making sure everyone in the vicinity knew I belonged to him. I shudder at the thought.

The funny thing about reflection is how differently you start to view things. I used to think it was nice Dean wanted me on his arm all night, showing me off, parading me around. I thought he was proud of our marriage.

But if I strayed for too long or was found catching up with someone Dean didn't approve of, you'd find us in the alley behind the bar where most come to smoke. Not us, though. Of course not.

Dean would need to pull me aside to scold me. He wanted to remind me of who I was: his *wife.* But the word never sounded as good as I imagined it would. It felt...wrong, if I let myself be honest.

I let it go, though. Every single time. I used to apologize and promise I would make it up to him when we got home. He would tell me to do better and pat me on the head like a fucking dog. I'm embarrassed looking back now.

I really wish I could say it wasn't all bad. I wish we got to organically end and coexist like every other couple who didn't survive high school graduation, to be normal like everyone else in this packed bar.

Hold the Goddamn phone.

If Dean is here...where in the hell is Katie?

The song ends, and I scan the room for a head of icy, blonde hair. Unfortunately Katie St. James *also* lives for the reminiscing high she gets off tonight. I don't see her and breathe a sigh of relief.

I mean, we're not in the clear yet. The night is young, but still.

Daisy thrusts a water into my hands, the official mother hen on a night like this. "You're alternating tonight. Don't argue with me on it. I'm not cleaning puke out of the back of my car for you ever again."

"It was one time, Daze. And I apologized a million and a half times," I whine before chugging the ice cold water that I'm actually extremely thankful for.

Thanksgiving fell exactly one week after I kicked Dean out of the house, and against everyone's wishes for me to have a chill night in, I demanded to go out. I drowned myself in whiskey and have sworn it off since.

"I never cared for an apology. Just your blood oath of a promise to listen to me and drink the damn water, babes." Daisy leans in and kisses my cheek. I smooch her right back.

"Can we talk about how fucking hot you look tonight? Who are you trying to take home?" I ask her.

Daisy rolls her eyes and pretends to smooth out her black bodysuit. We're basically matching, almost every woman in this bar is. She has on tight, dark wash jeans that hug every curve of hers, with holes perfectly ripped right above each knee and white tennis shoes. Where her head is normally covered by a bandana, her big, jet black curls have been let free tonight, framing her face and falling to hit her lower back.

"No, really Daze," Margot interjects. "You're an absolute fucking smoke. I bet every guy in here is going to be lining up to lay you down tonight."

Daisy's face scrunches up and just when I think she's about to have some retort for Margot, I follow her line of vision to see the cause for her stank face.

"Daisy Stiles wouldn't be caught dead slumming it with anyone in here. Wouldn't want to ruin her perfect princess reputation," Gus says without a hint of a joke in his voice.

"You smell like the bottom of a fucking dumpster, August," Daisy spits out.

"Do I?" Gus lifts his arm and pretends to sniff. "Huh, the girls I was just talking to must be into it."

"Well, seeing as how you're over here with us and not still with them, I wouldn't bet on that. But that must be hard for someone with such a small brain to comprehend. Anyway…" Daisy dramatically turns her body to face away from Gus. "That was too many words for him. We need to move away now, please."

Sawyer crashes into Gus' back and they both stumble forward

into the makeshift circle we've kind of formed here. I take the moment of disarray to look for my favorite head of curls. I turn my head every which way and can't see him anywhere among the crowd.

Why isn't he with Sawyer and Gus? Would he really leave without telling me? Did something happen to Penelope?

Before I have the chance to dive further into this panic, firm hands grip my waist from behind, and I finally let out a deep breath. Before I lean back into Miller's chest, I see Miller grab two drinks from Chris at the bar to head over to our group.

Wait.

I whirl around in shock, loosening from hands that don't belong anywhere near me. I face ~~my worst nightmare~~ Dean. "What in the fuck do you think you're doing?"

"Happy Thanksgiving Eve, baby," Dean slurs while trying to invade my space *again*.

I open my mouth to tell him exactly where I wish he would shove it when Miller crosses my path and pushes Dean into the wall behind him. His back slams into the wood, and he bounces forward. He's off balance thanks to the amount of alcohol he's probably ingested and loses his footing.

The next few seconds are a blur. Gus is at Miller's side almost immediately, and I feel Margot grab my arm, pulling me away from the scene unfolding. There's yelling, but I can't make out who's saying what to who over the music. People around us have started to stare, and I'm rightfully super nervous we're about to be thrown out, or worse.

I'm not going to think about the worst case scenario.

I finally snap out of my fog and pull myself away from Margot to get to Miller. I need to get him away from Dean. He cannot fuck his life up over this, over *me*.

"You're wasting your time with her. She's just confused." Dean's lies rock through my head, but I keep pushing through the crowd that has now formed.

"Would you shut the fuck up for once in your miserable life?" Gus retorts, successfully holding Miller back. Thank *God.*

"What's your stake in this, Burton? You trying to finally get in Red's pants, too?"

"Why would you even think to say something like that?" I scream and at the exact same time—because of course that's my fucking luck—the music cuts.

Miller's head whips to me. "Gwen, you don't need to be here for this. We're good. I'm good."

"That's zero percent reassuring, actually," I snap before turning back to Dean. "You want a show? Fine. I'm done protecting the peace. Here it is. We go around and around with this conversation far too often for me to let it keep happening. We're done. Divorced. I *hate* you. Every single part of you."

For as drunk as he probably is, I see every word I say register on his face. His eyes go from antagonizing to cold within seconds, and if I didn't have Miller and Gus on either side of me, I'll admit I'd probably be scared right about now.

"You're...You're a—" Dean sputters.

"Say it," Miller breathes. "Say whatever was about to pour out of your fucking mouth and watch what happens." At this, Gus lets go of Miller, and he takes one step forward, closing in on Dean's space.

Ben and Dylan, Dean's two right hand idiots, stand off to the side, clearly ready to jump in if needed. Until and unless that's necessary, they aren't bothering with the show.

"Fitzgerald." A deep voice booms from behind us, a voice I haven't heard in a while. I turn to see the only officer in the entire department who isn't a braindead loser. Dean's boss, Mark.

I should say he's Dean's old boss as he's retired now. He never said much about the end of his career, but most of us know it has to do with the inner workings of how the department operates, who they hire, how they run things; it's not great. He left because he was done with the bullshit, and Dean took that as his opportunity to run wild.

"Get the fuck outside *now*," Mark commands.

There's no room for argument, and Dean doesn't press for one. Because even with Mark out of his official role, when he steps into one of authority even temporarily, Dean listens. He always has. I don't fully understand why, but at this moment, I don't particularly care. Dean nods his head once, not even bothering to give us another look before storming through the crowd of people surrounding us. His baboons follow him while Mark trails the three of them to make sure they find their way out.

The DJ awkwardly brings the music back up to a normal volume, and everyone around us tries to shake off the last five minutes. I keep my feet firmly planted in place, trying to get a hold of my emotions, but I feel my lip start to quiver. I hate that I'm a fucking crier when I'm angry.

I jump when a hand finds mine and pull back in fear of my comfortability wronging me again. But Miller's voice finds my ear. "It's me, Gwen. God, I'm so sorry—"

I pivot to throw my arms around him and bury my face in his neck. I don't want him to apologize. He has nothing to be sorry for. I breathe him in while his hands slide up and down my back as I take deep breaths.

"Come on, let's go take a minute," he whispers. I keep my head down and hold onto Miller's hand like a lifeline as he pulls me through the bar.

We make it to the bathrooms that are tucked into the back corner, and by some miracle, one is open. Miller guides me inside and without a word, picks me up and plops me onto the sink's counter. His hands continue to comfort me, now sliding up and down the tops of my thighs.

When his head finally lifts, and I get the chance to get lost in those green eyes, my hands instantly find his face. I caress his sharp jawline and take in all of Miller's features. His long, thick, black eyelashes bat at me when he blinks. I feel my fury begin to dissipate as the comfort that is Miller Caswell's presence washes over me. I even crack a smile at the freckle that lives so perfectly right above his lips, lips I've come to love getting to know.

I reach up and flick off his hat, letting his curls loose so I can make a mess of them. We both say nothing, and it's the most comfortable silence.

"You said you had to tell me something," I finally say.

"I did," he confirms.

"It'd be nice if you informed me of that thing like, now. Now would be cool."

"First, I need to know you're okay."

"I am," I assure him. "I don't want the focus of tonight to be on that. Please."

He leans forward and captures my mouth with his. I'm lost in him instantly, pulling him closer in between my legs so his chest is flush with mine. It helps to feel that he's really just fine after all of that, sturdy as ever. We get lost like this for a minute until he pulls away.

"I HAVE A BIG, fat crush on you, Gwendolyn Bozelli. It's more than a crush, actually. I like you, a lot. Penelope does, too. And I'm pretty fucking sick of pretending I like the friends who kiss label we have going on."

Clear words and grand declarations I never would have asked for. But (not so?) secretly longed for. A sort of peace washes over me that has me feeling more than ready to get the hell out of here and only focus on the sweet man in front of me.

"Can I ask you a favor?"

"I'll do pretty much anything you ask, beautiful. I've only told you a hundred times." Miller presses his forehead into mine. His voice is shaky.

Oh, I do not ever want this sweet boy to have a single doubt about how I feel about him. He needs to know exactly where I'm at. He deserves that. Although, I'll never understand how he doesn't see it. He goes to bat for me with everything, he picks up where I leave off. I'm the one who feels like I have to play catch up to be someone he wants and needs.

"Take me home, Miller."

The smile that breaks out across his face could end our search for world peace, I'm sure of it. He lifts me off the counter and without letting me down, brings my face back to his. Miller leaves light kisses, and I giggle into him. I wrap my legs around his waist, refusing to let go.

He continues to carry me, and when he unlocks the door, we almost slam right into Margot. Sawyer is standing behind her, leaning over to rest his head on her shoulder. "Heyyyyyyout-wooooo," Sawyer slurs while wiggling his eyebrows.

"Big guy over here is ready to call it an early night," Margot tells us, slapping his chest lovingly. "I saw you head in this direction and wanted to make sure you were good before we took off. You *are* good, right?"

I tap Miller on the shoulder so he knows to let me down. "More than good. We're about to leave, too." I bring Margot in for a hug and hold her tight. "I love you, thank you," I whisper so only she hears.

"I love *you*," Margot replies and lowers her voice to match mine. "You deserve this; right here, right now. Not what happened before. Don't let him take your joy."

"Never again," I tell her confidently.

Miller claps Sawyer on the back and checks in with Margot to see if she needs any help hauling all six-foot-three inches of Sawyer Hale out of here, but she assures us she's fine.

I catch Daisy with a group of girls we used to have class with and tell her goodbye. We scan the room for Gus but can't find him anywhere. It seems impossible that we could miss him because normally he's the biggest guy in the room anywhere he goes.

Miller pulls out his phone and sends him a quick text when we get outside. We didn't last long enough to need a designated driver so Miller guides me around the back to where he parked his car so we can go back to the house. Thankfully there's no Dean or his cronies in sight.

We walk hand in hand, and I smile down at our fingers intertwined. When we both hear Miller's phone go off, we're happy to see Gus responded, letting Miller know he was fine.

Typical Gus to take off and think no one was going to notice or care about his disappearance.

"You know," Miller says, pulling me out of my head. "We could just head on up to the apartment."

"I know." I swing our arms between us. I look up at him with a smirk. "But my bed's bigger."

CHAPTER 22: MILLER + GWEN

MILLER

*I*f someone had a gun to my head right now and asked me what Gwen and I talked about the entire drive back to her house, I'd be a dead man.

I actually think I might already be a dead man. Because there's no way real life Miller is going home with this woman.

After putting my car in park in her driveway, I turn off the engine and look at Gwen in the passenger seat. She put that big head of hair of hers up into a ponytail once we left the bar, and I'm having thoughts I've never had before about taking it and wrapping it around my—

Gwen interrupts my thoughts. "Are we going inside or do you plan on staring at me, practically screaming your dirty dreams in my face, for the remainder of the night?"

"I—What? Me? No." I stumble to throw my door open and loop over to her side to whip the passenger door open. "Okay, maybe me a little. I'm sorry, you're just—"

Gwen steps out and places her hand on my chest, and I

instantly feel warm. "I like it, Miller. I like your attention a lot. I'm telling you right now that I'm probably into whatever it is you want to do because I like you. A lot."

I needed to hear that, and I wasn't man enough to admit it. How she knew isn't something I need to dwell on for too long, because it's Gwen, and she always seems to know what someone needs.

My breath comes out in a whoosh, and I follow her up her front steps and into the entryway after she unlocks the door. I squat down to untie my boots, and leave them by the door. I pull my sweatshirt up and over my head, and find an empty hook, placing my hat on top of it. "I'm not sure what I should be doing right now," I tell Gwen with embarrassing honesty.

She guides me into the living room without a word, and stops in front of the couch.

My cock stirs as I watch her sink to her knees in front of me. She's looking up at me with those big, doe eyes. A dichotomy of innocence and sin. I swipe my hand down my face trying to keep my shit together as she toys with my belt. Once undone, she makes quick work of the button and zipper on my pants.

I'm fully hard in an instant.

This is the single hottest moment of my life, and she's barely touched me. I haven't even gotten my hands on her yet. I let out a stifled moan through my hand when her fingers wrap around me. The smallest bit of her touch is already sending me over the fucking edge.

"Gwendolyn," I say through gritted teeth.

Her hand gently glides up and down my length, like she's getting used to the feel of it all. There's a small smile on her face when she looks up at me again.

"Is this okay?" she asks.

"I'm not opposed to begging at this point."

I swear to God I see a twinkle in her eye. She leans back on her heels, not stopping her slow stroking. "You'd beg."

I think it's a question, but it comes out more like a shocked statement. I manage to pull myself together to pin her chin with my thumb and index finger. "You don't know the things I'd do to get those pouty lips on me right now."

I swipe my thumb over her bottom lip, and she parts her mouth for me in answer. She pulls my thumb in and sucks as her tongue lolls around it, in what I can only assume is a preview of what's to come. She releases me with a pop, and I start singing my ABC's backwards in my head to keep from coming from that alone.

"Sit," she commands as she pushes me back so I have no choice but to fall into the couch. I wouldn't have tried to object anyway.

I'm in so over my fucking head right now, but I'm finding the will to give a shit nonexistent. I have the most beautiful fucking woman in the world on her knees in front of me, and I don't have an ounce of the control pulsing through this room.

Gwen leans forward, rubbing the palms of her hands up and down my thighs while my jeans sit pooled at my ankles. She grips the base of my cock with her right hand and looks up at me again.

"Tell me what you want."

How do I tell her everything? How do I tell her I don't have a fucking clue what I'm doing and my experience in all of this is next to none without her thinking I'm not going to put my all into making this good for her? I want to get this right.

Gwen's head tilts to the side in question. She's probably wondering what the hell is wrong with me.

"I'm sorry." I sigh while pulling on the ends of my hair to the point of pain to snap myself out of this.

She sits back on her heels again, and I feel the loss of her touch instantly. "What're you thinking about, Miller?"

Fucking *Christ*, her saying my name like that right now makes my cock twitch again.

"I've never done this," I blurt out.

Gwen's eyes pop out like a cartoon. "Done…this?" Her hand snakes up my thigh again, her fingers wrapping around the base of me, and I shudder.

"Yes," I manage to get out.

"Ever?"

"Ever, Gwendolyn."

I watch the goosebumps spread up her arm. "But, you're a dad…You've…"

"I stumbled into losing my virginity at sixteen, and wound up with a pregnant girlfriend within two months. Having a baby young doesn't equal experience, Gwen."

I try to not be embarrassed about it. I've watched porn. I've *had* sex. Obviously. But, I've been raising Penelope on my own, not trusting anyone. Date nights haven't been a thing for me to broaden my horizons with. I turned that part of my brain off a long time ago. My hand and I have gotten by just fine, until now.

The smile that breaks out on her face is downright diabolical.

"Let me take care of you then," she says as she lowers her head to my tip.

Any inkling of embarrassment disappears as I watch her swirl her tongue around me like a fucking lollipop, and I try to keep my eyes from rolling to the back of my head. My hands instinctively find themselves running through her hair, grasping it. Gwen takes me in her mouth, and I have no willpower left to do anything but let her fully take over.

"Holyfuckingshit," I get out between breaths.

She takes me deep and continues to stroke with her hand at the base. I feel myself buck and hit the back of her throat. She moans around me, and I now picture sheep to count to keep myself from coming on the spot.

Yeah, this is a top ten moment for me. Scratch that, top five. Hell, maybe even top three.

"Holy shit," I hiss.

I see the corners of her lips tip up. I watch her suck me in over and over again. Her cheeks hollow out, and I black out.

I let my head fall back, and I close my eyes while continuing to run my fingers through Gwen's hair as she works me. Somewhere along the way, her ponytail holder slipped off and seeing Gwen like this has ruined me.

I'm probably supposed to be thinking of words and saying them out loud, but full transparency, there's not a thought floating through my brain beyond telling myself to keep up and not come.

I look down to see her eyes meet mine and caress her hair. "You're fucking perfect, you know that?"

* * *

GWEN

They say it's always the tall, skinny guys, and boy, were they fucking right.

I work the base of Miller's cock with one hand while taking as much of his length as I can in my mouth. I grip tightly and suck until my cheeks hollow out. The moans he lets out send shivers down my spine, and I know without the need for confirmation that I'm soaked through my thong.

There's so much power in knowing how good you can make someone feel like this. Yeah, I might be the one on my knees, but Miller here would probably do anything I asked while in this position.

I release his tip with a pop, continuing to stroke him while I look up to see he still has one hand gripped in my hair and the other pressed in a fist against his mouth.

"Miller?" I say in a low voice.

He tenses up, and I find way too much joy in his inability to keep it together for it to be normal. But I don't care. I want him completely undone for me.

"I need words, baby." I drag my tongue along the bottom of his shaft.

"Words? *Jesus Christ—*" he mutters more to himself than me. "Gwen, I'm trying to not blow on the fucking spot here."

My only answer is taking him deeper, until he hits the back of my throat again. And with a hand pressed into the back of his leg, I hold him there for a moment and release when I hear him let out a breath with my name on it.

"Gwen," Miller pants. "Gwen, I'm gonna come."

I run one hand up and down his thigh, and I feel goosebumps break out every place I touch. I grip him hard and continue sucking until I feel him tense up again and let his release down the back of my throat.

"Gwendolyn," Miller moans my name like a fucking prayer as I swallow him down.

I loosen my grip and gently slide him out of my mouth, lightly licking his tip before looking up at him. His hair has been pulled in every direction, his chest is heaving. Miller looks downright demolished sitting here on this couch half undressed and rumpled.

I. Am. Obsessed.

His eyes are pinned on me with a look I can't quite place. It's awe and adoration, and I think I'll be chasing the high of it for a long time.

Before I can lean back on my heels again, Miller moves. He kicks his pooled jeans off and hoists me up. He tosses me so my back hits the couch cushions, and suddenly I'm trapped by a half-naked Miller hovering over me.

"That was…" He's still panting, and I'm trying not to squirm under him. Forgoing the need for words, his mouth meets mine. I'm sure he can taste himself on my tongue. He has one hand braced near my face while the other roams my body.

His fingers pause when they reach the fabric of the bodysuit covering my breasts. I know he's noticed them before, but has always been too polite to ask. Miller gently and slowly—so, *so slowly*—pulls each strap down over my shoulders, exposing my chest to him.

The streetlight casts a glow into the living room that makes the metal of my piercings glint.

"They're arrows," I tell Miller while he stares. "For staying on my true path, or at least that's what the piercer told me when I got them done."

His face lowers and he shoots his eyes up to me. "Can I touch them?"

"Please," I breathe, not looking away.

He flicks his tongue on my left nipple, and I jump at the contact. I've always been sensitive and after I got them pierced that only intensified. But I've been the only one testing out touch since I got them done, so this is all new to me.

His mouth captures my nipple, and I feel his tongue swirl as I twist underneath him. My hands find his hair—their favorite place to be apparently—and I play with his curls at the same time he plays with me.

Miller's tongue tangles with mine while he fumbles with the button on my jeans. I lose my patience and reposition to help him drag the denim off me. He tosses my pants along with his shirt across the room.

It's when he's toying with the clasps on my bodysuit, and I can hear his frustration through his small sigh that the first giggle escapes my lips.

"I'm so sorry," he exhales and lifts himself to sit upright on the couch next to me.

I prop myself onto my elbows. "Do *not* be sorry right now."

"It's just…you're you. You look like *this*." Miller gestures to my near naked body, and I feel the heat creep from my chest up to my face. "You just did *that*." His hand motions down, and I have to hold back from slapping my own hand across my mouth. "I knew I was out of my league here, but wow."

"Miller." I scoot over and grab the throw blanket hanging off the back of the couch to place on top of us. "That's silly. I want *you*. There's no league or whatever. I…Would it help if I told you this is hard for me too?"

I trace his jawline with my finger as he nods.

"Okay, trigger warning, I'm going to mention Dean."

"I feel like I should put clothes on for this conversation…"

"No!" I drape my legs over his thighs, keeping him right where he is. "I like you like this, please." He offers me a soft smile and my nerves loosen.

"Okay, so I've never actually said this out loud before. And now we're here and uh, yeah, okay."

Miller grabs my hand and squeezes. "Gwen, you can talk to me about anything. Your past is a part of who you are. I'm good. You're safe here."

Hearing the word safe opens up a floodgate of emotions I wasn't prepared for. I also wasn't prepared for how absolutely true it feels to hear Miller say that. I'm safe here with him.

I let the words I've held in in fear of judgment for so long fall out. "Dean and I had a shitty sex life. He had to be the one to initiate things, or he would call me needy. It was done when he was done. There are…*things* I think I'm really into that he would put me down for. There was a lot of name calling. It just—it just wasn't fun. It wasn't the way I think sex with your partner is supposed to be."

My words hang, and I feel the need to keep going. "I don't care that you don't think you know what you're doing. My underwear is wrecked right now because of how much that blowjob turned me on. I don't want you to feel like you need to keep up or be someone you're not when all I'm looking for is you."

"He never deserved you," Miller mutters down to his lap where our hands sit cozily together.

I grab at his chin and pull him to look at me. "Nope. But I think after years of therapy and self-reflection, I see that, and I deserve another chance at happiness. I'd like to take that chance with you."

"And you're okay with uh, teaching me?" He winces at the last part.

"Miller, baby." I snake my hand under the blanket and graze his abdomen with my fingertips, loving the way he jumps beneath my touch. "That tongue doesn't seem to need much teaching. But, yes. I'm more than eager."

"These light touches are killing me." His hand wraps around my wrist. "Wait, Gwen. Before you get me hard again, and I start thinking with the wrong head. Can we…God damn it, is it okay if we take this part of things slow?"

"Yes," I answer without a second thought. "Of course. I don't want to do anything you're not comfortable with."

"It's dumb, really—"

"No it's not," I cut him off. "Your boundaries are important. That's like, the number one rule of sex-ed. So, consider this your first lesson. Miller, you're allowed to say no."

"Thank you," he says with closed eyes.

My hand trails farther down, and I find myself toying with the happy trail of dark hair on the lower part of his stomach. "For clarification purposes. I'm about to invite you upstairs to my bedroom. You are in no way obligated to accept this invitation, but I also need you to know it's not some ploy to get in your pants. Well, your lack of pants."

Miller pulls me into him, and he laughs. "To sleep?"

"To sleep," I assure him.

"But if I wasn't ready to sleep just yet…" The hand that was rubbing circles on my back starts to play with the hem of the body suit that's currently still somehow stuck to me.

"Miller Caswell, are you propositioning me?" I ask in a mock transatlantic accent.

He shakes his head and pulls me closer to him, and I nuzzle into the crook of his neck. His arms wrap around me tightly, and I think about how I've never felt this relaxed and wound up at the same time in my life.

"Let's get that fine ass of yours upstairs," Miller mumbles into my hair.

Gwen directs me upstairs, saying she has to take care of something in the kitchen, and she'll be up in a minute. I climb the staircase with the throw blanket wrapped around my waist and peer into each room along the hall until I find the door that's hers. Of course it's the last one.

Gwen's bedroom is just about as perfect as I expected it to be. The floors are a dark and worn hardwood, covered with rugs of all different shapes and sizes. Some overlap others, and it doesn't seem like there was a method to laying them down, but it somehow works.

Her bed, which is absolutely without a doubt bigger than mine, sits against the back wall in between two windows that must overlook her backyard. There's a good six or seven empty and half-filled water bottles on one nightstand while the other has a single book on it.

I walk over and pick it up to find it's the book of affirmations I gave her. I return it to its spot with a smile on my face. I sit on the edge of the bed, unsure what I should be doing.

I didn't bring any clothes or a toothbrush or literally anything else. I didn't even grab my phone downstairs before heading up here. Actually, that's irresponsible. I need to go get that.

I crash into Gwen in the doorway and step back a few steps, falling into her closet door I didn't realize was right there, like an idiot.

"Shit! Sorry!" I yell.

Gwen dumps the tray of snacks and drinks she brought up on the cushioned bench she has at the end of her bed. When she looks up at me her eyes go wide. "You're good! You're fine! Everything's cool!" she says in a high pitched voice, slamming the closet door shut.

She's definitely acting weird, but I overlook that when I see she ditched the majority of her clothes. I don't know if the scrap of fabric that's left covering her bottom half constitutes clothing. Those silver arrows pierced through her nipples are holding almost every bit of my attention.

The way her body responded when I flicked my tongue across them. The way her breath hitched. I want to learn every single way she reacts to every single kind of touch.

I step into her space, ignoring the pain in the back of my head from its connection with the edge of the door.

"Is your head okay?" Gwen asks, reaching up and brushing my hair out of my face.

"Gwen, I don't give a fuck about my head," I say before pulling her into me. We pick up where we left off earlier, and I palm her now bare ass with both hands.

The blanket falls, and I walk us back until Gwen's calves hit the side of the bed. She falls into the mattress, and my lips continue their mission to learn every inch of this woman's body.

She shimmies up to the head of the bed, and I follow, hovering over her. I kiss her mouth dand her jaw, stopping to nip and suck on the side of her neck. I let one of my hands play with her nipple, testing out pinching and rubbing it between two of my fingers. Gwen's shallow breaths and mews lead me to believe I'm doing something right.

It's when I toy with the metal bar with my tongue that her hips press into me. "Miller, oh my *God,* that feels good."

My hand drifts over the plane of her stomach, inching lower until I reach the lace covering her pussy. She wasn't lying, the material is soaked.

"Can I?" I ask with a voice shakier than I intended.

Gwen's hand snakes under mine, pulling the tiny thong to the side. My hand moves with hers as she starts to slowly rub featherlike circles around her clit. "You can. But does it help if I show you, too?"

I can't take my eyes off our two hands moving together. I don't even think I'm breathing, but I nod so Gwen at least knows I can hear her. I just don't have the capacity to speak right now.

She moves faster, pressing harder into herself, and her wetness coats our fingers. My middle finger slides into her, and she moans. Gwen plays with her clit in tandem with me gliding in and out of her, following her to keep pace.

"Another," she breathes. "Please." My index finger enters her, too, while I keep my thumb on the top of her hand.

I can't take my eyes off her.

With her hair cascading across the pillow and the light from the moon shining in from the window, Gwen looks like a fucking dream right now. I keep fucking her with my fingers, coaxing every noise I can out of her. I thought she sucked the life out of me earlier, but I'm hard again seeing her like this.

"You're perfect. I've told you that right?" I ask after she lets loose a cry louder than the last.

"Once or twice," she answers, breathless. I find a rhythm and feel her pulse around me. "Yes, just like that."

Her fingers leave her clit, and before I can gather what she's doing, I feel her hand wrap around my cock. She uses the wetness from her pussy to coat me, pumping me until I'm panting along with her.

"Fucking hell," I say before kissing Gwen deeply.

"You're gonna come with me, okay, baby?" she whispers.

She's been calling me baby all night. It's sick how much I love it.

"Yes, ma'am." I nip at her neck, not caring if it leaves a mark.

"God, why was that hot?" she asks.

I drag the tip of my tongue up to the spot right under Gwen's ear, knowing it drives her fucking crazy. When I test out curling my fingers inside her slightly, I feel her muscles tense.

"Miller!" Gwen cries. Her back arches and as impossible as it would seem to be able to do so, she gets even tighter around my fingers. I keep moving them in and out while she comes. Her orgasm triggers mine. I don't even have the chance to grab some-thing—*anything*. I coat Gwen's stomach with my release. It jets up across her breasts, and before I can start the apology tour of the fucking century...

I see Gwen smile.

It's a devilish grin that I'll have burned into my memory for the rest of time. I'm more than sure of it.

When she releases me and drags her finger up the middle of her torso, stopping to swirl my come around each nipple, I see stars. I slowly slide my fingers out of her pussy and do the only thing that feels right.

I suck both of them into my mouth, savoring the taste.

I move to get up, to get something to clean up the mess I made. But Gwen pushes me to the side, causing me to fall onto the bed next to her. "Sor—"

She cuts me off. "Do *not* fucking say sorry right now, Caswell."

"It's just—I—"

Gwen sits up and grabs a T-shirt off the floor. She wipes my come off herself as she says, "You can't apologize for something I like. I like that I made you come, twice. I like that you couldn't help yourself, that you had to finish, in me, *on* me. It's hot. I'm into it."

"Oh." I think I blacked out again because she didn't just...

"Great. Now you think I'm sick in the head or something." Gwen moves to get up, and I grab her wrist, holding her in place.

"I need you to not leave me right now and just listen, okay?" I pull her into me until her back is flush with my chest.

She gives me a *harumph* and presses her ass into me. I rethink my *take things slow* plan for a second but shake it off. I push her hair to the side so I can see her face.

"I don't have a fucking clue on what I'm doing, Gwen. I'm following your lead here. But I want you to feel respected and as beautiful as I see you, inside the bedroom and out. If you're telling me you have a kinky side, I'm fucking here for it. But I don't know where the line is. So yeah, I was trying to say sorry for coming on your tits. But if you liked it...well, then, I'm not sorry and thank you." I kiss the top of her head.

"Oh my God, can you say *kinky side* again?" She giggles.

I grab the comforter and wrap it around us, snuggling closer to her, if that's even possible. "Shut up. It's time to sleep. Goodnight." I squeeze my eyes shut, fighting off the embarrassment of my inexperience, grateful as fuck that Gwen doesn't seem to care. I'm kind of obsessed with the fact that we can play with each other like this.

She wiggles until I loosen my arms around her. "No way, I'm showering and eating. You are, too. Come on, up you go." Gwen stands and holds her hand out until I grab it, pulling myself up.

We do exactly as she says. We shower and take turns washing each other's hair. I learn that not only is her bed bigger, but her towels are softer, too. I find my discarded T-shirt and boxers to throw on. Gwen puts reruns of a 90s sitcom on while we sit up in her bed, eating the chips and salsa and chocolate cake from the cafe she brought up earlier.

We brush our teeth side by side after I thank her for the extra toiletries she had stashed in the cabinet. I look at the two of us standing in the mirror and think about how far off this version of life felt only months ago.

Gwen falls asleep first. Before dozing off myself, I sneak downstairs to grab my phone, I find hers next mine and grab it to plug both in upstairs. Before I reach the staircase, I check the lock on the front door, flicking off the porch light on my way by.

These are small things I could find myself getting used to quickly, but I push that thought away, knowing how fast it could all come crashing down, knowing the damage Caswell men seem to cause everywhere they go. I then shake that thought, too.

I'm not my father, I repeat until I finally close my eyes and drift off to sleep.

* * *

DAYLIGHT BREAKS before I'm ready to open my eyes. But when I do…

It feels like the world stops.

Gwen fell asleep with her head on my chest and my arms wrapped around her, and I thought the view couldn't get more perfect, but I'll admit right now, I was wrong.

The last time we were in this position, I was scrambling for a way out of it in fear I was somehow messing up Penelope and didn't get to savor the sight that's Gwen in the morning light.

But now I can't look away. I don't want to look away.

Her hair falls down her back in waves. It's perfectly in place, as if neither of us moved all night, afraid we might separate for even a second throughout the night. Her breaths are shallow and even, still sound asleep.

I try to move as little as possible to reach for my phone on the nightstand. I pull up the group text Melanie and Beth threw me in last night to see a message delivered about an hour ago. I wince when I realize Penelope must have woken up no later than six. Hopefully Melanie and Beth are still used to small early risers.

My heart rattles when I look at the picture attached to the text. Penelope's on a stepstool against Beth's kitchen counter, the small chef hat on her head and an apron tied around her. There's an *S* embroidered on the front, telling me this thing is Sawyer's from when he was young. She still has her nightgown on, smiling so big with a wooden spoon in her hand over the mixing bowl filled with enough batter to make at least a couple dozen pancakes.

The thing I notice above all is how happy Penelope looks. She's beaming with her cheek pressed right up against Beth's for the picture Melanie must have had them pose for mid-mix. I feel a rush of guilt for keeping her all to myself for so long when she could have had a group of people to love her just as much as I do.

I made my decisions out of fear. I thought I was doing the right thing, keeping us closed off, never giving either of us the opportunity for something more.

I type out a quick reply, telling Melanie to have P call me whenever she wants, and that I'd be by shortly. I snap a picture of Gwen, too. I don't want to forget what she looks like in this moment.

Laying in the quiet of the early morning isn't something I'm used to. I can hear the rustling of the trees outside and the faint sound of someone walking their dog. Gwen stirs, and I keep running my hand up and down her back, wanting her to sleep as long as she needs.

The arm that lays snug under my shirt moves and her hand starts to slowly roam the span of my chest and then further down. She hasn't even opened her eyes yet when one finger slips under the waistband of my boxers.

"Waking up to Miller Caswell in my bed? I kind of like the idea of this," Gwen says with the most gravely voice that shoots right to my cock.

"Y-you and me both," I stutter.

Her hand continues its journey further down until she starts to lazily stroke me. I pull her face to mine to kiss her deeply, ignoring any self doubt because as long as this woman wants me, I'm here.

"You know, normally I just take care of myself in the morning," Gwen whispers. "Sometimes I use my fingers, sometimes one of the toys I have in that nightstand there..."

"Fuck me," I sigh.

"You'd like that, huh, Miller, baby?" That sinfully playful voice in my ear will be the death of me.

She slides precum along my shaft and picks up her pace. The grip I tighten on her ass right now could very well leave a mark. The thought of that drives me insane.

"Oh my God," I groan.

Gwen continues to stroke me, and I think about how I've never had a better morning in my entire life.

One of our phones start to vibrate, rattling on the nightstand that apparently contains *toys* of Gwen's–toys I'm going to need her to show and tell with the class pretty fucking soon now that she's mentioned it. The class is me.

I feel the loss of Gwen's touch immediately. I almost whine like a toddler, but then see her reaching for my phone.

"I just want to make sure it's not P," she says.

Shoot me dead. This woman can have me worked all the fucking way up one minute, and the next be prioritizing my kid without a second thought.

"This bitch." Gwen slides her finger across the screen to answer the call, and I know the only person this could be even before hearing her voice on the other end. "Someone or something better be on fucking fire, Margot Dorothea."

The maniacal laugh that comes through the speaker ruins any chance of finishing what Gwen started.

"Payback, my love," Margot finally says. "Anyway, Happy Thanksgiving. Wanted to check in and see how you're doing. Sounds like you're good. My mom already texted Miller, but pancakes are hot if you guys want 'em. Sawyer and I are about to head over. Beth's already started on the turkey."

"You're evil. You know that?" Gwen responds.

"Yeah, yeah, whatever. Get your ass to the riverside. Or don't!" The call ends.

"I feel like that could have been a text," I exhale.

"It could have been. But then it wouldn't have been fun for her," Gwen tells me. She tosses the phone on the nightstand and throws herself back into the mattress, grabbing the comforter to pull over her face.

"I don't think I understand female friendships," I admit.

Gwen throws the comforter back down, sits up against the headboard, and runs her hands through her hair. "Eh, you don't have to. I cockblocked her. She cockblocks me. It's all love." She shrugs her shoulders, and I sit up next to her.

"Good morning, by the way." I lean over to kiss her again. I don't think I'll ever get sick of kissing her.

"Morning," she says with a sleepy smile. "I don't know about you, but I slept like the dead."

"I can honestly say it was the best night of sleep of my life," I tell her.

"I know this is a big deal, and I'm cool with whatever you decide, however you want to handle this, but you're welcome to stay here whenever. Penelope, too, of course. I have three empty bedrooms waiting for someone to use them. And it doesn't have to be right now! Or ever! But I like you, and I like this and—"

I shouldn't take this much joy in seeing Gwen completely

flustered like this, but I do. It's nice to know I'm not the only one here struggling to keep my cool all of the time.

"Gwennie girl, hold on," I stop her and open my arms until she shuffles back into them. "I'd love that. And Penelope would, too. I know it's a big deal. But it's a conversation we need to have. Do I know what that kind of conversation looks like or how I'm supposed to handle things? No. Not even a little bit. But if there was any reason to figure it out, it'd be you."

"Me," she says to herself.

"You're worth the biggest of deals, Gwen."

"Oh." Gwen keeps her focus down, so I can't read her face, and I start to worry I said the wrong thing. "Well, let's uh, let's start with pancakes. Then we have to get through Thanksgiving dinner and then, yeah. Let's…let's figure this out. Together." She toys with the ring on my pinky and looks up at me.

Her eyes show nerves that I know match mine, but there's joy there, too. She doesn't need to voice it, but it's the joy in tackling something with someone. I know, because I feel it, too.

"Yes, ma'am," I answer before my lips find hers.

CHAPTER 24: GWEN - CAN'T BE HATEFUL, GOTTA BE GRATEFUL

My body is humming with so much energy I don't even know what to do with it.

The dinner table is set, and decorated perfectly, I might add. The appetizers I was in charge of are lined along the counter to start us all off. The charcuterie board I made that's big enough to probably feed two or three parties worth of people has cheese shaped like pumpkins and salami roses, everyone's favorite.

I scattered fake fall leaves along the three tables I pushed together to fit everyone in proper fashion. There's a burnt orange linen napkin folded into a boat (because it's the only shape I had time to watch a tutorial on the other night) placed on top of each plate. And the deep crimson tablecloth has tiny turkeys along the border, because I knew Penelope would lose her shit for something cute and silly like that.

Speaking of Penelope, her place setting is extra special. While everyone else also has little name cards I made for them, hers includes a bundle of double sided crayons and holiday themed coloring pages and mazes. I have her sitting right in between me and Miller. No "kids table" bullshit. We're all one big family today, the way it should be.

This is the calm before the storm, when I stand by myself in silence in the middle of what I've created and quadruple check that it's ready to rock and roll.

I love hosting. I love that every little detail comes together at the last second after being scattered to the wind to the point where you think there's no possible way it'll all work. It's special to see it actually happen after spending countless hours worried it'll be too over the top or worse, already done and boring, that the effort and energy will all be for nothing. But then you take a moment to feel the magic settling. You know at any second, the doors will open, and you'll be greeting familiar faces, giving them the chance to experience something worthwhile.

This is the feeling that keeps me coming back to unlock the doors and open Red's, even on the days when I feel like I made too many mistakes somewhere along the way, an error or two that led me to owning and operating a business that I don't feel my soul beating through as much anymore.

I bite my bottom lip, nervous at the thought of letting that kind of dark secret out. I don't even want to begin to think what people would say if they knew I cared less and less about being everyone's favorite cafe owner each passing day.

Yeah, let's forget about that right now. Lipstick. I forgot lipstick. I find my purse in my back office and stand in front of the full length mirror I have attached to the back of the door.

Our lord and savior Miss Swift, only uses Pat Mcgrath, therefore, big same. I line my lips and fill in the rest with Elson 4 and rub them together until it looks just right. I also channeled my inner Waldorf for outfit inspiration today, and I feel Queen B level confident. It is Thanksgiving, after all. It's the most sacred holiday in the world of Upper East Siders, which I am not, but damn it, I can pretend.

After breakfast at the riverside, I split off from everyone to prepare myself and the cafe. I do my due diligence as a daughter and video called my parents to wish them a Happy Thanksgiving at sea. I blow out my hair and pin half of it back, securing it with a bow. My favorite cream sweater that falls perfectly off one shoulder slouches and sits right on top of the corduroy tan mini skirt I paired it with. Suede booties that match the skirt hit my ankles. Tying everything together are my dangly autumn leaf earrings, a gift from Daisy on my eighteenth birthday.

I hear a key enter the—repaired thanks to Miller and John—lock from the other side of the back door and a tiny voice talking a mile a minute along with it. I smile to myself as I pick up the end of the conversation.

"...But *why* do they have two different names? They're the same thing! Circles and sweets! It makes no sense, Daddy!"

"Penelope, honey, my little love," Miller says with a voice that tells me this isn't the first time this topic has come up. I lean against the doorway to my office and watch them both walk in. "Some things don't make sense. There are pies, and there are cakes. Today we're having pie."

"Dumb," Penelope mumbles. Her entire demeanor changes when she spots me. "Gwen!" she shrieks, diving into my arms.

"Hey cutie girl, what's the drama with pie?" I ask with a laugh and a look at Miller silently telling him to not correct her with that silly, formal *Miss* at the beginning. I like being her Gwen. His Gwen. Their Gwen. Just Gwen.

She pulls away from me with a very serious look on her face that forces me to match mine to hers. "I think pie and cake are the same thing. Daddy says I'm wrong."

"Well..." I pause, thinking of how to word this without making things worse. It's important to fuel children's curiosities and questions, and the second you put up a roadblock, intentional or not, shit goes south. "You're not *wrong*. You just...need new information!" I tell Penelope excitedly.

Miller's face is one of pained confusion. Penelope has her head tilted to almost a right angle.

"Listen, I order goodies and sweets for the cafe all the time, right?" I wait for P's acknowledgement to continue. "Okay, cool. So, the place I order everything from has everything set up into little sections. Bagels, muffins, croissants, pies, cakes…make sense?"

P nods again, and I keep going, hoping I'm helping and not hurting. "Funny enough, I had a similar question to yours. I thought *what makes a pie a pie and what makes a cake a cake?* And guess what I found out?"

Penelope looks to the floor and shuffles her little pink flats. "I dunno."

"All a pie needs to be a 'pie' instead of a 'cake' is a pastry crust with a filling. Could be sweet like the apple pie over in your daddy's hands there, or it could be savory, like a chicken pot pie."

"But what about cake?" she asks exasperatedly.

"Cake is like pie's party sister. It's sweet, *always.* It can be any flavor, so long as it's sugary goodness."

Penelope mulls over my explanation, and Miller watches on nervously.

"That…that makes so much sense! Thanks, Gwen!" P's arms wrap around my neck again with a strong hug, but before I know it, she releases me and dashes off into the cafe.

"How did you just do that?" Miller asks, placing the box of pie on the counter, shaking his head, and walking the few steps towards me. "How did you break that down so easily for her?" He doesn't wait for my answer, instead pulling me into him to kiss me.

When we part, I pick our conversation right back up. "Learning every little thing about life is hard. Us adults forget how heavy it felt because we're so far past those early days. Sometimes we just gotta back it up and slow it down for them."

I won't lie, knowing I just absolutely fucking crushed that is puffing up my ego.

Miller takes a step back, holding my hand up so I twirl around his finger. He's looking at me like *I'm* a pie or a cake. "You look gorgeous, by the way. Stunning, beautiful, all of the adjectives." He pulls me back into him, and I rest my hands on his chest.

The flustered, sincere compliments inflate me even more.

"You're not looking too bad yourself, Mr. Caswell." I smooth out the collar of his maroon button up. It has small cream colored foxes all over it, paired with slim fit khakis and low top shoes. His mess of curls is classic Miller.

"Oof, you wanna say that again?" he whispers in my ear.

"Fishing for compliments?" I whisper back.

"No, I just really like hearing you say my name."

I peck his freshly blushed cheek before taking his hand to walk out front together. "Am I allowed to say I missed you, *Miller Caswell*? Is that stage five clinger weird?"

"Nope." Miller's fingers intertwine with mine. "I mean, maybe it is. But I'm clinging right back. Missed you too. When's everyone else showing up? Are we the first ones here?"

"You live upstairs. Are you really surprised? They'll be here soon. I just finished all of the set up. Now all that's left to do is feast."

Just as I finish my sentence, I see Margot and Sawyer walking past the front windows, hand in hand. Guests are arriving, and it's showtime.

* * *

"I CAN'T POSSIBLY EAT another bite!" I drop my fork and dramatically push my plate away.

"Tell me you didn't forget to leave room for dessert. I brought pie!" Miller says on my right in mock shock.

I make quick work of scooping my fork back up. "Change of plans. It's pie o'clock."

This couldn't be going any better. The food has been fantastic, drinks are flowing, and the company is some of the best I've ever had. I'll admit, even though I wasn't surprised my parents bailed on the holidays *again*, I was still hurting. It's normal to crave a sense of family around a time like this, and Mom and Dad aren't the best at filling that void.

It's not their fault.

Okay, it is a little bit, but I'm trying not to think about it.

Instead, I look around the table at these beautiful people like I have all night. Beth had us go around and each say what we were thankful for before diving into our overflowing plates. It was so touching to hear how each of us helped one another in some way over the course of this last year that led to gratefulness being expressed right here, right now.

Maybe it's the red wine making me extra emotional. I'm more than certain it's not though.

I'm the most content cat. All I need to make things perfect is Miller's lap to curl up on with a cozy blanket wrapped around us and a movie to laugh along to. It's a very specific daydream I could get lost in right now as the conversations of the people I love most chatter around me.

A knock at the front door causes me to jump. I turn my head to see Daisy standing outside with an oversized flannel wrapped around her, swiping mascara from under her eyes, trying to angle herself in a direction so that no one inside can see. I scoot my chair back to rush over and unlock the door.

If there is one thing consistent and true about Daisy Stiles— well two things actually. She does not lie, and she does not cry.

Everyone's eyes follow me as I pass, so when I swing the door open, I lower my voice, "Daze, what's wrong?"

Before she can answer, it's the voice from behind me that has my eyes bulging out of my head. "What happened?" Gus barks.

"Nothing, you big fucking clod," Daisy snaps, swapping tears for rage.

"Shut the hell up and tell me why you're out here crying in the fucking street, Stiles," Gus gives it to her right back. Like they always do.

"That doesn't even make sense. Do you hear yourself? Are you that dumb?"

Gus opens his mouth to probably throw another foul-mouthed retort, but I cut him off before he can.

"Eeeeeenough." I put my hands up in between my two sparring friends. "Daze, come inside. We'll talk later. We're about to have dessert. The both of you better keep your mouths and hands to yourselves. I'm not breaking up another fight. Got it?"

They both nod in understanding. "Nope, that's not working for me. I want to hear it. Say *Yes, Red. We would never disrespect you, Red.*"

I haven't called myself Red in weeks. It's funny how weird it feels to say now when just a short bit ago, that's all I felt like I knew.

Daisy and Gus both grumble their acknowledgements and find their way to everyone else inside. Beth has already pulled up a chair for Daisy...a chair that also happens to be seated right next to Gus. I look up to the ceiling in silent prayer.

To my surprise, Margot has already started getting the post-meal coffee ready, pulling out mugs, creamers, and sugar. I hear the drip of a fresh pot brewing. Miller is busy placing the pie and other baked goods I had set aside on the table.

Miller makes eye contact with me, and I feel fuzzy all over when he places a freshly poured glass of wine at my place setting.

"Sit," he gently commands. "You handled all this, so we got the rest, okay? Time to relax." He kisses the top of my head as he passes by, and I hide behind my glass to keep the blush creeping up my neck to myself.

I'm not used to others taking care of me like this.

"Shit. Fuck. Miller, you're making me look bad!" Sawyer's chair scrapes against the flooring as he gets up to meet Margot behind the counter. He starts collecting mugs by the handles in one hand and grabbing the creamer carafe from Margot with the other.

"Language, my boy," Beth teases. Penelope is now situated on Beth's lap, drawing out their next game of tic tac toe on the blank back of one of the coloring pages.

"Oh yeah, because Beth Rivers is the epitome of on the straight and narrow when it comes to swearing," Gus jokes.

"I'm surprised you even know the word epitome." I roll my eyes at Daisy, knowing she couldn't help herself.

"And I'm not surprised you already broke your promise to Red to watch your fucking mouth." Gus's joking tone has left the building.

"What's that supposed to mean?"

"You're untrustworthy. Not loyal. A snake in the weeds."

Well, the feeling of gratefulness and a sense of familial bonding has now officially skedaddled.

"Of course *you* wouldn't bite the hand that feeds you."

God, this is ugly, and it needs to stop immediately. But as fast as their mouths are moving, the rest of everything feels like it's going in slow motion.

"Why are you even fucking here, Daisy? I can't imagine you'd pick roughing it with a bunch of misfits like us when you have some fancy ass meal to attend with your perfect ass family. Or did they kick you out? That why you were bawling your eyes out out there?"

"Shut *up*," Daisy hisses. New tears well on her water line.

"Oh? Only you get to show up and be nasty? Can't take what you dish out?"

"Gus," I whisper. That's all I can manage right now. We all normally stop things before they get this bad, but it seems as though we're letting it play out. This is never going to end well.

"No, I just don't want to hear the opinion of some nobody asshole." Daisy tries to keep her voice steady, but I hear the wobble.

"Go fucking cry some more about it."

"I have had it!" Melanie yells, slamming her fists down on the table. The mom voice is in full effect and causes everyone to pause. "You both should be deeply embarrassed by your behavior. And I mean *deeply*. How can two people individually be so incredible and amazing but when put in the same freaking vicinity act like feral toddlers? Grow the hell up or get out."

Gus stands, towering over everything and everyone. He takes a deep breath and looks at Melanie, then at Daisy. "I'm sorry." It's a blanket statement to everyone, not just Daisy, but it's an apology nonetheless. He storms off to the back without another word.

Sawyer moves to follow, but Gus holds a hand up along the way without looking back. "Don't bother. Need a minute."

"Shit," Daisy mutters. She starts to stand and then thinks better of it. She clears her throat and addresses everyone the same way Gus did. "I'm sorry, too. I was wrong to show up here like this."

"You're always welcome here, Daze. We just all need to be able to coexist." I lean over and pat her thigh.

We salvage the rest of the night, Gus returning after a couple minutes. He smartly picks the seat on the other side of the table next to Melanie. We dish out the dessert, and I send everyone home with to-go containers holding a little bit of everything.

Miller puts Penelope to bed and meets me back down in the cafe afterwards to help me finish cleaning up. Thankfully, he gets a little distracted along the way. He pins me up against the wall and kisses me senseless a few times before watching me drive off towards my house.

I didn't give him the chance to ask me to stay. There are conversations to be had. If we have any shot of making this work, we have to do things the right way. For Penelope. For Miller. For me. For us.

CHAPTER 25: MILLER - PUT A RING ON IT

That's a very vague text. I shoot Sawyer a reply, letting him know I can stop over before I snag P from school in a little bit. He thumbs ups my message without further explanation.

Huh. Weird.

I pocket my phone and continue cleaning up my work inbox. I set up in one of the back booths at the cafe, stealing glances and quick touches from the pretty girl running the show behind the counter.

Beginning of December is busy season at the bank, with everyone withdrawing new bills for gifts and depositing money to spend. The mass influx of customers causes our systems to sometimes go haywire. It's a lot of work for the IT department as a whole.

But I'm just thankful I'm not one of the tellers. I feel for them, I really do. They're out there on the front lines fighting off

Karens and Debbie Downers, trying to keep spirits high, while all I have to do is click away until the tech fixes its shit.

My eyes find Gwen chatting it up with a customer while Chris gets to work on their order. As…odd as that kid is, he's not a bad addition to the environment here at Red's.

Gwen's wearing this sweater dress that hugs every inch of her, and I've thought no less than ten times about stripping it off of her. It hits right below her knees, and she's got those cute as fuck ankle boots click clacking around.

She winks at me without missing a beat of her conversation, and I feel like the luckiest nerd in the whole Goddamn world.

Have we put a title on things? Nope. Have I worked up the courage to have a conversation with my daughter about the future of the Caswell family going from two to three? Also no. And I'm ashamed of that.

But the last couple weeks have been filled with unspoken glimpses into everything that's to come. What's funny is that beside the fact that there's a lot more kissing and touching when P isn't in the room, not much else has changed with our dynamic. We've been in each other's orbits comfortably for months.

I'm embracing the idea of natural change. Turning over a new leaf, or whatever.

Gwen slides into the booth across from me, pushing a fresh cup of coffee onto my side. She does this every hour, on the hour. I'm pretty sure there's such a thing as caffeine overconsumption but, I'm not turning down a thing from this woman.

"Have I told you how much I don't want to go to this thing tonight?" Gwen asks. Her forehead hits the table.

"Yeah, but you can tell me again. I don't mind." I don't. I'd listen to her read the owner's manual to a kitchen appliance.

"I wish I could just tell them no."

"I mean…" I start.

She holds up a hand. "Don't say it."

"No. Sorry, beautiful. You need to hear this. You can, and you should say no. Merrymount's Blueberry Festival Committee will survive you bowing out this year, or permanently, if it would make you happy."

She lifts her head slightly, letting only her chin now rest on the table. She has the most adorable pout on her face. "It would make me happy. But then I'd think about how many people I'd be letting down. That would make me sad. It's a sick cycle."

I reach out until she offers me her hand, and I take it in mine. "Gwendolyn, you're letting yourself down by pulling yourself in every direction for everyone else. Come on, tell me one thing you want to do just for yourself."

Her response practically falls out of her mouth. "I want you to fuck me."

How do you say *asdfghjkl* out loud? Because that's what my brain just did. I picked the wrong time to take a sip of my coffee because it takes everything in me to not accidentally spit it right in Gwen's face.

"I'm sorry!" She laughs as she pulls the mug out of my hand to move it away from me. "It was the first thing that came to mind! I'm not pressuring you, I swear!"

I dab my mouth with the napkin and slide my hand down my face. "Oh God, please don't be sorry. That's just embarrassing."

"Miller, there is nothing to be embarrassed about. I'm fine with taking things slow."

That's the thing, I'm not, not anymore. But I also don't want the first time I'm inside her to have to be hushed behind closed doors, or ending with having to say goodbye almost immediately afterwards. Piecing sex into a lifestyle that went so long without it is complicated as hell.

I've been meaning to talk to Margot about a sleepover with Penelope. I've been meaning to tell Gwen how I feel, more than just telling her I have a crush on her. I've been meaning to do a lot of things, and apparently as smooth as things feel like they're sailing, I'm still falling short. Like always.

My dad's rants about how much of a disappointment I am ring in my head, and I actively work to tune it all out. I need to figure my shit out.

I grab her hand again. "Believe me, I'm right there with you. I just want it to be right."

"No, I get it. I mean it, I have no timeline. I'm perfectly content with the way things are."

"No you're not, don't do that. Don't treat me like everyone else, placating me to keep me happy."

"That's not fair, that's not what this is—"

"I'm asking Margot and Sawyer to take Penelope for the night this weekend." Like I said, I've been meaning to ask. I'm going to see Sawyer in a little bit anyway for whatever the hell he wants to talk about. It all works out.

Gwen flusters, but recovers quickly. "Well, that's great! She'll love time with her aunt and uncle. I think that's a great idea."

"Mhm," I hum. "So, that's handled. Now, quit the committee."

"I can't just quit—"

"You can. You should. And you will." I try to leave little room for argument.

"Don't use your daddy voice on me," Gwen teases.

"Why?" I lean in, lowering my voice. "Is it working?"

She slumps back in the booth and grumbles, avoiding eye contact. "Maybe…"

"I'm not saying completely change your ways. You're Gwendolyn Bozelli. You can still help out with the festival. It's town tradition and all that, I get it. But stepping away from this whole committee thing gives you the chance to help when you *want* to, not all of the time just because you *have* to."

Do I selfishly want more time with her? Yeah, no shit. But this whole volunteer and work herself to death thing has got to stop at some point for her own well being.

I watch Gwen mull it over. I can see the gears in that pretty head of hers turning. She's weighing her options and her feelings with any outcome. My girl's a planner, and when I see the defeated shake of her head and smirk, I know I won this battle.

It takes everything in me to not fist pump right now.

"Judy is going to be so pissed." She chuckles.

"You employ her precious grandson and host her inappropriate book club. She'll live. Plus, think of all the extra time you'll get to spend with your favorite person now."

"You're so right. Penelope and I are going to have a *blast*," she teases.

"I walked into that one." I sigh. "I gotta go meet Sawyer. He wants to talk to me about something." I start to collect my belongings that have scattered across the table.

Gwen's jaw practically falls off. "About what? Is everything okay? Oh my God, do you think Margot's pregnant?" She whispers the last question, lifting her ass off the bench to lean into me.

"What?" I ask, shocked. "No. I think you'd be the one to know that first." I stand, slinging my laptop's backpack over one shoulder. I hold out my hand for Gwen to take hold of before standing. I kiss her, not caring who sees.

"You have a point," she says into my mouth. "Well, keep me posted. I'm gonna go rip the bandaid off with Jude, then probably catch up on some paperwork."

"You got any plans tonight?" I joke.

She rolls her eyes, but drops the act when she plants another fat kiss on me. Yeah, I'll be seeing her later.

* * *

I PULL up to Rivers River and park my car next to Sawyer's Jeep. It doesn't take me long to find him, seeing as he's pacing the front porch of the main cabin.

This whole place is sick. I plan to spend a lot more time here next summer with P. The fact that Beth and her husband created this whole business and life from nothing is just fucking incredible. The security of being able to pass down something so solid and real is inspiring.

"Hey!" I call out.

Sawyer stops and quickly drops the hand he had rubbing the back of his neck. "Miller! You came!"

"Uh, you did text me, right? Like, you meant today?" Jeez, I wasn't nervous before, but with the way he's acting and Gwen's reaction to me just mentioning this whole thing, I'm at least a little worried now.

Sawyer shakes his head. "Yeah, bud. Sorry, I did. I'm just—Do you want a beer?" He gestures inside.

"Normally I would." I'm lying, I hardly drink. "But I've gotta get Penelope from school."

"Shit. Yeah. I knew that. Uh, you wanna take a walk with me?" He steps off the porch and starts heading towards one of the trails marked with a green arrow without confirmation that I plan on following him. There hasn't been any early snowfall this year so while it's cold as shit, I guess everything is still open to use.

Glad that I'm wearing my leather jacket, I jog a little to catch up. "Alright, tell me what's going on."

"Nothing's going on," Sawyer sputters.

"Dude, why the hell am I here?!" I don't mean to yell, but a group of birds that were perched in a tree scatter to the winds.

Sawyer twists around to face me. "I'm asking Margot to marry me!"

Woah.

"Holy shit," I say. I stop and stare out at the river. The edge is littered with fallen leaves, bare branches sticking up this way and that. A shiver goes down my back at even the thought of getting near that freezing water.

"Yeah," Sawyer breathes. He stands beside me, taking in the same view. "I know it's crazy, and I know it's fast, but she's it for me. So, I thought, why wait?" When I turn and see the smile on his face and the look in his eyes, I know it would be hard for even the world's biggest cynic to muster up an argument.

I know I don't *know* Sawyer and haven't been around a long time, but the change in him since Margot came crashing into his life is obvious. Everyone sees it. Everyone comments on it. It was like she brought him back to life. I'm so unbelievably happy for them, and I feel lucky to get to watch it all play out. But—

"I don't want you to take this the wrong way. This is awesome. But, uh, what'd you need me for?"

If I thought it was impossible for Sawyer to look even more like he was going to puke, I would have been wrong. This is a guy who is always sure of himself, the one making the decisions, and calling the shots. He looks beyond lost right now.

He finally shrugs his shoulders. "You're...fuck, I don't know how to say this." He straightens himself out. "Look, I didn't ask you to come here to ask for your permission. On account of the fact that I'm sure Margot would slap me upside the head if she knew I was asking anyone else besides her if it was okay to propose. But you're her brother, and it's important to me. So, I'm asking her to marry me, and I hope I have your blessing."

"Are you kidding?" I laugh. "Fuck yeah, you have my blessing, Sawyer," I clap him on the shoulder, "I'm new to all of this–having family, friends, people who look out for each other with no strings attached. I feel so lucky every day that Penelope and I get to be included. Please marry my sister."

There are a lot of emotions coming to the surface right now, and crying in front of my soon-to-be brother-in-law is not something I'm on board with. I'm touched, I'm honored. To know that Sawyer thinks so highly of me means a lot. But I can't look like a fucking dweeb in front of him.

Sawyer's sigh of relief could probably be heard from the next town over. "Dude...thanks. I've been stressing about this for weeks."

"Weeks?" I ask, surprised. Not surprised he's been planning this for some time now, I mean, that makes sense with needing to coordinate a ring and all of that. But why the hell would he need to work up the courage to talk to me?

"Yeah. Truthfully, I would have gotten down on one knee before the summer ended. But there was a lot going on with… Well, you know what was going on. And then I got in my head about what you or Melanie would say. She's ecstatic, by the way." Sawyer's grin reaches ear to ear. "Talked to her while she was here for Thanksgiving. But you're a dad. You're responsible and serious. I didn't want you thinking…I dunno."

"I would have been on board from the jump. I am. No question about it."

Sawyer pulls me in for one of those movie style bro hugs where he claps me so hard on the back, I think my fucking spine cracks. "Brothers!" he yells.

Thankful as hell that I don't have to continue further into the woods, we head back to the cabin. Gus meets us outside while Sawyer shows me his mother's ring he's proposing with. I don't know anything about jewelry aside from the plastic stuff Penelope picks out and the ring I wear for her, but this is really nice. It's a simple gold band with one oval shaped diamond. Margot's going to love it.

Sawyer fills me in on the plan, it's all going down Christmas Eve. I ask if they have plans this weekend, and when I tell him why I'm asking, he has Margot on the phone in seconds. Her squeals of delight loud and clear.

Damn, what a day.

CHAPTER 26: GWEN - PSPSPSPS

I'm standing in a crowd of moms and dads—some of whom I went to school with—holding up this flimsy piece of bright pink construction paper with *Penelope Caswell - Grade 1* printed across it.

I really need to laminate this thing for Miller so it doesn't disintegrate into shreds. I should have brought a beanie or something because it's cold as shit. The way everyone is waving these namecards around feels very reminiscent of those scenes you see of the guys on Wall Street in New York City.

All these thoughts exist to distract me from the fact that I feel like a complete and utter imposter.

But Miller, sweet Miller, who tries so hard every single day to ask nothing of me because he sees how everyone else piles it on without a second thought, got caught up with a big bank-wide outage of some sort and asked me to pick P up from school.

So, here I am. Ready to throw elbows up to get to the front of this crowd to claim Penelope and get us back to the cafe for a girls afternoon. I know as soon as I'm out of this claustrophobic scene, I'll be able to breathe and see clearly again.

Until then, I'm looking around at all of these parents, some familiar faces, some not. I wanted to be a part of this chaos so badly. I dreamed of the moment where I would see my kid's face light up through the glass door when we made eye contact. They'd run out in a sprint to jump into my arms, and we would walk hand in hand to the car as they chatted about their day.

I do realize it was a very detailed and specific dream. Don't judge me, I've had a lot of time on my hands to conjure it up.

A voice breaks through my thoughts. "Red Bozelli, is that you, sweetie?"

I turn to my right and see Holly Montag, my co-captain from cheer…and Katie St. James's very best friend. A decade has gone by, and I still hate her fucking guts.

What can I say? Sometimes I hold a grudge.

She's holding a pink slip of paper identical to one in my hand. She has a son that, now if I do the math, is probably around the same age as P, maybe a year or two older. She parts her way through the sea of people to stand beside me.

"Oh my God, it *is* you! Well, what in the heck are you doing down here at Merrymount El? Did you pick up another babysitting gig?" She asks question after question in the most condescending way, and I weigh my options on the most effective way to bash her face in.

I backburner the plan of physical violence and put on my fakest, happiest facade. I'll do anything to get me out of here faster. "Hey, Holly. Just picking up my…Miller's daughter."

My Miller? Seriously, Gwen?

"Well isn't that just so sweet of you. Gosh, you're exactly what a parent needs, a good helping hand. You're the village we all look for!" Holly places her hand on my shoulder and gives it a squeeze that has me flinching to shake her off.

"Sure," I say with a tight lipped smile. If I stick to one word answers, maybe I'll survive this. And shit, when are they gonna let these kids out?

Holly continues rattling off information I didn't ask for. "I'm waiting for my boy, Brayden. He's in the fourth grade now. The *best* kid. Ugh, I'm so lucky. And I'm sure you've heard—" She stops short. "I mean, of *course* you've heard about Katie's son. Now we get to raise our boys together! B and B, isn't that the cutest?"

"The. Cutest," I say through clenched teeth. Is she this dumb, or is she really trying to rile me up in the front of a fucking elementary school? Aren't we past this level of pettiness? We're almost thirty for crying out loud.

Thankfully the doors open. A flood of kids barrel out searching for their grown-ups, and our conversation mercifully halts. I spot Penelope before she sees me, and when I get to witness her face light the hell up when she finds mine, every bit of negativity from two seconds ago disappears as if it never existed.

"Gwen!" The call-out could be heard around town. My favorite little girl crashes into my waiting arms, and I get smacked in the face by the big white puffball on the top of her hat. "This is the best surprise ever! Ever, ever!" She's jumping up and down, and while I could blame the crisp air for the tears prickling my eyes, we all know that's not why they're there.

"There's my favorite tiny human. Jeez, I thought they'd never let you out. Daddy's caught up with work so he thought it'd be okay if I scooped you. What's up? How was the day?" I pull her backpack off to carry it for her. The thing is practically bigger than she is. She grabs my hand without a second thought, and we walk along the sidewalk together to get to my car.

"It was good. We had a spelling test…" Her voice trails off as she looks to the side. Right where bitchass Holly and her twerp son are standing.

"Hey." I bump Penelope. "Do you know that kid?"

"Uh, sort of." She's being quiet. It's very un-Penelope-like.

I stop us both and squat down to her level. Her cheeks and the tip of her nose are the cutest shade of pink from the cold. "Spill, now."

She sighs. "Brayden." The amount of disdain in that one word out of her tiny body holds a lot of weight. *Don't worry, girlie. I feel the same way about his mom.*

"And what did Brayden do?" I coax.

"Everything. He *sucks*." She tugs at my arm to keep moving. I follow, but I'm not dropping this.

"Did he touch you, Penelope?"

"No. He just…sometimes he says mean stuff. Actually, he always says mean stuff. Daddy doesn't let me ride the bus anymore because of him."

Realization dawns on me. Miller told me about this fucking punk. He bullied Penelope. Oh, I am going to have *words* with Holly—

I try to pivot to circle around back to Holly and her turd-faced kid, but P keeps her feet planted on the ground and her hand locked in mine. "Can we just go?"

"Penelope. I can't *not* say something. You're my girl, you know that, right?"

"Please," she pleads. I immediately fold. I don't want to make things harder for her, but shit, I was ready to rip an eight-year-old apart.

I again redirect us, and we continue our short journey to my car. "Fine. The discussion is not over though, got it?"

She nuzzles into my side, and I scoop her up. "You sound like Daddy when you get bossy like that," P tells me.

"Yeah, well. Sometimes it's needed."

"Sometimes it feels like you're my mom," she says it offhand-edly, like it's an insignificant statement that didn't just alter the course of the rest of my life. I must stay quiet for too long because then she adds, "Is that weird?"

"No, P. Not at all. That means a lot to me."

"Because you want to be a mom, right?"

I nod, not trusting my ability to find the right words without Miller here as backup. "That memory of yours is in tip top shape, girlie. Come on, in you go." I open the door to the back seat and plop her into her carseat.

"Would you want to be my mom?" Okay, guess this conversation is not one I'm going to breeze over.

"I want…" This feels like something I need to talk to Miller about. Not because my answer is no. Not because I don't see her as the daughter I always dreamed of, but because she is. Nothing would compare to being honored with the title of Penelope's mom. But I don't know my place here. I could just be the village Holly mentioned.

God, I hate her.

Penelope waits eagerly for my response, and I instantly feel guilty for keeping her hanging. "I would want that very much, P. It's one of those big things we have to talk to Daddy about though, okay?"

"Ugh, complica-cated."

"You know what's not complicated though?" I offer.

She eyes me skeptically.

"How much I love you. I mean it. Call me Red, Gwen, Mom. I don't care. It doesn't change how I feel about you." I bop her nose, and she bops mine back with a giggle.

After quadruple checking the straps are secure, I blast the heat and drive us back in the direction of the cafe. We drop the family dynamic and Brayden topics, and I listen to Penelope chat about the ins and outs of first grade.

It was pizza day at lunch (that's her favorite). She crushed her spelling test (I'm not even a little bit surprised). At recess she played some weird version of tag I've never heard of (but Penelope assured me it's the coolest thing ever).

Everything is a big deal, and I love to hear about every single second of it.

I pull into my usual spot in the back of the cafe and practically smack my head on the roof of the car when Penelope screams.

"What's wrong?!" I yell, whipping around to do…well, I don't know what I need to do. But I'll do it.

"There's something moving! Right there!" Penelope points to the dumpster, unclicking her carseat to free herself.

And sure enough, there's a little black and white puffball pilfering through the cardboard boxes that are stacked against the trash.

"I think it's a raccoon or a skunk, babe. We can't get too—"

Penelope's out of the car, sprinting to whatever this feral animal is before I have the chance to finish my sentence. Fucking shit, this kid cannot catch a case of rabies on my watch. I'm fucked. I am so fucked.

"Penelope Caswell! *Stop!*" I scream across the alley, while trying to extricate myself from the driver's seat. To P's credit, she stops to stand as still as a statue the second I shout, mere feet from the furry creature. She looks at me with practiced doe eyes. God damn it, she's as smart as she is adorable.

I'm ready to read her the riot act about car and animal safety when the smallest of meows come from the little puff's mouth.

"Wait…Is that—is it a cat?" I move closer to inspect the situation, holding Penelope back by the shoulders.

The situation in question waddles its little fluffy body towards us, and I confirm, it is indeed the tiniest little kitten. "Ohhhhhmygawd," I squeal, squatting to capture the baby. I pick it up and bring it close to my chest, completely disregarding the possibility of getting ringworm. It would be worth it for this sweet angel.

"O-M-G, it's a kitten! Gwen, it's a baby kitten!" Penelope jumps up and down beside me, trying to pull at my arm. I bend down to her level so we both can get a closer look.

This teensy thing is young, probably too young to be away from its mama, and my heart cracks at the thought. There's no collar. I haven't a single clue on how to tell whether it's a boy or a girl, but it has the poofiest black fur sticking up every which way, except its little paws are white like—

"He's wearing little slippers!" Penelope cries out. Yep, just like that.

"He is, isn't he?" I coo as I snuggle the kitten. "Wait, we don't know if he really is a he. What made you say that?"

"I dunno." P shrugs. "Just a guess."

"Hmm, well, what the heck do we do with a kitten?"

I keep Penelope close to me as we walk up and down the alley, peering into any small nook and cranny looking for this baby's mom or the rest of its litter with no success.

I have no issue with a kitty cat trotting through the cafe, but without the proper licenses, the Department of Public Health does. I opt to use the spare key for the apartment and guide us all up the stairs.

Penelope keeps a constant stream of facts and questions about cats going to fill any chance of silence. I love listening to her brain pick things apart.

Something tells me Miller isn't going to be thrilled with the prospect of a temporary roommate in the form of a feline, but too bad, so sad for him. I'm certainly not throwing this baby back out on the streets.

I find a small bowl to fill with water and place it down on the floor in the bathroom, plopping the kitten in front of it so it knows where to find the water when it needs it.

I need to stop calling it an it. That's rude.

"We're just gonna keep him in here for now." I quickly scrub my hands and arms and then shut the bathroom door behind us after we leave. "We have to head to the store for kitty litter and some food, okay? At least until we know what to do with him," I tell Penelope.

"What do you mean? We're keeping him! He's our baby now!" she declares.

"You do remember you have a dad who has told you no every single time you've asked for a kitten?" I raise an eyebrow at her.

"That was before you. Daddy never wants to say no to you. Plus, the kitten found us."

Kind of hard to argue with that logic.

I blow out a breath and bring Penelope into my side. "Alright, we'll cross that bridge later. First, The Store. Let's go."

* * *

"No way."

"Fix the attitude before you walk through that door and disappoint her," I tell Miller with a hushed voice at the top landing of the staircase. The door is closed, and I'm giving Miller a quick heads-up about what he's walking into.

"Gwen, you texted me and told me you're harboring a fugitive cat in my apartment. I'm telling you it's getting booted."

"He's just a baby! He shouldn't even be without his mom yet. We practically saved his life. We have to give him a home."

Am I laying it on a little thick? Sure. But in the past two hours, Penelope and I have bonded with this kitten. He has a name and a family with us, and I'm not letting grumpy Miller Caswell burst our bubble of love and fun.

"Him, huh?"

I shrug my shoulders. "P thinks it's a boy. We won't know for sure until his vet appointment tomorrow but..."

"You already booked a vet appointment?" he asks. Miller steps into my space and gently tucks a loose strand of my hair behind my ear.

I scoff. "Of course I did. He needs to be checked out. He needs vaccines and to be chipped in case he ever gets lost again. And we do actually need to confirm he's a *he*."

Miller presses his forehead into mine. He's melting in front of me, and I'm fucking living for it. "And does *he* have a name?"

"Of course, what kind of monster do you think I am? But I'll let Penelope tell you." I sneak a kiss. "She loves him so much already. I knew there was no way you could say no."

He grumbles something inaudible into my mouth, but I get the feeling that he's conceding. He steals another kiss. "I don't remember saying yes."

"But you're going to, right?"

"One condition," he states.

"Always with the conditions to our deals, Miller. Aren't we past this?" I let one finger trail down his chest slowly. His breath hitches, but he doesn't back down. "Fine, lay it on me," I say.

"You're staying tonight. I'll take the couch, and you can have my bed. But I've done the first night with a newborn before, I'm not doing it alone again. Even if it is for some furry four legged *thing*."

He's teasing, but there's real and raw honesty there. I don't want to make his life harder, only brighter. I nod my head over and over, the smile growing across my face. I don't think he means for this to feel like a test, but I think the universe does. I'm in this. I'm *so* in this. With him. With *them*.

Miller pulls me back into him by the nape of my neck, and I sigh with contentment when he kisses me until I'm breathless. It's not long, maybe a minute, but I let myself get lost in him. When we pull apart I reach behind me, opening the door into the living room.

"Daddy!" Penelope exclaims from her spot on the couch. The poof is curled up in a little ball, wrapped in a blanket, sleeping peacefully in her crisscrossed lap as her hand gently pets down his small back. Well, he was until two seconds ago. "This is Ladybug!"

"Ladybug?" Miller questions, side-eyeing me.

"Yes," I declare, ready to back Penelope up five hundred percent on her name choice. Miller kicks off his shoes, drops his work bag, and walks towards the couch. I continue, "Ladybugs are good luck. Plus, we were watching A Bug's Life and the ladybug is a boy."

"Isn't he so cute and perfect, Daddy?"

"Yeah, isn't he, Daddy?" I joke.

Miller pets the kitten behind his ear and looks over his shoulder at me with heat blazing in his eyes. He stands and gives Penelope a kiss on the head. "He's adorable, Penelope. Can't argue with that."

"So we can keep him?!" The amount of hope in this tiny girl's body is enough to make my heart shatter. If I didn't convince him before he walked through that door, there's still no way he would have won this battle.

He sighs and takes Ladybug off of P's lap. Miller holds his tiny body up like Rafiki holds Simba in *The Lion King* and then pulls him back to rest against his chest. "Yeah, P. We're keeping him."

CHAPTER 27: MILLER - CAT DADDY

So, I'm a cat dad now.

I'm embracing it, if only for the unfiltered joy this little furball brings Penelope *and* Gwendolyn.

I've We've survived a full week of litter box training (why can't cats use the toilet or go outside like dogs?), the middle of the night bursts of energy where he tries to dash across my face, and the meowing. Damn, the meowing doesn't stop. He's a chatty little thing.

And yes, he is a he. The vet officially confirmed Mr. Ladybug Caswell for us, and thankfully confirmed he's perfectly healthy and flea-free.

All last week, Penelope didn't want to leave the kitten's (or Gwen's) side for even a minute except for school, so we postponed the Auntie Margot and Uncle Sawyer sleepover until this weekend.

After I declared to Gwen she was staying, I quickly realized I needed to have a conversation with Penelope to get the all clear. I got halfway through bringing up Gwen potentially staying for a sleepover with the newly found Ladybug before P was screeching and sprinting throughout the apartment about it being the best day of her life.

The overnight bag is packed and sitting by the door. P now feels comfortable leaving Ladybug with me and Gwen for a night, because Gwen hasn't left us except to retrieve clothes in a week either. Don't hate that, I can tell you that much.

The me sleeping on the couch, her in the bed thing never worked out. I don't know why I even entertained the idea. If I'm waking up to Gwen Bozelli in my apartment, I'm waking up next to her in my bed. She sleeps with no pants on. Do you know how fucking lucky I am?

Work has been an absolute shit-show, and the extra set of hands helping coordinate drop-offs, pick-ups, and meals has been such a fucking lifesaver. I'm in a branch more than I've ever been in the last five years, and I would be drowning if it wasn't for Gwen. I thank her every night, in more ways than one.

Now that I've tasted her, licked paths all over her body, and made her come undone, I'm an addict. There isn't enough of her. I always want more. The way she wants me back just as much fuels it all, adding fire to an already out of control flame.

Sitting at the kitchen island, I'm trying to keep the focus on this last piece of P's homework while she makes no effort, ignoring the math problem in front of her to dangle one of Ladybug's toys in his face so he swats at it. Gwen's closing down the cafe, and then we're dropping Penelope off at the cottages.

"Penelope, can we try to wrap this up, please?" I tap the pencil on the paper.

"Can't we save it for Sunday night?" she pleads. I hated homework growing up, and I try to keep things positive, so she doesn't have the same negative feelings towards it. Today is a struggle.

"But if we finish now, then we don't have to worry about it at all for the rest of the weekend. Doesn't that sound good?" I offer.

"Not really, no. I don't want to worry about it right *now*."

I'm not above bribery, I'll admit it. "What do I have to give you?"

"Disney."

"Not happening. Yet," I add in quickly. I wish it was. P has been on a roll about going ever since she cracked open Gwen's photo albums. I have it on my list to ask Gwen if she'd be willing to help plan something within the next year if I can. Maybe she'll even come with us.

I can see the gears turning in Penelope's head. She's not finishing this homework until she gets something worth her while now that it was offered, and damn it, I have to respect the hustle.

"Can Gwen stay?" she asks timidly.

I wasn't expecting that. We still haven't talked about anything permanent because I've chickened out and avoided the subject. But my girl is apparently ready to tackle this head on.

"Is that…is that something you'd want?"

"Yeah, duh," Penelope says. Like it's the most obvious thing in the world. "You're funnier when she's here. She likes to play dress up, and she makes better cheesy chicken than you. And I…I saw you kiss her on the lips. That means you like her, right?"

I grab her hand. "I like her a whole lot, Penelope. This is a big kind of deal, though. It's not something we decide on to get you to do your times tables. But, I'm happy you brought it up."

"Does she not like you back? Gabby at school says her mommy doesn't like her daddy so they don't live together anymore."

Yikes. I try to laugh off that interesting fact. "No, babe. I think she does like me back. It's a little different than Gabby's parents. Remember how we talked about how all families don't always look the same?"

She nods, and I continue, "Okay, cool. So sometimes you have a daddy and a mommy, or just a daddy, or just a mommy. Sometimes you live with Grandma or Grandpa, or an aunt and uncle, right? Well, sometimes when you live with just one parent, they meet someone new—"

"Someone like Gwen," Penelope adds.

"Yeah, someone just like Gwen," I tell her. "They get to know each other, and if they're lucky they, uh, they fall in love. And then that someone sort of joins the family."

"So, Gwen would be like my mom?"

Wow, did all of the air in this apartment get sucked out, or fucking what?

"Umm? Uh? I—she—" I stumble and stutter and feel myself flailing with nothing to hold onto. "That's a great question, Penelope. It's something I'd feel better talking about with all three of us sometime soon. Is that an okay answer?"

"Mmm, yeah. That's okay. She kind of said the same thing." She picks her pencil back up and focuses on the remaining multiplication problems in front of her.

I scoop up Ladybug and bring him to my chest, rubbing behind his ear the way he likes so much. I'm just gonna say it. I fucking love this little guy. When he's not waking me up at 2:00 a.m., he likes to sit around my neck. He'll hang with me as I walk around the apartment. It's cute as hell.

Realization hits me suddenly.

"P, what do you mean she said the same thing?" I awkwardly ask.

I know Penelope and Gwen have this connection between them. But to hear P say she could see Gwen as a mom? Are we really at this point? I mean, it's been months, but I haven't given myself the chance to think about it enough.

Penelope doesn't look up from her homework. "I asked her. You know, about being a mom and stuff. She said she had to talk to you."

Gwen became intertwined in our lives before I even knew how it felt to hold her in my arms, to see her tuck my daughter in with unconditional care and love. Is that short amount of time enough to know for sure? Can you ever even know something like this without a doubt?

I picture Gwen in the morning, right before she wakes up, and I get to take in the sight of her all to myself. A wave of peace washes over me. It's the most simple view in the world, and it brings me the easiest answer. Yes.

I wouldn't say I was ever someone who believed in fate. It's hard to when you grow up in the kind of environment I did, but there's a part of me that has this absolute feeling that we were always meant to find Gwen. Or she was supposed to find us. Either way, it all just inexplicably makes sense.

I fully intend on showing and telling Gwen all of this repeatedly over the course of the next twenty-four hours we're going to have alone together.

Well, us and the cat.

* * *

"Okay, bye!" I barely have the car in park, and Penelope already has her carseat unclipped and her hand on the door handle to leave. She reaches down with her other hand to grab hold of her backpack.

In the passenger seat, Gwen tries to quiet her giggles. "P, let the guy park the freaking car before you ditch us."

Penelope huffs. "I'm just excited. I've never had a sleepover with Auntie M."

"I know, kid. She's so pumped, too. You don't even know. She told me today she and your Uncle Sawyer have so much planned," Gwen easily assures her.

"I'm gonna miss you, though. And Ladybug. And Daddy."

"We're gonna miss you too, princess. But we'll be here bright and early tomorrow morning for breakfast. Does that sound good?" I throw in. I'm trying to add to the conversation, reminding them I'm here. Because I've basically been dubbed the chauffeur since we got in the car, Penelope and Gwen ignoring me to keep the flow going amongst themselves.

I don't mind, though. It's given me the time to let my mind wander through everything I want to say to Gwen, everything I want to show her and do for her—*with* her. I want it all. I'm taking a page out of Sawyer's book and just going for it.

When you know, you know, right?

"Not *too* early though," Penelope says.

Gwen turns her upper body around to face P. "You got it, dude."

"Are you guys gonna kiss while I'm gone?"

Gwen's eyes practically pop out of her head, and she slaps her hand over her mouth. She jerks her body back to face forward and flings her door open, jumping out. Gwen then proceeds to pretend to have a dramatic coughing fit.

She's leaving me in here alone, and I'm gonna get her back for that, damn it.

"Uh, that's, umm, that's not an appropriate question," I say, praying to literally anyone who will listen that it's a solid enough answer.

"Why?"

Fuck.

"Because it's private?" I offer.

I watch P's head swivel and turn to see Margot walking outside, officially catching Penelope's attention.

"Huh," she says absentmindedly. "Okay, Daddy." She picks up her backpack, slings it over her shoulder, and hops out of the car like a tiny teenager. How'd she grow up so fast? Where does she come up with all of the whys of the world?

Silently thanking Margot, I'm last to exit the vehicle, out just in time to see Penelope throw her arms around Margot's neck like she hasn't seen her in weeks, when really it's been maybe a day.

I hope my sister and future brother-in-law are okay with

never moving out of Merrymount because I don't think I could ever live in a world now where my kid, or *kids* if I really give it some thought, don't live down the road from their aunt and uncle. And maybe their own children someday.

After a short visit with Margot and Sawyer, Gwen and I say goodbye and goodnight to them and Penelope. Gwen hangs out the window waving her arm like a gorgeous lunatic down the whole dirt driveway. She doesn't slink back in and buckle up until the cottages, and more importantly Penelope waving back at her on the porch, are out of sight.

I drive us a few towns over to an Italian restaurant I found while scouring reviews for a decentish place to take Gwen for a real dinner date. I can't take my eyes off her. Not a soul could as we are walked to our table in the back by the hostess either. Can't say I blame a single one of them.

She has her hair in those big curls that make her look like a freaking Hollywood star and another one of those skin tight sweater dresses that hits right below her knees. Can't say I've ever had anything with the word sweater in it turn me on like those things do.

Gwen lets me hold her hand in the middle of the table, and I don't think there's ever been a time when I've felt so wholly happy in my life. My daughter is safe with family who's not just me. I'm sharing a meal with the smartest and most gorgeous woman I've ever met in my life, and she's mine. At least, I'm hers, and she feels like she's mine.

I think I can count good memories from my childhood on one hand and somehow Gwen pulls every single one out of me effort-lessly. For each one of mine, she gives me one of hers, and I pocket them all, committing them to memory.

Our server places a slice of raspberry cheesecake in the middle of our table with two spoons. I let Gwen take the first bite, and she dives into another story.

"Oh! Have you ever been camping?" I shake my head, not wanting to stop her.

"Katie invited me once," she continues.

I raise an eyebrow at the mention of the name.

"Yep, that Katie. This was like, right before she became a complete wackadoo. She, Sawyer, Gus, and I went up to Barefoot Lake and pitched a couple tents as, like, an end of summer hoorah before school started. Everything's chill and normal when all of a sudden this older man comes strolling through our site!

"He makes sure we know to lock any food before we go to sleep—because of animals and stuff—and then just sits by us around the fire. At first I was like *Uh, what the fuck?* But then he turned out to be cool as shit, and told us ghost stories that honestly kind of terrified me. He had those eyes that just told you he was kind, you know? Sorry, I'm rambling. I know, I do that a lot. Hey, there's Red the rambler, yapping away—"

"Gwen," I squeeze her hand and she pauses. "You're Gwen here, with me, always. I want to know every little thing about you, so ramble away. Hell, let me record you, and I'll play it back in the car like it's my own podcast."

"You're ridiculous," she laughs and sets her spoon down. She stretches her arms up. "Would it be cliche of me to tell you to take me home again?"

"Baby, I want to hear that line every day for the rest of my life."

CHAPTER 28: GWEN - OH, SO THIS IS WHAT IT'S SUPPOSED TO FEEL LIKE

*L*adybug slinks in between both of our legs as we enter the apartment.

"Hey, cutie boy," I coo.

Miller scoops him up, holding him close to his chest while he rubs behind one of Ladybug's ears, just like he does every time he comes home. For as much grumbling that this guy did about taking in a kitten, he sure has warmed up speedy fucking quick. Ladybug climbs up Miller's shoulder to rest his little body around his neck. Two peas in a pod.

I kick off my heeled boots and line them up next to Miller's, silently admiring how they look together, alongside a pair of Penelope's rain boots. After hanging my purse on the coat rack, I nuzzle my face into Ladybug's in greeting.

"I think I want to shower," I tell Miller.

"Am I invited?" he asks.

I make my way to the bathroom and say nothing until I stop in the doorway and look back at him over my shoulder. "Silly question, Miller baby."

His eyes go wide, and he pries poor Ladybug off his back

without a second thought, gently plopping him back down on the ground. "Scram, kid."

A giggle escapes my lips as I turn the knob in the shower to the hottest setting. I tried to make it sound sexy inviting Miller in here with me, but the horny part of my brain must have forgotten how ridiculously small this stand-up shower is. What-ever, a quick rinse off in small quarters with Miller Caswell isn't something I'd ever find myself complaining about.

After stripping off my dress and ankle socks, I hook my thumbs into the waistband of my thong to drag it down to the floor, and step into the stream of scalding hot water. I savor it until Miller joins me when I adjust the temperature down a few degrees.

Miller steps in behind me and his hand moves my hair to hang over one shoulder. His lips find the side of my exposed neck.

"That dress drove me fucking crazy all night," he whispers into my skin.

"Good. That's the whole reason I wore it." I bring my hand up to entwine my fingers in his hair.

"I wanted to be the one to take it off."

"There's always next time," I say in a sing-song voice.

"Oof, I love the sound of next time," he says before nipping at my neck again.

I twist to face Miller, and we're a mess of hands and kisses and moans. There's absolutely no point to this shower aside from getting as close to each other as possible. I can't get enough. I pull him towards me even though there's nowhere for him to go. When Miller isn't gripping my ass, his fingers are grazing my spine.

"I need to lay you down, Gwen. I need to be inside you. I'm desperate. I'll do anything."

I toss my head back, and Miller's mouth envelops my left

breast. After flicking at my sensitive nipple until I cry out, he looks up at me.

"Please," he begs.

He. Begs.

That one word sends my body and my brain into overdrive. I smash my fist down on the handle, turning the water off abruptly. I take in his face, my fingers outlining that perfectly sculpted jaw I love so much, and bring it to my own face. Miller catches what I'm trying to put down and lifts me until my legs wrap around his waist.

His hard cock presses into my stomach. Anticipation pools low in me. I've had Miller in my mouth and my hand. His tongue has explored just about every inch of me. In a way, it feels like we've been building up to this for forever.

Apparently, we're forgoing the need for towels. Miller walks us, sopping wet, out of the bathroom into his bedroom, the bedroom that's basically been taken over by me this past week.

He tosses me onto the bed and falls over me, one hand on the mattress holding him up, one hand roaming my body. He parts my thighs. He licks a trail between my breasts and then takes his time swirling his tongue around each pierced nipple.

"Still fucking love these," he murmurs.

I lose control of my body and find my hand pressing his head down as I moan.

"You want me to eat your pussy, Gwennie?" Miller asks with devil eyes looking up at me.

Since fucking when does this guy know how to use his words like this? Since when do I not have words to form? I manage to nod, and he grins before fucking devouring me.

"Oh my *God*," I breathe as Miller finds my clit with ease.

For someone who said he didn't know what he was doing, he sure knows how to keep tempo or pace or whatever the fuck it's called to get me to the edge faster than any toy I've ever used.

When he inserts a finger, then two, into me, my back arches.

He sucks and flicks with his tongue and fucks me with his fingers until I'm coming. I pull at his perfect curls and try to catch my breath as I try to regain my senses.

"That's one," Miller says with a grin.

"One?" I ask.

He crawls up my body and kisses me so I taste my release. His voice is like gravel. "I have tonight to hear you scream. I plan on listening to the sweet sound of you coming plenty more than once. So, yeah, that was one."

"Who even are you?"

"Yours."

"Mine." I cup the side of his cheek. We have a silent conversation, exchanged only between our eyes, and when he kisses me, I get the very distinct feeling that I'll never believe in a world worth living in again without Miller Caswell.

"I brought condoms," I blurt out. "All kinds of them! Flavored, ripped, magnum, sheepskin—because I realized I didn't know if you had a latex allergy? I even grabbed one of those warming ones, but to be honest, that kind of freaks me out. So, unless you're really interested in trying that out, I'm respectfully asking to pass."

I tap Miller so he'll let me sit up and reach over to the bag I left stashed in the nightstand. "I came prepared."

"Jeez, Gwen. Did you raid the sex shop?" Miller asks nervously, eyes wide and fixed on the plastic bag in front of him.

"No! Well, yes. But it was online. I just—I wanted you to be comfortable. I'm on the pill. I take it every single day at the same time for maximum effectiveness. But I also know that no birth control is one hundred percent, you know? This way, you hopefully don't have to worry."

"You're too good for this world, Gwendolyn." His praise washes over me.

Miller sifts through the bag of foiled rubber I just threw at him until he finds one that catches his eye. He tosses the bag back on the floor. I watch, propped up on my elbows with parted lips, as he silently tears at the wrapper and rolls the condom onto himself.

He falls over me again, and my head crashes into the pillow. My hands find his shoulders, arms, hands. I want him every-where all at once. I want to be wholly consumed by Miller.

I think I already am, though.

"You're okay?" I ask.

"I'm about to be more than fucking okay, Gwendolyn."

He notches his cock at my entrance and while his tongue plays with mine, I feel him sink every single individual inch inside of me. When he moans into my mouth, goosebumps break out over my entire body. I feel whole in a way I haven't in a long time. Now that I think about it, I'm not sure I ever have.

"I need a minute," he pants.

I try my fucking hardest not to wiggle under him, but I feel so full and the pressure keeps building. "Miller, you feel—"

"Don't tell me how good I feel right now. I'm holding on by a fucking *thread* here—"

I lift my hips, somehow pulling his cock in even deeper. I want him wild and unhinged.

"Oh my *fuck*," Miller sighs. His hands grab hold of my knees, spreading me wide. We both look down where our bodies connect, and he drives into me over and over.

I feel my pussy flexing around him, squeezing his cock. The rhythm Miller has going right now is bringing me towards the ledge I love to swan dive right off of when I'm with him.

"You're fucking me so good, Miller. It's so good. It's *so* good," I repeat.

"Gwen, holy shit," he pants, but he doesn't slow down. "I wanted to make this last, I wanted this to be—"

"Come inside me, Miller baby. *Please.*"

His mouth finds mine again, and when he shudders with my name on his lips, it triggers my second orgasm of the night.

Miller kisses the side of my face, my neck, my shoulders, each breast. With each peck, another phrase of praise falls out of him. I'm beautiful, I'm perfect, I'm incredible.

He doesn't stop until I start to really believe him. When he slips out of me, I feel the loss immediately. I'm emotional in ways I didn't expect. I don't know why but I think—

"Hey, are you crying?" he asks softly. There's no judgment, just total concern. Miller's thumb swipes a tear from my cheek.

"I don't know…I mean…That's never happened. It's never felt like that before."

"Like what?"

"Like it wasn't just sex," I say it so quietly, I don't think he heard me.

Miller brushes back my wet hair and looks so deeply into my eyes.

"Because it wasn't, Gwendolyn. Come on."

He pulls me up, grasping my hand and refusing to let go as he leads me back into the bathroom. He discards the condom and restarts the shower. He holds me in the stream of hot water and wraps me in the fluffiest towel he can find when we're done.

He doesn't elaborate, and he doesn't ask me to explain any more about where I'm at in my head. He chooses actions over words, and I feel a sense of calm wash over me.

Once he changes the sheets to warm, dry ones, we crawl back into the bed, bodies pressed together as one again. My eyelids feel heavy, and I know when I wake up, I'll be mad at myself for missing out on a wild night of uninterrupted sex with Miller.

I don't linger on that thought, though. Instead I drift off to sleep in Miller's arms, and I imagine him kissing me on the top of my head, whispering *I love you.*

Except there's a part of me that wonders if I didn't imagine it at all.

CHAPTER 29: MILLER - MR. AND MRS. CLAUS

"**G**wennie, don't drink that—"

I try to stop her in time, but unfortunately, the effort isn't good enough. Instead, I have a front row seat to watch Gwen attempt to swallow down hours old room temperature milk that Penelope left out for Santa Claus.

She understandably gags and rushes to the kitchen sink to spit it out.

"Oh my *God*," she heaves.

"Yeah, so normally I just sort of pour it down the drain. Penelope doesn't know the difference."

"You didn't think to tell me that five minutes ago?"

I bite into one of the chocolate chip cookies P left out for the big man and place the remaining bit back onto the ceramic plate. "I didn't think you were going to try to actually drink it!" I argue.

"Lesson learned for next year..." she grumbles. I smile to myself because the thought of her already planning for the next Christmas season with us has me feeling jolly.

I don't think we've spent more than a few hours apart since our night together. Gwen's practically moved into the apartment and while space is limited with three humans and a cat, there's never been a place that feels more like home.

I love her. It's the easiest kind of love too, requiring no thought. I wake up and know that if everything else goes to shit, I'll still have Gwen to call mine.

I do need to tell her that, though. For some reason I'm having a hard time vocalizing my feelings. I don't think I'm scared of them not being reciprocated. I'm actually for once confident in the fact that someone out there loves me back. But I'm scared that once it's out there, something will swoop in to take it all away.

"So, what's next on the agenda? Is it safe to bring out the presents now?" Gwen asks.

Checking the time to confirm it's past the window of uncertainty, aka when Penelope might wake up and come out to see Gwen and me placing *Santa's* gifts under the tree, I nod. "Yeah, we should be good."

We pull out the pile of gifts we've been wrapping the past few nights from my bedroom closet, and I watch Gwen stack them all strategically under the tree. It looks like a picture in a magazine with all of the matching wrapping paper and bows. I hope P doesn't notice Santa really upped his game this year.

I hold a poorly wrapped box in my lap. After wracking my brain for weeks on what to get Gwen, I settled on something that's either lame as fuck or going to make her cry. When she turns around, she sees me toying with a corner of the wrapping paper.

"What's that?"

"It's for you. I want to give it to you now so you don't have to feel pressured around P to pretend like you like it or anything," I explain, nervously jutting my arm out to hand her the box.

"Unless it's a box of dicks, there's no way I would need to put on an act. Don't be ridiculous." Gwen takes the gift and rips off the paper, revealing a photo album.

She's silent as her hand roams over the fabric on the cover. I don't dare make a single move. It's agonizing watching her flip through each page so slowly, spending a few extra seconds on more than a few of the pictures.

When she gets to the last page, she closes the book and holds it tight to her, still as quiet as a mouse. I hold my breath waiting for Gwen to say just about *anything*.

"You see me."

I heard her. She didn't stutter or mince words or beat around any sort of bush. It was clear as day. But I still find myself asking, "What?"

Gwen looks up with tears streaming down her face, the photo album of every picture I've taken of her and Penelope in secret these past few months still clutched to her chest. She's in her plaid pajamas that match mine and P's. We all picked them out together.

"You see me. Who I am, and what I want, it's all right here."

She opens the photo album again and flips to the first page. It's of her reading Penelope a bedtime story, one of the first I took of them together. She has the most animated smile on her face while she reads, and Penelope is looking at her half asleep, but also like Gwen hung the moon. Every page has a little caption to go along with each picture.

This one reads: *The two most beautiful girls in the world. My girls.*

"This was before…before everything. And yet—"

"I feel like I've always seen you," I finish.

"How do you do that?" she asks.

"Do what?"

"Say the right thing and actually mean it. It's like you're reading from the script of World's Best Boyfriend, but it's genuine, and I cannot for the life of me figure it out."

I reach out for her, pulling her into my lap. "The truth is that you make it easy. You're kind and smart and funny as hell. You treat my kid like she's your own, and you rescue stray cats. I see you set out to make someone's day every single day and never go to bed without accomplishing it. I'm fucking crazy about you, Gwen. This was the only thing I could come up with to try to show you."

I avoid the three words I should be repeating to her over and over until she gets it. I gotta work my way up to that. My hands weave through her hair, and my lips desperately find hers.

Gwen breaks the kiss first. "Your gift is combined with Penelope's. I'm torn, because half of me wants to make you wait till tomorrow. The other half kind of wants to spoil the surprise now, in fear you might blow a gasket."

I laugh. "I can wait, I trust you."

"Thank you," she breathes. "For your trust, and for the most beautiful gift I've ever received."

"I'm sorry it's not more—"

Suddenly, I'm being whacked on the arm with the photo album.

We finish setting up before crawling into bed. And even though I check the clock and see we have mere hours before Penelope comes barrelling through the door, stocking in hand, ready to get the festivities rolling, Gwen and I keep each other up.

I rock into her from behind, breathing in the scent of her shampoo when we finish at the same time. Afterwards, we talk about next Christmas and how to do things bigger and better, like a team. When she falls asleep, I kiss the top of her head and whisper an *I love you*, the same way I've been doing every night.

* * *

NOT TO BRAG, and not without Gwen's help, but I fucking crushed the whole Christmas thing this year. P's never been so happy in her life. Maybe it has more to do with the fact that

Penelope now has Gwen to ooh and ahh at every present, adding to the joy, but nevertheless, I'm stoked.

Few things hold a candle to a child's happiness on Christmas morning. It's hours of wrapping, days worth of pay, and very strategic planning all coming together. When you have a kid as good as mine, it's hard to not go totally overboard.

Torn wrapping paper covers just about every inch of the living room. Poor Ladybug is trying to wade through it all as best as he can. Penelope has graciously thanked us and Santa for every single gift she's opened. But there's one giant box left, and it's taunting P in the worst way.

"Who's that one for?" she finally asks.

"Why don't you scoot your little butt over there and read the label?" Gwen offers from her perch on the couch, Mrs. Claus coffee mug in hand. I have the Mr. Claus one beside me.

Penelope does exactly that and after quickly seeing it's addressed to both her and me, she squeals. "Daddy, it's for us!"

"Bring it over here. You can open it for us."

I don't have to tell her twice. Penelope bounces up, snatching the last remaining gift that's tucked underneath the tree, and throws herself and the box at me. After half a second of adjusting herself on my lap until she's comfortable, she tears at the paper.

When Penelope pops the cover off the top, we both peer inside to see two white envelopes at the very bottom, and nothing else.

"What the heck?" P says.

"Oh come on, open them!" Gwen's impatient.

Penelope tosses me the one with my name scratched out and *Daddy* written underneath it. She tears at the opening of hers and scans the paper.

I do the same, not believing a single word I'm reading. "Gwendolyn…"

Anything I was about to say is cut off by Penelope's scream. If anyone was still asleep in Merrymount before, they sure as shit aren't now. She's on her feet, clutching that poor piece of paper in a death grip of a fist.

"ARE YOU SERIOUS?!"

Gwen is sitting next to me on the couch with her hands tucked underneath her thighs, like she's forcing herself to stay where she is. She nods once. "Mhm. Yeah. So, Merry Christmas, we're going to Disney World."

Penelope zooms around the apartment going no less than a million miles a minute, screaming and singing. Ladybug hides underneath the couch. I look back down at the print out. There's flight and hotel information along with the 10-Day Weather forecast for packing, dining reservations, and park tickets. It's too much.

Gwen notices my hands are shaking, and she grabs hold of them, forcing me to look at her. "Hey, you both deserve this. I can't take no for an answer, so don't even try."

"This is…" I don't even know what to say.

"A long overdue and incredibly deserved vacation. A gift. From me to you. The only catch is you have to let me come along for the ride." Gwen winks and then points to the dates. "I know it's short notice, but it was the only time I knew you'd be off work and she'd be off school. We leave tomorrow. And Daisy has already agreed to cat sit Ladybug."

"We don't have passports," I tell her.

"Well, good thing traveling from Massachusetts to Florida doesn't require one. Is that your only argument?" She laughs.

Shit, I knew that.

Penelope launches herself on top of the both of us. "Are we really going to Disney?! Like, for real life?!" The volume of her voice might be permanently stuck like this.

Gwen looks at me, reading every emotion on my face and without the need for words, confirms I'm not mad. "Pack your bags, girlfriend!"

"Thankyouthankyouthankyouthankyou!" Penelope chants over and over, squeezing the three of us together so tight.

Gwen walks us through the plan for the next three nights and four days. Turns out I would have never been able to do this on my own, seeing everything that goes into making a vacation of this magnitude possible.

Between times designated for the popular rides, maneuvering all of the different ways to get around this theme park that seems more like its own city, firework shows, and dining reservations, I feel like I'm going to need a vacation from the vacation.

Gwen tries to sneak in the little fact that one of our dinners includes Mr. and Mrs. Bozelli, because they just so happen to be docking while we're there and for once they felt like they couldn't miss the opportunity to see their daughter.

It's laughable considering they basically abandoned her here. But, I'll be on my best behavior.

While Gwen is explaining the lore behind some purple dragon thing to P who's hanging on to every word Gwen is saying, her phone screen lights up with a video call from Margot. I know there can only be one reason why she's calling right now so I pass Gwen the phone, urging her to answer it.

"I'll call her back," she says, trying to wave me off, engrossed in her conversation with Penelope. She's always making sure P knows she has her undivided attention.

"You're gonna wanna answer this one," I encourage her.

Gwen gives me a funny look and swipes to pick up the call. Penelope cranes her neck up to get a good view, too. "Merry Christmas, Auntie M!"

"Merry Christmas, babes! I'm so happy you two are together! Lil P, where's your dad?"

"Why's your face so red and splotchy?" Gwen pulls the phone closer to her face.

I try to stick my head in the frame. "Right here, Marge. Merry Christmas."

"We're getting married!" Margot announces, holding up her left hand and grabbing Sawyer. He has the goofiest smile on face, like he knows the rest of his life just got a hell of a lot brighter.

"Shut the fuck up right now!" Gwen exclaims, tears already filling her eyes.

The next five minutes involve a lot of cheering and crying. Penelope already has her flower girl duties planned out, and after I congratulate Margot and Sawyer, I get to work on the post Christmas morning clean up.

We have a big family dinner later to celebrate the holiday and now an engagement. And apparently we also need to pack. Because we're going to the world of Mickey Mouse tomorrow.

Once the excitement of the morning dies down a little, Penelope is playing independently with some of her new toys alongside the kitten, and Gwen is getting herself ready, I let myself take some time to process.

To think this is just the first Christmas of many to feel like this is wild. To think I thought I knew what it was all about before is laughable. Penelope and I were fine, but Gwen has shown me that fine wasn't ever going to be good enough for us. We deserve this kind of life.

Surprises and love and laughter and a real shot at a family. Everything that didn't seem attainable is now here in my reach, and I'm taking it. For all of us.

CHAPTER 30: GWEN - THE HOUSE MEETS THE MOUSE (PART 1)

I love flying, and I mean that whole heartedly. Silently judging others who don't have their shit together in the TSA line, people watching from your gate, the little snack mix and soft drink combo once you hit ten thousand feet in the air–there's nothing like it.

Now, watching two people who you care about very, very much fumble through the process with wide eyes during the busiest season for the very first time? Priceless. Kind of wish I recorded Penelope and Miller during the whole thing.

Penelope kept her face glued to the window of the plane while Miller gripped the armrest as if his life depended on it the entire two and a half hour flight. Now we're riding Orlando International Airport's Automated People Mover from our terminal to the main building to load up on a bus that will take us to our resort for the next three nights.

The sound of Mayor Buddy Dyer welcoming us home to The City Beautiful over the speakers feels like a warm hug.

I've lost count of the number of times I've taken this exact route for this specific type of vacation, but never have I ever been so excited to introduce someone (*someones, in this case*) to the place that holds my most magical, happiest childhood memories.

I guide us down to baggage claim to retrieve our luggage and Penelope's stroller that we checked before boarding the plane and walk us over to the area where the buses pick everyone up. After giving the sweet cast member manning the kiosk my last name and the hotel we're staying at, she directs us to the bus that will bring us to what I deem one of the most beautiful and classic resorts. Miller has an obsession with 90s sitcoms, and everyone knows the real ones always went to Disney World for an episode or two. I'm really hoping he recognizes it.

Penelope again has her face plastered to the window of the bus, calling out every time we pass a billboard with a familiar character on it. When we reach the famous arch, signaling our arrival on property, I remember to record it to watch back for years to come.

Miller's quiet, which is not unexpected. He's an observer who needs to take everything in. But he also hasn't let go of my hand once, and it's getting harder and harder for him to hide his bright, curious eyes. I think he's trying to put on some act to be the responsible adult. He doesn't get that once you're in a place like this, everyone's a kid again. I'll teach him.

The red roof and white siding of the iconic hotel come into view, and when Miller squeezes my hand and sucks in a breath, I know that all of the secret planning and scheming to make this happen was worth it.

"No fucking way are we staying here," he whispers to me.

It takes everything in me to not scream confirmation that we indeed are. Instead I repeatedly nod my head with the biggest smile on my face. "Yeah, Miller baby."

After retrieving our stuff and tipping the driver, we enter the lobby, and I head to the check-in desk while Miller and Penelope take everything in. I remember seeing the giant bird cage elevators and the characters tiled into the floor for the first time. The

Christmas decor, life size gingerbread house included, adds to the magic.

I hear Miller gasp, "Uncle Jesse played that piano."

We took the first flight out of Boston so it's still fairly early, and our room isn't ready yet. We drop our bags with Bell Services, and I fasten First Visit buttons to Penelope's and Miller's shirts. Miller pulls me in for a kiss, whispering thank yous and other sweet things, like how he can't wait to bend me over the bathroom counter later. You know, sweet things.

It's at this moment I realize Vacation Miller has been unlocked.

I've planned just about every minute of this trip because there's a lot that goes into a successful theme park vacation, and because it's busy as hell with the holiday crowds. But I've left a few things up for Penelope to decide.

First up, "Okay, kid. Monorail or boat?" I put my hands on my hips and wait for her to pick. Both are solid options, so she really can't go wrong.

"Monorail, Monorail, Monorail!" she cheers, jumping up and down.

"Let's go!" I lead them, Miller pushing the stroller while Penelope swings our hands together in between us, to the elevators. Once we pass through security, we pack ourselves like sardines into the overcrowded compartment.

Don't forget to stand clear of those closing doors.

Once we're through the line and have officially entered the park, I pause before we head into the short tunnel that will lead us to the Town Square.

"Alrighty, we're here. We're officially in. I know this is all foreign to you, but we're tackling the park counter clockwise, starting in Tomorrowland, followed by Fantasyland, then we'll break for lunch. Got it?"

Penelope nods her head vigorously, probably ready to agree

to just about anything. Miller hoists P up, smiling. "You're the captain today."

Miller proudly parades through the park with the goofiest smile on his face in his Princess Protection Program T-shirt I packed, and I don't think I've ever met someone who was more made to be a girl dad in my life.

* * *

"WHAT DO YOU MEAN IT'S A BATHROOM?" Penelope stops dead in her tracks in the middle of a sea of people. Miller and I stumble to halt with her.

Penelope has a pair of purple floral ears with a sparkly tulle veil and butterfly fastened to the front on the top of her head and remnants of a mouse-shaped chocolate ice cream bar hanging on for dear life in the corners of her mouth. The princess dress I made her for Halloween was the only outfit option when getting dressed today.

There's also a betrayed, disgusted, furious scowl on that cute little face. It takes everything in me to not burst out in laughter.

"Oh shit." Miller chuckles.

Penelope guffaws with her hands on the tops of her thighs. "This is the silliest thing I've ever seen!"

Today has been…today has altered my brain chemistry. We've ridden rides and gotten themed snacks. The shopping bag dangling from the stroller is the biggest one they had in the gift shop and is filled with merch we couldn't say no to. Miller surprised me, insisting we needed a balloon. I think his phone is going to hit capacity on pictures and videos, too.

My favorite people in my favorite place.

I had a feeling the Tangled Toilets were going to throw P for a loop, so I have a reservation for us to meet our favorite lost princess in the castle to make up for it. I could have told her.

Maybe I should have. But the look on her face was priceless, and it'll be a funny story to relive when she's older.

After finding all of the chameleons hidden in the area and inspecting all of the wanted posters of ruffians, Penelope hops back in the stroller, bubble wand waving in the wind, and we head in the direction of the castle.

Miller pulls my hand up to the stroller's handlebar and covers it with his own as we push forward.

"She's having the best day. Fuck it, *I'm* having the best day. I didn't know it would be like this. I mean—I knew when we eventually got here, it'd be fun. But I couldn't have pulled half this shit off. Seriously, I don't know how you did it."

"I can plan a vacation in my sleep, Miller baby. I'm just glad it's living up to your expectations."

"Exceeding them, Gwendolyn." He leans over and pecks my cheek with a light kiss. "So, what's next on the agenda?"

I already have the app pulled up on my phone that houses all of the park's information. "The carousel only has a ten-minute wait, so I thought we could do that and then head into the castle to meet some princesses?"

"Love that plan. For the record, I would have said that about anything you suggested."

"Even if I told you we were all signed up to get our faces painted?" I joke.

"Yep," he says matter of factly. "Can they make me look like the racecar?"

"Don't tempt me. I bet it could be arranged."

We park the stroller in the designated area off to the side of the ride and hop in the short line. When we get to the cast member standing post at the front of the line, Penelope is ready with three fingers raised high in the air before he can even ask how many there are in our party.

"Three, please!" She's my little expert, catching on to how things work around here so fast.

"Right this way, princess," the man guides us to join the waiting queue of people for the next go-around. "Just remember to have Mommy or Daddy ride alongside you."

Penelope whips her head around to me and Miller. *"You hear that?"* she mouths, hooking her thumb in the direction of the poor man who unknowingly just rocked our worlds, categorizing us as a perfect little family.

Miller silently takes my hand in his and we follow P up and onto the horse of her choice. We stand on each side of her as we spin around and around, laughing and singing.

After princess twirls and hugs that felt like they lasted a blink and forever simultaneously, we feast on a classic park day lunch of chicken tenders, french fries, and fountain soda.

Then we all agree we could use a break from the crowds. I check my email and texts to see our room still isn't quite ready yet, so I opt to walk us over to a different resort to explore before hopping on a bus to the next park of the day.

CHAPTER 31: MILLER - THE HOUSE MEETS THE MOUSE (PART 2)

I don't think I've ever walked so much in my fucking life.

I check my watch to see we just crossed twenty five thousand steps, and we're still not in our hotel room yet. I stupidly thought once we made it back to where we dropped our luggage, our room would be a floor or two up. Turns out, it's about three buildings down this walkway.

Is it common knowledge that a Disney trip requires miles of hoofing it? I didn't get that memo.

I'm running off of fumes and adrenaline right now. After the 3:00 a.m. wake-up and a full day of two different parks with tens of thousands of other people, I'm a version of exhausted I've never felt before. I can't believe people do this multiple times a year. Fucking athletes, I swear.

Penelope is already passed out in her stroller. The excitement of the day finally caught up to her as we were leaving Epcot after the fireworks. Incredible show, by the way. Gwen tells me I'm not ready for the one back at the castle tomorrow night. I thought they'd all be the same, but hey, what do I know?

"We're right up here on the left!" Gwen calls out from a little ahead. A damn miracle. She's effortlessly walking with two of our three suitcases, a pep still in her step.

After Gwen taps her watch to the Mickey head above the doorknob, she swings the door open, and I follow her in. When she flicks a lightswitch on I have to basically pick my jaw up off the floor.

"This is a hotel room?" I ask in shock. I look around at the full-sized kitchen and dining area that leads into a whole ass living room. Sheer curtains cover the doors that lead to the balcony overlooking that lake we saw earlier. Knowing I haven't spotted a bed or a bathroom yet, I already know this is bigger than my first and second apartments.

"Well, technically, it's called a one-bedroom villa." I feel my eyes bulge. "It sounds bougier than it is though!" Gwen adds, trying to lessen the stress of the amount of dollar signs I see floating around in my head. "Remember that timeshare program my parents signed up for? Pays for itself at this point."

"This is insane," I breathe.

Gwen's arms wrap around my waist from behind. "You deserve every bit of it. Come on, let's get our girl to bed."

Our girl. Fuck if I could hear that every damn day.

I need to tell this woman I love her. And that I want to give her as many babies as she wants and let her plan a trip like this every year for the rest of our lives. She deserves to know the wait for our version of happily ever after is over. I'll walk a million miles to see it happen.

I've known that for what feels like a while now, but I kept getting smacked in the face with the realization and the desperate need to tell her throughout our whole day today. It feels impossible to keep it in now.

We leave Penelope snoozing peacefully in the stroller while we bring down the queen sized murphy bed in the living room. Gwen finds P's stuffed cat and blanket in one of the bags and gets the covers untucked while clicking the TV off, but not before showing me the screen that reads *Welcome Bozelli and Caswell Family* with light piano music playing.

Once we get the little one situated—somehow we get the sleeping sack of potatoes out of her costume and into some actual pajamas—Gwen shows me *our* bedroom. There's a second TV, a king-sized bed, and a bathroom that has a giant ass tub along with a shower. I've never experienced anything fancier in my life.

When Gwen shows me the second set of doors from our room that lead out to the balcony, I actually feel like I lose the ability to breathe. You can hear the music piped in from all around and boats are floating in the lake. Light reflects off the water from the other hotels and Magic Kingdom itself surrounding it.

"This is one of my favorite views. It's not always guaranteed, but I put a note in about how special this trip was when I booked it, really hoping the stars would work in our favor. The wishing paid off," Gwen explains.

Fireworks boom, and I try not to jump. We can see the top of the show from our view here. It's a sign. This is it. It's now or never.

I take Gwen's hand but quickly drop it, in favor of pulling her closer to me from the back of her neck. She looks up at me, and her eyes show the reflection of the fireworks. I get caught up in how truly beautiful she is. From her freckles that cover so much of her skin, to the way the pieces of hair in front of her face curl up in the humidity. A soft variation of her perfect, and more importantly, genuine smile that has been plastered on her face for every second of the past twenty-four hours has me sucking in a breath to tell her—

"I love you."

It's exactly what I'm thinking, but it's not my voice that says it.

"What?" I ask.

She doesn't understand that I've never heard anyone say those three words to me aside from my daughter. Gwen doesn't know that I gave up the hope of ever finding someone who feels that way about me a long fucking time ago.

"I love you, Miller. I love Penelope so much, sometimes it feels like she's my own. I love Ladybug. I love this life. I'm still scared, but I want this. I want us."

Bringing her mouth to mine, I pour every bit of who I am and how I feel into her. "I love you," I pant. "She's yours, we both are. I love you so much. This is it for me, Gwendolyn."

She tugs at my hair and her tongue practically dances with mine. I hold her as tightly as I can, thinking about how I never plan on letting go. At the risk of being the world's most insecure, broken piece of shit on the planet I ask, "Can you say it again?"

"I love you. I'll tell you every day, multiple times a day. I love you, I love you," Gwen reassures me over and over, without judgment. Because she's Gwen.

I went from thinking I was incapable of receiving love to being completely engulfed in the feeling. There's a fire blazing inside of me that is dying to get out.

Guiding us back inside, I poke my head into the living area to see Penelope sleeping like the dead before making my way to the bathroom to meet Gwen. She's busy taking out her earrings in front of the mirror. I grab a condom from one of what seems like dozens of packing cubes Gwen brought.

I need to be inside her right now. I come up behind her and push her hair to one shoulder, peppering kisses and licks and nips up her neck while my hands explore the rest of her body. She sighs with content, leaning into me.

Gwen's wearing one of those black athletic dresses that taunted me, swishing every fucking which way all Goddamn day. I snap one of the straps, urging her to peel it off her body immediately. I step back as she strips, and I pull my shirt over my head, tossing it to the floor. I drop my shorts and boxers and roll the condom on.

"Someone's eager," she teases. But I'm not really in the teasing mood.

"Drop your panties, Gwendolyn."

"Yes, sir," she says in a surprised but low voice.

"Hands on the counter."

I watch Gwen shiver as she does exactly as she's told. A couple of nights ago, she admitted that as much as she normally loves to be in charge in her everyday life, sometimes she wants someone else to call the shots. She wants to try letting someone else take control, especially in the bedroom. Now seems like a good time to make that happen.

I rub a smooth circle with one hand around her asscheek while Gwen waits so patiently for my next move. The yelp she lets out when my palm smacks against it shoots right to my fucking cock.

"Oh my God, again. Please," she pants.

"Since you asked so nicely." Smack.

Her head falls forward, and she wiggles her backside at me. "Where's my sweet Miller?"

"Here. Always here," I correct her, massaging her. "But I really need to fuck you right now, and there's nothing sweet about the way I want it."

When Gwen lifts her gaze, and I see the heat and love in her eyes that I'm sure as shit matches my own, I slide my fingers between her thighs—her breath hitches—and find she's already wet.

"Yesss," she hisses, head falling again when I find her clit. I play with her, working her all the fucking way up. I want her needy and desperate. I want to plow into her until I have to cover her mouth with my hand to stifle her screams.

I grip the base of my cock and glide it through her wetness, coating myself. When I notch my tip inside her, she wiggles again, trying to pull me in.

"Not so fast, Gwennie girl." I gather her hair into my fist and pull until she faces me in her reflection again. "I want you to watch this." I slowly thrust, feeling her pussy clench around every inch of my cock as I enter her. "I want you to see how fucking perfect you look when I'm inside you."

She whimpers and rocks back into me. I keep the hand wrapped with her hair right where it is, and the other grips her hip, letting me control the pace. I'm relentless, not letting up as I watch her heavy breasts bounce in the mirror.

"Look at you. Look at us," I manage to get out in between rocking into her.

Gwen's hands slip on the granite, inching her forward. She moans, and it fills the room.

I slow, rubbing a hand up and down her back gently. "You have to keep quiet, Gwennie. Can you do that?"

She nods enthusiastically with softer moans this time. "I want it hard, though. I'll be good. I promise."

"You're always good, Gwen. Such a good girl. Let me take care of you."

I get lost in her, like I always do. I watch her breasts bounce in the mirror, and when she chances taking a hand off the counter to toy with one of her piercings, I lose the ability to contain myself.

"You like getting fucked like this?" I ask gruffly.

Her smile looks like pure bliss. "I love it. I love you."

"Again."

"I love you," Gwen says with a cry, and her muscles flexing triggers my own release. I don't pull out, letting myself pump into her.

I let go of her hair and fold over her, whispering how much I love her into her skin. After we clean up and get situated in bed, Gwen's head comfortably on my chest and listening to the TV's default channel's music on a low volume, I finally work up the courage to address the tiny elephant in the room.

"So, you got called Penelope's mom today..." I start.

Her fingers stop their swirling on my stomach. "Mhm."

"Kinda need a little more than that, Gwen."

She sits up abruptly, folding her legs in so she's sitting criss-cross next to me. "I have to tell you something." She takes a deep breath, and I hold mine, having absolutely no clue where she's heading with this. "P told me a few weeks ago she thinks of me like her mom, and I've been ridden with guilt since."

"Why?" I ask, dumbfounded.

"Because I should have told you immediately. She's your daughter. I'm not—I mean, I get what she's saying. Sometimes I forget myself. Actually, it's most of the time, if I'm being honest. I love every second with her. But...I'm just Gwen. Shit, you still insisted she add a *Miss* to my name until fairly recently. I'm the fun friend who has kind of attached herself to you guys."

"Baby..." I reach out for her, pulling her back into my chest, running my hand through her hair.

"I don't want to be some fill in." It sounds like an admission.

"You don't get it, so let me try to help. There wasn't an open position. I wasn't interviewing for Penelope's Mom. P and I were perfectly fine as just the two of us. But, then you blew into our lives and changed every version of our future.

"Now, that's not to say you don't have a say in this. There never has to be a title put on things if that's what makes you comfortable. If you hate the idea of marriage and only want to be P's fun friend, Gwen, Red, I don't care, and neither would she. I'll have to sit her down and talk to her, obviously, but, we're just asking to be a part of your life. We can have days just like this. We can be happy. I'm telling you, I'll take whatever I can get."

"I don't want that," she whispers, and it feels like the wind just got knocked out of me.

"Oh."

Gwen swings her leg across me and lifts herself up so she's straddling me. She shakes her head. "Miller, I love you. I don't want you to only take scraps of that. You're worth more than that. God, we both lived our whole lives thinking we weren't worthy of great love, and now that it's here, we're both too scared to accept it. You're offering me everything I've ever wanted and I'm trying to argue my way out of it for fucking what? This has to be the dumbest fight ever."

"We're fighting?" I ask.

"Yeah, but with ourselves and our dumbass brains. We're overtired. Today was a huge deal. Come on, let's go to bed." She leans over and kisses me long enough that I accept the conversation is over for now.

We're on the same page, but we're not. I'm done with the back and forth and dancing around how we feel, dipping our toes into the commitment and getting scared. I'm willing to fight for this and risk it all. I just need to know Gwen is too.

CHAPTER 32: GWEN - MEET THE PARENTS

I'm kicking my past self right in ass for agreeing to a dinner with my parents on the last night of the most perfect vacation of my life. I know before we even walk into the restaurant that this is going to be a colossal mistake.

After not having seen dear old Mom and Dad face-to-face for over a year, introducing them to *my* Miller and Penelope feels wrong. I don't want to share them, I don't want to share any part of my life with my parents now. I don't know how we got to this point where the people who birthed and raised me feel like complete and total strangers, but it's where we are.

I'm angry, but it hurts more than anything.

I put on my fakest smile and turn to Miller and P before we approach the doors. "Okay, here's the rundown. They're Larry and Jean. Don't call them Mr. and Mrs. Bozelli. They hate it. They're weirdo hippies who actively choose to live on a cruise ship. Please don't take anything they say to heart. I try my hardest not to. Argue nothing. P, if you're confused by anything they say, just smile and nod. It'll get us out of here faster. When it's all said and done and we get to say goodbye, I'll buy you each an ice cream scoop bigger than your heads. Deal?"

Penelope perfectly executes a smile and nod. Her mouse ears flop on the top of her head. She hasn't taken them off since we entered the state of Florida. That's my fucking girl.

Miller is harder to convince though. He raises an eyebrow at me. "Is there a reason we need a military level debrief before walking in here, Gwen?"

I blow out a breath. "Ugh, no. I'm probably overreacting. But I'd rather us all be extra prepared. Let's just…can we just get this over with please?"

Miller leans in and kisses my forehead, warming me all over, and easing my mind instantly. "I got you," he whispers.

I straighten my shoulders and take the hand he's offering. He opens the door and holds it for us, and the three of us enter the packed restaurant. I pretend I don't see my mom's big head of grey curls tied up with a red bandana bobbing as she waves her hand frantically back and forth to get my attention.

My dad's approach is just as subtle. Meaning it's not. "Red! Get over here! Red!" My dad elbows the man sitting at the table next to him. "Look at our daughter, the beauty!"

Yep. That's me. The shiny trophy signifying every box in life is checked off.

"Hey, guys," I greet as we arrive at their table, kissing both of them on the cheek. Miller doesn't let go of my hand, but holds out the other to shake my father's.

"Hi, Mr. Bozelli. Miller Caswell, it's very nice to meet you. Thank you both so much for making time for us tonight."

"Please, son, call me Larry. Jean will ask the same of you, so don't even try."

"Told you," I mumble to Miller. He squeezes my hand in answer.

"Hi Jean, it's a pleasure. This is my daughter, Penelope." Miller puts his hand on Penelope's shoulder in front of us, and she offers a shy wave.

My mother turns her attention to Penelope who's been

twisting her head every which way, trying to keep up. "Oh, hello there, little one. Aren't you just the prettiest thing I've ever seen? A doll, she's like a real life doll!" Mom coos. "Sit, sit, everyone get comfy. We want to know everything. Give us the scoop. How's Merrymount?"

We all get settled in our seats and the server brings over three more menus. "Home's good. The cafe is basically running itself."

"As it should. We planned it that way for you, Red," my dad interjects.

"Yeah. Thanks," I acknowledge him. "As I was saying, things are fine—"

"Have you had to see Dean lately? What about that baby of his?" This time it's my mom's turn for interruptions.

"I'd appreciate it if we don't mention my ex-husband and his escapades, thank you." I keep my voice level and look over the menu, silently looking for the option I can scarf down the fastest.

"Well then I apologize for mentioning someone who has always been such a large chunk of your life," my mom says after a sip of her wine. I feel Miller's grip tighten on my leg, and I cough to avoid further comment.

We place our orders and all manage to keep conversations polite and surface-level as the food arrives. I feel like I'm sharing a meal with complete strangers. It's making my skin crawl.

Miller is trying his best. I can tell he's biting his tongue with every backhanded compliment from both of my parents and trying to distract himself with extra attentiveness toward Penelope and by keeping a hand firmly planted on my thigh.

I thought I had a good relationship with my parents; we looked like the perfect family in pictures. But when I try to break down what we meant to each other, it's really hard for me to see any sort of connection. They don't know anything about me. They never bothered to try.

"So, Miller. Our Little Red here tells me you live above our cafe. How are you liking things?"

"We're extremely grateful things worked out the way they did. The apartment is great."

"Love to hear it, son. Our Red isn't always known to make the best choices, but it seems like she got it right this time." My dad pats my head.

Miller places his napkin on top of his empty plate. "With all due respect, Gwen is the smartest woman I know," he says it matter of factly, not breaking my father's eye contact once.

"Gwen?" my mom scoffs. "You hear that, Lar? Gwen! Barely know her!"

"Yeah, I've gathered that," Miller retorts.

"You wanna try that again?" My dad leans into the table, the act of sincerity ditched.

Fuck.

"It's this silly thing. You call me Red. Miller calls me Gwen. Names! Am I right?" I have no idea what I'm saying, just word vomiting to get us out of a potential brawl.

"Listen, Larry. I'm fine to sit here and talk about your travels, because Gwen asked me to. But you're not going to directly or indirectly insult her in front of me again."

"I would never insult my daughter. I'm just aware of her capabilities. That's why we set her up."

"You're joking, right? Did you ever stop to think she might not have needed that? Or wanted it, for that matter?"

"Miller, honey…" My mom tries to mediate. "Clearly, you care deeply about our daughter. That means a lot to us."

"Does it?" Miller snaps. "Because I would think you'd have made an effort to show face at any point over the past year."

"We're busy people with our own lives. When you get older, you'll understand the juggling act—"

"Age has nothing to do with this. Please do not patronize me. I've handled more in my short twenty-three years than you could imagine. You've spent your only meal with your only daughter lobbing offhand comments about her intelligence and *capabilities* instead of begging for a chance to see a glimpse into her world–the world she created completely on her own."

Miller pushes away from the table and stands. "I'll handle the bill at the front. This was…insightful. Thank you."

I follow his lead, tapping at Penelope's placement for her to get up as well. Poor kid is wide-eyed and confused as hell. She's getting a double scoop of ice cream.

"Sit down," my dad tries to command.

"No," I plainly state.

"Red, I don't know what this is all about, and I know he had his issues, but Dean would *never* speak to your father this way," my mom says.

"Oh for Christ's sake, I don't give a fuck what Dean would do. Are you kidding? That's where you go with this? Miller's right. It's like you never cared, and now I don't think I care. Don't be surprised if you don't hear from me for a while. I'm busy. With my family." I pick Penelope up and march towards the sweet sight of freedom on the other side of the restaurant's doors.

Neither my mother or father try to follow. I'm not sure why I thought they might.

* * *

OKAY, so the return airport process is never as fun as when you're leaving for the trip. The only thing keeping the three of us from not completely moping at the gate is the fact that we get to go home and see Ladybug.

I'm swiping through all of the pictures with Penelope that Daisy sent me while we've been away while Miller is busy stocking up on overpriced snacks for us.

"Do you think he misses us?" Penelope asks while resting her head on my shoulder after a particularly cute picture of Ladybug snuggled up on her pillow.

"Duh," I assure her.

"Good, because I miss him. And Auntie Margot."

"Me freaking too, tiny human."

I haven't updated anyone on everything that went down with my parents last night, so that'll be a fun catch-up with Margot when she picks us up from the airport.

It still feels too raw, and I don't want to take away from the rest of the trip, because up until that dinner, it really was picture perfect.

Getting to experience something I felt like I knew like the back of my hand through the eyes of a child for the first time is indescribable. Penelope watched and sang along to the firework show with tears streaming down her face. Every character she got to meet, she hugged for what felt like an eternity. I wish I could bottle up her squeals of delight from every ride.

I'm itching to toss every other photo album—aside from the one Miller made me—into my junk closet and only display my Christmas gift and the one I'm going to get to put together from this trip. Between the hundreds of pictures, I don't know how I'm going to narrow them down. Maybe I won't. Maybe I'll just have multiple books.

When Miller said *I got you* last night before we walked into the restaurant, he meant that. He held me as I silently cried for hours in bed, well into the early hours of the morning. For as much work as I've put into therapy and bettering myself, I kept the dam locked on my emotions relating to my parents for as long as I possibly could. It was excruciating to have them all flood out unexpectedly.

Today is better. Today I don't have to go home to an unbearably empty house filled with broken dreams and promises.

But damn it, it still really fucking sucks.

"For you." Miller holds out a coffee, and I snatch it up, inhaling that first sip greedily. "And for you." He then hands Penelope a cake pop, which she chomps down on.

"Thank you," we both manage to mumble.

We still have some time before boarding so Penelope digs in her backpack, pulling out her kitty cat headphones, and plugging them into her tablet.

"So, I have an idea," I say to Miller.

"Sounds good." He sips on his own coffee.

"I haven't even told you what it is yet!"

"So? If you came up with it, I'm on board. You know that. Come on, baby. Lay it on me."

"What if you and Penelope and Ladybug came to like, stay at the bungalow…"

"Tonight?" he asks.

"Tonight, tomorrow, uh, whenever?" I don't know why I'm being so awkward. I've been staying at the apartment for weeks, and it's completely illogical when I have a giant ass house that's collecting dust.

"Easiest yes of my life. Fair warning, I still want to punch your neighbor."

CHAPTER 33: GWEN - PLAYING HOUSE

"Wicked witch incoming," Margot warns me. I lift my head up from the paperwork I'm trudging through to hear the jingle of the bell on the door and see Katie St. James and Holly Montag waltz into the cafe.

My cafe.

Of course today of all days we don't lock the door after closing.

"What the fuck?" I whisper.

I've been back in Merrymount for a little over a week and besides needing to distract myself from how things went down with my parents, it's felt right to be home. Miller, P, and I finished up winter break holed up in the bungalow with visits from the newly engaged Margot and Sawyer and letting Ladybug get a lay of the land in a new, much larger space than he was used to in the apartment.

We rang in the new year with take out and Penelope declaring she'd make it to the ball drop. She was snoring in between us on the couch by ten. It was perfect.

Miller and I decided it was best to not rock the boat too much in terms of our living situation so we did end up moving the party back to the apartment the night before school started back up. The last thing we wanted to do was disrupt Penelope's routine before any of us were ready. We've tackled it all as a team. I'm proud of us.

So of course we're taking three steps forward and now two steps back with some petty, catty mean girl drama to shake things up.

Katie's carrying her son in his car seat, but Holly's demon spawn is nowhere to be found. They both have smiles on their faces that signal to me that they're up to no good. Because why would they be?

"Can I help you?" Margot asks, putting in very minimal effort to appear cordial.

"We're simply paying a visit to our local coffee shop," Holly says.

I exercise even less of an attempt at hospitality, "We're closed."

Completely ignoring me, Katie directs her demon eyes to Margot's left hand. "I hear you have my ring. Congrats," she hisses, placing the car seat on the counter.

The comment rolls right off of Margot. As it should, seeing as that ring was never Katie's, and we all know Sawyer only has eyes for Margot. She adds insult to injury by raising her hand to inspect the ring. "Hmm, funny. I don't remember hearing about him proposing to you. I do remember when he asked me though. It's like, the cutest story. Do you wanna hear it?"

Katie's eyes narrow. "No."

"Shame," Margot exhales with an antagonizing smile. God, I love her.

I glance down at the baby and get a look at him up close for the first time since our one shitty interaction in front of Mrs. Johnson's house. He's sleeping peacefully, all cozy with a blanket draped over him. Poor dude has no idea how much his parents suck.

"This is embarrassing, even for you," I interject.

"Oh, you want to talk about embarrassing?" Holly adds. "When are you going to give up the little mommy act?"

"What's that supposed to mean?" Margot snaps.

"Red here parades around town with a kid that's not hers, playing house with her fake family. She'll never know what it takes to be a real mother." Holly turns her head to me, "He'll get bored, you know. Just like Dean did. Maybe you should have gotten knocked up like—"

"Shut up," I say with a shaky voice. Shit.

"It's nothing you haven't had to try to convince yourself isn't true. But it is, Red. We see right through the act. You think you can replace what you lost."

It's not true, at least not all of it. I didn't lose anything, I took out the fucking trash when I kicked Dean out of my life. My life with Miller and Penelope isn't even comparable. But fuck if every other word wasn't a kill shot.

"Oh my God, I'm done with this. Eat shit and get out," Margot barks.

"But what about our coffee?" Katie asks in a sickly sweet voice.

"I said we're closed," I repeat through clenched teeth. I'm not doing this with them.

Katie lifts the car seat up and chuckles with Holly. "That's a shame. God, Red. You used to be more fun than this. Where's that feisty bitch we all used to know? I guess things really do change. Well, it's been a treat!"

Margot follows them out, locking the door behind them and flipping them off. "Would you fire me if I keyed their cars?"

I try to laugh, but nothing comes out. Margot's by my side in a second. "Hey, everything they said was bullshit, you know that."

"Do I?" My eyes are starting to water, and I know I have mere seconds before the floodgates burst and I'm openly sobbing.

"Yes. You do. Don't do this, Red. Don't go backwards." Margot rubs my arm, trying to comfort me.

"What if he does get bored though? Or he realizes playing pretend isn't worth it? What if one day I wake up and it's all taken away from me? We keep circling each other and then shutting down any conversation of a future together. I told myself I wouldn't put myself in this kind of position again. I love him, Margot." Great. Now I'm crying. "I love Penelope and our fluffy cat, and I want more babies. I want to be a wife and a mom who hosts birthday parties and campouts in the backyard. I daydream about getting railed in the laundry room, for crying out loud! Domestic shit, Margot! And I'm too chicken shit to risk anything for it."

"Marge, do you mind giving us a minute?" a soft voice comes from the back. A voice I'd recognize anywhere now. I try to swipe at my eyes as fast as I can before Miller walks over with his hands in his front pockets. He's wearing that dark green hoodie of his I've been sleeping in most nights.

"Sure thing, lil bro." Margot squeezes Miller's arm before hugging me as tight as she can. She grabs her tote from under the counter and lets me know she'll be at home when I need her.

When I hear the back door click shut I face Miller. "How much of that did you hear?" I breathe.

"Do you want me to lie, or can I say every word?" He pulls me into his chest.

"We don't lie," I mumble.

I feel his lips on the top of my head. "You're absolutely fucking right. Now, let's talk about it."

"What do you mean?" This feels dangerous.

"I'm ready to lay it all out there, Gwen. I'm done with the back and forth, the doubt, and letting our pasts control us. Let me just —let me just say what I need to say, okay?" He holds me at arm's length to level with me. I can feel him shaking.

Definitely dangerous. I give him a shallow nod.

"I need you, Gwen. But it's the same way I think you need me." I'm frozen in place, hanging on to every word. "More than that, I *want* you. I want your crazy hair, sticking up in all different directions in the morning. I want to see you having a dance party with Penelope when I know it's time for bed, but the extra five minutes of you two doing your thing is more important. I want every inch of you that you're willing to give me because I love you."

"But—"

"No. Keep listening. It's you, Gwendolyn. I love *you*–the person, *my* person–not what you can offer. There's no hidden agenda or favor I'm about to ask. My days—my whole fucking *life* —are better because of your presence in it, and I want to make sure it stays that way."

Some variation of an *I love you* leaves my mouth in between the stream of tears falling down my face. No one has ever made me feel more seen in my fucking life.

Miller keeps going, clearly not finished with his declarations. "You could never make me a cup of coffee again. I'd be fine with seeing you ditch this entire business, town, and life if that's what your heart wanted. I'd follow you anywhere, as long as there's room for Penelope and Ladybug in the backseat. The only thing I can't do when it comes to you, is walk away when I know that we both know this is it for us."

"I don't want to confuse Penelope…"

"What does that even mean, Gwen?" He runs his hands through his hair in frustration. "You think you're not a real mother because you didn't birth her? I know you don't believe that. Tell me you don't believe that."

"I don't."

"Then don't hide behind that excuse. I'm just asking you to love us as much as we love you. I swear it'll always be the only thing I ask of you."

"The easiest thing I've ever done is love you. Both of you. All of you, actually. If we count the cat." I shrug. "I have all of this ugly self-doubt, and I don't know where to put it. I never remember being so unsure of myself. It's killing me, Miller."

"I believe in you, and this enough for the both of us. At some point I'll need you to catch up, but I can carry it for now." He's offering me the world and taking nothing in return. Because that's Miller.

I throw my arms around his shoulders and cling to him like a spider monkey. He holds me tight, just like he always does. "Gwen..." he says apprehensively. I feel myself stiffen. "I want you to take the weekend."

"What?" I pull back. Not to sound like the world's biggest clinger, but we haven't spent a night apart in weeks.

"I don't want you to agree to all of this right now and then run away and hide later," he admits. Ouch. "You're a planner, Gwen. Plan it all out for me: the house, the kids, the life we could have together. If you can't see us rocking on a front porch together in fifty years...well, then we need to have some sort of conversation about it. Because I can picture it all clear as day. I'll be here when you're ready. I've got nothing but time when it comes to you. I've told you that. I just want you to be sure."

Fresh tears sting the corners of my eyes. He kisses me deeply, promising me everything I've ever wanted with no words needed.

The only thing standing in the way of it all is myself.

CHAPTER 34: MILLER - THE BOOK OF ADVICE BY MELANIE LECLAIR

I haven't heard from Gwen in three days, and I'm starting to think giving her space was about the dumbest fucking thing I could have done.

Okay, not completely true. She's called every night to wish Penelope goodnight. She just doesn't really have much to say to me. I don't press her. I'm the one who told her to take her time. I know she's been to the apartment because Ladybug had new treats and toys stocked up that I know I didn't buy. That has to be a good sign, right?

But, fuck I don't know what to do. There's nothing else I could say that could convince Gwen this is it. We found what we were looking for, and we deserve it. Both of us.

So, here I am being smacked in the face with the strong smell of chlorine as I walk into Hopeford's community pool center. I dropped Penelope off at Margot's this afternoon so they could do whatever it is that nieces and aunts do together, and I drove the hour out here. I spot Melanie LeClair wrapping up her class as she waves to me. I wave back and take a seat in the bleachers.

I need to get Penelope into swim. Maybe I could pay Melanie to do private lessons or something over the summer. Water safety is important. I watch Melanie gather all of the kids to do one last jump in the pool before dismissing them and grabbing a towel to dry off and head over to me.

"Hi honey, I'm so happy you made it out!" Melanie calls.

"Hey Mel." I lean in for a quick one-armed hug to avoid getting soaked.

"Walk with me to my office?" she offers.

We walk down the short hallway that leads to her office. The desk is covered in paperwork, picture frames, and seashells. There's a giant mural of the ocean covering the wall behind her desk. Melanie must notice me inspecting it.

"Margot painted that in high school," she tells me.

"I didn't know Margot was into art."

"Eh, she's not. Well, not this medium at least. The photography has stuck, but my girl has gone through many phases in her life. This was one of them. Do you paint?"

I laugh. "No. Definitely wouldn't be able to put together anything that made sense."

She tries to reassure me. "I don't believe that. Everyone can mix colors together to make something beautiful."

"And when you can't make out which color is which?" I ask.

"Miller, honey, are you colorblind?" Melanie asks, wrapping the towel around her waist to sit down. She gestures for me to do the same on the other side of her desk.

"It's called Protanopia. I can't see reds for shit. I didn't get the official diagnosis until I was older because my parents never bothered, but the school nurse clocked it pretty early on. It really doesn't affect my day to day life dealing with numbers and computers and all. P has a freaking field day with it though."

"Can't see reds, huh?" Melanie eyes me with a brow raised.

Never Red. Just Gwendolyn. "Ironic, I know. Speaking of..." I start.

"I know why you're here, Miller."

"Hey, I also came by to to check out the place and because I miss you." Both are true. I've never had a motherly figure like Melanie. "But, yeah. Gwen," I sigh.

"Margot doesn't fill me in nearly enough, you're going to have to catch me up to speed."

So that's exactly what I do. I recap the last six months, from admiring Gwen from afar when she didn't even know my name to the other day when I basically gave her my heart on a fucking platter. Melanie doesn't interrupt. She nods and waits patiently for me to get everything out. My throat feels hoarse by the end of it.

"You're not going to like what I have to say," she admits.

"I'm clueless, Mel. Fucking stuck with this fear that I had it all, and I'm about to lose it. Penelope, too. I can't even think about that."

She puffs out a short breath. "The ball is in her court, Miller. Like you said, you laid it all out there and told her she needed to ruminate on it. That's exactly what she's doing. You have to be patient."

"But what if she doesn't come back?" I sound desperate. I am.

She reaches across the desk and takes my hand in her own. There's a soft smile on her face. It's comforting in a way I haven't experienced. "Faith and trust, hon. Everything's going to work out just fine. Your Gwen didn't go anywhere. She just needs some time to sort herself out. You're one of the good ones, honey. She knows that."

"I just want her to choose me. Choose us. Not out of obligation or anything, but because she sees what I see, you know?"

Melanie LeClair has the ability to make anyone comfortable to the point where they'll spill their guts. Clearly I'm not immune to the spell.

She shakes her head like I'm missing something. "That girl has been choosing the two of you for quite some time now. Does Red have an issue with boundaries and saying no, extending herself to the point of exhaustion? Yes." Melanie sighs and clasps her hands together. "But that's not even close to what's happening here. It might be hard for you to see, and it's not your fault, but how she shows up for you is unconditional love in its purest form. It all started with that little apartment she offered you with no strings attached."

"You think so?" I ask apprehensively.

"I know so, Miller."

"Margot was lucky to get you out of the parenting deal." It's something I've thought about for a while. I'm not bitter about it, because things really did turn out okay, but it comes out a little off, and I immediately wish I could take it back.

"Oh, Miller. If I knew...There are a lot of things I wish I had done differently. I hoped so deeply that Michael would be different for you, and I'm so sorry he wasn't. You deserved better. I know it doesn't make up for the past, but I'm so incredibly honored to be here for you and Penelope now."

"That sounded bad, I'm sorry. I didn't mean anything by it except that you really are great. I'm grateful to have you, Mel. I'm serious."

"Always. And I mean that. There's no getting rid of me now. Just ask Margot," she jokes. Melanie stands and walks over to the little bar cart she has set up with a coffee maker. "It's not as good as anything served up at Red's, but you want one?" She plucks a pod into the compartment and the machine whizzes to life.

"I won't say no to that." I ring my hands together, twirling my ring around nervously. "Umm...Do you think I could ask you something?"

It's been bothering me basically my whole life. I never had anyone to talk about it with because there was never anyone who could truly get it.

"Of course," she says with concern.

"Am I like him?" I let the question hang and then follow it up with, "*Could* I be like him?"

It takes no time for Melanie to register who I'm talking about.

She freezes, and her face becomes stern. It's kind of fucking terrifying. "No."

The only sound in the room is the drip of the coffee into the mug.

"You have his eyes, as does Margot, as does Penelope, as will most likely any future children the two of you have because for some damn reason those genes are strong. But all similarities stop there. You're everything I think he wishes deep down he could but never will be." Melanie clears her throat. I look up to meet her eyes and see she's getting emotional.

"Michael is a poor excuse for a human being and an even worse example of a father. I will not sugarcoat that. I do not forgive or forget the hurt he has caused so many of us." Melanie walks towards me and places her hand on my shoulder to squeeze. "Your mother included. But he gave me Margot. She has always been my dream come true, my loudest happy, as she would say. And now we have you and Penelope. I think, and I hope you'll agree, it's time we leave him to his own devices, in the past."

A weight that felt permanent until right now lifts from my chest.

Melanie and I spend the next hour or so drinking our coffees and catching up on less heavy subjects. She gives me a tour of the community center, walking me through the years she's spent getting this place to what it is now. Mel admits she feels like more of her heart is in Merrymount now than here. I tell her it's not the worst place she could relocate to.

I FULLY INTEND on taking Melanie's advice to leave my father and everything that comes with being raised by him in the past. I just have to make this one stop first.

When Margot texted me asking me to keep myself busy for an

extra couple hours, I didn't question it. I'm sure she and P are having fun doing some project together or something. But I have nothing in Merrymount to keep myself busy that doesn't remind me of Gwen, so I wound up here.

I parked across the street, and I'm leaning against my car with my arms crossed over my chest, staring at the house of horrors I grew up in. The lawn looks like fucking shit, per usual. It's riddled with empty beer cans and grass that's taller than Penelope, folded over and dead from years of neglect.

The garage door is definitely broken, stuck slightly ajar at an angle. You can see a glimpse into the space, filled with useless junk and trash, no room for the two cars it's supposed to be able to fit.

Speaking of cars, it looks like dear ole dad didn't even bother shutting the driver's door of his rusted beater of a truck before calling it a night last night after he parked it crooked in the driveway. Dents that I'm sure appeared after he drunkenly smashed into God knows what cover too many spots for him to still have the ability to hold a driver's license.

Not a fucking thing has changed.

I mean, I didn't think it would. I had zero expectations of things looking even remotely better when I questioned over and over again why I had to do this on my way here. I still don't have the answer for that, but I'm here regardless.

There's no shot he gives a shit about someone hanging outside, so I'll have to go to the door. I'll probably have to bang on it to the breaking point for him to even register someone's trying to get his attention from the outside.

But imagine the shock on my face when I cross the street, climb the porch steps, and raise my fist to begin knocking, just for the door to fly open.

My father, Michael Caswell, stands at my eye level, squinting at the light of day. He's staring at me like he's hallucinating, and I probably look like I might throw up.

"What the fuck do you want?" he sneers. I can smell the alcohol on his breath.

"Excellent way to greet your son after over five years of no contact. Hey, Dad."

"You're lucky I don't bash you upside the head. I'll ask you again before I slam this door in your face. What the fuck do you want, Miller?"

I'll admit a part of me, the smallest, most minuscule part, kind of hoped he would have been a little remorseful. Maybe he could have wanted to know anything about how I'm doing, or at least his granddaughter. But, this is reality.

"I wanted a better father—" He moves to whip the door shut, but my palm connects with it to keep it open. "No, you're gonna listen to this."

He grunts. I start again, letting my heart do all of the talking because my brain couldn't put two thoughts together if it tried right now.

"I wanted a better father, so I became one. I used to sit up late at night and wonder how you could hate your kid so fucking much. I thought about what I could have done wrong. And now that I have one of my own, I question it even more. Do you know how easy it is to love her? Easier than breathing, I'll tell you that."

I'm shaking, but I take a breath and continue, "And then I found Margot." I watch the shock and recognition register on his face. "*And* Melanie," I add for good measure. "They make love and family look easy. They took us in as their own and haven't wavered since. And I realized it was never me. It was never about fatherhood or being a parent in general. You're just a piece of shit. And hey, maybe a little bit of that rubbed off on me too, because I'm only here to tell you that to your face."

He lunges, but it's sluggish, and I dodge with time to spare.

"You think you're better than me?" he spits.

"No, I know I am. Look." I gesture around us. "Look at the world you live in, Dad. I got out. I wish Mom did too, but I can't change that, just like I can't change you. But, I'm going home to people who love me. I have purpose. I wish that I wished you'd find that, but I lost that hope a long time ago. I am who I am despite you, and I'm finally proud of that."

I walk backwards down the steps and begin the journey down the walkway back to my car. He doesn't follow but stands as still as a statue on the porch, watching me.

"Are you happy?" my dad calls with malice in his voice.

I get in my car, start it, and roll the window down to answer him one last time. "Happier than you could ever imagine."

Letting that truth out makes the journey back to Merrymount so much lighter. I keep the windows cracked to let the crisp January air bite my face as I put everything together in my head about where things go from here with Gwen and Penelope. And the cat, I add. I take a page out of Melanie's book of sage wisdom and advice and remind myself that everything has a way of working out. And for once in my life, it's going to. In my favor.

CHAPTER 35: GWEN - IT'S GRAND GESTURE TIME, PEOPLE

Your fam just left the cottages. Go get em, girl

*D*amn fucking straight that's my family. I shoot Margot a ridiculous amount of hearts in response and toss my phone in my purse to continue dashing around the apartment putting the final touches on everything.

I never should have let Miller give me the weekend to *mull things over*. What the hell does that even mean? There's nothing to think about. It's them and me. It's us. It was always supposed to end up this way. I let my fears of the past fester the point where I almost lost it all for nothing.

Never again.

No one in my almost thirty years of life has seen me or loved me the way Miller does. No one has made me feel more whole than Penelope. They breathed life and purpose back into me when I thought those kinds of feelings were hopelessly gone forever.

Miller told me he'd follow me anywhere but there's nowhere else I'd rather be than in Merrymount together. I'm here to show them, in my own way, that this is it. Not the end, but our very own beginning.

Ladybug parades through the mess I've made, and I swoop down to pick him up, whispering into his soft fur as if he gives a single shit about what I have to say.

"Do you think they're gonna think I'm crazy, LB? Psh, you're right. They already know I am."

I readjust the blue bow collar Penelope picked out at the pet store for him so it sits right under his little chin like a sophisticated bowtie.

"We're gonna be a big, happy family at the bungalow. Maybe we can convince Daddy to get you a friend." The kitten nuzzles his face against mine, and I swear he's responding to me. "I know, it's going to be the best."

I walk through the apartment admiring the work I've done to get everything looking exactly like it should. Miller has spent months showing and telling me all of the ways he loves me, and now I get to do the same.

I'm a ball of anxious jitters, pacing, readjusting, and just basically wearing myself out until I hear the distinct sound of my favorite tiny human climbing the stairs. I didn't bother hiding my car, parking it in its usual spot in the back of the building, so she must know I'm here.

The confirmation of that comes almost immediately when I hear Miller calling from down below. "Penelope, slow *down*."

"She's here, Daddy! I gotta—" The door swings open, and I stand in the middle of the living room with my arms plastered to my sides not making a single move.

"Woah," P exhales.

"Hi, baby," I greet her with a small wave and a big-ass smile. I've missed her so fucking much. I don't care that it's been barely a few days and I've called her every night, I miss her every second we're apart.

Miller enters next, and I swear it feels like all of the air in the room gets sucked out as he looks around at the absolute mess I've made of his apartment.

Small sticky notes—identical to the dozens he's given me over the course of knowing him—cover almost every surface. Some have scribbles of words, others doodles. Each one was made with care and love and intention.

He picks up the first one, right next to the door.

Let's line up our shoes next to each other's for the rest of always.

-Gwendolyn

I hold my breath and say nothing.

Penelope is, shocker to no one, the first to break the silence. "What the crap?"

Miller and I burst into laughter, and all feels right again.

"I missed that laugh." The admission falls out of me.

Miller crosses the room, scoops Ladybug and plops him right on the floor. He grabs me into his arms in the next second. He picks me up and spins me around and suddenly his lips find mine. It's quick and hard and when we break apart Penelope is crashing into our legs, wrapping her arms around the both of us. "Cuddle puddle!" she yells.

"Gwennie girl, what the hell is going on?" Miller finally asks.

I clear my throat. I'm ready. I'm prepared. I can do this. I pull apart from both Miller and Penelope and stand straight, ready to show up for them the same way they always have shown up for me. "Alright, here goes. No interrupting, got it?"

Miller picks Penelope up and they both nod once in confusion. Good enough for me.

"Cool. So, P—" I direct my eyes to her and focus on her cute little button nose. "Remember when you said you sometimes feel like I'm your mom?" She nods more enthusiastically now. Good. Good. This is good. "I feel the same way. I love you so much. More than I ever thought I could love someone. I'd do anything for you—"

"Like squash Brayden's face in?" she asks. The no interruption rule lasted about as long as I thought it would.

I chuckle, saving me from crying. "Yes, exactly. And that's taught me that's what being a mom is all about. You can call me whatever you want: Mom, Gwen, Red. The title doesn't matter to me. I just want you to know I'm here for you, I'm always going to love you, and there's absolutely no chance of getting rid of me."

I hear Miller suck a breath in, but I don't look at him. Not yet. If I do, I won't be able to get the rest of this out, and I need to.

"Really?! Well, duh, I love you, too!" P declares. "I'm gonna go check on Ladybug. I bet he missed me." Miller lets her down, and she trots into her bedroom.

"He sure did, tiny human," I tell her retreating back before finally looking up to Miller.

My sweet Miller who is shaking like a fucking leaf with tears in his eyes. I fucking hate that I've kept him waiting. I hate that he might have doubted us for even a millisecond.

He takes a few steps into the kitchen and picks up a pink square of paper.

The best (and last) first kiss of our lives happened here.

-Gwendolyn

He pulls the purple note off the sink's faucet.

You wash, I dry forever, ok?

-Gwendolyn

Wordlessly he walks throughout the entire apartment picking up each note, reading them silently to himself. Sometimes he shakes his head, sometimes he laughs. Miller piles them on top of each other, clutching them in his hand.

I follow closely behind him, waiting on bated breath for any type of response. He saves the bedroom for last. There's only one blue note in here, placed right in the middle of the bed.

He picks it up and finally faces me.

My bed is still bigger. Move in with me.

P.S. You can't say no. Consider this an eviction notice.

-Gwendolyn

"Gwen, I'm trying really hard to hold it together. Today was kind of a big day, and I need you to spell this all out for me. Please." He stands with his back towards me facing the bed.

"I want it all, Miller. The house, the babies, the vacations, everything. But only if you're the one doing it with me." I wrap my arms around his waist and breathe him in.

He twists around and cups my face with his hands. "You're s-sure?"

"I was sure before you kissed me goodbye in the cafe three days ago. I just needed time to figure out how to show you. This" —I hold up his hand still grasping at the stack of sticky notes— "Was the most Miller and Gwen way I could show you. That first note you left for me, and every single one after, saved me. They— *you*—pulled me out of this dark hole I thought I was comfortable living in."

His hands move further back, burying into my hair, as he keeps looking at me with more love than I thought possible. "Is this real?" He presses his forehead into mine.

I pinch his butt, and he jumps. "See? Very real. Not a dream."

The next kiss starts softly. Miller's lips barely graze mine. It's slow, like we're committing this moment to memory. I stroke my fingers up and down his back in rhythm. He hums into me when my tongue glides across his bottom lip, begging to be let in to tangle with his.

He tastes so good. Like the early rays of daylight and whispered plans of the most golden future. My body sinks into Miller's, and I let myself forget the rest of the world exists.

Until Penelope bursts in and starts jumping on the bed. "Are you guys gonna do that all the time now that Gwen's my mom?"

Miller and I look at each other trying to keep our shit together and a silent conversation passes between us. We both dive onto the bed, tickling Penelope in between us, her laughter trilling throughout the apartment.

CHAPTER 36: GWEN - KARMA IS A CAT

"**I**'m gonna go put this box of shit out for free on the sidewalk!" I call to Miller from the front door.

I throw my old UGG boots on and grab one of my black puffy coats from the rack to throw my arms into before stepping into the freezing February air. I drag the box of old plates and bowls from the entryway to the porch outside and hoist it up to carry down the walkway.

Don't get me wrong, I love Merrymount and have every plan to live here forever but fuck, why does Massachusetts have to be so Goddamn cold like, nine months out of the year?

Two weeks ago, after Miller and I finally found ourselves on the same page. We sat down and planned out combining our lives for real and not just this kind of weird in between. We've successfully moved him, Penelope, and Ladybug into the bungalow and cleaned out the little apartment above the cafe. It's empty and ready for whoever is lucky enough to call it home next.

I'm obsessed with how space in the house is filled now. The first thing Miller did was update the picture frames throughout, no more stock images or old school pictures of me that held no meaning. Penelope has her own bedroom, and we set up another one of the rooms as a play and reading room for her, with bookshelves and a desk for art and writing. Her toys are scattered throughout in a way that shows this is a home that's lived in. We've left the last bedroom empty, in case we ever need a nursery down the road. I really hope we'll need a nursery down the road.

I've never been happier dashing from the bedroom to the kitchen, making breakfasts and packing lunches in the mornings before zooming to make it to school drop off in time and then heading into the cafe. We're busy in the best kind of way.

We brought back that idea of family pizza night with Margot and Sawyer, adding Daisy and Gus to the mix, even if the two of them pretend the other doesn't exist. There's no fighting, so it works.

My parents haven't called. Or texted. Or emailed. And I haven't put an effort in either, so I guess I can't fault them. But it doesn't hurt as much when there's so much love coursing through every other part of my life day in and day out.

I reach the curb and pull the permanent marker out of my pocket to write *FREE* on the front of the box when I set it down. I turn to run back into the warmth of the inside, but I stop dead in my tracks before crashing into a wall of annoying ass fucking caveman.

"What do you want, Dean?"

He ignores my question. "You let them move into our house?"

I bite back a snort and straighten my shoulders. "It's my house. Mine. Always has been. You live there." I point to Mrs. Johnson's old place. "We've gone over this too many times to keep having the same conversation."

"I want to know what changed. Where's the Red I knew?" His

hand comes up like he's going to try to move my hair, and I flinch away.

"She died, Dean. I truly, and I really mean this, don't care what you do from here on out, but you need to leave me alone."

He looks like I slapped him across the face, as if I haven't said a variation of the same words hundreds, if not thousands, of times over the last couple of years. It's insane how dense he is, and I'm sick of catering to it.

"Do you remember back in November when I told you I hated you?" I ask.

Dean scoffs, and I know he's not ready to hear how truly insignificant he is. But for once, I don't care about how someone else feels about what I have to say.

"Sure, yeah." He tries to sound absentminded, but it doesn't land the way he intended.

"I don't hate you." I wait for the tiny speck of hope to dawn on his face. "But it isn't love either, it's just indifference."

"You're such a—"

"Bitch? Cool. Good one." I stand with my arms across my chest.

I watch him struggle to come up with a response, anything to tear me down. But he comes up short, because he always will. He backs up one step. Then two. Followed by a third.

I should walk away now. There really isn't anything left to be said except—

"There is one thing I have thought about a time or two, you know. I do hope you get everything you ever wanted. Really." Dean's eyes practically bulge out of his head. "I hope it's never enough."

I stand here in front of my house, and he stands in front of his, the line of the sidewalk at our feet, a physical reminder of the permanent divide between us. I look at Dean Fitzgerald and see him for everything he is, and I can't help it—I laugh. A big, ugly bark of a laugh that would have earned myself a stern talking-to later behind closed doors if I was still legally attached to this miserable loser staring with his mouth agape at me.

I manage to pull myself together as I step back to head inside my house to my little family.

* * *

"Can we frame it?" Margot asks. She's holding a copy of the Merrymount Daily. It got dropped off this morning like any other day, but this one was something special.

"We don't want to scare customers away with that face." I laugh and click my tongue.

I don't know who he pissed off at the town's local newspaper, but they sure as shit wasted no time plastering Dean's mugshot on the front fucking page. The article outlines his arrest after he wrapped his cruiser around a tree a couple nights ago, the arrest that his old boss, Mark, called in when he found him passed out in the driver's seat, still holding a bottle of whiskey.

I'm just beyond thankful no one else was involved or injured.

The article goes into detail on how this fuck up of his has shed light on every little and big thing that the department has covered up to keep Dean's hands clean the last however many years. I've never seen karma work quite like this. This was all after I watched déjà vu play out in real time when Katie piled all of his shit on their front lawn.

I thought about offering her words of support or something, but I'm busy keeping my side of the street clean.

Will it be the wake-up call he needs to be a better person for himself and his son? Probably not, seeing as his parents blew into town to bail him out and ripped him out of Merrymount immediately after. But hey, good luck or whatever.

"This isn't even a good mugshot. Like, he didn't even pose," Margot continues to inspect and judge, the way a best friend should.

"I don't want to look at that," Miller says as he approaches the counter.

"Then go somewhere else. You know, you don't have to work from the cafe every day." Margot rolls her eyes and snaps the newspaper to hold it up in front of her face.

"I don't," he argues. "Sometimes I stay home with Ladybug."

"Lovesick idiot," Margot mutters.

I swat the paper into her face. "Takes one to know one, bitch. It's dead, you can take off for the day if you want. You have a shoot later, right?"

Margot drops the newspaper, and I get the honor of watching her face light up at the mention of her passion. But of course, she tries to downplay it. "Don't make it sound like it's legit or whatever, it's just like…pictures of some kids like, to help out."

"*Some kids*," I mock with air quotes. "The karate studio is literally paying you. Be proud! The rest of us are!"

"Yeah, Marge. Seriously, it's cool as hell." Miller bites into a muffin.

"Thanks, guys. Sawyer tried to hype me up this morning, too. I don't know. I don't want to get my hopes up that this is the thing that sticks."

"If the last year in Merrymount taught you anything, Margot, it's that you've found plenty of things that stick."

"True that." Margot shoots her dorky finger guns at me before grabbing her bag, saying her goodbyes, and taking off.

"So, what are we feeling for dinner tonight?" Miller asks with an elbow resting on the bartop.

"Sushi, please. I don't feel like cooking."

"I can—"

I cut him off before he offers to pick up the slack. "I don't want you cooking either," I lower my voice. "I have plans for you, baby."

Miller's eyes widen. I love how he gets flustered when I get flirty like this. Which is funny, seeing as how I'm ready to pounce on him at just about every chance I get.

"God, I love you," he says before pulling me into his orbit to kiss me in the empty cafe. I taste my odd but favorite combination of his mango chapstick and coffee, mixed perfectly with sparks and butterflies.

CHAPTER 37: MILLER - THE BLUEBERRY FESTIVAL

"Margot has texted me no less than five times ensuring we're not going to be late. I don't know what her problem is, but I'm ready to smack her," Gwen grumbles while slipping into her sandals. She bends over, and her sundress rises up to the point where her thighs meet her ass.

"Mhm, yeah," I answer distractedly, thoroughly enjoying the view.

"I mean, we're not late for *everything*. Just like—" She stands back up to her full height after getting the buckle on her shoe secured and turns around to face me. "Were you checking me out?"

"Mhm, yeah," I repeat, slowly nodding. I'm still doing a full intake of Gwen standing in front of me. Her dress is one of those strappy tank top ones, with a low neckline to show off her perfect breasts. It hugs her tightly until it flows out at the waist, and when she does a spin, letting it dance around her, I grab her and pull her into me. I can't help myself, there's no such thing as too much of her.

"I happen to like that," she says while peppering light kisses up my neck. Her lips follow my jawline until they connect with my own. She palms my already hardening dick through my shorts, and I do the math in my head to see if we have time to dive into the laundry room so I can properly hike that dress up and bury myself inside her.

She's been off birth control, and I haven't touched a condom in months. We're filling that nursery up as soon as possible.

I grab a handful of her ass and press myself into her. She moans in response. "Come on, baby. We have a few minutes."

Gwen grips me harder and just when I think she'll follow along with my little side quest, I feel the loss of her hand immediately. "No, we don't. Penelope Grace, pack it up!" she calls up the stairs.

"Evil woman," I mutter.

"That you love so much!" Another kiss to placate me.

"Always, baby. Always." It's not like she's not going to wind up naked in our bed later.

I make quick work of readjusting myself in my shorts while Gwen grabs her purse. We hear Penelope clomp down the stairs in her plastic princess heels. The argument of the week has been trying to get her to understand that leaving the house in those things risks a broken ankle or two. She assures us daily she's fine. Her clumsiness disagrees.

Gwen wordlessly holds out a matching pair of sandals of her own in a smaller size to Penelope who sighs so deeply for a six-year-old with not a worry in the world on summer vacation. She kicks off the dress-up heels and puts on the ones Gwen offered. Smart girl.

"You look beautiful, tiny human," Gwen compliments her.

And like always, Penelope's face lights up. She's still Gwen's number one fan. "Thanks, Mom." She does a twirl that mirrors the one Gwen just did moments before and grabs her hand.

My girls.

"I'm just gonna make sure LB has food and water before we head out," I tell them before kissing Penelope on the top of her head as I pass by down the hall to the kitchen.

"Meet you at the car, Daddy!" Gwen calls.

I'm never going to get sick of this life.

* * *

MARGOT'S BEING WEIRD, and we haven't seen Sawyer or Gus since we showed up on Main Street for the festival over two hours ago. Penelope has dragged us all–myself, Gwen, Margot, Beth, Melanie, and Daisy–to every booth to try every free sample available and has eaten her weight in popcorn and cotton candy.

It's been a great time, don't get me wrong. But there's a part in the back of my brain that's telling me something is up. Call it a hunch.

Gwen thought I was overreacting for a little bit, but as time passes on and Margot continues to wave us off when we ask where the hell her fiancé and his best friend are, her suspicions have begun to rise.

She leans into me while we all watch Melanie and Beth hop into the wagon filled with hay attached to the tractor that's giving free rides around the block.

"I think they're up to something," Gwen whispers.

"Yeah, no shit. Look at her."

We both try to inconspicuously tilt our heads in Margot's direction. She's standing off to the side chatting with Daisy, but she's looking every which way and keeps fidgeting with the sweater she's been carrying in her hands. That's another thing, it's almost ninety degrees. What the hell does she need the sweater for?

"First she pesters me to the point of annoyance to get here on time, and now she's acting like she's being followed, in the witness protection program or something. And where the hell are Sawyer and Gus? Why are they MIA? Do you think she's mad at us? What could we have done? Is this about the camping trip? Margot doesn't even fucking *like* camping!"

Oh, my girl's spiraling now. We gotta figure this out fast.

"Marge!" I yell across the way.

Margot jumps, swiveling her head. She points to herself, acting like she's unsure if I was addressing her. I roll my eyes. "Get over here!"

I watch her gulp down a swallow and she tentatively starts the short journey that takes a hell of a lot longer than ten steps in this direction should take. "What is up, my dudes?"

"Tell me what the hell is going on, or I'm uninviting you from the bonfire later," Gwen snaps.

Margot scoffs and readjusts the sweater to hang from one arm to the other. "You wouldn't dare. Besides, Penelope wouldn't let you. Everything's fine. More than fine actually." She tucks one side of her hair behind an ear, and I see the skin underneath her freckles darken.

Gwen's hand darts out to grab my wrist in a vice grip and realization washes over me.

"You're pregnant," I say.

Margot opens her mouth and closes it. Tears start spilling out of her eyes and she starts nodding her head with the biggest smile on her face. Gwen crashes into her in an instant.

"You are! You're pregnant! Holy fucking shit, you're *pregnant!*" Gwen squeals. The two women are fused together and jumping up and down, both crying. They look deranged. It's incredible.

"Wait, shut up!" Margot yells, abruptly halting their celebration. "I need Sawyer here! We're supposed to tell all of you together! I had a plan, and you just ruined it!" She's still yelling and crying, but there's no bite in her voice.

When the two finally separate, I pull Margot in for a hug. "Congrats, Margot. This is huge."

Sawyer jogs over to us holding a brown paper bag. "Shit, I'm so late."

Margot's eyes narrow on Sawyer, and he holds his hands up, bag still swinging in one, in surrender.

"I'm sorry, I'm sorry!"

Boy, do I feel bad for him the next however many months.

"They know, Sawyer. I tried to hide it as long as I could, but they sniffed me out, damn it."

Sawyer turns to me and Gwen. "Sorry, guys. I had to go tell my parents first. It was important to me. It took a little longer than I planned." Margot's face softens instantly at the mention of Sawyer's parents. We all get exactly what he's talking about.

"So, you guys hear I'm gonna be an uncle? Dude, you too!" Gus claps me on the back, and I lurch forward at the contact.

Margot holds her hand up. "Enough! We haven't told you everything yet and I'm not letting another bit of this surprise get ruined by you impatient bitches."

She journeys over to where the tractor is dropping everyone off, and she herds our gang to the cafe. Once we're all situated in our seats, Margot stands in front of all of us and whips out that brown bag Sawyer carried over. Sawyer wraps his arm around her waist.

She clears her throat. "A year ago we all gathered here for the first time as one giant makeshift family. The Blueberry Festival feels like a really special kind of day." Margot looks up at Sawyer, and he kisses her temple, urging her to keep going. "Actually, everything about Merrymount feels really special. It's this little town bursting with hopes and dreams, and I swear it feels like magic. I feel so lucky to get to experience it every day. I feel even luckier to say our babies will get to experience it, too."

Margot pulls out the smallest, white onesie with an American flag that has tiny blueberries making out the stripes. She turns it around to show us that it reads *"Baby Hale"* on the back.

The collective gasp fills the room, and Melanie is darting towards Margot in an instant, basically tackling her daughter. Beth, for once, is speechless when she pulls Sawyer in, sobs wracking her body.

But since Gwen's initial shock has worn off, with Penelope bouncing on her lap truly just happy to be here with everyone, she's the first to speak up. "Margot…"

Margot peaks her head over Melanie's shoulder. She still has her daughter in a bone-crushing embrace. There's a smirk on her face. "Yes?"

"What else is in that bag?" Gwen passes Penelope to me and stands, walking over to snatch the bag out of Sawyer's hand. She pulls out a second onesie that matches the first.

"Oh, Sawyer, you dirty dog," Daisy laughs.

"Twins?" I ask in disbelief.

Sawyer pulls Margot into him again, beaming from ear to ear. "Twins!" they shout simultaneously.

After another round of hugs and cries of celebration, Margot settles us all down again. "Okay, okay, we have some important things to go over." The room falls silent.

"Jesus, it's nothing bad," Sawyer assures us.

"Are you okay? Are the babies healthy?" Melanie ignores Sawyer, jumping into mom—now grandma—mode.

"I'm great. I mean, I don't know where the fuck they're going to fit in a couple months." Margot laughs and swipes a hand over her stomach. "But all three of us are perfectly healthy. They're baking just fine in there. Grandmas." Melanie and Beth grab each other's hand. "You have, give or take, eight months to figure out what you want to be called. P, buckle up, because your new cousins need to learn how to be your carbon copies. Red, Mills," Margot faces us, "Will you be Baby A's Godparents?"

Gwen is swiping makeup from under her eye with her other

hand that's not intertwined with mine. I answer for the both of us, "We're honored, Margot."

"August, Daisy," Margot turns to the two people who have the ability to clear out a room with their battles. "Baby B needs you. Both of you. On the one condition you get your everloving shit together to be there for them."

A beat and a moment pass between the two enemies. For once, they seem to come to a silent understanding. It's Gus who speaks up. "We can manage."

Holy shit, the family is growing again.

A year ago, to the day, Penelope and I were apprehensively walking into what felt like a tight knit group as outsiders. We didn't really feel like we had a place besides with each other. Family felt like an untouchable fairytale we happily read about at bedtime.

Now, I share my life with the most beautiful woman in the world. I'm gonna marry her by the end of the year, mark my words. My daughter is no longer just mine, but ours. We spend our days laughing and singing and experiencing new things together.

I don't think about the darkness of the past, it doesn't matter now that I'm standing tall in the daylight on the other side.

EPILOGUE: PENELOPE

I barely recognize myself in the reflection of the bathroom mirror. Mom spent hours on my hair and makeup to make me look like the reference pictures I've been showing her in the weeks leading up to this night. I check to make sure the pearl butterfly clips that are fastened in my curls are secure. I shouldn't be surprised that they are though. My mom, Gwendolyn Grace Caswell, is nothing short of a perfectionist.

We've been talking about my senior prom since she told me about her own when I was just a little girl, when she first popped into mine and my dad's life. Although, it's hard to remember what life was like before her now.

My mom...she's my best friend. There's really no other way to put it. She's the kind of mom to punt a kid across a football field for calling me or my sister names and open her home to every child who might need a safe place. Biologically, we're not related.

But like, that woman was meant to be a mom, *my* mom. And she's never made me feel like there was any other option.

I've spent my entire school experience listening to my friends and classmates rant about their parents–how they're overbearing or weird. I've never been able to relate, honestly, not even a little bit. Is my dad kind of a nerd? Yeah, but like, in a cool could probably hack into the government or something kind of way. And his whole existence revolves around loving me, my little sister, Goldie, and my mom. Oh, and LB. My grumpy old man of a cat.

We're one of those obnoxiously close-knit, insufferable kind of perfect families you read about in books or watch in movies. Yeah, I've threatened to punch Goldie in the face for stealing my chargers and clothes, but only I'm allowed to do that. Anyone else goes near her, and they're dead. And okay, sure, some screaming matches over curfew and some of my outfits have occurred. But we all follow the "don't go to bed angry" rule, and you never leave without an *I love you*.

I'm sure I have mere minutes before Goldie and our cousins try to barge in here to see me in my dress first. I can hear them conspiring in the hallway, and I'm running out of time to ignore them. I smack my lips together after applying my lip gloss and open the door to see Kit, the youngest but feistiest of our crew (although there's only months between the four littles), with a fist raised, ready to knock.

"Yes?" I lean against the doorway.

"You look like a princess, Penny!" Nora yells. I still hate that nickname. But the twins are an exception. I'll always have a soft spot for each of my cousins, seeing as I'm the oldest.

"No, a queen!" Drea adds.

"Dang, sissy. Noah's gonna flip a shit," Goldie finally chimes in. Everyone thought once she could finally pronounce Penelope, she'd switch to calling me that instead of sissy. She did not.

Noah is my best guy friend, *not* my boyfriend, despite

everyone thinking otherwise, by the way. We're going to prom as friends. Again, despite what everyone else thinks.

"Noah's going to say what now?" Our mom comes around the corner with a hand on her hip, but the smile on her face gives away that she's not serious about any sort of scolding. "Oh, my not so tiny human." She raises her hand to her mouth with tears lining her eyes. "You're perfect."

"Oh, this?" I twirl so the purple tulle of my dress fans out and the sparkles twinkle in the golden hour light shining through the windows.

Mom's choking up now and trying to wave it off. "We have to get you downstairs for pictures. Your father's going to have a field day with this." She ushers us all to the stairs, and once I'm halfway down, I hear my dad suck in a breath. I look at him and yep, he's already crying.

His hair is starting to grey in his early thirties, but my mom's obsessed with his curls so he still keeps it long. He has bright, emerald green eyes that match mine. And my sister's. And Auntie Margot's. And the twins', Nora and Drea. He can't gain weight for anything, so he stands tall like a green bean in his classic black boots, dark jeans cuffed over, and black T-shirt combo. My (literal) day one dude.

"Hey, Daddy," I greet him.

"Hi, princess," he answers with a wobble in his voice. He's standing right in front of the framed collage of sticky notes he and my mom have exchanged over the past however many years. Like I said, there is no shortage of the obnoxious, sickly sweet kind of love in this family.

I hear the distinct sound of my aunt's camera clicking away once I reach the bottom landing. I turn and see her crouched down in the hallway. "Lord woman, are you crying too!?"

"Don't give me shit, lil P! You're the first baby to not be a baby anymore!" Auntie Margot swipes her eyes.

"Let her be emotional, kid. I think everyone in this family is," my Uncle Sawyer says, leaning against the wall.

He's right. But when we head outside and everyone (my parents, sister, cousins, aunts, uncles, and grandmas) all crowds around to take picture after picture and send me off, I remind myself I wouldn't have it any other way.

There's no place like Merrymount.

THE END

"Look, Daze," My first mistake is making eye contact with her. My second is every word that falls out of my mouth from here on out. "You hate me, I'm never going to be your biggest fan." She scoffs. Typical. "But for some reason everyone here still gives a shit about us. We need to drop it. For them. For the babies."

Daisy shakes her head, clearing whatever emotion was trying to break out of her. I watch the metaphorical light bulb go off above her head. "Want to make it a competition?"

"Huh?"

"The twins have some time to cook, right? We agree to put our differences aside for as long as Margot's pregnant, and when you break the truce-"

I bark out a laugh. "Don't go assuming it'll be me."

"Whatever. *If* one of us breaks the truce, the loser walks away. Not like, entirely. I'm not evil, asking you to hightail it out of Merrymount, although I wouldn't hate that..." she mutters the last part to herself. "But the winner gets first dibs on all family get-togethers and events going forward."

"That's insane."

"No it's not. If we can't coexist for the most innocent forms of life, then there's just no use in trying. Frankly, they-" Daisy motions to our crowd of people, "don't deserve us at our worst anymore."

If it was coming out of anyone else's mouth, I would have instantly agreed. It's actually kind of genius. I'm not telling *her* all of that though. "Hmm," I start noncommittedly.

"I know you're only not saying it's a good idea because I came up with it. Don't be fucking dense, August. For once."

"Ah! There it is." I wag a finger at her. "You'll never survive this. You'll be out before we find out the genders. You know what? Sure, Daze. Let's shake on it. Nine months, me and you, buddy-buddy." I hold out my hand.

When her tiny fingers attempt to wrap around mine, I almost pull back at the shock. Static electricity must be weird today, I don't know. For how small her hand is, the grip is tighter than I expected. It'd feel fucking amazing wrapped around something else.

And that's the thought that tells me I haven't been laid in a while, if I'm thinking about Daisy Stiles anywhere near my dick from a simple handshake. Nothing a quick trip to the bar can't fix. Nothing to cause alarm.

"As much as this pains me to say...Deal," Daisy agrees. She snatches her hand back in the next second and takes a step back towards Margot and Red gushing over ultrasound pictures. "For the record, Gus, I don't...I don't hate you."

For some reason the only thing my brain can come up with is a one word answer. "Okay." With that, she turns her back to me.

It wasn't a compliment, it wasn't an admission of affection or close to anything you'd write home about. But for the first time in ten years, Daisy Stiles said one singular sentence to me that wasn't an insult or jab. It was just a simple fact she felt the need to drop on me.

And I have no fucking clue what to do with that kind of world shattering information.

Because Daisy Stiles hates me. It's one of the few things I've known with complete sureness.

And if she doesn't then…

Well, if she doesn't then it changes nothing. She's still the most insufferable, stuck up, bitchy, unreliable, messy woman I've ever come in contact with. We still mutually can't stand the sight of each other and when she loses the dumbest kind of bet she could have come up with, I'll get to enjoy this makeshift family I'm somehow included in without her breathing down my neck.

**merrymount book three
coming late fall 2025**

ACKNOWLEDGMENTS

Did I seriously just type *the end* on my second book?

I flipped back and confirmed, I did indeed do that. It wouldn't have been possible without you, dear reader. Thank you for being here, always.

B, I'd find you in every life. Thank you for loving me through it all and being my biggest and loudest and proudest fan. (And packing up and moving us 1100 miles to our happy place while navigating a new job, a child, a cat, and allowing me the space to write more love stories.)

HJ, to know you is to love you. I want to simultaneously show the world how incredible you are and selfishly keep you to myself forever. Penelope Caswell exists because of you.

Wanda, we did it again. No one sees the overly emotional pisces vision quite like you do. Thank you doesn't even begin to cover it. Back to Merrymount, we go. I LOVE U.

Kim, look at us. Sister authoring x2 now. This journey would be dull and meaningless without you to scream into the void with. I actually wouldn't be on this journey if I didn't have you. Stuck together forever. Ilyilyily.

Kay, THANK YOU. Thank you for your kindness and seeing my vision without explanation. Your hype comments and voice memos made editing feel painless and full of joy. I can't wait to do this again with you.

Maribeth with Legends Literary Management, thank you. Your organization and support and encouragement has been amazing.

Jessi and Mads, my hype women, my WAGs, my cheerleaders. Thank you for loving me and my characters unconditionally.

Parker, thank you for yelling about Gwen and Miller from the first draft. It means the world to me. Parker's Paragraph Time forever.

Mom and Dad, thank you for always loving me not despite, but regardless. Nightloveyaseeyainthemorning.

My family & friends in the real world, thank you for supporting me like you do. I couldn't ask for anything more.

Honey Lemon Sugar Pie Sikorski, the weird emotional support cat of my dreams. Thank you for existing in this world at the same time as me.

And finally, to Taylor Alison Swift & Alani Nutrition energy drinks. My books come to life because of you.

Chapter 22
Chapter 23
Chapter 28
Chapter 31

Ila is a hopeless romantic who loves to write small town stories with found family, banter, happy endings, and a dash of spice.

Born and raised in Massachusetts—now calling sunny Orlando, FL home—an overly emotional pisces, she is a girl mom to the coolest kid ever, married to the boy she had a crush on in high school, and completely obsessed with her cat.

When she's not writing, you can find her and the family checking every Disney destination off their bucket list, speaking in song lyrics, binging early 2000s tv shows, reading books that make her cry, and sending ridiculously long voice memos to her friends.

Let's be friends!

@authorilasikorski

9 7989 9 0 6 0 7 9 1 0